THE LAST
TEA BOWL
THIEF

Books by Jonelle Patrick

Nightshade

Fallen Angel

Idolmaker

Painted Doll

THE LAST
TEA BOWL
THIEF

JONELLE PATRICK

Inquiries should be addressed to
Start Science Fiction
221 River Street, 9th Floor
Hoboken, New Jersey 07030

PHONE: 212-431-5455
WWW.SEVENTHSTREETBOOKS.COM

10 9 8 7 6 5 4 3 2 1

978-1-64506-022-2 (paperback)
978-1-64506-029-1 (ebook)

Printed in the United States of America

引き取る

hi-ki-tō-rū

1. to take over; to take back
2. to retire to a private place; to withdraw; to get out
3. *iki wo hikitoru*: to draw one's last breath

CARRYING CLOTH

TEA BOWL BOX

TEA WHISK

TEA SCOOP

TEA BOWL

PROLOGUE

Feudal Japan

F E B R U A R Y ,   1 7 8 8

Edo (now known as Tokyo)

H e's not used to waiting. The guard who greeted him at the temple gate feared him enough to hustle him into a private room instead of making him stand outside with the coughing and miserable rabble, but his irritation is ratcheting up by the minute. What's keeping that head priest? Feeling naked without his swords, the *daimyō* of Yodo Castle clutches a wooden box, pacing the bare anteroom. Three there, three back, three there, three back.

The door slides open, revealing a shaven-headed figure in white linen robes, forehead pressed to the floor.

"His Reverence extends his apologies for keeping you waiting, Your Excellency." The priest rises. "If you'll come this way..."

The two retainers posted outside the door fall in behind their commander, and the scent of smoking sandalwood grows stronger as they near the chapel where the carved figure of the Kinkokoro Jizo awaits.

The temple staff must have been burning incense day and night since the outbreak, because the long chains of golden lotus surrounding the altar disappear into a sacred haze before they reach the coffered ceiling. The head priest is bowing front and center, clad in magnificent gold brocade vestments for the occasion, flanked by a dozen minions.

The *daimyō*'s eyes dart around the chapel. Who are all these fools? He doesn't need—Ah, there it is. Oblivious to the pomp surrounding it, the face of the shoulder-high, wooden saint radiates serenity. Healing. The kind of healing he came here to obtain.

Introductions are made, polite phrases exchanged. The burning sticks of incense in the offertory urn grow shorter, along with Lord Inaba's patience. Why are they wasting time with needless—

"What brings you here to petition the Jizo-san today, Your Excellency?"

Finally.

"My son," he growls. "It's the pestilence." The pestilence that has claimed more than a tenth of his household, the pestilence that struck down his favorite concubine, the pestilence now trying to take his son.

He motions to the retainer on his left, who steps forward to extend a bulging doeskin pouch. It clinks softly as an under-priest receives it with a low bow. The retainer on the *daimyō*'s right steps forward, offering a shock of rice, representing the tithe of his holdings that he will pay in perpetuity to Senkō-ji temple from this day forward. It, too, is received with ritual gratitude.

Then the warlord himself limps forward, holding a box. He'd commanded that it be brought from the family stronghold in Kyoto, but he still hesitates before offering it. His father would have forbidden him to allow its luck and influence to escape their clan. The tea bowl in this box had cemented his House's hold on Yodo Castle, consolidating allegiance among the nobles who exerted power through a devious command of culture and custom, not their swords.

But there will be no House of Inaba if his son dies. The *daimyō* hides his desperation behind a fearsome scowl as he extends the box with both hands.

"Please accept this humble offering and appeal to the Jizo-san to spare my son's life." He bows. "I beg you."

And the tea bowl named Hikitoru passes out of one circle of influence, into another.

1.

Nori rings the doorbell for the third time, then peers through the rusting metal bars that crisscross the pawnshop's display window. She squints into the darkness beyond the red "silk" wedding kimono and a pair of questionable samurai swords.

Nothing moves but a fly, trapped against the glass. If she were taller, she might be able to see past the display and get a better idea what kind of place this is. Too bad she takes after her grandmother. She reaches to press the bell for a fourth time when a light flicks on deep inside, silhouetting a figure in the hallway beyond. She steps back to the door as two locks *thwap*, and it opens with a sticky sound. In the narrow crack allowed by the security chain, a woman's lined face appears.

"We're closed."

"I know. But my grandmother told me that Miura-san might be very interested in something I have to sell." She thrusts a note stamped with her grandmother's *hanko* through the gap.

The woman takes the slip of paper and reads it, frowning. Pursing her lips, she unchains the door.

"I apologize for troubling you." Nori steps inside. Bows. "I'm Chiyo Okuda's granddaughter, Nori."

"I'm Miura's daughter."

The woman isn't as old as Nori had first thought. Threads of white are beginning to streak her dark hair, but the lines in her face are deep with suspicion, not age. Early forties, maybe? Younger than her mother would be now.

The woman closes the door and flips on a dim overhead light, revealing a room crowded with wooden chests, miscellaneous bric-a-brac cluttering every surface. Plates from the 1970 Expo are stacked beside iron teapots and boxes of jumbled kimono cords. Souvenir geisha dolls sit atop crumbling boxes that might hold anything from soup bowls to ceremonial sake sets. It doesn't look like any of it has been moved in years. Had her grandmother made a mistake sending her here?

"Is that it?" the woman asks, flicking a glance at the flimsy convenience store bag in her hands.

"Yes." She makes space amid the miscellany on the nearest chest. Setting down the bag, she draws out a square box, wrapped in green silk.

"I'll take it to my father and ask him if he's interested." The woman reaches for it.

Nori's fingers tighten.

"I'm sorry, but my grandmother wouldn't be happy if I let it out of my sight." She's not letting it disappear down that hall.

The woman sighs. "All right. Wait here. I'll see if he's feeling well enough to see you."

Once she's gone, Nori wrinkles her nose. Something smells of mildew. She moves away from the suspect basket of secondhand kimonos, and catches a glimpse of herself in a tarnished silver platter. She snatches off the kerchief her grandmother makes her wear while she's working. Crap. She can't believe she came here looking like a shop-slave.

She reaches up to smooth the spikes of hair escaping from her too-short ponytail. It's finally growing out again after she let her best friend chop it off for a beauty school exam. Yu-chan had convinced her that if she looked more confident, she'd *be* more confident, but the dismayingly boy-like clip had only given her confidence in her decision not to return for a trim until her hair is long enough to pull back with a rubber band.

Raising her eyes past the scratched silver plate to the cabinet pushed up against the far wall, she sees that its shelves are stuffed with wooden boxes the same size and shape as the one she brought. She glances at the doorway that swallowed Miura's daughter, then crosses to the cabinet and picks one up, inspecting the calligraphy on the lid. She puts it back, pulls out another. The artists' names mean nothing to her, but their general state of dusty neglect adds to her fear that Mr. Miura is no longer any good at selling pieces as valuable as the one in her bag. Has he fallen on hard times since the last time her grandmother had dealings with him? Can he really afford to pay what the tea bowl is—

"We don't keep the good stuff out here, if that's what you're looking for."

She spins around, half-guilty.

The woman regards her impassively from the lit doorway. Setting out a pair of guest slippers, she says, "Come on back. He says he'll see you."

Nori sheds her shoes, steps into the slippers. Following the woman down the hall, she wonders if her mother's hair has begun to gray too. Of course, it wouldn't show as much in her mother's bleached curls. Unless she'd stopped coloring them. What if her mother has let her hair revert to its natural black? She'd never thought of that. Would she even recognize her if—

The woman stops before a door marked Private, and Nori nearly bumps into her. She knocks, then stands aside for Nori to go in first.

The pawnshop office is eerily similar to the one behind her grandmother's pottery shop on Kappabashi Street. Shelves sag with the same kind of sales ledgers her grandmother uses (although these have blue spines, not red), the local merchants' association calendar features a photo of too-pink-to-be-believed cherry blossoms, and the *tatami* mats underfoot are worn in the same dark path from the door to the low lacquered table in the center of the room.

Behind the black table sits the man she came to meet. He's swimming in a stiff, wide-lapel suit that nearly stands by itself around his thin frame. His face is as seamed as her grandmother's, his thinning gray hair combed straight back from a forehead stenciled with age spots.

She bows.

"I'm Nori Okuda, Chiyo Okuda's granddaughter."

"I'm Miura," he replies, returning the greeting. "Mariko," he says to his daughter, "could you bring us some tea? And get the boy. I'd like him to see this."

With a grumble of assent, the woman disappears. The pawnbroker turns his sharp eyes on Nori.

"Why didn't your grandmother come with you?"

"She . . . wasn't feeling well." It's not exactly a lie.

"I'm sorry to hear that. Nothing serious, I hope?"

Her grandmother is lying unconscious in a hospital bed, but she's spared from answering by the arrival of a skinny boy in black-rimmed glasses, the unselfconsciousness of childhood only slightly tainted by the awkwardness of adolescence. Twelve, maybe? Thirteen? A cheap— but huge—digital watch slides freely around the bony wrist poking from his white uniform shirt, and the inch of sock showing between his loafers and the hem of his uniform pants suggests he's growing so fast his mother can't keep up with letting them out. He's already half a head taller than her.

"You wanted to see me, O-jii-san?"

"Yes, come in. This is Nori Okuda. She brought us something I'd like you to look at. Okuda-san, this is my grandson, Daiki."

"*Hajimemashite*," the boy says, following the formal pleased-to-meet-you with a bow.

His buzz cut is a topography of light and dark patches, and Nori feels a twinge of sympathy. She'd been subjected to many home hair-cuts herself.

Miura waves the boy closer, and he lopes across the room, sta-tioning himself behind his grandfather, like the Emperor's most trusted retainer.

"Well, Okuda-san," the pawnbroker says, folding his hands before him. "Let's see this famous tea bowl."

She kneels on the thin cushion across from him. The bag rustles as she draws out the box and offers it to Miura. The grandson moves closer, peering over his shoulder.

The old man unties the green silk wrapper and peels back the corners one by one, revealing an unvarnished wooden box, darkened by time. It's tied with a blue cord, grown stiff with age. The pawnbro-ker's gnarled fingers tease apart the knot, and the cord falls away. He lifts the box from its wrappings, sweeping them aside. Daiki crouches at his grandfather's elbow, peering at the hand-brushed calligraphy and the square, vermilion stamp on the lid.

"Read it," the pawnbroker says to the boy.

"It's called . . ." He studies the writing, draws back, puzzled. "Hiki-toru? That can't be right. Who would call a tea bowl 'Taking Back'?" He glances at his grandfather, hoping for enlightenment, but none comes. He returns his attention to the box. "Looks like it was made by . . ." he sounds out the characters in the artist's stamp. "Yoshi Takamatsu?"

"Well done." The grandfather allows himself a small smile. "Now tell me, is the box genuine?"

"How am I supposed to know *that*, O-jii-san?"

"How would you find out?"

The boy turns to his phone.

"What are you doing?" Miura sounds annoyed.

"Looking for a picture of the box, so I can compare it with this one."

"And what's wrong with the senses you were born with?"

"O-jii-san," the kid moans. "How many times do I have to tell you? Everything is on the internet now. We don't always have to do things the hard way, you know." He scrolls through the results on his phone, grows impatient, keys in a new search. "Huh. It can't be that famous. I can't find any pictures of it."

"That's because there aren't any," Miura says, with satisfaction.

"But here's another one made by the same guy," Daiki says, refusing to give up. "It's called . . . 'Snow Bride.'" He scrolls some more. "And . . . yes! Here's a picture of it with its box." He zooms in and holds the photo next to the box on the table. His eyes flick back and forth between them. "The artist's stamp looks the same."

"So . . . do you think this one is genuine?"

"Well, they look the same to me," the boy says warily, sensing a trap. "But I guess one of them could be forged." He shoots Nori an apologetic glance. "Sorry."

"How are we going to find out?"

"I guess we could get a sample of the ink from Snow Bride's box and compare it to a sample from this one and—"

"Or we could use the faculties the gods gave us," the old man snaps, seizing the box and holding it to his nose. Giving it a sharp sniff, he nods, then holds it out to his grandson.

Daiki takes a cautious whiff. "Smells like . . . charcoal?"

"It smells like Senkō-ji temple burning to the ground in March of 1945," his grandfather informs him. "The box is genuine."

The pawnbroker sets it on the table and eases off the lid. He lifts the brocade-swathed tea bowl from its nest, then stops. His eyes narrow. Placing it before him, he unfolds the covering. With a grunt of disapproval, he fixes Nori with an accusing glare.

"Is this some kind of joke?"

"What?"

"This isn't Hikitoru. Did you think you could fool me?"

"No! I didn't know! I mean . . ."

She stares at the pale irregular bowl with dark drips running down one side. It looks like an expensive tea bowl to her. And it was inside the box her grandmother had hidden in the secret place under their *tokonoma* alcove.

"How . . . how do you know?"

Miura hands it to his grandson. "Tell her."

"What? That's not fair, O-jii-san! You didn't give me time to . . . I mean, I can't just—" With an exasperated groan, he pulls out his phone to study the description of Snow Bride again.

"Okay, this other Yoshi Takamatsu tea bowl came from Sasayama, which means it's, uh . . . Tamba-ware?"

He glances at his grandfather. No correction comes, so he returns his attention to the bowl, brow creased.

"This one is white with brown drips like the one in the picture, but they're only on one side, so . . . maybe it wasn't really made by him?"

His grandfather shakes his head.

Daiki sighs. Hefts it.

"It's . . . too heavy?" he guesses.

"Yes. A genuine piece of that quality would be lighter. And?"

The boy flips the bowl over and studies the bottom. Laughs.

"Oh. It's stamped Yamamura. Not Takamatsu."

Nori's face burns with shame. How could she have been so stupid not to have checked whether it matched the box or not?

But Miura doesn't notice, because he's telling his grandson, "Even if it was stamped with Yoshi Takamatsu's name, that tea bowl wouldn't be Hikitoru."

"Why not?" asks the boy.

"Because the artist who made it died in 1724, and there shouldn't be a mark on the foot at all. Signing one's work is a modern conceit. Remember that, Daiki. Someday it may save you from buying a fake from a forger who didn't do his homework."

He shifts his attention to Nori. "But passing off fakes isn't Chiyo Okuda's style. Your grandmother didn't bring me many things to sell, but they were always the genuine article. So why is your *o-baa-san* suddenly sending me the right box with the wrong tea bowl inside?"

She has no answer. Had 'Baa-chan lied to her? But she's sure her grandmother had been deadly serious about the stuff hidden beneath the main room's *tokonoma* alcove. When Nori had surprised her opening the secret storage well a week ago, she'd been told to forget she'd seen it. Not to even *think* of investigating the shadowy recesses she'd glimpsed before the slab of polished wood was latched firmly back in place. Yes, the things stored there were valuable. Rare. But they weren't to be touched, except as a last resort. This was their insurance, said the grandmother who didn't trust banks.

What had happened between then and now? Had the real tea bowl been stolen while she was sitting at her grandmother's bedside in the hospital, willing her to open her eyes and be well again? Or maybe 'Baa-chan had secretly sold it without telling her?

"She didn't really send you, did she?"

Nori swallows. "Well . . . not exactly. But that note I gave your daughter—did she show it to you? It was inside the carrying cloth, so I know she wants me to sell the tea bowl if—" She clamps her mouth shut. Never let a buyer guess how desperate you are.

"If she wants you to sell it, why isn't it in the box?"

"I don't know." What had 'Baa-chan done with it? "Maybe she sold it to someone else. Without telling me."

He shakes his head. "Anyone who'd buy a tea bowl that valuable without the box to authenticate it is a fool. And I've known your grandmother over sixty years, long enough to know that she doesn't deal with fools."

He retrieves the discarded cord and the green silk carrying cloth. "If she changed her mind about wanting you to sell it, I'd wager she hid it somewhere. Somewhere you'll never find it."

He pushes the wrappings across the table with a sigh. "But if you do, call me."

2.

Art authentication specialist Robin Swann shoves her front door shut with her hip, dumping the mail and her handbag atop the shoe cupboard with a sigh of relief. Why is it that no matter how big her purse is, the stuff inside expands to fill it? Rubbing her aching shoulder, she scuffs her feet into the fluffy pink slippers waiting beyond the edge of the entry tiles and trudges down the hall toward the kitchen. Detouring to the pocket-sized bedroom on the way, she trades her pantyhose and suit for sweatpants and a t-shirt, zips a faded college hoodie over the top. Then she grabs a shapeless sweater and pulls it over her bush of blond hair, because it's still two-sweatshirt weather in her apartment. People have been posting bursting blossoms online for weeks now, but anyone who has read the haiku masters and lived in Japan for eight years knows that's just an invitation for a late dump of snow.

Ugh, has it really been eight years? She takes off her glasses and rubs her tired eyes. She's over thirty, still living year-to-year on a precarious academic visa that has to be renewed every April, and has had a longer relationship with her goldfish than with any man since she arrived. Speaking of which . . . she crosses the room to the clear glass bowl and peers in. The orange fish lurks near the bottom, not moving, but not belly-up either. She taps in a few flakes of foul-smelling food, and it waves its feeble fins, rising slowly to the surface to nibble.

At first, she'd kept the unwanted pet in a pickle jar, expecting it to move on to goldfish heaven within the week. Instead, it was her romance with the Japanese chef who'd won it for her at a shrine festival that died a quick death, while the stubborn orange fish lived on. After being ghosted by two more prospective boyfriends—neither of whom had been able to deal with her being taller and heavier than they were, even at her skinniest and in flats—she'd reluctantly bought the fish a clear bowl with a fluted blue rim, sprinkled some colored gravel on the bottom, and given it a name.

Fishface is now two—no, three—years old. Surely that's some kind of record for a festival goldfish. She keys a search into her phone. Nope, apparently, she and Fishface would have to live here thirty-eight more years to challenge that one. The very idea makes her want to . . . what? Scream? Drink wine straight from the bottle? Eat a whole carton of green tea ice cream?

She tucks the canister of fish food back behind the framed photo of her solid Middle American parents, flanking a beaming, longer-haired Robin who's squinting into the sun and clutching the diploma proclaiming her a Bachelor of Arts in East Asian Studies. She'd been so excited that day, a week shy of stepping onto a plane to begin her graduate program in Kyoto. So many shining roads had stretched before her, and on that sunny afternoon she still had no idea that the one she'd chosen would lead her further and further from the Japanese poetry master who was her passion, and turn her into a reluctant expert on Yoshi Takamatsu's tea bowls instead.

The truth is, her fairytale life in Japan is slowly grinding to a halt. She has a dead-end job authenticating antique ceramics, a month-to-month studio apartment near an inconvenient train station, and a marked-up fourth draft of her PhD dissertation languishing on her laptop, the file unopened since mid-December.

That reminds her, she still hasn't gotten the letter from her thesis advisor that's key to renewing her visa for another year. If she doesn't submit her application next week, she'll be in deep trouble. Retracing her steps, she scoops up the wedge of mostly pizza flyers and utility bills, shuffling through it until she spots a fat envelope with her academic advisor's return address in the corner. Whew. If she makes the dreaded pilgrimage to the immigration office next week, her visa renewal should nip in under the deadline.

Abandoning the junk mail, she returns to the kitchenette and tugs on the overhead light's grubby string pull. The fluorescent UFO overhead stutters to life as she opens the refrigerator. There's a gap where the wine bottle usually stands. She groans, remembering that the last of her chardonnay had contributed to last night's vow to get out more, meet new people, maybe even sign up for a matchmaking service. As if.

Turning to the cupboard, she discovers that her wine supply has dwindled to a single bottle of pinot and the dusty bottle of champagne she'd received when she finished her master's degree. She twists the top off the red and pours some into the glass that never quite makes it back into the cupboard from the dish drainer. A nightly glass of wine is her one indulgence, and although American wine is more expensive than French in Tokyo, she considers drinking California chardonnay and Oregon pinot among her few remaining acts of patriotism.

She takes a sip and plops down at her low table with the envelope from her advisor. Slits it open, to make sure everything has been signed and sealed.

It has. But a note is paper-clipped to the renewal form, and her smile fades as she reads. The professor, who supervised her research establishing that the tea bowl discovered in the Jakkō-in convent's treasure house had indeed been made in the 1700s by Yoshi Takamatsu, regrets to inform her that if she doesn't submit her doctoral dissertation within the coming academic year, he'll be unable to sponsor her visa again.

Robin's heart sinks. If she fails to finish her dissertation, she can't stay in Japan. And if she can't stay, where will she go? Certainly not home.

3.

The clay flows between his fingers. Thinner . . . thinner . . . and stop. Yoshi Takamatsu lifts his hands from the rim of the bowl spinning on the potter's wheel. A smile blooms on his face. This one feels *right*. As the wheel slows, he reaches for the cord used to cut a newly thrown piece from its mounting, but it's not where he left it.

"Nobu?" he calls to his younger brother. "Did you take my cutting cord again?"

"It's not your cord," grouses Nobu from across the studio.

Actually, it is. But to be fair, it was Nobu's before it was his, and their father's before it was Nobu's.

"Can I have it back so I can get this bowl off the wheel before it dries?"

"Only if you explain again how you do your glaze," comes the sulky reply. "You must have left something out when you told me last time, because mine didn't turn out at all like yours. Father said it looked like I'd slopped mine on with an old rag."

Yoshi sighs. The truth is, he doesn't know how he does the glaze. He just gives it a stir, swipes it on, then lets the gods of the kiln do the rest.

"Maybe if you close your eyes," he suggests, "and do it without thinking."

"Close my eyes? How am I supposed to do anything with my eyes shut, stupid? That'll make it worse, not better."

"Sorry, I don't know what else to tell you. Maybe if you didn't care so much about how it turns out . . ."

"Easy for you to say." His brother's voice drips with resentment. "You don't have to."

Which is true. He doesn't. Yoshi is older by six years, but it's his younger brother who's being groomed to take over the family business. Someday Nobu will become Honzaemon IV, if he ever learns to glaze his tea bowls properly.

Yoshi had been destined to become Honzaemon IV for the first five weeks of his life, until his parents' delight at being granted a son turned to despair. They finally had to admit to themselves—and then to each other—that their baby's eyes weren't tracking any fingers, or focusing on any faces. The priest at the local shrine regretfully confirmed their fears: Yoshi was blind, and likely to stay that way.

A pity, everyone murmured when his parents were out of earshot, since he was otherwise a beautiful child. From his mother, he'd inherited curved lips that tilt up at the corners and expressive features that eloquently telegraph his joys and sorrows. From his father he'd inherited thick black hair that resisted being confined in a topknot, and long, sensitive fingers filled with hidden strength, perfect for shaping clay. The only thing he lacks is sight.

To be honest, Yoshi doesn't really understand why not being able to see is such a big deal. He's overheard more than one of his father's patrons offering to buy his work. His formal training stopped the day his brother was old enough to sit at a wheel, but he's still allowed to fill empty spots in the kiln after his father and brother have arranged their pieces for firing. It makes no sense to him that he has to be able to see in order to do anything important, but that—everyone tells him—is the way of the world.

Fortunately, unlike blind men from families without means,

Yoshi will never have to eke out a living as a masseur on the back streets. But his drop from number one son to the bottom of the pecking order means that nobody spares him much attention unless there's some left over after the other four children have been prodded and coddled. Even his sisters are more valuable to the family than Yoshi; their womanly arts and pretty faces will buy the Takamatsu family valuable marriage alliances.

He does contribute to the family fortunes in one way, though: despite being blind (or perhaps because of it), he's especially good at preparing the clay. The chunks of earth they gather from a secret spot outside town must be wetted down with just the right amount of water, then he treads the virgin clay with bare feet until all the stones and impurities are worked out. When he feels the consistency is just right for his father's work—not too stiff, not too soft—he finishes the job by cutting and kneading it until there isn't a single air pocket left.

His brother Nobu hasn't quite got the hang of it yet. He's too impatient. He's earned more than one beating when he quit working it too soon, and his pieces exploded in the kiln, taking some of Father's work with them.

Yoshi hears the missing cord drop onto the table beside him. Winding the ends around his fingers, he stretches it taut, then draws it beneath the foot of his bowl, separating it from the wheel. Then he dips his hands in the nearby water basin and gently lifts the still-pliable vessel. He holds it before him, taking pleasure in the feel of it, allowing the delicate walls to bend slightly inward, becoming one with his cupped hands.

This is what Kiri's face would feel like, if he could hold it. The smooth skin, the gentle curve.

"That's wrong, you know," Nobu informs him. "That shape. Father scolds me and makes me do it over if it's not round."

That's not why he makes you do it over, Yoshi thinks, settling his bowl onto a drying shelf. More than one famous tea bowl isn't round. But until an artist learns to follow the rules of making tea ceremony ware, he's not allowed to break them. Good thing he isn't burdened with the curse of sight, or he'd have to follow the rules too.

He cleans the wheel and tidies his tools, then feels his way toward the bath, hoping it's still too early for his father to be taking his turn. On the way, he checks the cupboard where he's been hiding his tea bowls. Poking his arm deep between the folded bedding, his fingers walk up the stack, counting . . . three, four, and five. All still there.

He has to hide them, because his work has a way of disappearing if he leaves it in the studio. Two water jars and a tea bowl have gone missing since last spring. His father told him he needed more shelf space, so Yoshi's pots had been tossed on the trash heap to make room for his own. That's his privilege, of course, as the named artist of the household, but it still hurts Yoshi to be reminded that his work is of no consequence and never will be.

Not as far as the outside world is concerned, anyway. But Kiri will appreciate it, and she's the only one who matters. Today's tea bowl will be the last he'll make before he decides which one to give her. He pulls his arm back and slides the cupboard door closed, smiling to himself, imagining her cry of delight when she holds his gift in her hands for the first time.

Today he's in luck—the bath is empty, the water hot. By the time the townsfolk outside the garden walls are hurrying home for their evening meals, he is scrubbed and soaked and wrapped in a cotton kimono, dangling his legs over the edge of the polished wooden veranda encircling their house. Although the temperature is dipping toward freezing, Yoshi still glows with inner heat from soaking neck-deep in the cedar tub. Breathing in the crisp autumn air, still pungent with the ghosts of burning leaves, he tilts his face to the sky. Snow is coming, late tonight, or early tomorrow morning. He always knows before anyone else. He sits, languid and content, listening to the faint whir of bat wings dipping and diving over the garden as the crows argue in the trees, contending over the best roosts for the night.

Today's tea bowl could very well be the one. He'd made it a little smaller than the others, remembering Kiri's delicate hands. He'd held them only once, but the memory fills him with joy, again and again. It had been like holding a pair of wild doves—soft and smooth, beating with life.

They've known each other for almost seven years now. Would he even have met her if he'd been able to see? He thinks about that for a moment. Probably not. Not to talk to, anyway. She's the third daughter of an official in Lord Katahachi's government, and no matter how sought-after the Takamatsu family's tea utensils become, samurai are samurai and artisans are artisans.

The only time they really intersect is at tea ceremonies. The Takamatsu family teahouse had been built by his grandfather, Honzaemon II, and every social climbing samurai worth his rice allotment longs to receive tea in the room that had once hosted the shōgun himself. Honzaemon II hadn't been a top-notch artist, but he was a genius at selling tea bowls to the culture-hungry warrior class. Nothing predicts an imminent increase in rank quite like being invited to a tea ceremony hosted by a superior and performed by a famous tea master. Guests never fail to fall all over each other in their eagerness to buy everything they touch that day, and commission much more.

On the day he met Kiri, he'd been banished to the garden, ordered to stay out of sight and shoo away the crows. They like to perch in the tree that's smack in the middle of the famous view framed by the teahouse's window. If they just sat there, they wouldn't be a problem, but their cawing is too distracting for the nervous guests, who already have plenty on their minds. The choreography of a tea ceremony is as strict as the rules governing how and when a samurai may draw his sword, and mistakes can be just as deadly to a career.

Yoshi hadn't minded the crow job. He'd much rather be out in the garden on a warm spring day than inside the teahouse. He remembers sitting on the bench by the pond, breathing in the heady fragrance wafting from the wisteria arbor, listening to the waterfall's gentle music and idly waving the gardener's broom in the air to keep the crows from settling.

Deep in a daydream, he'd been imagining what he'd do if he were the valiant Kintaro and met a bear in the woods, when a girl's voice piped up behind him.

"What are you doing?"

He'd dropped the broom, startled.

"I *was* scaring away the crows." Falling to his knees, he felt around for the broom handle. "Who are you? And how did you get in here, anyway?"

"I came with my father and brother. They're at some stuffy old tea ceremony."

Yoshi climbed back on his bench, resumed his shooing.

"Why aren't you inside with the women?"

"It's so boring. All they do is talk. And I can't exactly kneel on the floor all day, can I?"

"Why not?" He waved the broom. "Don't you practice? If you practice, it gets easier."

"Not for me." Offended. "Don't pretend you didn't notice."

"What do you mean?" He'd turned toward her voice, puzzled by her anger. "I'm sorry, but I'm not sure what you're talking about."

Then there was a telltale pause, as she took in his milky eyes, his unfocused gaze.

"Oh," she said. "You can't . . ."

He felt her draw near, inspecting him like everyone does when they first realize he's blind. Why do they do that? What does that tell them that they don't already know? It always feels like a violation, and he'd instinctively shifted away.

"I'm sorry. I didn't know," she said in a small voice. "Have you always been . . ."

"Since I was born."

"Me too."

That surprised him. "You're blind?"

"No. But there was a big fire. When I was a baby. They didn't quite get me out in time so . . ."

"You got burned?"

"Yeah. That's why I can't sit *seiza*."

"Oh." Must have been pretty bad, if she couldn't kneel on the floor like everyone else. On the other hand, having an excuse not to sit with your feet tucked under you for hours might actually be pretty convenient. You wouldn't be expected to sit *seiza*, just to be polite. When Yoshi kneels before his wheel shaping a pot, he's too wrapped up in what he's doing to notice the discomfort, but sitting respectfully while adults drone on about the dull things grown-ups talk about puts both his brain and his legs to sleep.

He resumed his broom waving.

"Does it still hurt?"

"No."

"But you can walk, right?"

"Not very well."

"Oh. How did you get in here, then?"

"I use a stick. My maid helps too. Sachi goes everywhere with me."

And years later, the faithful Sachi still does. That day in the garden was the first time he'd heard Kiri's voice, but it wasn't the last. Over the years, they'd devised ways to run into each other on the day of the Sheep, when Kiri is on her way home from painting lessons, and sometimes on the day of the Rooster, when she and Sachi are allowed out to the shops. Being different from everyone else is what first drew them together, but over the years, their friendship has become something more.

Oddly, nobody forbids their meetings. Kiri's comings and goings seem as little regarded as his own. Yoshi has decided that invisibility is one of the best things about being "handicapped," although it still annoys him when people talk about him like he's not in the room. Do they think that being blind also makes him deaf?

It does occasionally allow him to learn something to his advantage, though. Last spring, he'd overheard two visiting samurai wives tut-tutting about what a pity it was that Kiri's face had been so disfigured in that fire. If the damage had been confined to her limp, they might have considered a match with her powerful family for one of their younger sons. The poor girl, she'll never marry.

Which had kindled a hope Yoshi had never dared consider. Kiri's face doesn't matter at all to him. It's her ready wit, her soft hands, and the way her silken robes smell of flowers and rain that he cares about. And her voice. When he'd told her she must be prettier than his sisters because her voice is so much nicer than theirs, she'd laughed in a slightly bitter way and said that was the first time anyone had ever said that to her, and would probably be the last.

If he hadn't already been convinced that having the gift of sight isn't as important as everyone claims, that clinched it. Having two good eyes somehow blinds them all to the fact that Kiri is the most beautiful girl in the world.

He slips his newest tea bowl into his father's next firing, waiting impatiently for the kiln to cool off enough to dig it from the ashes. And when he does, he finds the waiting was worth it.

This is the one. He knows right away. Running his fingers over the cascade of delicate rivulets spilling down its curves, he can feel the magic that the kiln gods worked with their fiery breath.

Just to be sure, he retrieves the other candidates and holds each between his palms, but they only confirm its rightness. Tossing the rejects onto the trash pile, he wraps the bowl in a piece of linen, settling it into a fresh wooden box and tying it with a blue silk cord. Finally, he stamps his artist's mark on the lid with vermilion ink.

The days pass with maddening slowness until his next meeting with Kiri, and when the hour finally arrives, he's waiting for her on the bridge, nervous as a fledgling sparrow teetering on the edge of its nest. He invites her to a nearby shrine to stroll in the garden, so he can give her his gift in the most secluded public place he knows.

Just as he'd hoped, she gives a small cry of pleasure when she opens it.

Pure joy shines from his face as he waits for . . . why isn't she saying anything? He hears a sniff. And another. Is she . . . crying? He's been imagining this moment for months, but tears are not what he—

"It's . . . it's beautiful," she quavers. "I'll take it with me, and treasure it forever."

"Take it with you? What do you mean?"

"I'm being sent away. Right after the new year."

"What?"

"My father . . . two nights ago, he sent for me and told me I'm going to Jakkō-in." She draws a ragged breath. "It's a convent. Near Kyoto."

The bottom drops out of his world. "For how long?"

"He says . . . he says that soon I'll be old enough to marry, but he won't defy the gods by finding me a match. That any man in search of a wife would take one look at my face and know that the *kami-sama* have other plans for me. That no man from a decent family will marry a woman who attracts such bad luck. And since I'll never have children, it's . . . it's my duty to spend my life praying for those who will."

No. He doubles over. This can't be happening.

"Yoshi? What's wrong?" She steps closer. "Please don't . . . are you all right?"

How could he have been such a fool? He'd been so busy imagining the moment he wins her heart, he hasn't given any thought to how impossible it will be to win her hand. A crippled girl and a blind boy. A samurai's daughter and an artisan's son. He doesn't have a prayer of persuading her father to give his blessing to a pair the gods have so doubly cursed.

"Please don't worry about me," she begs. "I hear Jakkō-in is a beautiful place. And the nuns there don't have to give up everything, not like at some temples. I can still wear my favorite kimonos, and I can still paint." Her voice breaks. "I can still drink tea from your tea bowl."

"I didn't mean for you to drink it alone!"

"I won't be alone. I'll . . . I'll have Sachi. Sachi is coming with me."

Sachi is not who he meant.

"What about others? Will you be allowed to see . . . others?"

"No." He can hear her gulping back tears. "Once I take my vows, I won't be allowed to see anyone from outside. Not even my family. Not until . . . not until we meet again in the next life."

Then her cough becomes a sob, and her composure crumbles, overcome by the despair she's been trying so hard to keep inside.

He reaches out to her, but they're in public, and he manages to pull back just in time. Touching her will draw attention, make everything worse, not better. All they can do is stand there with wet cheeks, throats too choked to speak, their misery and longing expanding to fill the space between them.

Somehow he finds the words to part with her and stagger back home. Bereft, hollow, he drags himself through the side gate and locks himself in the outhouse, where he can finally bury his face in his wadded-up cloak and surrender to his anguish.

For the next two days, he rages against fate, see-sawing between anger and grief.

How could the gods do this to them? Haven't he and Kiri had more than their share of bad luck? Isn't it someone else's turn?

Then his fury hardens to resolve. If the gods are powerful enough to set Kiri on this path, they're powerful enough to derail it. He just has to convince them. He visits the family shrine many times a day, plying the gods with coins and prayers. He even makes his servant take him across town to the Ōjiyama Inari shrine to climb the tunnel of a thousand red *torii* gates.

But the weeks fly by, and preparations for Kiri's journey proceed unchecked. The gods aren't listening. Either they aren't mighty enough to change her destiny, or they choose not to.

But if they don't care enough to save her, surely they won't mind if he does.

4.

FRIDAY, MARCH 28

Tokyo

N ori can't get away from the pawnshop fast enough. She speedwalks down the sidewalk, and ducks into the first alley. Falling back against an uneven brick wall, clutching the Family Mart bag to her aching chest, she tries not to cry. The pawnshop she'd hung her hopes on is a dump, her grandmother's friend thinks she's trying to cheat him, and the valuable tea bowl she thought would save her is missing.

After opening the utility bill, she'd been afraid to look at the one from the phone company. Unless the shop gets a big order, by next month she'll have to choose between food and internet, even if she cleans out the petty cash box. What's she going to do?

One thumb is already hovering over her best friend's phone number before she remembers that Yu-chan had never called her back. On the day 'Baa-chan had been rushed to the hospital, she'd interrupted her best friend's dinner, desperate to cry on a sympathetic shoulder, but the friend who'd been there for her since primary school couldn't give her more than a fraction of her attention while keeping her children from killing each other. Nori had hung up, fighting tears, sure she'd call back later, offering the kind of sympathy that Nori would have showered on her if their situations had been reversed. But she never did. Had their friendship really dwindled to the gossipy chats that only happen when she occupies the chair at the cut-rate clip joint where Yu-chan works?

She scrolls half-heartedly through her contacts, hoping a sympathetic name will pop out, but none do. Layers of work, weddings, family obligation, and kids have silted up between them, making it hard to get together without moving mountains. She hadn't called a single one of them when her grandmother had her stroke, so she can hardly expect sympathy now. Besides, none of them can help her with her real problem: she has no money, and no way to get it. Not unless she finds the real Hikitoru.

And she doesn't even know what she's looking for. She hadn't caught a single glimpse of what was inside the box when she discovered 'Baa-chan opening the hiding place a week ago, because her grandmother had packed her off to restock their cleaning supplies. An hour later, when she'd called from the drugstore to ask whether to get their usual brand of cleanser or buy the one on sale, 'Baa-chan hadn't answered the phone. She'd dashed back to the shop to find her grandmother sprawled on the floor behind the counter, unconscious. In the maelstrom of ambulance, hospital, and one discouraging doctor consultation after another, she hadn't thought about the tea bowl again until she dug the box from its hiding place this morning.

Nori tips her face to the sky, but the clouds melt and blur. A tear escapes down the side of her face, and she swipes it away angrily. Don't cry, *think*.

Where could that accursed tea bowl be? Miura said it couldn't have been sold without the box, so . . . stolen? But if it was stolen, why would a thief leave the box and replace the real bowl with a fake? Only her grandmother could have done that.

And that's a good thing, she tells herself. If 'Baa-chan hid it, it's got to be somewhere in the building. If she tears the place apart, surely she'll find it.

But first, she has to know what she's looking for. She consults her phone. Searching for the tea bowl Daiki found, she discovers there's a second Yoshi Takamatsu tea bowl. Waterlily. From the side, Snow Bride and Waterlily are both rounded—not straight-sided, like most—and both have drips of glaze running down the sides, but there the similarity ends. Snow Bride is a pale beauty, glazed an ashy white, with regular drips of chestnut trickling down from the rim in perfectly imperfect stripes. Waterlily is a muted brick red, overlaid with glossy drips that are both finer and wilder. Are the drips two different colors? Or are they the same glaze, the contrast tricking her eye? She zooms in on Waterlily's thumbnail, but that just turns it into blurry squares. There are more photos, but they don't help. In one, the rivulets seem to be a solid medium-brown, in another, a much lighter golden color, and in a third, somewhat greenish. One hints of a bubbling texture in the glaze near the rim. Is that because the photo is especially good or especially bad? She can't tell from the tiny square on her phone, so she navigates to the source and gets her answer. It must be good, because it's from the Tokyo National Museum.

Holy crap. A tea bowl by the same artist who made Hikitoru is in the National Museum? She checks the time. If she hurries, she can make it to Ueno Park before they lock the doors.

Nori scowls at the prices posted above the ticket window. She has to *pay* to get into a public museum? Shouldn't she at least get a break, because it's nearly closing time? Sorry, says the ticket lady.

She grudgingly pushes a thousand-yen note through the window. A museum is the last thing she wants to spend money on, but until she knows what she's looking for, it would be pointless to turn the house upside down trying to find it.

More people are streaming out than in as she squeezes past them through the heavy front door. She makes it halfway across the lobby before being slammed with the sensation she's been here before. But the reception desk had seemed taller, the floor closer. The gray granite had been wet, the afternoon drizzling with rain. It was a few weeks after her father died, and she'd spotted a hundred-yen coin lying unclaimed at the foot of the reception desk, but 'Baa-chan had been gripping her hand so tightly it hurt, and she didn't dare pull away to pick it up.

Earlier that day, her grandmother had packed her onto a bus and taken her to a neighborhood so devoid of landmarks, it had taken her years to find it again. 'Baa-chan had sat her down on the bus shelter bench and given her a picture book to entertain her while she crossed the street to take care of some "business." But Nori had looked at that book so many times, it only took her a few minutes to finish flipping through it. She'd glanced up and caught 'Baa-chan ringing the bell at an apartment block across the street. When the door opened, her mother was standing there, her mane of bleached curls and way of standing as familiar to Nori as her own body. But in the months she'd been gone, it was her mother's body that had changed. A growing baby was making a bump under the front of her dress.

Nori had leapt up and clapped her hands with delight. That's why her mother had gone away! She wanted to surprise Nori with the little sister she'd been asking for. Nori had jumped up and down and waved. But whether she was too far away, or the rain was coming down too relentlessly in the street between them, her mother hadn't waved back before closing the door on her grandmother.

When 'Baa-chan returned, Nori had taken one look at her face and swallowed her questions. Her grandmother's lips were set in the grim line that meant she might be dealt a swat on the bottom for reasons she didn't understand.

So she watched and waited. She didn't know how long it took to make a baby, but the months dragged by, and still her mother didn't return. It was more than a year before she mustered the courage to ask why they'd never been back to meet her new brother or sister. Her grandmother's face had hardened as she said, "You don't have any brothers or sisters," and walked away.

Nori didn't understand, but she knew better than to ask again. If she wanted to know anything about her mother and the baby, she'd have to find out for herself. But by the time she was old enough to sneak out and find the nondescript building across from the bus stop, nobody with her mother's name lived there.

She drags herself back to the present. Less than thirty minutes to closing time.

She unfolds the map that had come with her ticket, and her heart sinks. There are dozens of galleries. Scanning the lobby, she locates the information desk. Swimming toward it against the tide of exiting visitors, she calls up the photo of Waterlily.

"Excuse me," she says to the uniformed woman behind the counter. "Can you tell me where to find this tea bowl?" She hands over her phone.

The attendant studies it, consults her exhibition list. A crease appears between her brows.

"I'm afraid that might be difficult."

"Difficult? Why? It says right there that it's in your collection."

"It is," the woman replies, handing back the phone. "But it's not on display right now."

"Not on display?"

"Our collection is huge. Only a fraction of the works can be exhibited at any one time. The rest are in storage."

"But . . . I need to see it. I came all the way here to see it." She'd spent money she didn't have to see it.

The woman keys a search into her computer.

"The last time that piece was shown to the public was . . . two years ago, in a show of art from Buddhist convents. You might check the gift shop," she suggests apologetically. "There were lots of nice pictures in the exhibition catalog, and there might be a few copies left."

Disappointed, Nori thanks her and crosses the lobby to the museum store, but there are a dizzying number of books on display. She backtracks to fidget in line before the register, while the only employee in sight rings up twelve postcards for the customer in front of her.

"Excuse me," she says, stepping up to the counter. "Can you help me find a book with photos from a show that happened two years ago? I think it was art from Buddhist convents, or something like that."

The clerk leads her to a section in the far corner and pulls out a glossy hardcover with a golden, hundred-armed deity on the front.

"Is this what you're looking for?"

Sacred Treasures from Behind Convent Walls, the title reads, in inch-high letters. Sure enough, halfway though, there's a lavish photo of Waterlily, bigger than life. It's not as good as seeing the real thing, but at least she now knows that Hikitoru could be either grayish white or brick red, but the glaze dripping down the side will certainly be the same glossy chestnut. She scans the page to find out how big it is, but her attention is hijacked by something else: Waterlily was named a National Cultural Treasure in the year Heisei 29.

A tea bowl by the same guy who made Hikitoru is a *National Cultural Treasure*? That would mean Hikitoru isn't just valuable—if it's anything like Waterlily, it could be priceless.

5.

Yoshi stamps his feet, trying to keep warm. He's waiting on the bridge spanning the Sasayama River, at the place he always meets Kiri after her painting lesson. A brisk wind is blowing from the north, and the night air has become bitterly cold as the hours count down to midnight. It's less than a week until New Year's Day, when everyone becomes a year older. Yoshi will turn nineteen, and Kiri will be sixteen, old enough to enter the convent and begin earning eternal benefits for her family.

The wind pries at his robes with icy fingers as fellow travelers scurry past, too intent on getting out of the cold to wonder why Yoshi isn't somewhere warm, or at least trying to get there.

A distinctive *clop clop* sounds from the wooden planks at the far end of the bridge. Yoshi tenses, feeling exposed. Only samurai are allowed to ride horseback, and they can stop to question anyone, at any time. That's the last thing he needs tonight. Best to keep moving. Hitching his traveling bundle more securely onto his shoulder, he walks toward the approaching warrior, one hand on the railing to guide him.

As the horseman and his attendant pass, he relaxes, realizing he needn't have worried. This one came from the direction of the pleasure quarter, and even above the odors of horse and leather he can smell the sake fumes. Samurai are forbidden to frequent the so-called "teahouses" or waste their stipends on courtesans, but most of them do anyway. This one is probably slouching home under the kind of deep straw hat designed to conceal his face, hoping not to be recognized.

Yoshi makes it to the other end of the bridge and feels his way to the shelter of the shuttered noodle shop to get out of the wind. It's a little warmer in the lee of the wooden building, but he dares not tarry. He doesn't know if Kiri will be able to see him here, and he doesn't want her to worry if she doesn't find him waiting where they'd agreed. He sets out across the bridge once more. This time he meets no one. When he gets to the end, he turns and starts back.

Shivering, he wraps his cloak tighter. What time is it? He'd arrived early because he didn't like the idea of her standing alone in such a public place, but he's been pacing back and forth for some time now. It must be nearly midnight. Listening for her footsteps, he makes his way back across the span, but neither of the townsfolk he encounters have her halting gait.

A plume of snowflakes lifts from the branches of a nearby cedar grove, pricking his face with minty stings. His robes flap about his knees as he bends into the wind, makes another circuit. The town watchman cries midnight, and still she doesn't come.

Maybe the weather is delaying her. Or—more likely—it's delaying her father and brothers as they make their way back across town, pretending they haven't been ignoring the shōgun's prohibition against the red light district. On a bitter night like this, the men of her family would be reluctant to leave their favorite pleasure houses.

He tells himself he should be happy she'd listened to him when he warned her not to set out until she's certain everyone is asleep. She's probably sitting in the dark right now, packing and repacking her carrying cloth right up to the last minute, changing her mind about which things she can't live without.

He hopes that one of them is his tea bowl. If she brings the tea bowl, he'll know she understood his unspoken message: that it wasn't a gift for her family, it was a gift for her. A personal gift. The kind she could only properly accept from a family member or lover. They had never explicitly reached such an understanding, but he's sure she feels the same way he does. He hasn't imagined the warmth in her voice, or the way she contrived to draw out their meetings. He hasn't misinterpreted her faithfulness, meeting him even when it was pouring rain.

He too had packed and repacked his bundle, but he'd never removed the new tea bowl he'd made for her as a sort of wedding gift, even though they'll never officially be able to marry. They'll have to lose themselves among people who've never heard of the samurai's crippled daughter who shamed her family by running away with the artisan's blind son. There can be no wedding papers with their real names on them, no new family register. But they'll be together, and that's what matters. He'll help her with the chores of daily life that her leg makes difficult, and she'll help him do the things that the world makes difficult, and together they'll be happier than either of them expected to be.

He reaches the end of the bridge and turns around. His sandals and leggings are soggy with snowmelt, his feet aching with the cold. He should have worn the warm hemp travel clothing in his pack instead of his festive silk kimono.

The town is completely still now. Nobody has passed for some time. Even the pleasure seekers are home, or holed up with their favorite women. Only the sharp claps of the night patrol's sticks periodically break the silence.

Now he's beginning to worry. Had Kiri's cough returned? Her whole household had been stricken this winter—the pestilence had carried off an old servant and the cook's baby—but she'd assured him she was on the mend, well enough to travel.

Had she changed her mind? He quickly banishes that thought, telling himself that even if she had, she'd never let him stand out in

the snow all night. At the very least, she'd come to explain. Or send
Sachi to—

Running footsteps. It can't be Kiri, though. Kiri can't run.

He hears his name, recognizes the voice.

"Sachi!" he cries. "What is it? Where's Kiri-san?"

"She . . . she . . ." The maid lurches to a halt before him, breathing
hard. "The guard . . . outside our gate. Stopped her."

No!

"Took her to her father. Woke him up. He . . . he locked her in her
room. When I took her to the privy, she told me about . . . about you."
Now there's accusation in her voice. "She told me to come here. To tell
you she's sorry." Sachi begins to weep. "They're taking her to Jakkō-in
a week early. They're taking us both. We have to be packed and ready
to go at first light," she wails. "I won't even have time to say goodbye
to my mother."

Yoshi can't sleep that night. And he can't go home. He already has one
foot firmly planted in the world where he and Kiri live happily ever
after, and he can't go back.

Wrapped in his cloak, he's hunkered down in the shelter of the
noodle seller's doorway. He'd promised to save her from the future she
didn't choose, and he's not going to give up now.

It's not impossible. Nothing is impossible. Just a little more difficult.

Following her won't be hard—even though he's blind—because
he knows where she's going. Tomorrow, she'll set out for Kyoto, and
three or four days after that, depending on the weather, she'll pass
through the gates of Jakkō-in.

He decides against trying to intercept her mid-journey. Even when
his far more humble family travels, they don't set foot on the road
without a couple of armed guards to discourage brigands and enough
servants to keep them comfortable. As the daughter of a government
official, Kiri will be traveling inside a palanquin with her maid, plus
four bearers, a cadre of trusted family retainers, and a detachment of

seasoned fighting men to guard her. Men who will be twice as vigilant, since she tried to run away.

It would be easier to liberate her from behind the walls of the convent, where her only jailers will be nuns. Maybe Sachi will help him. Kiri's maid doesn't want to be shut away in a convent any more than her mistress does. No one consulted her either.

The wind dies at daybreak. At the public bath, he changes into his humble brown traveling clothes and packs away his finery. As soon as the town begins to stir, he recruits an enterprising urchin to guide him.

"I'm making a pilgrimage to the famous healing Jizo at Jakkō-in," he tells the boy. "There's a bonus in it for you if you can find a comrade who knows his way around a staff or knife, to protect us on the road."

As he hoped, the boy has an "older brother" who fits the description, and the three are well on their way by the time the pale winter sun climbs high enough to warm their faces and send snowmelt racing into the roadside streams. Fortunately for Yoshi's unseasoned feet, Jakkō-in isn't actually very far away. But because the convent perches at the end of a valley, deep in the mountains outside Kyoto, the journey by foot will take them two days. It will take Kiri and her more ponderous escort at least three.

They reach Jakkō-in by late afternoon of the second day, and he finds an inn near the walled temple complex, in the settlement that has sprung up around the pilgrimage site like a patch of unruly moss. Outside the gate, florists hawk thin bouquets of chrysanthemums to those paying their respects at family graves. A pickle stand tempts hungry pilgrims as they arrive to petition the healing Jizo, and a cacophony of vendors sell incense, rosaries, and small carved replicas of the famous saint.

He pays his two companions what they'd agreed, but apparently they felt a little additional appreciation was due, because he wakes the next day to find his gold lacquered medicine vial has disappeared with them. Not that he's really surprised—that's why he sleeps with his money pouch tied securely beneath his robe. He'd brought along the small but valuable *inrō* in case he needed to pawn it in an emergency, but the gods must have decided that his guide and guard needed it more.

In any case, it's long gone now. Nothing to do but thank the *kami-sama* for lightening his pack.

In exchange for that, they send him some luck. By the next afternoon, he's standing before the gates of the convent, dressed in the ragged robes and conical hat of an itinerant monk who gladly accepted a shiny coin in exchange for his clothing, staff, and begging bowl. For another coin, he'd taught Yoshi the sutra he chanted at arriving pilgrims, hoping to persuade a few to stop for a blessing.

Yoshi has already dispensed several fake blessings by the time Kiri's retinue plods to a halt before the great wooden gate. When her name is announced by the men-at-arms, he's ready. Just as he'd hoped, she recognizes his voice and hears her name when he inserts it into the sutra he's loudly chanting, even though she's sequestered behind the bamboo blinds of her palanquin. She asks her entourage to pause long enough for her to send her servant back with a small coin for the blind monk. He's able to have a whispered exchange with Sachi, while pretending to give his blessing. The maid agrees to meet him at the narrow back gate of the convent at midnight.

But when she slips through the portal later, her news isn't good.

"Her cough is back, worse than before, and she burns with fever." Sachi wrings her hands. "She never should have defied her father. The gods are punishing her. They're punishing both of us."

"Nonsense," Yoshi says firmly, as if saying it will make it so. "She's not being punished, she's heartsick. Of course she'll pine away if all she can look forward to is being shut inside convent walls for the rest of her life. If you want her to recover, you have to help her escape. And," he adds, "it's not just her health and happiness that's at stake, is it? What will happen to you if she dies in the convent? Have you thought about that?"

Sensing the maid wavering, he presses his case.

"You won't be left alone and penniless if you help."

He shows her a string of coins that will make sure she gets safely back to Sasayama, with a dowry big enough to marry the water vendor's son she's been in love with forever.

That does it. They part in agreement, the first shiny installment tucked into the folds of Sachi's sash.

6.

Nori navigates the now-familiar route through the twenty-four-hour fluorescence of the hospital, the mingled odors of disinfectant, floor polish, and illness catching her attention before they become the new normal. As she rounds the corner by the nurses' station, the head nurse emerges from her grandmother's room, a clipboard under one arm. She spots Nori as she closes the sliding door, and they greet each other with the familiarity that grows up around chronic illness.

"I'm sorry, but there's been no change," says the nurse, in answer to her unasked question.

Nori didn't expect there to be. She bows her appreciation for the nurses' diligence and slips through the heavy door.

The room seems darker than before. The lights over the closer bed have been switched off, the crisp white sheets pulled tight as a drum. Where's the elderly woman who had been her grandmother's room-mate? Nori had wondered why she was occupying a hospital bed in the first place, but everyone knows that small doctor-owned hospitals like this one often turn a blind eye to elderly people being parked there by relatives who need a respite, even when all that's really wrong with them is old age. As long as the family and the National Health pay the bill, neighborhood hospitals are happy to act as a sort of medical hotel and take their money. Patients can stay as long as the bed isn't needed for someone whose complaints aren't quite so vague, or until family caregivers are rested enough to take them home. Is that what happened with the lady in the other bed? Because she certainly didn't seem in any danger of—*Stop*. Don't go there. Even thinking it can attract bad luck.

Speaking of bad luck . . . Nori groans. Is that why everything fell apart today at Miura's? She pulls up the online astrological calendar, already knowing what she'll find. Sure enough, today is *butsumetsu*. Bad luck all day. She kicks herself. 'Baa-chan never would have charged off to the pawnshop before making sure it was an auspicious day to sell the tea bowl.

With a sigh, she pockets her phone and crosses the room. Her grandmother lies in the bed next to the window. The green lines on the monitor overhead silently trace and retrace the faint beating of her heart, but Nori still anxiously studies the motionless figure beneath the covers, holding her own breath until she sees 'Baa-chan's chest rising and falling.

When her grandmother had first been admitted after her stroke, she'd been surrounded by banks of blinking machines. As her condition stabilized, but she still didn't regain consciousness, they'd been withdrawn, one by one, trundled away to monitor patients in more acute danger. Now, she's mostly observed by the cadre of nurses who look in around the clock, as she inexplicably sleeps on. The human mind is an unpredictable thing, the doctors tell her. They've done all they can. Patience is what's needed now.

Nori studies the familiar face, which looks curiously unlined and serene, the fiery feelings that had so often transformed it now buried deep. Oxygen tubes snake into her nostrils and a bag of clear fluid drips into her arm, tethering her to her sickbed. Nori smooths a stray hair from her grandmother's brow, then pulls the visitor's chair to the side of her bed. The nurse told her it's good to talk to people, even if they're unconscious. Stroke victims can sometimes hear you, she'd said, even if they can't open their eyes. It's good to let them know you haven't given up on them.

"Hi 'Baa-chan. How are you feeling?" she begins, pretending her grandmother is just resting her eyes. "I've got something important to ask you, so I hope you're listening. Remember last week I told you I didn't think I'd have enough money to pay the bills this month? Well, they came this morning, and I don't. I know you don't trust banks, so you must have a stash somewhere, but I can't find it. I didn't know what else to do, so I opened the hiding place under the *tokonoma*. The note you left with that tea bowl said to take it to your friend Miura. So, I did."

She studies her grandmother's face, hoping for a response. Nothing.

"He knew right away the bowl inside the box wasn't Hikitoru. Why did you do that to me, 'Baa-chan? What did you do with the real one? He said you couldn't have sold it without the box. That you must have hidden it. Did you? Why didn't you tell me, 'Baa-chan? Why did you hide it from me?"

She's talking too loudly. Rising abruptly, she turns to the window, pushes aside the curtains to gaze, unseeing, into the darkness. Thunder rumbles and rain begins to streak the glass. Crap. The astrology forecast isn't the only thing she forgot to check this morning. She didn't bring an umbrella.

Returning to the bedside, she clasps her grandmother's limp hand in hers.

"Tell me, 'Baa-chan. Please," she begs, willing the sleeping eyes to open. "Please wake up and tell me where it is. At least give me some idea where to start looking."

Her grandmother's heartbeats flare and fade across the monitor, but her eyelids don't even flutter.

Nori rounds the corner, her sodden hair straggling into her eyes, the worthless tea bowl drooping from her wrist in its fraying Family Mart bag. At least she's finally on Kappabashi Street, where the wooden awning held up by carvings of the street's impish mascot will keep her from getting any wetter.

The restaurant supply district wasn't spared in the firebombing that leveled great swaths of Tokyo during the war, and the Okuda & Sons building is one of many Western-style structures that sprang up afterward, replacing the more gracious ones that had been reduced to ash. Time has not been kind to these hastily built postwar boxes. Their aluminum-framed windows vacantly reflect the shops opposite, weeping dreary tears down stucco walls that the decades have stained a grimy gray. Many of the stores have been renovated and enlarged as their owners' fortunes improved, but Okuda & Sons is still just one room wide and three stories tall. The large wooden characters spelling out the Okuda name across the top once gleamed proudly with gold leaf, but over the years, it has mostly weathered away, the shiny remnants no longer hiding the dull brown primer beneath.

The shop occupies the entire first floor, with the family's living quarters on the second. Above is an empty attic, with a bucket to catch the leaks when it rains. The goods that used to be warehoused on the third floor are now crammed into a small lean-to behind the shop, tacked onto a back room that serves as the office.

Nori shivers and breaks into a trot for the last half block, spurred by the recollection that the tea bowl wasn't the only bundle hidden in the secret storage space. She'd ignored a softer one in a faded cotton carrying cloth because the silk-wrapped tea bowl looked much more valuable, but now she wonders. Anything that would keep the lights on for another month would help. If it's a kimono—a wedding kimono, perhaps?—it could be worth something.

She climbs the steep staircase leading to their flat, then hunches over her purse in front of the door, digging for her key. The worn lock complains as it gives way, and she plods into the tiny, stone-floored entry, dripping. Shedding her coat and shoes, she steps into worn Hello Kitty slippers, flipping on the lights as she makes her way down the narrow hall to the eight-mat *tatami* room that's still used for everything but cooking, bathing, and sleeping. Pulling the cord to switch on the overhead light, she automatically glances at the bear-shaped stain up in the corner to see if it has spread with the rain. A little, but not too much. Good. Roof repairs are the last thing she can afford right now.

She sets the wet bag on the low, lacquered table that serves for eating, TV watching and—before she'd quit school—homework, then kneels in front of the *tokonoma* niche. Framed in peeled cedar saplings, the floor-to-ceiling alcove designed to display a seasonally rotating collection of scrolls and vases is the only reminder of the more gracious building that stood here before the war. Not that any valuables survived the firebombing—the vase she now shifts to the *tatami* is a cheap design that failed to sell in the shop downstairs. It's filled with a spray of dusty fake cherry blossoms that are only in season once a year.

Feeling around under the lip of the polished hardwood shelf, she snaps aside the hidden latch and uses both hands to dislodge the slab. Dragging it onto the floor, she peers into the shadowy well beneath. There's the other bundle, pushed into the far corner.

She lifts it out. It certainly feels heavy enough to be a kimono, but as she pulls apart the knot, she discovers it's not. Just ordinary workman's clothing—a pair of cotton tie-waisted trousers, a jacket that crosses left over right, and a head wrap, all dyed indigo, so blue they're almost black. But as she unfolds each piece, hoping there might be valuables sandwiched between the layers, she finds they're not as new as the dark color led her to believe. Fabric this patched and threadbare ought to be faded nearly white. Why had someone taken the trouble to redye them? Out of pride, to hide the wear?

She sits back on her heels, wondering who they'd belonged to. Holding up the jacket, she measures a sleeve against her arm. It's a little too big. Since the style dates from the time before milk drinking made the entire Japanese population taller, it had probably belonged to a man. Her grandfather? Her great-grandfather?

The bigger mystery is why 'Baa-chan had kept them. The clothes are old, but not the least bit valuable. Why would she hide a pile of worthless rags in the most secret place in the house?

7.

Feudal Japan

DECEMBER, 1680

Jakkō-in Convent, Kyoto

Yoshi waits by the back gate with his possessions in hand and traveling cloak on, but Sachi arrives alone, her voice tight with worry.

"They called the doctor and he gave her some herbs, but every hour she grows worse."

"Worse?" He stiffens with alarm.

"We've been chanting the sutras for her, but what if she dies? What will happen to me if—"

"Did you tell her I was waiting for her?" he interrupts, cutting her off before she names his worst fear. "Did you remind her that she can spend the rest of her life living it, not just praying for others?"

"I told her your words exactly, Takamatsu-san."

"And what did she say?"

"I'm . . . not sure she heard me. When she speaks, she makes no sense. If she . . . what if she . . . what will happen to me if she . . ."

"Don't say it!" Yoshi barks, his fear making him harsher than he means to be. More gently he adds, "I'll see what I can do."

But what *can* he do? The next day, he visits the apothecary, but there are no herbs in his storeroom that haven't already been sent to the convent, no remedy that hasn't been tried. Helpless to do anything but hope, he pays a scribe to write Kiri a letter, urging her to fix her eyes on the future, to find the strength to do what her heart desires, hoping it will lend her the strength to get well.

He delivers the note into Sachi's hands that night, then spends the next day making offerings at every shrine and temple within walking distance.

But the next night, Sachi's news is worse, her voice edgy with fear and exhaustion.

"I've barely slept for days," she whimpers. "When she's awake she has trouble breathing, and when she's asleep, she tosses and moans."

"Did you give her my letter?"

"Yes, but she was too ill to read it, and I—" Sachi can't read.

All he can do is increase his prayers, double his offerings.

The next night, pacing back and forth before the gate, he hopes for good news, but as the snow hardens to ice, and the maid still doesn't come, he fears the worst. Is Kiri dying? Is she already dead?

For three nights, he keeps his vigil under the steadily waning moon. Hunched against the cold, heart filled with dread, he stamps his feet and shivers until the clack of the night patrol's sticks warns him that early morning deliverymen will soon begin to arrive. He spends his days tossing coins and praying fervently at the shrines and temples. The traveling money he'd scraped together by pawning his fine clothing and the two dusty ink paintings he'd spirited from his family's treasure house is dwindling, but he dares not give up.

On the fourth day, he has to know. He rises early, goes to the public bath. Then he dons his last silk kimono and visits the barber to have his tonsure shaved and his topknot oiled.

He hammers on the front gate of Jakkō-in. The gatekeeper tells him that men aren't allowed past the entry hut, but he refuses to take no for an answer.

"I'm the son of Honzaemon III and this is a matter of great urgency," he insists, mustering the voice his father uses for uncooperative tradesmen. "I need to see a woman who's staying here. Her name is Kiri."

"I'm sorry," says the porter, a veteran of such demands. "The nuns aren't allowed any contact with the outside world."

"She's not a . . . never mind. Let me speak with the abbess, then."

"I'll find out if she'll see you. Wait here, please."

Yoshi takes a seat on the hard bench provided for visitors. He leaps to his feet twice, thinking he hears footsteps, but it's some time before the gatekeeper returns with the abbess. Hearing them stop before him, he rises.

"This is the gentleman who asked to see you, Your Reverence."

He bows and introduces himself, adding that he's from Sasayama. If that means anything to the abbess, she doesn't say.

"I understand you have a message for one of our nuns."

"She's not a nun. She just arrived a week ago. But she's been sick, and—"

"Ah. Are you referring to the postulant we've been petitioning the blessed Jizo-sama to deliver from her grave illness?"

"Yes. That's her. Her name is Kiri."

"I'm afraid it's not," the abbess says, in a gentle voice. "Not anymore. This morning she received a new name."

"She's . . . dead?" He sways, gropes for the gatepost. It can't be true. But it must be—they've already given her the name she'll use in the afterlife.

"No young master, I'm afraid you misunderstand," the abbess replies. "All our nuns give up their old names and receive new ones when they take their vows."

8.

The rows and columns of Robin's spreadsheet blur. It's not yet dinnertime (her stomach is a liar), but deep in the windowless bowels of the university library where she still enjoys academic privileges, it might as well be midnight. Except for two bespectacled women and a skinny man who looks like his four straggly chin hairs could finally use a shave, she's alone in the stacks on a Saturday night.

Pushing her laptop aside, she drops her head onto her folded arms. She's not a numbers person. She's never been a numbers person. So, how the hell did she wind up doing her dissertation on "Methodologies for Authenticating Edo-Era Ceramic Pieces Using Thermo-Luminescent Imaging"?

She rolls her stiff shoulders, stretches her back. Being on the team that authenticated the Yoshi Takamatsu tea bowl squirreled away in Jakkō-in's treasure house for nearly three centuries is a respectable achievement, but her first love is literature, not art. Specifically, the poetry of Saburo, the only Japanese haiku master whose name had penetrated the Midwestern backwater where she grew up. The first Saburo poem she'd read in her World Literature class had spoken to her so powerfully that she'd gone straight to the high school library after class and binge-read everything he'd ever written. Everything that had been translated into English, that is. From then on, instead of devouring Sailor Moon comics still warm off the delivery truck, she began haunting online haiku forums and teaching herself Japanese. By the time she submitted her masters' thesis on "Mapping Traditional Buddhist Sins to Saburo's *The Eight Attachments*," she was living in Japan and hoping to turn her years of Saburo obsession into something that would earn her a living. The main reason she'd signed on to do a PhD with the research team studying the newly discovered trove of art at Jakkō-in was because it was rumored there were unpublished Saburo poems among the cache of scrolls.

Sadly, there had been only one, and it had been snatched up by a rival grad student with a degree from the same university as their thesis advisor. That poem ended up being merely "school of Saburo," though, not an undiscovered gem written by the master himself. Last she heard, the doctorate based on that disappointing research hadn't vaulted its author into anything loftier than an untenured assistant professorship in rural Ohio. Recalling this dodged bullet still fills her with half-guilty schadenfreude. At least her research had been conducted on a piece that was named a National Cultural Treasure within a year of its discovery, and had debuted with great fanfare in a blockbuster exhibition of convent art at the Tokyo National Museum.

For a few weeks, that had rekindled her enthusiasm for finishing her dissertation, but it didn't last. The only thing that had ever really sparked her interest in authenticating the tea bowl was the growing evidence that the potter Yoshi Takamatsu and the poet Saburo had crossed paths, maybe even influenced each other. Scholars generally accepted that they had encountered each other on Saburo's first poetry pilgrimage, and it was none other than her undergraduate advisor who'd discovered that the potter had given one of his tea bowls the same name as a poem in Saburo's famous collection, *The Eight Attachments*. Robin had secretly hoped that the tea bowl lying unstudied at Jakkō-in would also turn out to be named after an *Attachment*. If there were two, it would bolster the theory that one artist had inspired the other. Unfortunately, it turned out that Jakkō-in's tea bowl had never been known by any name but Waterlily, and it had been in the convent's collection since before Saburo was born.

By then, though, she was helplessly ensnared by the sideways drift of academic research, which pushed her further and further from Saburo's poetry. By the time she found herself scraping microscopic samples of clay from Waterlily and subjecting them to high heat in order to pin down age and origin, it was too late to steer her career back on course. Her experience fine-tuning thermo-luminescent testing as an authentication tool for Edo Period pottery had landed her the job at the Fujimori Fine Art auction house, but she's stuck in the ceramics section, not the one that deals in literature. And finishing her dissertation will just propel her faster in the wrong direction. The only scholars who might invite her to join their research teams will be studying potters like Yoshi Takamatsu, not poets like Saburo Shibata.

But it's no use crying over spilt milk, as her Missouri grandmother would say. And the father who gave her a loan so she wouldn't have to shoulder another Sallie Mae would remind her that a PhD in the wrong specialty is better than no PhD at all.

Until a better option presents itself, she'd better get to work. She wakes her laptop. Scrolls. Counts how many rows of data still need to be uploaded into tables.

Ugh. Far too many.

9.

Yoshi staggers against a rough-barked tree trunk and slides to the ground, sinking into knee-deep snow. Behind him, his path zigzags between the cedar trees, plowing a tumbling line down steep wooded slopes, punching through the thin ice of countless ice-cold streams, and up the other side. His feet stopped hurting hours ago, reduced to numb stumps at the end of his stumbling legs.

Night is falling, and he's deep in the mountains, far from any road. He's a full day's walk from Jakkō-in now, but he doesn't know where. And he doesn't care.

Kiri took her vows. He still can't believe it. How could she? They must have forced her. Or tricked her. Took advantage of her weakened state and— She never would have become a nun of her own free will. She loved him. She wouldn't have agreed to run away with him if she didn't.

He'd refused to believe the abbess, demanded to speak with Kiri's maid. But the abbess told him Sachi was gone. When it came time for her to take her vows along with her mistress, she was nowhere to be found. Yoshi searched the town for two days, asking at every inn and shop, until the pickle-seller finally told him she'd seen a nun among Lord Matsubara's retinue two days ago, and wondered how a camp follower had acquired a postulant's robe from Jakkō-in.

He lets his bundle slump down beside him and leans back against the unforgiving bark. He's tired. Bone tired. Too tired to think. And, finally, too tired to feel. It's quiet here, amid the trees. Snow drifts unnoticed over his cloak and settles into its folds, as an unexpected warmth steals over him. He closes his eyes. If he and Kiri can't be together in this life, maybe they'll be luckier in the next. He drifts off.

And wakes up in hell.

It must be hell, because everything hurts. His toes, his fingers, his ears. His bones ache, his skin is on fire, his whole body cries out in agony. This must be the torment reserved for unfilial sons, the hell so vividly described to him as a child after he'd knocked over one of his father's vases in a fit of pique.

He's desperately thirsty, but his mouth is too parched to call out. Struggling to sit, he feels a hand on his back, helping.

"Here," murmurs a steadying voice.

The smooth rim of a cup presses against his lips. He drinks. The water is cool, fresh.

"Where am I?" he croaks.

"Just a moment."

The water-dispenser disappears and the quiet settles around him like a winter quilt. The room feels small, but it must be deep inside a larger building, because he can't hear the wind whistling through the eaves. The mingled fragrances of fresh straw and incense tell him that the *tatami* mats in this room are new, and his futon had been aired somewhere that's perfumed with devotion.

Footsteps whisper toward him across the mats, and a new presence kneels beside his pallet.

"Where am I?" he asks again.

"In a better place than you were."

The newcomer is an ancient pine, his voice as deep as the waters of

Lake Biwa. The fragrance of sandalwood drifts from his robes, which rustle with the stiffness of silk.

He says, "You're lucky you chose to die near the hot spring we use for bathing, or you'd have been a Buddha before your time."

"It *was* my time," Yoshi replies bitterly.

"Apparently, the powers-that-be decided otherwise," the voice corrects him, with a touch of asperity. "Fortunately, you were not allowed to rush into another cycle on the Wheel of Rebirth still bearing such a heavy burden."

The cup returns to his lips. He drinks. Lying back, all he wants to do is sleep, but the old pine isn't finished with him yet.

"What attachment is tormenting you so much that it drove you to that place, my son?"

"'Attachment'?"

"'Life is suffering, and the end of suffering. Suffering is caused by attachment—attachment to what we desire, and to that which we wish to avoid.' Which is it, young man? What drove you to try to flee your fate?"

Suffering. Attachment. Now he knows where he is.

"Is this some sort of temple?"

"Yes. A monastery."

"And you're some sort of priest?"

"Yes. My name is Rinkan, the abbot of Sengen-in."

"Sengen-in?"

"You haven't heard of us?" Dry laugh. "I'm not surprised. Our founder set us apart intentionally."

"Why?"

"Worldly pleasure is the first attachment most of our monks must give up when they arrive. Greed, ambition, lust—it's easier to let go of them when the nearest temptations are more than a day's hike away."

In the silence that follows, Yoshi shifts his aching limbs, feels himself being studied.

"I don't believe worldly vices are the source of your despair, though," the *rōshi* reflects. "If you want to live without the kind of pain that drove you here, I suggest you work on giving up love instead."

Yoshi is shocked out of his misery for a moment. How did he know?

"You were delirious for a day and a night," the abbot explains. "Her name is Kiri, isn't it?"

10.

MONDAY, MARCH 31

Tokyo

In the waiting room at the Immigration Bureau, Robin glances at the nearest monitor glaring down on the ranks of airport-like seating. Now serving number twenty-three. She sighs, tucking the slip of paper bearing number fifty-one into her coat pocket. Unwinds her muffler. Getting in line twenty minutes before the door opens usually lands her in the first thirty, but the god of visa renewal is not smiling upon her this morning.

She leaves her coat on, sensing that the waiting room might be more Siberia than Sahara today. Excusing her way toward a swath of empty seats in the middle of a row, she squeezes past a hijab-wearing woman and three men whispering in something that's not quite Chinese. Leaving a polite empty seat between herself and an amulet-rubbing Vietnamese lady, she pulls out her phone to kill time, scrolling past the storybook weddings, rosy babies, and gap-toothed children of her increasingly distant friends and classmates.

#29. #30. #31.

Robin looks up. That was fast. Eight numbers in fifteen minutes. If everyone takes care of business that quickly, she'll only have to use half a day of her unpaid leave. On the other hand, previous experience tells her it's far more likely those hapless applicants failed to bring some minor piece of documentation, or fill in every box to the exacting requirements of the bureaucrats behind the windows.

She spares some sympathy for the dejected Nepalese woman now zipping her parka as she heads for the exit, remembering what it was like to be on the receiving end of bewildering instructions delivered in rapid Japanese, instead of getting the coveted rubber stamp.

#34 and #35 are dispatched quickly. Too quickly. She's not immune to the irrational fear that others' misfortune could be contagious, so she rechecks the papers in her battered plastic folder. Passport, visa extension form (signed), academic transcript (stamped and sealed), and the all-important letter from her advisor, guaranteeing that he's overseeing the research (and, by extension, the ability to behave according to Japanese rules) of Robin Swann, PhD candidate.

The time between numbers stretches. She won't be done before lunch after all. She stands, tugs at her slacks so they cut into a different spot on her hip. She'll have to give up something until they fit again, but she already stopped eating rice two weeks ago, and she can't bear the thought of giving up wine right now. The only thing getting her through endless days of testing a tedious lot of Bizen-ware is the prospect of a glass of pinot when she gets home.

But give it up she must. At her thinnest she took up more than one seat on the subway (even though she tried not to) and she knows from humiliating experience that not a single pair of pants in all of Japan will fit her. She won't have a chance to buy new ones until she goes home to Boone Falls for Fourth of July.

The annual family reunion. She's not looking forward to it. Even if she spends all her free time between now and then working on her dissertation, three months is too soon to have it in the bag. She'll have to come up with a fresh excuse for why she's still not Dr. Robin Swann. Her aunt will enquire how she likes her job in China. Her uncle will tell her that he doesn't understand how anyone can live in a place where all they eat is raw fish. And she still won't have the heart to tell her mother that not only do they have McDonald's in Tokyo, the food is a lot better than the desiccated "welcome back to civilization" cheeseburgers that unfailingly await her in the oven when she arrives. By the end of the week, she'll be counting the hours until her parents go off to church, so she can dig out the plastic Sailor Moon chopsticks she'd insisted on using at every meal in high school, and employ them to ferry her emergency supply of seaweed-flecked potato chips from the bag to her mouth.

Even on her darkest nights, she doesn't consider moving back to Boone Falls for long. But now the clock is ticking, because without a doctorate to roll the employment dice for her, where else can she go? There's not a single assistant professorship or post-doc she can hope to land—not in Boone Falls, not anywhere—without those three crucial letters after her name.

#48. #49.

Clutching her plastic folder, she gathers her muffler and purse onto her lap, ready to go when called. After work, she'll go to the library and transcribe numbers until closing time. And if she manages to finish that table tonight, she'll put off giving up her nightly glass of wine until tomorrow.

11.

C rap, she's late. Late, late, late. Nori dashes headlong down the stairs, cursing herself for forgetting to set her alarm. She'd been up until the small hours, searching every corner of the flat, but even after midnight, when the astrology forecast ticked over from *senshō* (bad luck after noon) to the more auspicious *tomobiki* (good luck all day, except at noon), she'd found no sign of the missing tea bowl.

And now it's nearly nine-thirty, half an hour past opening and an hour past the time she usually goes downstairs to ready the shop. And late is bad. Their best customers tend to come early, hurrying back to their restaurants before lunch prep ramps up in earnest.

Vaulting over the last step to the sidewalk, she dodges a bicycle, its front basket piled high with soup bowls, and tosses an apology to a startled knot of tourists, chattering away in a language she doesn't understand.

Hers is the only store on the block that's still closed. She rams her key into the half-rusted padlock, yanks on the handle and rolls up the wide front shutter with a clatter. When the opening is barely waist-high, she ducks under and pulls it down quickly behind her.

Inside the windowless store, it's pitch black with the shutter down, but Nori has made her way to the light switch so many times she could do it in her sleep. Feeling her way between the sidewalk displays that she pulled inside yesterday at closing time, she flicks on the lights, illuminating thousands of dishes, all shapes and sizes.

From one-bite appetizer plates to wide-mouthed ramen bowls, pottery is stacked on floor-to-ceiling shelves lining every inch of wall space. Deep green Oribe, black and tan Mashiko-ware, ochre and brown Seto-yaki, blue and white from Kutani. The patchwork of colors comes from every corner of Japan, fashioned by kilns that Okuda & Sons has done business with for generations. Tables crowd the narrow space between, tempting customers with the most seasonal wares. Unlike the forever-unchanging fake flowers in the vase upstairs, the store displays are kept meticulously up to date, anticipating the next season a month in advance, so restaurateurs can stock up on dishes for seasonal specialties before they're needed. It had taken Nori months to learn her grandmother's system of organizing, but now, when a restaurant manager leaves a message that he needs thirty Seto-yaki soy sauce dispensers with the pine design, she can find them in minutes.

The shop is unheated, so she keeps her coat and muffler on while she switches on the space heater behind the counter, readies the cashier station, and checks the answering machine. Two messages. She prays they'll need everything from appetizer plates to dessert bowls.

The first is a disappointment—onesie-twosies to replace last month's breakage. But the second voice belongs to Masao Watanabe, owner of the busiest conveyor-belt sushi restaurant in Asakusa. He's opening a smaller, more premium branch and plans to stop by first thing in the morning to choose the plates that will tempt patrons to eat more than their fill.

She leans on the counter, weak with relief. A big order from Watanabe-san will not only pay the bills this month, it might pay next month's as well. Plenty of time for her grandmother to get well, or to find Hikitoru and sell it to the highest bidder.

Then she remembers the time. How early is "first thing"? Scuttling to the front of the shop, she heaves the shutter open and peers up and down the street, searching for the shaven-headed restaurant owner.

She greets the wizened chopstick seller from next door, who's out sweeping his sidewalk, and bows to two shoppers strolling past. No sign of Watanabe-san. Good. If he'd arrived earlier and found the shop still closed, surely he'd have left another message on the machine.

She's just begun maneuvering the heavy sidewalk displays into position when she spots someone coming out of the shop next door. Tall. Bald. Watanabe-san?

She takes a step toward the restaurant owner, then freezes as the patriarch of Itoh Fine Ceramics follows him out to the sidewalk, performing the kind of deep and obsequious bow a shopkeeper reserves for customers who have just spent lavishly.

No. He wouldn't . . . !

Her hackles rise. It's not the first time the Itohs have tried to steal a customer, if half the things her grandmother has hinted at are true. The store next door hasn't been in business quite as long as the Okudas, but its frontage is three times as wide. The Itohs somehow came out of the war far richer than they'd been before—suspiciously richer, according to 'Baa-chan—and they'd bought up the two neighboring shops, replacing them with one wide building. Theirs is now topped with seven stories of rentable real estate, plus a penthouse for themselves. Unlike Okuda & Sons, with its traditional open front that allows passers-by to see all the stock at a glance, the Itohs' store features an air-conditioned interior and tastefully styled displays behind plate glass windows.

Tetsu Itoh holds his deep bow as Watanabe-san takes his leave, but as he straightens, his eyes meet Nori's and widen in alarm. He whisks back into his shop, like a weasel into its burrow.

The restaurateur turns and catches her staring. His brow furrows, trying to place her.

She forces a smile.

"Good morning, Watanabe-san. Remember me? I'm Nori Okuda." She gestures to the open storefront behind her.

"Oh." His face reddens. "You're the granddaughter, right?" Stepping closer, he hesitates, suddenly awkward. "How is she? Your grandmother, I mean. Itoh-san told me she's in the hospital."

"She's . . . recovering." Best not to air the details out on the sidewalk. "I'm sorry I was a little late this morning. But I got your message, and if you're ready to choose dishes, we just received a few things that I'm sure you'll like."

She nudges aside the displays blocking the shop entrance, but when she looks up again, Mr. Watanabe is still standing on the sidewalk a few feet away, radiating discomfort.

"Ah. The thing is . . ." Sideways flash of eyes, downward curve of mouth. "I didn't know when—or if—you were going to reopen. My new place's hard opening is scheduled for Saturday the thirteenth, so I, uh . . . well, I'm sorry, but I already found what I needed next door."

The bottom drops out of her stomach.

"I . . . I see," she stammers. She manages to babble something about remembering them in the future if he needs anything else, then bows to hide how stunned she is.

Mr. Watanabe asks her to give his regards to her grandmother, then makes his escape.

Nori staggers back into the store and leans against the soup bowl display, reeling. She'd only been half an hour late! How could he have outfitted an entire restaurant so fast? And where did he get the idea they might be closed indefinitely? Did he go next door, to ask the Itohs?

Yes, that's exactly what he did. Her blood begins to boil. He'd gone next door to ask about 'Baa-chan, and ended up buying all his dishes. No, he hadn't *bought* all his dishes, Itoh-san had *sold* him all his dishes.

She stalks back out to the sidewalk and stares daggers at the shop next door. The spotless sheen of the display window reflects her clenched fists, her stony face. Then her shoulders slump. It's too late. A done deal. The order is signed and sealed with Watanabe-san's *hanko*. Even if she was as fearless as her grandmother, the kind of person who could march right in and confront old Weaselface, it wouldn't accomplish anything.

Nori retreats, defeated. Mad at Itoh, mad at herself. She tugs the dust covers off the sidewalk displays and rolls them into a bundle. Trudging to the back, she stuffs them beneath the counter, then stares bleakly through the deserted shop as people saunter by outside, without a glance in her direction.

The only saving grace is that 'Baa-chan wasn't here to see this. Nori had quit high school to help run the shop when her grandmother had her first "spell," so she doesn't have many career options if 'Baa-chan decides she's too much like her father. He ran the family business for only a year after her grandfather died, but that was long enough. Afflicted with an uncanny gift for sensing trends a little too late, his enthusiasms packed the lean-to behind the office with unsellable goods. He nearly bankrupted them before her grandmother had to step in and take over again. Nori had only been five at the time, so she hadn't realized that was the beginning of the end.

But it was, wasn't it? Six weeks later, her mother left, and a month after that, her father was found by the side of the road, the victim of a hit and run. A car? A truck? Nobody knew, nobody saw anything. At the hour he'd been returning from wherever he was drowning his sorrows that night, all good citizens had been tucked up in their futons.

Her mobile chimes from her pocket. Unknown number.

"*Moshi-moshi*?"

"Okuda-san? This is Daiki. Uh, Daiki Miura. We met yesterday at my grandfather's shop . . ."

The boy? Why is he calling her?

"Oh. Yeah. Hi," she replies. Awkward silence. Obviously, he doesn't like talking on the phone any more than she does.

"Can I help you with something?" she prompts.

"I, uh . . . I was just wondering if you'd found it yet. Hikitoru."

"No. But I haven't had much of a chance to look, so—"

"Oh. Yeah. Sorry. But you're going to look today, right?"

Persistent little mosquito.

"Yes, as soon as I finish work. At five."

"Five, huh? Actually, my basketball practice is over at six, so if you need some help, I could come over and—"

"No," she says. Her grandmother would banish her to rural Aomori if she let a kid poke around in their business. "I mean, thanks for the offer, but the shop isn't that big, so there aren't that many places to look."

"Okay," he replies, disappointed. "But, you'll call right away when you find it, right?"

"First thing," she promises.

Another awkward pause, then, "When you call, uh, can you use my mobile number instead of the one on the card my mother gave you? The shop phone doesn't have an answering machine. I've tried to tell them a million times, but . . ."

Ha. Nori had badgered 'Baa-chan for over a year before they got one. Their grandparents had obviously been cut from the same cloth.

"Understood," she says. "I'll call you when I've got something."

"Great. Thanks. And, uh, good luck."

Nori adds the kid to her contacts list. She's got to give him credit—it took nerve to make that call. Had his grandfather made him do it? He's obviously being groomed to take over the pawnshop, but now she stops to wonder why. Maybe misfortune had visited Miura's family too. Maybe they need this sale as much as she does.

Reminded of sales, she glances at the old-fashioned black telephone crouching beside the cash register, silently accusing her. Her grandmother is diabolically good at sweet-talking customers into paying what they owe, but even thinking about phoning people and asking for money makes Nori's stomach cramp. If she doesn't do it, though, who will? She reluctantly opens the sales ledger to the first of the past due accounts. She'd flagged them all with post-it notes yesterday, to avoid making the calls, but she's run out of excuses.

Closing her eyes, she rehearses her pitch. Palms sweating, she makes the first call.

By the end of the morning it's gotten a little easier, just as her grandmother had annoyingly predicted. Four restaurant managers have promised to put a check in the mail, and if they actually do it, the lights and the internet will stay on for a few more weeks.

A distant construction siren goes off, releasing her like the school dismissal bell. Cheered, she flips the ledger shut. Time to grab some cheap curry, then use the rest of her lunch hour to find out more about that missing tea bowl. She can't start tearing the place apart until closing time, but the more she knows about Hikitoru and the guy who made it, the more she'll be able to guess what someone might be willing to pay when she finds it.

Ten minutes and a dash to the take-out shop later, Nori sets an old-fashioned silver desk bell on the counter, atop a dog-eared "Please ring for service" note in her grandmother's handwriting.

Shedding her shoes as she steps up into the office, she retrieves her personal chopsticks and plops down on a cushion behind the low table, keeping an eye on the shop through the open door.

She feels the office gods regarding her from inside their wooden shrine, high on a shelf that's swagged anew each year with a sacred straw rope and supplied monthly with fresh offerings of salt, sake, and evergreen *sakaki* sprigs. The 'Baa-chan in her head reminds her she'd better enlist their help before beginning her search for information on Hikitoru.

Folding her hands, she begs them to prove Miura Senior wrong about the internet.

An hour later, though, her prayers remain largely unanswered. A phone search for "Hikitoru" turned up lots of comic book characters and a book on Japanese death poems. Adding "tea bowl" confirmed that Senkō-ji temple had indeed burned to the ground in the fire-bombing of 1945. Hikitoru is on the list of art treasures saved from the burnt-out temple by valiant priests and townspeople, but there's no picture.

A search for "Yoshi Takamatsu tea bowl" delivers the now-familiar photos of Snow Bride and Waterlily, along with a few made in such different style that they must be the work of artists who share his name.

The potter's online encyclopedia entry informs her that he was the eldest son of a famous ceramics family from Sasayama that has been passing down the artistic name Honzaemon for sixteen generations. They're known for old-fashioned, wood-fired Tamba-ware, but oddly, it's not eldest son Yoshi Takamatsu who inherited the honorary artist name when his father died, but his younger brother, Nobu.

The internet serves up plenty of examples of Nobu's work. It's typical Tamba-ware, made from the region's pale ochre clay, slip-glazed a smooth reddish-brown, with drips of dark glaze running down the sides. But Nobu's tea bowls are straight-sided, not rounded like his brother's. Pages of critical exposition detail Nobu's career (iterative, not innovative), his patrons (every wealthy samurai family in western Japan), and his legacy (he's the father of an artist who is far more favorably regarded by art historians than he is).

There's less enlightening information about the older brother. Yoshi Takamatsu's personal entry is light on hard facts, and raises more questions than it answers. He left Sasayama to settle on the other side of Lake Biwa when he was barely twenty, but the entry doesn't say why. He captured the patronage of a powerful Kyoto warlord, but it doesn't say how. And it doesn't explain why so few of his works have survived. The only thing it clears up is why his younger brother inherited the family name: Yoshi Takamatsu was blind.

Nori blinks. That can't be right. The potter who made Hikitoru was *blind*? How could a famous artist be blind? Digging deeper, she finds an article by a professor of Japanese art history. Based on the fact that the hereditary artistic name bypassed Yoshi, the scholar suggests that he lost his sight early in life, but he doesn't explain how or when.

He must have done all his famous work before he lost his sight. That would explain why his pieces are so rare. Nori checks his birthdate, then scrolls down to the descriptions of Snow Bride and Waterlily. Both were made before he was nineteen. He must have become blind sometime in his early twenties. After he moved away from Sasayama? Or was that *why* he'd moved away from Sasayama?

She follows a link to Snow Bride, curious whether it's also a National Treasure. It takes her to a Fujimori Fine Art auction catalog from four years ago. Scrolling down, she scans the description. Rounded silhouette . . . thin lip . . . ten million.

Ten million. Ten million *yen.* Four years ago, the reserve price for Snow Bride was *ten million yen.*

She's stunned. Even if Hikitoru doesn't turn out to be National Cultural Treasure material, if it's worth anywhere near ten million yen, her worries will be over. Not just for now. Forever.

All she has to do is find it.

12.

The temple dweller known only to fellow novices as Yoshi sits outside the abbot's study, waiting to be summoned. This morning at first light, he'd sat his last *zazen* meditation, eaten his last breakfast of pickles and rice, and ritually wiped his wooden bowl for the last time. Today the abbot will send him out into the world with a task to complete before he returns to take his vows.

Yoshi sat his first *zazen* in the darkest days of winter, isolated and alone, not yet warmed by the friendship of the other novices. The ancient wooden meditation hall had felt vast and empty, despite the presence of nearly a hundred monks. But day by day, as the pain from kneeling for hours lessened, the pain of losing Kiri also began to diminish. By the time the tolling of the temple bell wiped the slate clean on New Year's, he was no longer freshly ambushed by grief every morning when he awoke.

After the new year, he slowly began to participate in monastery life, instead of being cared for like a broken sparrow. The first task the *rōshi* assigned was more practical than spiritual. Yoshi had quickly discovered how much he relied on others to set his meals before him, to make sure his clothes were clean and aired, to keep his tonsured head shaved and his topknot neatly bound. All through the deep snows of January, he learned to do those things for himself. By the time the scent of plum blossoms began to distract him through the meditation room windows, not only could he take care of his daily needs, he could also chop vegetables and scrub floors nearly as quickly as the other novices.

By the time he heard newly hatched swallows peeping hungrily from beneath the spreading temple eaves, the monk in charge of vigilance no longer had to tap him on the shoulder with his bamboo rod to remind him to straighten his back as he sat *zazen* in the drafty meditation hall. Oddly enough, his blindness helped him—he wasn't, after all, distracted by the sights that so easily diverted the other novices—and by the time the young swallows were whirring about the tower that supported the deep-voiced temple bell, his daily practice had calmed his soul enough that he'd actually found himself contemplating the future. Maybe he could learn to cook the temple's simple vegetarian fare, instead of just hauling its garbage. Or he could study to become the monk who strikes the ceremonial drum at worship, instead of merely chanting the sutras.

Then the abbot asked him to take part in a tea ceremony. It was an honor to be invited, and it turned out to be a far more moving experience than Yoshi expected. At home, tea ceremonies had been used to sell pottery, but at Sengen-in, they were elevated to a form of meditation. The unhurried performance of ritual gestures, the mindful appreciation of each tool, the divine moment when tea surprises the tongue.

It was a revelation. He began to wonder if the gods had led him to Sengen-in to become the temple's tea master. And that's when he realized that sometime in the past few months, he'd decided to stay at the monastery forever.

On the day the monks exchanged their heavy winter robes for lighter linen, he'd knocked on the abbot's door to ask permission to take his vows. But that interview hadn't gone as he expected. The abbot listened to his request and instead of giving him an answer, asked a question: had Yoshi ever learned a trade?

Rinkan-*rōshi* had never probed him about his past, except to learn the source of the despair that had driven him out into the snow to die. That first night, the abbot had explained that everyone who arrived at Sengen-in with the intention of becoming a monk left his old self behind on the temple steps and started at the bottom, regardless of his rank in the outside world. He'd gently assured the young man in the torn and soiled hemp robe that it was often those with the humblest beginnings who attained enlightenment most quickly.

Recalling those words, Yoshi was a little embarrassed to admit that he was the privileged son of an artist—a potter, who made tea ceremony ware—and that because of his father's position, he'd never learned a trade.

"But," he added, "my childhood toys weren't painted kites or wooden puzzle boxes, they were a fist full of clay and a potter's wheel. Before I left my father's house, I made tea ceremony utensils, but I'm sure I could make more useful things too. Would you like me to make something for the temple?"

"No, that's not why I asked," the abbot replied. He refused to say more, and sent Yoshi away that day without an answer.

Several weeks later, though, Yoshi had been called to the abbot's study and asked if he was ready to give up his first attachment.

"I've been thinking about that," he said, eager to show the abbot what a model monk he'd be. "I'm ready to give up all ties to the outside world."

"No," replied the *rōshi*. "Not yet. There's something you need to do first. I want you to go back out into the world. I want you to leave Sengen-in and work for a potter I know, over in Shigaraki."

The blood drained from Yoshi's face. Leave the safety of the mountain temple where he'd found peace? No. He couldn't face life outside the walls. Here, his work, his meditation, and his meals all took place in the company of his fellow monks. Outside, every time a woman opened her mouth, he'd be reminded that he will never hear Kiri's sweet voice again.

"I can't. I'm not ready. Let me do something else," he pleaded. "Anything else. I'll go later, when I'm stronger."

"I don't think you understand," the *rōshi* said, unmoved. "Until you give up your attachment to that girl, you cannot be fully present here. You're using this place to hide from your attachment, and it's chaining you to the Wheel of Rebirth. Until you give her up, you may not vow yourself to this temple."

A dove called plaintively outside the window. The silence deepened, but he couldn't bring himself to submit to the *rōshi's* request.

"You may go," sighed the abbot.

He'd dragged himself back to the kitchen in despair. The *rōshi* was right, but he couldn't give Kiri up. He held her memory close before he went to sleep each night, told her things that nobody else would understand, needed the ache that reminded him he'd once been loved.

Adding to his sorrows, this was the first time the abbot had been anything but kind. A distance widened between them, one he couldn't bring himself to close. Feeling abandoned and alone, he ate his meals, swept the temple steps, and meditated in lonely silence, acutely aware he was nothing but an outsider. The other monks might be diligent or lazy, they might achieve enlightenment or not, but they all belonged here. Everyone but Yoshi would be allowed to live out his days in service to the temple. The discipline stick rapped him daily, as his head drooped and his mind chased itself in circles, trying to escape the task he'd been set.

Then, one day in early summer, the tide turned. Little by little, he became resigned to his fate. One midsummer's day, he woke up with the strength to accept it. He knocked on the abbot's door and humbly asked for directions to the potter's kiln.

A week later, he sits on the sweet-smelling rice straw mats lining the corridor outside the *rōshi's* study, with his traveling bundle on the floor beside him and a wooden box in his hands.

"Come in," says the abbot.

When they're both seated, with fragrant wisps of steam rising from their teacups, the abbot presents Yoshi with a note, stamped with his seal.

"This is your introduction to my old friend, Takanori. We were novices together, but his father and elder brother were killed in the Great Yasu Flood of 1665. He gave up his intention and returned home to run the family business, but I think you'll find that he still walks the Eightfold Path."

He calls to a monk waiting outside in the passageway, introducing him as Brother Jin. Jin grew up in a village on the eastern shore of Lake Biwa, and knows the way well. He will accompany Yoshi and act as guide. It will take them two days to get to Takanori's kiln, deep in the mountains near the Yasu River.

"The Yasu River," Yoshi says. He doesn't know anybody who's been there. "What kind of pottery do they make in those parts?"

"Shigaraki-ware. Do you know it?"

He does. It's very different from his father's Tamba-ware, which is valued for the subtlety of its underglaze and the controlled drips that cascade down the sides. Shigaraki-ware is prized for its scratchy wildness, the way patches of rough, unglazed clay and natural impurities burst through slick smatterings of melted ash.

Yoshi has no experience making pots like that. Even his skill at preparing the raw earth might not be useful. How good would he be at treading out the kind of clay that has to be left rough, studded with chips of feldspar?

His doubts must have shown on his face, because the abbot reminds him, "The unknown is the soil in which learning takes place."

They contemplate this truth together, as the twitterings of birds in the cherry tree outside fill the silence. Finally, the abbot reaches for his teacup and Yoshi picks up his wooden box.

Drawing himself upright, he formally extends it toward the *rōshi* with both hands.

"This is one of my most treasured possessions," he says, "but it reminds me of the bride I tried to follow into the next life. As a sign that I intend to return only when I've given up that attachment for good, I humbly ask you to accept it, on behalf of the temple."

He bows low over the table, and as the abbot lifts Snow Bride from his hands, he feels his soul lighten, just a little.

13.

Closing time, at last. At the stroke of five, Nori wheels the sidewalk displays into the shop and bangs down the front shutter, slipping a pin on a slithery chain through a pair of bolt holes, to lock it from inside. She returns to the cluttered office and burbles hot water into the old stained teapot to prepare for the tea bowl hunt.

She stands before the shelves of dusty, expensive ceramics in the lean-to, holding her steaming cup, guessing that the box belonging to the tea bowl she'd taken to Miura's will most likely be among the foolish purchases made by her father.

Scissoring open the stepladder, she climbs it to search among the goods stacked on the top shelf. Checking one box after another, she's looking for one with a stamp that matches the mark on the bottom of that decoy tea bowl. Up and down, back and forth, she ferries anything that's roughly the right size to the office, just in case 'Baa-chan didn't just switch the two. She's made five trips before she uncovers the box with a Yamamura stamp on top. She picks it up, and knows right away it's not nearly heavy enough to have a tea bowl inside.

"'Baa-chan," she moans, "why do you always have to make every-thing so hard?"

Because that's the way you learn. Her grandmother's voice is as loud as ever inside her head, even though it's trapped in an unconscious body, six blocks away.

When Nori had skinned her knee as a child, her grandmother had handed her the first aid kit and told her to apply plenty of stinging disinfectant before the bandage. And every New Year's, instead of pre-senting her with a traditional red envelope filled with cash, 'Baa-chan hid it somewhere in the house. The year she turned eight, she looked high and low. The day wore on and her excitement dissolved into tears, but her grandmother refused to tell her where it was. That envelope remains hidden to this day.

If she changed her mind about wanting you to sell it, Miura had said, *I'd wager she hid it somewhere. Somewhere you'll never find it.* But her grandmother would never have told her Hikitoru was their insurance if it wasn't. The two of them don't always agree, but they've got each other's backs. Nori's parents are long gone, and 'Baa-chan's loved ones have been dead even longer. They're the only Okudas left.

She pries the lid off the Yamamura box, making sure it's really empty. But . . . it's not. A roll of yen notes as big as her fist is wedged inside. She pulls it out and stares at it. Snaps off the rubber band and counts. It's mostly small bills, but it ought to buy groceries for a month, if she's careful.

Message received, 'Baa-chan. If she wasn't in the midst of a real emergency, she wouldn't have to sell the tea bowl. At least not yet.

But with her grandmother's medical expenses piling up, she has to keep looking. Climbing down the stepladder, she tucks the yen notes into her purse and returns to the table, praying to the office gods that one of the boxes stacked on the table will contain another Snow Bride or Waterlily.

She angles the desk light onto the first one. Inside is a brown and cream Karatsu-ware tea bowl with a bamboo motif. Definitely not

Hikitoru. Box number two holds a glossy green Oribe bowl, and inside the third is an artfully rough piece of Shigaraki-ware.

The fourth lid is stamped with the mark of a kiln near Sasayama, the Takamatsu family's hometown. This one's more promising. It would be typical of 'Baa-chan to switch the valuable Hikitoru with a piece of ordinary Tamba-ware that's similar enough to fool someone who isn't expert enough to know the difference.

The bowl inside is a pale gray, with glaze dripping from the lip like Snow Bride, except the brown stripes are too regular, and its sides are straight, not rounded. She flips it over and holds it up to the light. There's no potter's mark on the foot. It's either old enough to be Hikitoru, or the kind of mass-produced touristware that the kiln doesn't put its name on. She hefts it, but since she's never actually held expensive pottery, she can't tell if it's lighter or heavier than it should be.

If the sides were rounded instead of square, she'd be confident enough to stop looking and call Miura, but it's not quite a good enough match. Setting it aside, she opens the last box.

This one holds a brick-red tea bowl with no stamp on its foot either. Its rounded shape is closer to Yoshi's other work, but although it resembles Waterlily, the glaze cascades from the rim in thicker drips, with a distinct greenish cast. She sits back, worrying her lip.

Which one is more likely to be Hikitoru? The white one that's the wrong shape, or the rounded one with the wrong drips?

She sets them next to each other. She could take both tea bowls to Miura, ask if he can tell her which is the real one. But what if his answer is "neither"? Or, even worse, what if one actually *is* Hikitoru, but he doesn't tell her? What if he makes her a lowball offer for it, then flips it and gets rich off her ignorance? No, she can't trust Miura.

But what about the grandson? Does he know how his grandfather plans to identify the tea bowl without its box?

Daiki Miura is definitely the lesser of two evils. If he doesn't already know how to spot the real Hikitoru, he can probably find out.

The boy picks up on the first ring. *"Mosh'-mosh'?"*

"Hello Miura-kun. This is Nori Okuda—"

"Did you find it?" he interrupts eagerly.

"I think so. But I'd like to be sure it's the right one before I waste your grandfather's time. Can you do me a favor and find out what he's looking for? I mean, how is he going to identify Hikitoru without the box?"

"Actually, I already know the answer to that."

"And?"

He hesitates. "It would be easier if I came over and saw it for myself."

No chance. He's sure to notice she's so clueless that she's trying to decide between two bowls that look nothing alike.

"I don't think that will be necessary," she replies smoothly. "If you could just describe the main points over the phone, I can save you the trouble."

"It's no trouble," he counters. "I can be there in . . ." silence, while he checks the giant wristwatch, ". . . twenty minutes."

"No, really," she insists. "Please don't trouble yourself. I'm sure I can—"

"The thing is, it's not something I can easily explain. Over the phone, that is. If I could look at what you found, I could tell you right away."

That gives her pause. Has she underestimated him? Because that's what she would have said, if she were in his place. Information is power, and as long as he's the only one who can tell her if it's the real thing or not, she can't sell it to anyone else. She'll have to let him see it.

"All right." If she stages it right, maybe he won't guess she's taking a shot in the dark. "You have the address I gave your mother? Message me when you get here and I'll let you in."

She ends the call and considers the two tea bowls. Decides to bet on the pale one that's the wrong shape, because it looks more like the picture of Snow Bride that Daiki found. Rewrapping it, she sets it aside. Then she packs up the others and puts them back on the shelf. If the white tea bowl proves a bust, they can always "discover" the dark red one in the lean-to.

Her phone chimes. That was fast. The kid must have run all the way from the station. *I'll be right out*, she types. Leaving the stepladder where it is, she whips off her kerchief and hangs up her work apron before hustling to the front of the shop to let him in.

The shutter rolls up, revealing scuffed black running shoes rocking back and forth, two hands shoved into the pockets of black uniform trousers, and a pair of narrow shoulders oppressed by a heavy backpack. Waving him under the half-open door, she rolls it back down behind him. He stands there surveying the shop through his black-rimmed glasses, blinking like a myopic turtle with a ridiculously weighty shell.

"Come on back," she says.

At the open door to the office, he slips off his shoes without untying them, then lopes to the table.

"Is this it?" he asks, staring down at the box.

"Yes," she says. "Tea?"

"Yes." Then he remembers his manners and adds, "Please."

She busies herself at the hot water pot, then looks up. He's still standing.

"Sit," she says, waving at the table.

He shrugs out of his backpack and lets it thud to the floor, then drops onto the thin cushion reserved for guests. He peers at the upside-down writing on the box in the middle of the table, while Nori arranges the teapot and two cups on a battered lacquer tray. She kneels across from him.

"That isn't going to tell you anything," she reminds him, pouring out the tea and handing one cup across the table. "Hikitoru's real box is upstairs, with the wrong tea bowl inside."

She unboxes the white bowl with straight sides and sets it between them.

"That's not it," he says.

That was fast. Too fast.

"How do you know? You haven't even really looked at it."

Unzipping his backpack, he tugs out a blue plastic sleeve and unclips the papers inside.

"You've seen these, right?" He hands her printouts of Waterlily and Snow Bride from the internet.

"Yes," she says, placing them on the table.

"What about this?" He offers a copy of Yoshi Takamatsu's unsatisfying biography.

"I saw that too."

"I bet you haven't seen these, though."

He hands her two black and white photocopies from a book that's so old, the yellowing around the edge of the pages shows up as gray shadows. The captions identify the tea bowls in the photos as Snow Bride and Waterlily, but they're shot from the top, not the side. Seen from above, both have a distinctive oval shape.

"Oh." Now she understands. "That's how your grandfather knew, isn't it? Before he even unwrapped the bowl I brought, he could tell it was the wrong shape."

"Yes."

"But that doesn't mean all of Yoshi Takamatsu's tea bowls are this shape," she objects.

"It doesn't," Daiki agrees, handing her the last sheet of paper. "But they are."

This photo shows another tea bowl—named Unmei, according to the caption—and it's oval too. But it isn't drippy or white. It isn't even Tamba-ware. The rough clay is studded with tiny chips of white and brushed with a bubbling glaze that leaves swaths of the bare surface showing through. It looks like Shigaraki-ware. If the Xerox had been in color, the clay would have been ochre, shading to deep red, and the glaze a grayish green. Her father had invested in enough Shigaraki-ware to outfit multiple restaurants, and it's all still gathering dust in the back room. It's beautiful, but sauces are hard to scrub from the nooks and crannies of the rustic surface, and not a single restaurant owner had been interested.

"Impossible," she says. "It's the right shape, but it's not Tamba-ware."

"I know. But according to this old book of my grandfather's, Yoshi

Takamatsu moved to Shiga province and started his own kiln, where he became known by the nickname Yakibō. He was working in a new region, with different clay and different glazes, but look at the shape. And the rim."

She sets the photo of Unmei beside the others, and once she looks past the rough surface, she sees it. It's the same shape as Waterlily and Snow Bride. And all three have delicate rims, far thinner than typical Tamba-ware or Shigaraki-ware.

She's still not convinced.

"Why don't any of the websites say he worked under two different names?"

The boy rolls his eyes.

"Because the kind of people who know the nicknames of Edo Period potters with hardly any surviving work write books, not articles for the internet. You may have noticed that my grandfather isn't a big fan. After you left, he showed me this book to prove his point. There's no picture of Hikitoru in it, but my grandfather says your missing tea bowl will be Shigaraki-ware, not Tamba."

"Why?"

"Look at the names. The Tamba-ware ones have pretty names. Snow Bride. Waterlily. But, Fate? And, Taking Back?"

He's got a point.

"Now that we know what we're looking for . . ." he bounces to his feet, ". . . where do we start?"

We. Nori regards him thoughtfully. Well, it wouldn't hurt for the kid to feel they're partners, at least until she knows more than he does. Which she might, as soon as she can get rid of him. 'Baa-chan has her own peculiar way of doing things, including how the dishes in the shop are arranged. The moment Daiki told her the potter's nickname, she knew exactly where to look for that tea bowl.

14.

Yoshi sits up, instantly awake. This must be the biggest typhoon to hit Shiga province in all the twenty-two years he's lived here.

Plink-plink-plink-plink-plink-plink-plink-plink—

Water is coming through the leak in the roof much faster now. By the sound of it, the pot he'd pressed into service at midnight is nearly full. Which doesn't surprise him, because the roaring gusts of wind that jolted him from sleep are now driving torrents of rain against the side of Takanori's old farmhouse. If the master had still been alive, he wouldn't have had to exaggerate this storm's ferocity to impress his drinking cronies.

The shutters rattle, buffeted by the wind. Is it still nighttime? Or morning?

"Hattsan?" he ventures. If his apprentice is still asleep, he's not snoring anymore. "HATTSAN?"

No reply. It must be morning. His anxious assistant has probably gone out to check the kiln, to make sure that the fixes they'd put in place last night are holding. They'd been up past midnight, covering the chimney and shuttering the stoking windows to keep the pots inside dry until firing, but no matter how short the night, Hattsan never sleeps past first light.

Plinkplinkplinkplinkplinkplinkplink. If that pot's not emptied soon, it's going to overflow. Yoshi stands, wincing a little at the stiffness in his joints. He'd been feeling it ever since Takanori passed away, as if he'd inherited the master potter's aches and pains along with his kiln. Six years now, nearly seven. After New Year's, he'll stop by the temple and talk to Uchida-*bōsan* about scheduling a service for the potter's death anniversary.

Yoshi rolls up his quilt, then measures four strides from the hearth to the corner of the room where he always stows it, so he won't trip over it during the day. Making his way toward the leak, he brushes a hand along the rough plaster wall until his foot encounters the clothing chest, then pivots to shuffle cautiously toward the bare patch where he'd pulled up the wet straw mat last night and set the pot in place to catch the leaks. With a grunt, Yoshi lifts the sloshing vessel and backs up to the wall, sliding along it until he reaches the stone-paved entry. Aiming his feet into his wooden *geta* clogs waiting in their customary spot at the edge of the mats, he shoulders the door open against the wind. The storm throws a fistful of rain in his face as he staggers outside to dump the water. He quickly ducks back in to replace the pot and wipe the floorboards.

His empty stomach reminds him that Hattsan would have been too polite to help himself to anything in the kitchen before heading out to his morning duties, and he'll be as hungry as a school of carp by now. Yoshi feels his way to the kitchen to scoop up handfuls of last night's cold rice and wrap them around salty-sour *umeboshi* plums and slices of pickled *daikon* radish. He eats two rice balls, listening to the pounding rain overhead and wondering how soon it will let up, then tucks the rest into a dish and ties a carrying cloth around it to protect it from the elements. Plucking his wide conical hat from its peg by the door, he knots the strings under his chin and shrugs into the new rain cape hanging beneath it. The shaggy reeds are still pungently damp on the outside, but he's pleased to find the inside warm and dry.

The wind is far too strong for the oiled paper umbrella he keeps propped next to the door, so Yoshi tucks his chin down against the slanting rain as he makes his way toward the kiln, trailing a hand along the blackened cedar siding of the farmhouse, then using the brushy bamboo lining the narrow path to guide his steps toward the outbuildings.

Hattsan isn't hard to find. Even the storm can't drown out the slightly bawdy song being sung with the gusto of someone who believes himself entirely alone in the clay treading shed. Despite the miserable conditions, Yoshi grins at a verse he hadn't heard before, then his foot catches on something lying across the path and he pitches forward so violently that the dish of rice balls flies from his hands. He lands, knees-first, in the mud. Palms stinging, kneecaps bruised, he rises, irate.

"Hattsan!" he bellows.

The song abruptly cuts off and the door bangs open.

"Yakibō!" cries the apprentice, so distressed at seeing his disheveled master that he accidentally calls him by the nickname people use for him in the village. "Are you all right? I'm sorry! Really sorry. I used that broom this morning to clear the path, but it was raining so hard, I thought I might need it again, so I leaned it up outside the door, and the wind must have . . ."

"How many times do I have to tell you—" Yoshi grumbles, stomping into the shed.

"I know, I know," Hattsan is scurrying to hang the errant tool on the wall where it belongs. "Always put everything back in its place. Here, let me—"

He kneels to swipe at the worst of the mud on the front of Yoshi's leggings with a rag, but Yoshi stops him and takes the cloth to clean his hands first.

The contrite apprentice says, "Sorry, I won't do it again."

Yes he will. Hattsan is a good boy, but not a fast learner. Yoshi carefully sets aside his irritation, however, lest it turn into another attachment binding him to the Wheel of Rebirth.

Instead, he says, "I brought you some rice balls, but they might not have survived the broom handle."

Hattsan thanks him and escapes to search the bushes.

When he returns, Yoshi asks, "Why are you out here preparing clay in the middle of a typhoon, anyway?"

"I thought we might need some new roof tiles," his apprentice explains. "That leak we discovered last night means at least one is missing or broken, and we may lose more if this wind keeps up. Since we're doing a firing anyway . . ."

"You're right. Good thinking." Gratitude chases away the last of Yoshi's irritation. Hattsan might not be the sharpest stick in the woodpile, but the son of a builder is way ahead of the son of an artisan when it comes to fixing anything that's not a pottery tool. Yoshi stoops to take a pinch of the clay his apprentice has been treading, rubs it between his fingers.

"Too wet," he says. "If you don't add more earth to make it stiffer, the tiles will be brittle after they're fired."

"They will?" Hattsan can't hide his dismay. "The ones I already turned out of the mold looked fine to me."

"Don't look," Yoshi says. "Feel. Close your eyes, if you have to. If you don't put those back into the treading pile and work in some more clay, we'll be replacing them again, come the next storm."

"I understand." He sighs. "I'll do it right away."

Satisfied that no more supervision is likely to be required for a few hours, Yoshi heads to the kiln. He has a long day ahead, arranging the pieces they'd hastily loaded in yesterday before the storm broke. Fortunately, the rain has diminished from gusting fury to a steady downpour, so he's able to pay his respects at the small shrine next to the kiln's entrance without getting much wetter. Like Takanori before him, he relies on the resident gods to bless each piece so it not only emerges whole and unbroken, but appealing to the eyes of his customers.

He crawls through the low entrance, reminding himself to give

Hattsan some coins to buy a good bottle of sake the next time he's in town, for the more elaborate offering they'll make before kindling the fire. He needs to stop by the temple to pick up more incense for honoring Takanori's death tablet on the home altar too. The kiln gods can make or break each batch of pottery, but it's Takanori's spirit to whom Yoshi owes daily thanks for teaching him everything he knows.

Work on mastering only one thing at a time, no matter how long it takes.

Practice makes perfect.

Listen to what the gods are telling you, so they don't have to hit you over the head with it.

The master's wisdom still informs Yoshi daily—not just for making pottery, but for the all-important work of shedding his attachments. When he'd first arrived, the *rōshi's* old friend had initiated him into the secrets of fashioning Shigaraki-ware, but over time, he also taught him how the repetitive throwing of everyday storage pots and grinding bowls could be a form of meditation. How turning out one nearly identical piece after another invited the gods to work through his hands, raising ordinary pots from the mundane to the divine.

That's how he got the idea to use his potter's wheel to master the attachment to Kiri he'd been sent there to renounce. He begged the gods to work through him, to elevate his sorrow to something pure and spiritual that would help him escape the Wheel of Rebirth instead of tying him to it. He'd made forty-three tea bowls representing "first love" by the time Takanori followed him to the firewood shed where he'd been stashing them. His master had stood for a long moment, contemplating the bowls stacked everywhere, then gently suggested that instead of making more, he ought to start throwing them away. That it would be better to choose one to pour his longing into, and discard the rest.

So Yoshi did, though he found it nearly impossible to decide which one perfectly captured the essence of "first love." He wavered back and forth, running to the trash heap to exchange the one he'd picked for one he'd just thrown away.

Takanori then pointed out he had merely traded one obsession for another. Until he smashed the alternates, he'd never be able to focus on giving up the one he'd chosen.

And that worked, for the most part. As the years went by, Yoshi discovered a number of other attachments and freed himself from them. Only First Love still mocks him from the shelf in the woodshed.

But that might be about to change. For the first time in twenty-two years, he's optimistic about getting rid of it. He'd experienced a flash of enlightenment yesterday while consoling the noodle maker on the loss of his wife, and when today's work is done, he'll put his new-found perspective to the test.

Turning his attention to arranging six new tea bowls around the mouth of the firebox, he holds each between his palms, feeling the slight variations in shape and glaze that differentiate the candidates representing Ambition, the lesser attachment he plans to deal with after ridding himself of First Love.

Working his way back through the kiln, he's oblivious to the storm drumming on the roof as he arranges the shelves of storage pots, water jars, and grinding bowls so that each will be blessed by the searing caress of the gods. Hours later, when he pokes his head outside again, he's surprised to hear the quiet *plip-plop* of water dripping from tree branches, instead of roaring from the heavens. Cautiously, he crawls out through the low opening, grimacing as he unbends his stiff body. He sniffs the air. It doesn't feel like the storm is over yet, but he ought to take advantage of this lull to test his new insight about First Love and restock the farmhouse's firewood before it starts up again.

Aiming for the sound of the swollen stream, he uses the half-buried rocks Takanori lined the path with to guide his feet, until he's pushing past shoulder-high azaleas outside the firewood shack. As the wind picks up, it stirs the dry leaves still hanging from the brushwood used to construct the small outbuilding. He yanks open the crooked door and steps inside. As always, it smells pleasantly of the pine stacked waist-high along the wall.

Before stooping to his chore, he reaches toward the shelf above the logs and runs his hands along the five tea bowl boxes atop it. He's managed to rid himself of Ude-jiman (misplaced "pride" in his own skills), Mikudasu (the "arrogance" which had prevented him from properly honoring Takanori's teaching when he first arrived), Kanzen-shugi (the "perfectionism" which stood in the way of trusting the kiln gods to help him turn out truly divine Shigaraki-ware), and Gankō (the "rigid thinking" that blocked him from accepting there could be more than one right way to do things).

But today he's here to consider Hatsu-koi. As the bowl representing First Love settles between his palms, he lets the silence surround him. Then he thinks of Kiri.

She'd be older now. He'd be able to feel the bones in her dove-like hands, and her musical voice might have acquired new depths from forty years of living. It's even possible that she's exchanged her fragrant silk kimonos for the incense-perfumed robes of an abbess.

Holding the tea bowl before him, he stills his mind. Then he probes his feelings, one by one.

His fear that she'd sickened and died.

His outrage that she'd renounced his love by taking her vows.

His anger that she'd given him up so easily.

His heartache that she might never really have loved him.

For years, those thoughts felt like open wounds, but today, for the very first time, the pain is gone. He sees them for what they are: distractions. It wasn't his love for her that had been binding him to the Wheel of Rebirth, it was his longing to be with her again in *this* life. After two decades, he has finally grasped that if they're truly connected by the red thread of fate, they'll meet again when they're reborn. And someday, when they both attain enlightenment, they'll dwell together forever in the Western Paradise.

Which is why he needs to hurry up and break this attachment, because neither of them is getting any younger. And Kiri has spent her whole life praying behind convent walls—she might very well go straight to the Western Paradise when she dies, and he doesn't want to keep her waiting.

When this storm passes, he'll go to the place in the woods where he hid the last two First Love candidates, and smash them. Then the only task remaining will be to let go of Hatsu-koi itself.

Rain is pattering on the roof again, so he puts the tea bowl back in its box, gathers an armload of firewood, and hurries down the hill to the farmhouse. As he nears the front door, he hears a moan.

"Hattsan?" But it can't be. It's coming from the wrong direction.

He dumps the firewood inside the front door, then feels his way down the track that leads to the road. He doesn't go far before his toe encounters a body, lying face down in the mud, soaking wet and stinking of sake.

15.

Feudal Japan

SEPTEMBER, 1703

Shigaraki

The first thing Saburo the Aspiring Poet becomes aware of as he swims up to consciousness is the smell of smoke. He opens his eyes a sliver. Then wider, because he still can't see a thing. It's so dark he can barely make out the peaked ceiling far overhead, supported by undulating beams blackened by age or soot or both.

His head hurts like a pack of vindictive demons is trapped inside. Reaching up, he finds his tonsure stubbled, his topknot awry. There's a tender patch high on his cheekbone and he winces as his fingers explore some scratches on his jaw that he can't remember—

Then it all floods back. The accursed typhoon, a late-season storm so fierce, he couldn't tell where the path ended and the forest began. The onslaught of wind and rain that not only pounded relentlessly from above, but blew sideways like the gods had turned the world on its ear. His traveling hat had been useless, his fine clothing soaked in minutes, and as he tucked his chin against the wind, his enviable goatee became a downspout, sluicing cold rain straight down the neck of his kimono. His feet were rubbed raw by plodding through the mud in sodden sandals, and his wet cloak felt like it had been fashioned by a blacksmith, not a weaver. Blinded by the driving rain, he must have taken the wrong track, because he hadn't encountered a single inn along the way. Just endless, endless trees that blocked the waning light long before sundown, and bushes that snatched hungrily at his garments from either side, as if they didn't get a chance to snare travelers very often.

The only thing that kept him from giving up was the bottle of sake he'd intended as a gift for the family acquaintance he was counting on to offer him a bed at his next stop. The alcohol had warmed him, dulled his aches and pains, or at least made him care less. Trying to make the final mouthfuls last, he'd spotted a track that didn't look like it had been made by animals, running up into the trees. He'd fallen more than once as he stumbled up the rocky path, his feet clumsy with exhaustion or drink or both. The weathered door of a decrepit-looking farmhouse is the last thing he can remember. But he must have knocked, and there must have been somebody home, because here he is, warmer and drier than he's been in two days. And hungover as hell.

"You're awake."

The gruff voice belongs to an imposing figure materializing from the gloom.

Saburo tries to answer, but his throat is too dry. The smoky smell diminishes as the man moves away, then returns as he's handed a roughly glazed cup.

"It's just water," the man says, "but that's probably the best cure for what's ailing you."

As the would-be poet struggles to sit, his rescuer splays one strong hand against his back to help him up. Saburo grabs the cup and drinks greedily, hands it back, asks for more.

"Later. Best to go slow at first. My name is Yoshi, but everyone calls me Yakibō. Who are you?"

"Shibata." He bobs an awkward bow. "Saburo Shibata."

How long had he been out cold? Is it the middle of the night? Or already the next morning? He squints into the gloom. The windows are shuttered tight against the storm, but slivers of light show around the edges. Must be daytime. Outside, anyway—it's midnight in here. The only light in the cavernous room comes from a fire banked low in the sunken hearth. It leaps up onto an iron teakettle suspended over the fire, then illuminates the underside of a carved wooden carp counterweight and the links of an iron chain disappearing into the gloom overhead. His rescuer's face is in deep shadow, the flickering light behind him silhouetting a shaved pate surrounded by wiry hair that's been pulled into the topknot worn by commoners and samurai alike.

"Where am I?" Saburo asks. "How long have I been here?"

"Since yesterday." The man adds a stick to the fire. "We found you lying in the mud outside. What were you doing in the woods all alone, during the biggest storm we've had in years?"

Saburo groans and falls back onto his pallet, reminded of the long list of calamities that had befallen him since he set out. His blistered feet, unaccustomed to walking long distances each day. His "winter" cloak, so inadequate for the mountain weather that it would have been laughable if it hadn't nearly killed him. And his utter failure to find the inspiration he'd been seeking.

"I was hunting poems," he sighs.

That got a guffaw. "Did you catch any?"

"No," he admits. "Not one." He ought to laugh along with his rescuer, but his throbbing sense of failure hurts more than all his aching bones combined.

"Well, then, Saburo Shibata, as a wise man once told me, you're lucky you didn't become a Buddha while still burdened with such burning desire. Be grateful you've been given another chance to rid yourself of attachments like that. You might find enlightenment yet, before your time comes."

Yoshi-known-as-Yakibō melts into the darkness again, and by the time he returns, the would-be poet has figured out what his nickname means.

"Why are you called the Pottery Priest? You don't look like a priest."

The man gives a short laugh.

"I'm not. A lifetime ago, that's what I wanted to be. I *am* a potter, though, for my sins."

Which is almost as hard to believe. He sounds educated, and doesn't have the nearly incomprehensible backcountry accent Saburo had encountered the last time he stopped at a village inn.

"You don't sound like a potter."

"Well, that's what the gods made me, this time around, anyway. Hopefully, it will be the last." Yakibō braces his hands on his knees and stands. "But right now, I've got wood to stack and a kiln to finish loading. You rest, get your strength back. If you're feeling better by tomorrow, Hattsan and I would welcome another pair of hands stoking the fire."

He shuffles to the door and lets himself out. A little rain blows in as it closes behind him, and Saburo sinks back into dreamless sleep.

The next time he awakens, it's even darker. Is this potter fellow too poor to afford a little oil for a lantern? Fortunately, he isn't too poor to afford food, because Saburo can smell pickled radishes and hear the soft *crek crek* of chopsticks scraping a rice bowl.

"Yakibō? Is that you?" He cautiously raises his head, relieved it doesn't hurt like the devil anymore.

"Ah, you're awake, young poet," comes the potter's voice. "Good thing you returned to the land of the living before I ate the bit I was saving for you."

"Why are you sitting in the dark? How can you even see to eat?"

"Seems to me I use my mouth for eating, not my eyes."

But the potter shifts from where he's sitting and a bamboo rice paddle knocks against the iron pot, scraping something into a bowl.

Saburo hopes it's for him. He's hungry enough to eat a wild boar, hide and all.

"Here." A warm bowl and a pair of chopsticks nudge up against his arm, and he gropes for them. Whatever is in the bowl smells delicious. Pickles, dried fish cured with soy sauce and sweet sake, and rice that's been in the pot long enough to acquire a toasty crust. But it's too dark to see the ends of his chopsticks. What's he supposed to do, stick his face in the bowl and eat like a dog?

"Yakibō-san? I'll need a little light if I'm going to eat."

"Sorry. I forgot."

"Forgot what?"

"You're handicapped."

Before he can ask what that means, a flint is struck, and a paper-shaded lantern begins to glow. As the flame lengthens inside, he sees Yakibō's face clearly for the first time. It's seamed and nut-brown, his wispy beard untrimmed, his milky eyes staring at nothing as he tucks away the flint and takes up his bowl and chopsticks again.

"Are you . . . blind?"

"Since birth," the potter replies, poking around in his bowl with the tips of his chopsticks. Encountering a chunk of *daikon* radish, he pops it into his mouth.

"But how can you . . ."

"Make rice? Make pots? Make a living?" He laughs. "I manage. And if you're about to start feeling sorry for me, I'd like to point out that I wasn't the one lying unconscious in the mud."

"Yes, but—"

"Look, young poet," the potter says, taking a swig of sake. "I've been blind my whole life, so I don't really understand this 'sight' thing you can't seem to live without. To be honest, at times I wonder how the rest of you muddle through the world, missing so much that's right in front of your noses."

Stunned, Saburo nearly drops his chopsticks. *You miss so much that's right in front of your nose.* Hadn't his poetry master said the same thing, the last time he had spared a word for Saburo's poems?

But the master's words hadn't been meant kindly. Saburo had been so stung by the criticism, he'd almost given up. But now that the same words have been uttered by a blind man who feels sorry for him because he can see, Saburo understands them in a whole new light.

This is a *sign*. He was meant to get lost in these woods. He was meant to be rescued by this potter. He was probably even meant to be eating this rice and these pickles. Maybe he's finally on his own version of Bashō's *Narrow Road to the Deep North* after all.

16.

MONDAY, MARCH 31

Tokyo

Nori promises to keep searching for Hikitoru, assuring Daiki she'll call the minute she finds it. Rolling the front shutter down between them, she slips the pin into its locking holes. Then she turns to face the empty shop.

Time to find that tea bowl.

The stock is arranged alphabetically by Japanese phonetic character, according to the name of the maker. *A-i-u-e-o, ka-ki-ku-ke-ko, sa-shi-su-se-so . . .* It's an odd way for a pottery store to be set up—most sellers group bowls with bowls and plates with plates—but it says a great deal about her grandmother's way of thinking.

The shelves weren't always arranged this way. The first Sunday after Nori quit high school and began working full time, she'd arrived at the closed shop in a foul mood, furious that her grandmother had summoned her to work on their day off.

She hadn't been sorry to leave the pointless homework and meaningless memorizing behind, but it turned out that sitting in class was a lot less tiring than staffing the shop. She'd been too stubborn to admit it, but every night, as soon as 'Baa-chan's snores began rattling her door, Nori had collapsed onto her own futon, asleep within minutes. She'd barely communicated with her friends all week because she fell unconscious every night, mid-message, phone in hand. By closing time on Saturday, she'd bowed out of their weekly shopping meet-up and was looking forward to sleeping until noon instead.

But early Sunday morning, her alarm woke her at the usual time, even though she definitely hadn't set it the night before. When she groped around to turn the bleeping thing off, she discovered a note telling her to be down in the shop by eight-thirty, and to bring rice balls for breakfast. 'Baa-chan had gone down early, and was waiting for her.

When Nori yanked open the front shutter, resentfully toting four rice balls fetched from the market down the block, she didn't recognize the place. The shelves were bare, every dish in the shop stacked on the floor.

Had 'Baa-chan gone mad? It looked like she'd decided to do *ō-sōji*, even though it wasn't December, when everyone scrubbed the nooks and crannies that only got cleaned for New Year's.

Without a word of apology or thanks, her grandmother bit into a rice ball and handed Nori a pad of paper and pencil.

"You'd better take notes," she'd said. "Until you learn the new system."

"What new system?" Their system was fine the way it was! Nori could find anything in the shop at a glance—bowls with bowls, plates with plates—even though she'd only been working there a week.

"Hand me those ramen bowls from the Akagawa kiln," her grandmother had directed. "The black ones with the brown crosses inside."

'Baa-chan climbed the stepladder to set them on the highest shelf on the right-hand wall, next to the entrance.

"Now the green Akiyama dishes with the pine design. Are you writing these down?"

Seething with mutinous thoughts, Nori did as she was told. But by the time the first section had been stuffed with dishware that looked so random she didn't know how she'd ever find anything again, she couldn't contain herself any longer.

"Why are we doing this?" she'd whined. "How will our customers ever find anything in this mish-mash?"

"They'll have to ask."

"How will *I* find anything in this mish-mash?"

"You'll learn," her grandmother said, fixing her with the stink-eye from the top of the ladder. "And when I'm dead and gone and it's time to restock styles that are sold out, you'll know who to order them from, won't you?"

Then she understood. In order to find anything, she'd have to memorize the name of every kiln and know what kind of pottery they made. And when it was her turn to take over, she'd be able to run the family business without thinking twice.

So, learn she did. She also grudgingly noticed an increased number of up-sells and add-ons, now that customers had to describe what they wanted instead of just browsing the shelves and finding it themselves. As usual, her grandmother had more than one reason for doing something. And, as usual, she'd made Nori figure that out for herself.

Which came in handy now. As Miura pointed out, if her grandmother didn't want her to have the tea bowl, she'd have put it somewhere Nori would never find it. But if she did want her granddaughter—and only her granddaughter—to find it, she'd put it in a place only the two of them would think to look.

That's how she knows Hikitoru won't be tucked behind bowls from the same region, or hidden amid others the same color. She'd searched all those places at Daiki's suggestion before he left, but now that he's gone, she goes straight to the shelf with goods made by kilns whose names start with the character "*ya*." That's where her grandmother would hide a tea bowl made by a potter known as Yakibō.

She moves aside blue and white soup bowls from Yakata, and red teapots from the Yamaguchi kiln, and . . . yes! There it is. A single, oval, tea ceremony bowl. Shigaraki-ware, just as Miura had predicted.

Elated, she takes it in her hands. Hikitoru fits into them like the potter had made it just for her. She closes her eyes, lifts it to her lips.

And freezes.

Holy crap, what is she thinking? This thing is worth ten million yen and she's standing over a concrete floor. With the panicked focus of someone crossing a rotten log that spans a bottomless chasm, she inches back down the stepladder and doesn't breathe again until Hikitoru is sitting safely on the low table in the office. Shaken, she makes some tea to calm herself.

Half a cup later (and back in her right mind), she pulls the tea bowl toward her and trains the lamp on it. A swash of glossy, gray-green glaze swirls around the outside and jumps the rim to the inside, leaving the rest of the exterior in its natural state—rough clay that deepens in a pleasing gradation from ochre to deep red, salted with white. But it's the inner surface that takes her breath away. Clear green glaze has melted into a pool at the bottom, reminding her of a secret swimming hole surrounded by boulders.

Even to her untrained eye, it's an exquisite piece, but it will be someone else's job to wax eloquent about its finer points. Her job is to fetch 'Baa-chan's magnifying glass and examine it for flaws, anything that might diminish its value.

She takes her time, makes herself look hard. But even though she examines it twice over, she doesn't find a single crack or the tiniest chip. It's perfect.

Face aglow with triumph and relief, she holds Hikitoru one more time. And feels it again. That *rightness*. She's never attended a tea ceremony, never understood why some people's idea of fun is getting trussed up in a kimono to spend an hour drinking a bowl of spinach-y froth and eating a snack that—no matter how pretty it looks—tastes like plain old sweet bean paste. But as Hikitoru nestles between her palms, she begins to understand. She lifts it, and as the delicate rim slides smoothly between her lips, she suddenly wishes there really was tea in it. Wishes she could drink from this thing of beauty, just once.

Then she comes to her senses. She dares not do anything that might lessen its value. Setting it carefully on the table, she goes upstairs to fetch the box with its name on top.

Time to turn this piece of rightness into money in the bank.

17.

Feudal Japan

NOVEMBER, 1703

Shigaraki

Saburo strains to lift the wooden board he'd stacked with water jars, then glances around to make sure nobody is watching, and offloads a few. Yakibō can lift twice as many, and Hattsan can carry even more, but they've been doing this their whole lives, after all, and he's only been doing it a few months. Balancing the tray, he staggers onto the short path between the kiln and the storehouse, exchanging grunts with the potter as they pass each other. Then he stops and turns to squint at the figure moving past the kiln. Why is Yakibō carrying a stack of pottery *away* from the shed where they keep the finished goods?

He doesn't find out until later that afternoon, when he returns to the farmhouse with a wet washcloth slung around his neck, fresh from scrubbing off the day's grime and soaking in the hot spring near the bridge.

"I'm back," he calls, untying his sandals in the stone-paved entry.

"Oh. It's you. *O-kaeri.*" Welcome home.

Saburo detours to the kitchen to hang up his washcloth, then joins Yakibō, who is squatting amid a circle of pottery.

The poet moves in for a closer look, hardly believing his eyes. Are those . . . tea ceremony bowls? How did a backwoods potter learn the art of making utensils for that elite ritual?

It's a subject that Saburo unfortunately knows all too much about. His eldest brother will someday inherit the title Tea Master of the Sorasenke School from their father, and his middle brother is making a name for himself as a master in the most prestigious flower-arranging guild. It has fallen to third son Saburo to become either a potter or a poet—tea schools, after all, need an endless supply of scrolls brushed with seasonal sentiments to hang above the flower arrangements, and bowls to drink their *matcha* from.

Unfortunately, his mind had wandered while the pottery master droned on about how a fine tea bowl must strike a perfect balance between the artist's intention and the whim of the kiln gods, and how essential it was to spend one's life cultivating an intimate relationship with those fickle deities. Saburo has little patience for anything that takes years to master, so his bowls sat awkwardly in the hands and his glazes looked haphazard, not artful. When the pottery master had damned his work with faint praise within earshot of Saburo's father, the mightily displeased patriarch had understood the message at once, withdrawing him from that apprenticeship (instead of waiting for him to be unceremoniously kicked out), and sending him (along with a generous donation) to sit at the feet of the crankiest of the poet Bashō's disciples instead.

But even though Saburo has no talent whatsoever for shaping clay, he can spot the work of a master in his sleep. Which is why he's staring down at the ring of Yakibō's pottery, dumbfounded. The Shibata family owns a number of tea bowls made by renowned artists, but every one of the pieces encircling the blind potter rivals the finest in the Sorasenke School's collection.

Oblivious to the effect his work is having on his temporary apprentice, Yakibō frowns.

"Help me decide, will you?"

"Decide what?"

"Which of these is *yabō*?"

"*Yabō*?"

Saburo has seen a lot of tea bowls, but never an "ambitious" one. How can a tea bowl be "ambitious"?

The potter offers the one he's been weighing in his hand. Saburo sinks to his knees and takes it, his breath catching as it settles between his palms. The kiln's fiery blast has blown ash across this one like a calligraphy master, melting crisscrossing strokes of glossy gray-green over half the outer surface. The other half is bare, an exquisite example of how small impurities can explode from the rough red clay during firing and contribute a rustic beauty all their own.

"I want you to hold each of these in your hands and tell me," the potter is saying. "Do any of them make you feel ambitious?"

Flattered he's being asked for his opinion, the poet holds the tea bowl in the light and turns it full circle. His admiration only increases as he considers it from every angle, noting that the bowl is lighter than it looks, and feels warm to the touch, even though it's nearly as cold inside the farmhouse as out.

Ambition. What a strange name for a tea bowl. But if Yakibō is crazy, at least he's crazy talented. Saburo tilts the bowl and peers inside, appreciating the sparkles of glassy green caught in the rough clay. He sets it down and picks up the next.

It's nearly identical. Puzzled, he picks up another. And another. There are slight variations between them, but they all have the same odd, oval shape that fits into his cupped hands like a bird settling into its nest. They all have rivulets of translucent green glaze cascading from their rims, ending in jewel-like drops that wink when the bowl tips toward the light. All are dusted with a sheen of ash that has melted to a glossy gray-green, the unglazed clay showing boldly through the gaps with a roughness that makes the smooth parts seem even smoother. And all have the hallmark of the rarest and most sought-after Shigaraki-ware: glassy green pools at the bottom, suggesting an eternally sublime sip of tea.

"I can't choose," he admits helplessly. "They're all beautiful."

"Beautiful?" The potter sounds annoyed. "Use your ears, poet. 'Beautiful' isn't what I asked for. Here," he says, thrusting the first bowl into Saburo's hands again. "This time, close your eyes. Don't be distracted by your precious sense of sight. Imagine the thing you want most in the world, the thing you'd do anything to get."

The potter sits back, folding his arms over his chest.

Saburo closes his eyes. Imagines returning to Kyoto, his writing box stuffed with reams of brilliant poems. His poetry master stands before a sea of disciples, solemnly naming Saburo his most worthy successor, while his father sits among the assembled luminaries, trying not to beam with pride, but failing.

Saburo picks up one bowl, then another. Turns them, studies them, tries to feel something. None of them make him feel ambitious. Just anxious. If he doesn't choose one soon, the potter will think him an insensitive oaf.

"This one," he says with false confidence, thrusting the one he's holding into Yakibō's hands.

The potter frowns as he hefts the bowl, running a thumb along the lip.

"Interesting. Not the one I'd have chosen. Nevertheless," he hands it back, "take this to the kitchen and find a box that fits. There should be some empty ones on the top shelf."

By the time Saburo returns, the potter has assembled an inkstone, a water dropper, and a brush.

"You can read and write, can't you?"

Saburo laughs. "I'd be a pretty pathetic poet if I couldn't."

"Good. You can save me a walk into town to ask the priest." Yakibō scoots aside.

Saburo kneels before the writing implements and positions the box squarely on the *tatami* before him, then rubs a stub of inkstick on the stone, adds a splash of water. He swipes his brush through the dark puddle.

Tip poised, he asks, "You're sure you want me to write *yabō*?"

"Yes."

He composes himself the way his calligraphy teacher taught him, visualizing the stroke order. Then he lowers his brush, and the characters for "ambition" flow across the lid. Not bad. Not bad at all. He looks up to find the potter waiting to exchange his name seal for the wet brush.

"Bottom left," Yakibō directs.

Saburo carefully stamps the stylized characters that read "Yoshi Takamatsu" in the lower left corner and hands the seal back to its owner.

"Why did you call it 'Ambition'?"

"Because it's time to give up returning to the monastery as a shortcut to enlightenment."

"What?"

The potter doesn't explain, just stacks the rest of the bowls as if they were everyday crockery and rises, aiming for the door.

Saburo watches, mystified, as the gathering twilight swallows the potter and his priceless cargo. Where is he taking them? Does the crazy bastard have any idea what people would pay for tea bowls of that quality? How revered he'd be if he lived in a decent-sized town, instead of the back of beyond?

If he could persuade Yakibō to let him take one back home, show it to his father . . . He imagines the look on the old taskmaster's face and laughs out loud. Neither of his brothers is famous enough yet to have relationships with artists who produce tea ceremony utensils of this quality. He looks at the box in his hands. Wouldn't they be surprised if he came back with a stack of brilliant poems and a masterpiece like *this* in his pack?

"*Oi*," says Yakibō, framed in the doorway. "Are you coming?"

"Oh, sorry, I was just . . ." The poet scrambles to his feet, Yabō in hand. "Those tea bowls. I didn't know you could . . . I mean, they're extraordinary. Do you have any idea how valuable they might be? I mean, this one alone might fetch more than you make in a year, selling water jars and grinding bowls."

The potter throws back his head and laughs.

"And what would I do with that kind of money?" He scoffs. "Money. I'm glad that was never one of mine."

"One of your what?"

"Attachments."

Saburo looks at him blankly.

"Life is suffering, and the origin of suffering is attachment," Yakibō prompts.

"Yes, yes, I know." He's heard the Pottery Priest blat on about the Four Noble Truths often enough, and he recognizes the Buddhist saying. "But what does attachment have to do with tea bowls?"

"Everything! Haven't you heard a word I've said since you arrived? Come. I want to show you something."

He strides away.

Dusk is falling fast, so Saburo grabs the lantern before trotting after him. The blind man trails one hand along the side of the farmhouse, reaches the corner, then pushes off into the darkening forest. At a fork in the path, Yakibō veers left without hesitation and shoulders through a stand of twiggy brown bushes toward a dilapidated shed.

Saburo had never noticed it before. It's easy to see why—it doesn't look like it was built by human hands, it looks like it grew there. Knocked together from unstripped branches and fallen limbs, dead leaves still flutter at the end of dry twigs, and a pelt of chartreuse moss spreads over the top. The potter tugs open a wooden door that hangs crookedly on leather hinges and ducks through the low opening.

"Don't just stand out there like a stone Jizo statue," he calls from within.

The shed is barely big enough for two people to turn around in, narrowed even further by a waist-high stack of split logs banked along the wall. Saburo squeezes inside, and the potter allows the door to bang shut behind them, plunging the place into darkness.

"This," the potter announces with satisfaction, "is where I keep my sins."

Saburo holds up the lantern, revealing five wooden boxes lined up on a plank that runs the width of the shed. All are of pale, unvarnished *kiri*-wood, with blue silk cords and names brushed on the lids in a tight, fussy hand. Yakibō takes Yabō from him and makes a space for it at the end. Then he picks up the box next to it.

"I've been working on this one for over twenty years." He hands it to Saburo.

The poet angles it toward the lantern so he can read the name. Hatsu-koi. First Love. What does Yakibō mean, he's been working on it for twenty years? Once pottery is glazed and fired, it's done. You can't really—

"A wise man once taught me that attachment is the desire to have," Yakibō is explaining, "and also the desire not to have. These . . ." he says, waving at the shelf, "are the attachments that have been chaining me to the Wheel of Rebirth."

Now Saburo's really confused. Is he so attached to them, he can't bear to die?

"May I open this?" he asks.

"Go ahead."

Saburo balances the lantern on the stack of firewood and opens the box. The bowl inside is the same shape as Yabō, but smoother, glossier. Red clay peeks through the pale glaze only here and there, like ash-cloaked coals smoldering with inner fire. He can almost feel its heart beating. The inner surface is liberally sprinkled with the tiny melted chips of feldspar called "dragonfly eyes," and a shallow pool of clear, glassy green has pooled on one side, forever preserving a final sip of tea. He closes his eyes and lifts it as if to drink, the thin rim pressing against his lips. Instead of being rough, as he'd expected, the delicate curve fits smoothly against his mouth. He can almost taste the tea slipping down his throat, delivering the kind of sublime experience that inspires poets to greatness. Opening his eyes, he gazes into First Love's depths with wonder. If this thing of beauty was a chain tying *him* to the Wheel of Rebirth, he'd be happy to go around again and again and again.

18.

The next day, Nori is so distracted by the treasure sitting in the back room that she gives one customer the wrong change and doesn't notice another wants to take a closer look at some bowls on the top shelf until he coughs to get her attention. At four-thirty, she gives up. She posts a note on the shop shutter, and twenty minutes later, she's in front of the pawnbroker's shop, tea bowl in hand. All too aware of what it's worth, she has wrapped the box in three hand towels and tucked it inside two extra plastic bags, worried that a single layer might catastrophically fail.

She hesitates before the door with its rusting mail slot, recalling the jumble of unsold goods inside, the smell of mold. Sighing, she presses the ailing bell. Miura might be past his prime, but the note her grandmother left tucked inside the silk carrying cloth gave her no other options.

This time it's Daiki who unchains the door. He herds her through the dark shop, bouncing impatiently as she exchanges her boots for slippers. Running down the hall ahead of her, he knocks on the office door.

This time, Miura rises to greet her, and after they've exchanged bows and pleasantries, the boy joins them at the table, vibrating with suppressed excitement as she unpacks her prize from its cocoon of bags and towels.

She offers the box to Miura. The old man's hands tremble slightly as he unties the cord. He examines the calligraphy on the lid, then opens it. Easing the bowl from its box, he unwraps it, lets the cloth fall.

A smile transfigures his face.

"Now *this* is the real Hikitoru."

He examines it inside and out, turning it full circle, gazing into its depths.

Nori allows him to worship at the shrine of potential pricelessness for a few minutes, resisting the urge to ask what it's worth, but finally, she can't stand it any longer.

"So . . . what do you think?"

Miura steeples his fingers. A car honks somewhere outside and a moth flitters into the circle of light, drunkenly bashing its wings against the lampshade.

Why isn't he saying anything? Had he spotted a flaw she'd missed? She clears her throat.

The pawnbroker still says nothing.

"Did you . . . see something that might make it worth less than the others?"

"No," Miura says absently. "It'll be worth more, if anything."

"More? How much more?"

"That . . . depends."

Her smile fades. "On what?"

"How much did your grandmother tell you about Hikitoru?"

"Not much."

"Did she mention the . . . special circumstances?"

"What do you mean, 'special circumstances'?"

"You'll have to ask her."

"I can't! I mean, the thing is, she's sick right now. I can't risk worrying her. And even if I asked her, I'm not sure she'd . . . can't you just—?"

"I'm sorry," Miura says, shaking his head. "All I can tell you is that pieces like Hikitoru need to be sold to a special kind of collector. And for that kind of sale, we charge a special rate of commission."

"How much?"

"Fifty percent."

Fifty percent? She can't have heard right. That's outrageous. Does he really think he can get away with gouging her like that? What kind of an idiot does he think she is?

Of course, she can't say that, not to his face. She drops her gaze to hide how insulted she is.

"Fifty percent seems . . . high," she murmurs.

"Your grandmother didn't think so."

Now the old snake is out-and-out lying. 'Baa-chan would never have agreed to terms like that. And she's not going agree to them either. She should have paid more attention to her instincts—this felt wrong, right from the start. The sooner she gets out of here, the better.

"Can I . . . think about it?" she asks, eyes still lowered.

"Of course." Miura bestows a cordial smile. "Take your time. You know where to find us."

Nori has wrapped herself in a cloak of flaming outrage by the time she steps off the train at the station near the hospital. Fifty percent commission? Criminal. And Miura knows it. Does he think he can take advantage of her because her grandmother is sick? Because she's a girl?

Unless . . . maybe that was just a negotiating tactic. In which case, she's got news for him. She's not the novice he thinks she is. She'll show *him* negotiating tactics . . .

She gives a curt bow to the white uniform on duty at the nurses' station and stalks to her grandmother's room. Nothing has changed since her last visit. The other bed still lies empty, and her grandmother still lies motionless as a wax doll.

Nori sits, holding the tea bowl on her lap, composing herself. Deciding how much to tell. Now that she's away from that dingy back office, all the clever and cutting words she *should* have said to the pawnbroker—words that would have told him exactly where to stick his fifty percent commission—crowd in to taunt her.

She's beginning to regret fleeing so spinelessly. She should have pushed back. If she doesn't tell this story right, 'Baa-chan will think she's as unfit as her father.

She gazes at the serene face, takes a deep breath. Begins with how she'd used her grandmother's organizing system to figure out where the tea bowl was hidden, then took the real Hikitoru to Miura.

"Everything was going fine," she says, "until he had the nerve to ask for fifty percent commission." Her sense of injury comes roaring back. "Can you believe that? *Fifty*, not fifteen! He said there were 'special circumstances.' What kind of a fool does he think I am? Did he think you haven't taught me anything?" She scoffs. "Why should he get five million yen, just for selling a lousy tea bowl?" Then she remembers her grandmother doesn't know about Snow Bride being worth ten million yen. She calls up the photo on Fujimori Fine Art's website.

"See this?" she says, holding the phone screen before her grandmother's closed eyelids. "This tea bowl was made by the same artist who made Hikitoru, and a company called Fujimori Fine Art sold it four years ago." She scrolls down. "See this number? Ten million yen. And that's just the *lowest* price they were willing to accept, so it probably went for a lot more. Maybe I should take Hikitoru to them." Why hadn't she thought of it sooner? "Yes, that's what I'll do. First thing tomorrow morning, I'll knock on their door and—"

Her grandmother's face pinches.

Startled, Nori cries, "'Baa-chan?"

The corners of her grandmother's mouth turn down, a line deepens between her brows.

She's waking up! Nori leaps to her feet and dashes out of the room to call the nurse. She's only gone a few moments, but when she returns with the nurse in tow, 'Baa-chan's face is as expressionless as before.

"She frowned," Nori insists. "I was telling her about some things that happened today and suddenly she looked like herself again. You have to believe me."

The nurse doesn't reply, busy checking the monitor, noting numbers on her clipboard. Then she stands for a long moment, regarding the still figure in the bed.

"I'll call the doctor on duty," she finally says, disappearing out the door.

Nori turns to the still figure, overjoyed. 'Baa-chan is finally on the mend. The doctor will confirm it. Everything will be all right now. She hovers, searching her grandmother's face for further signs of consciousness, hardly daring to blink, in case she misses something.

The nurse returns with a doctor whose nametag identifies him as one of the hospital's senior partners. She whirrs the blue privacy curtain around the bed, introducing Nori as the patient's granddaughter.

The doctor listens and nods as Nori recounts what happened. Then he bends to perform his own examination, pressing his stethoscope against her grandmother's thin hospital gown. Lifts one eyelid, and then the other, shines a light into her eyes. Moves on to test this and that, noting his observations. Nori hovers anxiously, awaiting his verdict. As he reads the monitor's data, the corners of his mouth turn down. He scribbles some notes on her grandmother's chart.

He turns to Nori, and her hopes dim. He's wearing The Look.

"I know how much you're hoping for your grandmother to wake up, Okuda-san, but I'm afraid that the 'response' you saw was most likely the kind of involuntary movement that afflicts the unconscious. However," he adds, "there *was* a spike in her vitals around the time you witnessed the change in expression—elevated cardiac rate, disturbed respiration— which might indicate a degree of returning consciousness. I'll ask the nurses to monitor her more closely and watch for a recurrence.

"But," he warns, "if it does—and even if it's a sign she's waking up—I want you to be prepared for what that means. On TV, patients open their eyes and take up their lives where they left off, but in real life, stroke victims have to work hard to regain function. And some never do. When she wakes up, your grandmother may face a long road to recovery. We just have to wait and see."

19.

Feudal Japan

NEW YEAR'S EVE, 1703

Shigaraki

"And that's the last of it," Saburo tells himself, indulging in a pang of premature nostalgia. All afternoon he's been shuttling fired water pots from the kiln to the shed, where they joined the miso jars and grinding bowls that Yakibō and Hattsan will sell at the temple's annual spring festival.

But he'll never lug another piece of pottery through this door again. He hasn't told Yakibō yet, but by the time there are enough pieces for the next firing, he'll be gone. It takes the potter almost two months to fill the kiln, and by then, the road will be free of snow, new shoots will be poking through last year's dead bamboo, and it'll be time for him to resume his poetic pilgrimage.

He marks the moment by swiping his brow with his sleeve, stopping (as is his custom now) to consider whether there's deeper meaning to be mined from the experience of sweating from hard work in deep winter, at the end of the old year. Could be, could be. He allows himself a small smile. He often catches himself thinking like a real poet these days. Once he's on the road again, he'll take out the observations he's squirreled away like ripe chestnuts, hoping that a few will grow into poems as good as the one he'd written on the day he'd helped name Yabō.

The potter and his friends had been several flasks of sake into one of their drinking nights when they'd prodded him into reading that one aloud. It was the big priest from Heizan-ji who had pointed out the poem's hidden layers of meaning, the insights that, to be honest, Saburo hadn't intentionally put there. Fortunately, he'd recalled something Yakibō had told him—that if poetry had to be explained, it wasn't any good—so he'd kept his mouth shut, letting them give him more credit than was due. Once the priest had pointed out the hidden meaning, of course, he saw it too. The poem *is* brilliant. He's astounded, actually, that he wrote it. He must be a better poet than he thought if he can convey sentiments that deep without even realizing it.

Saburo shoulders the shed door closed, then sets off down the well-worn track to the farmhouse. Tonight, they'll celebrate the end of the old year, the birth of the new. Unless the expected storm breaks early, they'll walk into town and take their turns ringing the great bronze bell at the Buddhist temple for the sake of their immortal souls. Then they'll stop by the Shinto shrine on their way home, to curry favor with the gods who grant more earthly desires.

The evening air has that crisp, clean, snow-is-coming smell—he's learned to predict it from Yakibō, who's uncannily accurate about such things—and, as if on cue, the clouds close over the full moon like curtains drawing across a stage. Saburo picks up his pace. As he brushes past snow-laden pine branches, he spooks a rabbit that bounds ahead of him down the path. A haunting call comes from the direction of the bridge, and he stops to peer through the trees in search of a shape coasting on silent wings. He now knows it's an owl, just by the sound of it.

The first flakes begin to drift down, gathering into clumps that soon plummet thick and fast around him. He snaps open the oiled paper parasol kept in the shed for when weather catches them out at the kiln. Climbing the last little rise before the farmhouse, he congratulates himself that he no longer has to rest halfway up.

Not only is he stronger, the past few months have changed him in other ways too. He and Yakibō have shared more than one bottle of sake while the potter expounds on the meaning of life, the mysteries of fate, the dangers of attachment. Saburo has learned to listen tolerantly to the religious blather—even the big priest secretly agrees the old zealot is more than a little unorthodox when it comes to the Four Noble Truths—but all that drunken philosophizing has made him aware that even the most ordinary moments can deliver revelation. And revelations are what poems are made of. The few he'd jotted between fetching and carrying and stoking and stacking are far better than anything he wrote when he spent his days cowering at the feet of his master.

Clearing the last cedar trees, he's cheered to see tendrils of smoke rising through the opening in the farmhouse's tiled roof. Slivers of light outline the shutters, and it occurs to him that Yakibō has changed too. The potter is frugal with everything that has to be bought in town, and lamp oil is an unnecessary expense for a blind man. He never used to remember to light the lantern at dusk, but tonight he has remembered his "handicapped" apprentice, who will enjoy his dinner more if he can see it.

Now that he's closer, Saburo detects the aroma of something grilling, and breaks into a trot. In the past few months, he's also learned how much better food tastes after a day of hard labor. Stamping his feet outside the farmhouse, he shakes the snow from the parasol and snaps it shut, then pushes the door open.

"Poet, is that you?" Yakibō calls from his seat by the hearth. Two skewered sweetfish are angled over the flames, fat sizzling, skins crisping.

"*O-tsukare-sama*," he adds, thanking Saburo for his day's work.

"Thank you for your hard work, too," replies the poet, returning the customary end-of-day greeting.

He props the parasol in a corner of the entry and looks around.

"Where's Hattsan?"

"I sent him home." Yakibō gives the skewers a quarter-turn. "The storm is coming in fast, and it feels like a big one. I didn't want him to get stuck out here. He should be home to ring in the new year with his parents, and help them through the snow to their first shrine visit tomorrow." He hands a large bottle of sake to Saburo. "Which means it's just you and me bidding farewell to the old year with this. Fetch the cups?"

When Saburo returns, he opens the bottle and fills the serving flask, then hands a cup to Yakibō before pouring for himself.

"*Kanpai*. Happy new year," he toasts.

"To the end of attachment," adds the potter.

Typical, the poet thinks, with an indulgent grimace. Fortunately, Yakibō can't see his face and suspect that giving up everything that makes life worth living isn't a goal he shares. On the contrary, he's looking forward to his fair share of fame, fortune, and first love. But brimming with sake and destiny, he's more patient than usual as the tide in the bottle recedes, and Yakibō's enthusiasm for his favorite subject increases. By the time distant temple bells begin tolling the hundred and eight Buddhist sins in their countdown to midnight, he feels that the world is wide, the future bright, and fame awaits him just around the corner.

He divides the last of the sake between their cups and they finish it together, toasting the new year as it replaces the old.

But instead of calling it a night and rolling into his futon, Yakibō stands and feels his way to the clothing chest. Considering how much sake he's drunk, the blind man is surprisingly steady as he bends over to root around, then tucks a folded carrying cloth into the pocket of his kimono sleeve.

"Where are you going?" Saburo asks, as Yakibō wraps himself in his reed cloak and makes for the door. He doesn't reply, just disappears out into the darkness.

What the hell? It's below freezing outside. Call of nature? The poet feels a slight prickling urge himself, but decides he can wait until morning. Warmed by the fire and the sake, he'd much rather curl up and go to sleep. He unfolds his quilt and lies down by the still-glowing coals. Closes his eyes. But the minutes tick by and Yakibō doesn't return. The unpleasant possibility of finding the old man face down in the snow and frozen stiff in the morning pokes at him until he casts off his blanket with an irritated grunt. Grabbing his cloak, he slides his feet into his still-damp wooden clogs.

The night air hits him like a slap in the face, but at least the fresh layer of snow makes it easy to see where the potter went. Rounding the corner of the farmhouse, he sees Yakibō's footsteps plowing off into the woods, in the opposite direction from the latrine. Good thing he followed, Saburo thinks. The potter must be drunker than he looked.

He has the benefit of being able to see where he's going, but Yakibō has a head start, so the poet doesn't catch sight of him until he's tugging at the brushy shack's door. It creaks in protest as he yanks it open, sweeping aside the snow drifted against it, then disappears inside. The old badger isn't going to pee on their firewood, is he?

No, Yakibō would never mistake the hut for the latrine. If there's one thing the blind man does better than anyone, it's smell. So . . . what's he doing? Fetching firewood to see them through the long night? Saburo hugs himself against the cold, breath pluming in the night air. A minute ticks by. Two. It's taking the old geezer an awfully long time to pick out a couple of logs. Maybe he's not fetching firewood after all. It would be typical of the Pottery Priest to have some weird ritual of making a First Visit to the Firewood Hut in the early hours of New Year's morning, instead of the customary rising before dawn to watch the First Sunrise.

The potter emerges with the carrying cloth looped over his wrist, knotted around one of the tea bowl boxes. What does he need that for, in the middle of the night? Saburo holds his breath, and steps off the path, hoping the blind man will pass without guessing he's there. He hasn't been invited to Yakibō's midnight tea ceremony, but now he's curious, and doesn't want to be sent back before he sees what the crazy old codger is up to.

He follows at a distance as the blind man hikes uphill into the woods. He stops only once, encountering the trunk of an ancient gingko. A mere shell of pale gray bark, it's hollow all the way to the sky, ringed with a braided straw rope that marks it as sacred to the Shinto gods.

Yakibō stoops to place a small coin between the roots, bows and claps twice, then folds his hands in a moment of reverence before moving on. Saburo feels a twinge of discomfort that nobody has told the blind man that the tree is dead, its gods departed, but now isn't the best time to break that news.

The poet stuffs his hands into his armpits and rocks back and forth to keep from freezing, watching the potter resume his wade through the snow. Yakibō stops on the bank of a narrow stream cutting deep through the blanket of white, still racing along, despite the freezing cold. The blind man braces one foot on a pointy rock as if he'd done it many times before, then pulls back his sleeve and plunges his hand into the icy water. Saburo's fingers ache in sympathy as he scrabbles around, his hand finally emerging with . . . another tea bowl? What's a tea bowl doing up here, at the bottom of the stream?

The potter empties it of mud and stones, rinses it, then dips it again, filling it to the brim with water. Then he puts the sound of the stream to his back, and paces deliberately across the clearing beyond, coming to a halt just short of a large, flat boulder the size and shape of the low, lacquered table on which Saburo had done his lessons as a boy. The potter raises the dipping bowl high above the rock, moving slowly back and forth as he empties it, dissolving the fresh pillow of snow on top.

Then he slides the carrying cloth from his wrist, placing it front and center on the glistening granite. Snowflakes sift down through the trees and dot the back of his cloak as he bends to work at the knot.

How can he have any feeling left in his hands? Saburo flexes his own fingers, which are painfully stiff, the tips numb. He hopes the old man won't fumble the tea bowl as he takes it from its box.

The wrapping falls unnoticed to the snow as Yakibō lifts the bowl in both hands like a chalice, its pale glaze shining in the moonlight. Saburo recognizes it. Hatsu-koi. He'd asked Hattsan what the potter meant when he said he'd been "working on" it for twenty years, and the apprentice had rolled his eyes before telling him that his master had made nearly fifty others before he chose that one to represent First Love.

The potter begins to chant, his long-ago priestly training welling up from deep within. The cadences of the True Faith Sutra rise and fall, gaining in strength as the powerful words expand into the darkness. The final line booms from his lips.

Then, silence. A reverent silence. A profound silence. A silence that even Saburo is finding somewhat moving. Eyes closed, he casts about for the right words to commemorate the moment in a poem. But when he opens them just a slit, to check whether the snow is "floating" or "falling," the potter's arms are swinging down in a powerful arc.

The tea bowl flies from his hands, exploding against the rock in a shower of glittering clay.

Saburo cries out.

The potter turns toward the sound, startled.

"Poet?"

"What are you doing? You drunken fool!"

"Is that you, poet?" The potter takes a step closer. "Why are you here?"

"Why did you break it?"

Yakibō stands there, puzzled. Then he says, "First Love has been my most stubborn attachment for over twenty years. And attachments are meant to be broken."

20.

Nori stands before the security guard's desk in the swanky lobby of the building housing the Fujimori Fine Art auction house. Everything about it is designed to repel uninvited visitors—the vast granite floor, the imposing arrangement of cherry blossoms on the reception desk, even the desk itself, fashioned from curved slabs of some dark, polished wood.

The blue-uniformed guard looks down at her, unsmiling.

"I'm here to see Eriko Hashimoto at Fujimori Fine Art," Nori says, trying to stand tall and muster some of 'Baa-chan's confidence.

The company website had provided the name of the auction house's Japanese ceramics expert, whose personal specialty is eighteenth-century blue and white porcelain—specifically, the kind manufactured for trade with Europe. But Hashimoto-san is clearly qualified to pass judgment on other types too, because she's listed as the expert on the Snow Bride sale.

"Do you have an appointment?"

"No." *Take the offensive*, prods the grandmother within. "But Ms. Hashimoto will want to see this tea bowl. It's called Hikitoru, and it was made by Yoshi Takamatsu." She displays the box in its green silk carrying cloth.

"I'll call up and ask," the guard says, sounding doubtful. "Your name?"

She gives it, reminding herself not to fidget while he dials.

After a brief exchange, his eyebrows arch, as if wonders never cease. He hands her a visitor badge.

"Go on up. Twenty-second floor. You can use the express elevator."

When the doors slide open on the empty waiting room at Fujimori Fine Art, she barely registers the plush carpet, the leather chairs, and the gold-leafed screen, because all hell is breaking loose. An ear-splitting alarm is whooping, and a towering foreign woman in a white lab coat is waving a teapot at the receptionist. She's like a pigeon among sparrows, definitely the kind of foreigner Nori would avoid sitting next to on the subway, even if it were the last empty seat. Her untamed bush of blond hair reminds Nori of the wig Yu-chan had dripped fake blood onto when she dressed up as a zombie nurse one Halloween.

Just as Nori decides it would be best to retreat until whatever's happening here is over, a gray-haired guard in a blue uniform arrives to stab at a security keypad behind the desk.

The alarm abruptly cuts off. In the sudden void, the foreigner is shouting, "... won't happen again."

The thoroughly annoyed receptionist looks past her, and in a voice tight with leftover disapproval, asks Nori, "May I help you?"

The white coat swivels toward her.

"Oh! Might you be the most honorable Miss Okuda?"

The foreigner speaks Japanese?

"Yes, uh, I'm ... I'm Nori Okuda."

How does this frightening person know her name?

"I'm Robin Swann, the most humble assistant of Eriko Hashimoto." Gold-rimmed glasses glint as she bows. "If our esteemed visitor would do me the honor of accompanying my unworthy self..."

Oblivious to Nori's state of stunned disbelief, she raises a warning palm to bid the guard not to reset the alarm just yet, and steams back through the security gate, teapot in hand.

As Nori scurries to catch up in the luxuriously carpeted corridor beyond, Swann apologizes for the tumult in the lobby. Using an inappropriately grandiose level of politeness, she tells Nori she'd been toiling in the laboratory of antiquities authentication when Madame Receptionist apprised her of the venerable Okuda's presence, and she'd made the grave error of bringing the teapot with her, regrettably forgetting it had been affixed with a modern electronic sensing device of utmost security.

It's the strangest Japanese she's ever heard. Robin Swann sounds like a cross between a time traveler from the samurai era and a politician caught with both hands in the till. Do all foreigners speak like that? Nori has never actually talked to one before—Okuda & Sons doesn't sell to tourists, only to the trade.

The flowery language is especially bizarre coming from a woman who's at work half-dressed. Robin Swann is wearing some sort of business suit under her lab coat, but her face is disturbingly naked. She's not wearing even a hint of makeup. Nori is far from a power user herself, but if she were Swann, she'd have buried the freckles on that otherwise enviable aquiline nose under some serious foundation, and wouldn't have set foot outside the house without making an effort to correct that unsightly pinkness. Unless . . . maybe she has an illness? A skin condition? Nori is trying to imagine what dread disease would prevent someone from concealing her imperfections in public, when Swann stops outside a door marked "Lab" and asks her to wait a moment while she puts the teapot back in the safe.

When she emerges, the white coat has also been left behind. Good. Now Nori can examine what she's wearing and more accurately estimate if this "Art Expert's Assistant" will be at all important to her mission.

The navy suit and white blouse suggest that her perplexing rank occupies a white-collar niche somewhere above "Office Lady," but the fabric is so shiny it must be polyester, and the style so generic that it's out of style and never out of style at the same time. And those shoes. Only someone on a punishingly slim budget—or perhaps someone whose feet are so long and narrow that nothing else fits her—would be forced to wear such hideous low-heeled pumps. Nori decides that despite the impressive-sounding title, an art expert's assistant isn't paid much. It will be safe to save her honorifics for the boss.

They halt before a door bearing a brass nameplate etched with "Hashimoto Eriko," and Swann sorts through her key ring.

"My esteemed superior is embarked upon an official voyage until next Tuesday," Swann explains, unlocking the door and pushing it open. "But my humble self will examine your noble tea bowl and contact you if she elects to view it for herself."

Wait, did she just say the expert is out of town? Why hadn't she mentioned that before? This underling can't possibly be qualified to evaluate what could very well turn out to be a National Treasure. She's not even Japanese.

"Excuse me," Nori says, balking. "Not to be rude, or anything, but I think it would be better if I brought Hikitoru back when your boss is here. Yoshi Takamatsu's work is pretty rare, so you might not be familiar with it. One of his tea bowls is in the National Museum. It's a National Cultural Treasure."

Swann recoils as if she'd just been slapped, then aims a withering look at Nori over the rims of her glasses.

"I actually know all about Waterlily, Miss Okuda, because I'm the one who authenticated it. Not to be *rude* or anything, but I have a master's degree in Japanese Literature from Columbia University and a nearly finished doctorate in Japanese ceramics, with a specialty in tea ceremony ware. So, unless you're a scholar I've not yet had the pleasure of meeting, there's not much you can tell me about Yoshi Takamatsu that I don't already know."

Now it's Nori's turn to feel slapped. Swann had switched from elaborately ingratiating to bluntly offended in less time than it took to swat a mosquito, delivering the message with the elegance of a native speaker. Nori has badly underestimated her.

And she's still standing there, holding the door, so Nori has no choice but to mutter her apologies and step through it . . .

. . . into another world. The sunlight streaming through the wall of floor to ceiling windows in Hashimoto's office is so dazzling, it almost hurts her eyes. The view soars out over the forested island of the Imperial Palace, past Tokyo Tower's orange Eiffel-esque spire, to the hazy skyscrapers of Shinagawa. The other walls are lined with venerable-looking reference books, interrupted only by a collection of tea bowls, displayed on individual plinths. Green Oribe, Nabeshima, Bizen, Tamba, Raku, and yes, Shigaraki-ware. They don't look any fancier than the ones gathering dust in the back room at Okuda & Sons, but they must be, because each basks in its own spotlight.

Half of Eriko Hashimoto's office is set up to offer hospitality to clients and colleagues, with a quartet of comfortable, but elegant, red chairs arranged around a low table that's topped with a celadon tea set. The other half is dedicated to the business of examining the ceramics that pass through the auction house on their way to collectors all over the world.

Nori refuses an offer of tea, and trails Swann to the working side's tall table, with its pair of high-intensity lamps and array of tools. She watches while the assistant trains both lights on the silk-wrapped box, dons a pair of white cotton gloves, and replaces her glasses with a boxy magnifying headset.

Swann unties the green carrying cloth. Somewhere in the luxurious hush, a clock ticks as she meticulously examines every centimeter of the tea bowl and its box, then lays the magnifiers aside and removes her gloves to type her notes into a blank form on her laptop.

Nori can't see what she's writing, but it's taking a long time. That worries her. Has she found something wrong with Hikitoru? Or maybe she's still mad about being disrespected, and she's writing nitpicky criticisms so her boss won't think Hikitoru is worth seeing. Nori worries her lip. She needs to get back on this gatekeeper's good side, but how? She's never dealt with a woman who isn't rich, elderly, or beautiful, but still has the nerve to demand respect.

Swann finishes tapping in her observations and crosses to the bookshelf to run her finger along the spines, stopping at a slim volume bound in brown cloth. She brings it back to the table, riffling through the pages until she finds what she's looking for. She sets the book next to Hikitoru, open to a photo.

Nori has seen the picture before, but only as a copy. It's the Shigaraki-ware bowl Daiki showed her, the one called Unmei. Seen side by side with Hikitoru, it seems obvious that the two were made by the same hand, but when Swann puts her glasses back on to deliver her verdict, her severe expression gives nothing away.

"Your tea bowl is in very fine condition," she begins, in a carefully neutral voice.

But...?

"I'd have to run some tests to make sure, but my initial examination suggests that your tea bowl is indeed a genuine Edo-era work by Yoshi Takamatsu."

Safe. Awash with relief, Nori says, "I'm glad you agree."

The assistant returns her attention to the bowl. Now Nori notes how unnaturally blank her face is. Robin Swann is trying hard not to betray her interest, but anyone who spends eight hours a day selling pottery can read the desire in her eyes. Maybe she won't have to do much bridge mending after all.

"How did you come to be in possession of such a remarkable piece?" Swann asks.

"I don't know the details, but it's been in our family a long time."

"You know nothing of its provenance?"

Unsure what she means by "provenance," Nori lobs the only fact she knows.

"It survived the firebombing of Senkō-ji temple in 1945. That's why the box still smells like smoke."

Swann bends down, curious, and sniffs.

"You're right," she says. "It does."

"So... what do you think?"

"Leave it with me. I'll show it to Hashimoto-san the minute she returns on Tuesday."

Nori is already shaking her head.

"I'm sorry, but I can't let it out of my sight. And," she's now confident enough to tell the merchant's favorite lie, "there are others who are interested."

Swann's eyes widen almost imperceptibly in alarm.

Nori not only catches it, she detects a satisfying note of anxiety as Swann replies, "I see. With your permission, then, I'll take some photos, and contact you as soon as I speak to Hashimoto-san."

Setting a ruler next to the tea bowl, she clicks away with a heavy digital camera, then scrolls back through the shots to make sure she's captured everything she needs.

When the bowl and box are documented to her satisfaction, she repositions her cursor and asks, "Are you the owner of record?"

Nori hesitates. Technically, Hikitoru belongs to her grandmother.

"Or," Swann suggests, "are you the owner's agent?"

"Yes. That's what I am. Her agent."

"And the owner is . . . ?"

Nori spells out the characters for Chiyo Okuda and provides their contact information.

A few minutes later, Hikitoru expertly repacked in the silk carrying cloth, they're back in the lobby. The graying guard steps in to check Nori's bundle, but Swann vouches for it and he backs off with a deferential bow.

The elevator dings.

Swann thanks her for coming, but as Nori takes her leave, she can't help but plead, "Please don't accept another offer before Hashimoto-san has a chance to see it."

Nori returns her bow, waiting for the doors to close before allowing a grin to spread across her face. Robin Swann might have all kinds of fancy degrees, but she'll never be half the merchant Nori is.

Sure enough, she has barely cleared the building when a message arrives, asking her to bring Hikitoru back to Fujimori Fine Art first thing Friday morning. But . . . isn't Swann's boss supposed to be out of town until next week? Is she cutting her trip short, just to see it? Does that mean Eriko Hashimoto is as eager to get her hands on the tea bowl as her assistant?

Nori taps out a reply. Regrettably, she's unable to make it downtown on Friday morning, but if they come to Kappabashi instead, she can meet them before work.

Ten minutes later, the meeting is scheduled for eight o'clock Friday morning at Okuda & Sons, and Nori has her answer: Eriko Hashimoto is very eager indeed.

21.

One arm flung wide, the potter sleeps like the dead, so spent he's not even snoring. But Saburo lies awake, too agitated to sleep. Every time he closes his eyes, First Love shatters into a thousand pieces. Again and again and again. He tosses and turns, unable to find a comfortable position. First too hot, then too cold. Last summer's spider bite begins to itch uncontrollably, and he scratches his ankle, even though the red bump is long gone.

Just because the potter made that tea bowl, did that give him the right to destroy it? In Kyoto, First Love would have given surpassing joy to generations of tea masters with the training to appreciate it, in the rarified setting it was designed for. It would have been cared for and admired, recognized as the masterpiece it was, not reduced to worthless rubble in a godforsaken backwoods. Everyone Saburo knows would agree: breaking it was deeply wrong.

But what's troubling him even more is that it's not over. There are more in that shed, and Yakibō intends to break them all. If he hasn't already—the other boxes might already be empty. Except for Yabō, the one he helped name. The one whose characters he had brushed with his own hand. The one that had inspired him to write the best poem he's ever written.

He can't let it happen. It's his duty not to let it happen. Even if the old fanatic believes his eternal salvation depends on destroying those tea bowls, what's one man's soul compared to the obligation to save great art from destruction? Every child in Kyoto has heard the cautionary tale of the selfish aristocrat who wanted to enjoy his family's priceless Sesshū scrolls in the afterlife, so he insisted they accompany his body into the cremation flames. Generations of scholars have lamented the loss, and his heirs are still criticized for permitting such an unforgivable act.

He has to do something. But what? Argue? Plead? Ask his father to intervene? He's spent too many evenings listening to Yakibō rant about the evils of attachment to think any of that will work. When it comes to interpreting the Four Noble Truths, Yakibō is deaf, as well as blind.

Action is what's needed, not words.

22.

Present-Day Japan

WEDNESDAY, APRIL 2

Tokyo

Nori arrives ten minutes early for visiting hours at the hospital. All day, she's been itching to tell her grandmother about her triumph at the auction house. If a payoff that could very well exceed their wildest dreams doesn't lure 'Baa-chan back to the land of the living, what will?

Draping her coat on the back of the visitor's chair, Nori scoots it to the bedside. She takes her grandmother's thin hand between her own.

"How are you feeling tonight, 'Baa-chan? I hope you can hear me, because this morning I found a way to get us a lot more for that tea bowl than if we sell it through that old highway robber Miura." She leans in. "Remember the picture of that other one I showed you? The tea bowl that's worth ten million yen? Well, this morning I took Hikitoru to the auction house that sold it, to see if they'd be interested in—"

Her grandmother frowns.

"'Baa-chan?"

This can't be a real reaction, because it's not the right one.

"I haven't got to the good part yet," Nori says, watching her grandmother's face like a pot that's about to boil over. "What I'm here to tell you is that the expert who sold that other tea bowl is so excited to see Hikitoru that she's cutting short her business trip to come to Kappabashi on Friday morning to—*Ow!*"

Her grandmother's hand is squeezing hers with the strength of ten grandmothers, and her expression has deepened into a definite scowl.

What the—

"'Baa-chan! Are you awake? Can you hear me? Let go, so I can call the nurse!"

She tries to pull away from the steely grip, but her grandmother won't let go.

The nurse flings open the door and charges in, stethoscope swinging.

"Is everything all right in here? Did you call for me?"

But Nori can't answer, because at the sound of the opening door, 'Baa-chan had dropped her hand like a hot chestnut and her face went slack.

"Was she showing more signs of consciousness?" asks the nurse, fingers clamped on her grandmother's wrist, counting. "Her pulse is a little elevated."

Nori narrows her eyes at the slight figure in the bed, once again far away in a world nobody can reach. Or *pretending* to be.

"I thought she might be waking up," Nori says slowly, "but I must have been mistaken." The crafty old so-and-so! "I don't think there's any need to call the doctor."

Not until 'Baa-chan gives up this charade, anyway. Because if she's decided not to let anyone know she's awake, she'll just keep making a fool of her granddaughter until she's good and ready to rejoin the living.

But Nori is fuming, and two can play this game. 'Baa-chan obviously doesn't need her sympathy, so no more chatty bedside talks. If she doesn't want to hear how her granddaughter rescued the Hikitoru situation with zero help from certain grandmothers, Nori isn't about to tell her.

23.

WEDNESDAY, APRIL 2

Tokyo

Robin shoves her front door shut with her hip, then breaks into the happy dance she's been suppressing ever since that life-changing piece of luck walked through the door into Fujimori Fine Art this morning.

The Yoshi Takamatsu tea bowl she saw today has the same name as the last poem in Saburo's masterwork, *The Eight Attachments*. Which confirms it's no coincidence that the one Saburo acquired on his first poetry pilgrimage shares the name Yabō with his sixth *Attachment*. If the authentication tests prove that Hikitoru really was made by Yoshi Takamatsu, it will be solid evidence that the potter and the poet are connected. More than connected. Saburo didn't compose *The Eight Attachments* until late in life—long after Yakibō had died—which strongly suggests the potter inspired the poet.

And she could be the one to prove it. A paper documenting the relationship between Yakibō and Saburo would rock the academic world. The professional journals would fall all over themselves to publish it, and she'd finally walk the graduation stage in the glow of early summer, wearing the cap and hood of a Doctor of Philosophy in

East Asian Languages and Cultures. A discovery of that magnitude would guarantee a long and glorious career spent unlocking new levels of meaning in one of Japan's most beloved pieces of literature.

She waltzes to the main room with the armload of research papers she copied tonight at the library and piles them next to her seat at the low table. Returning to the kitchen, she peers into her refrigerator. Half a pack of shiitake mushrooms. A lone carrot. A bunch of *komatsuna* that will be shriveled green rags by tomorrow. It's hot pot for one again tonight, unless she wants to gird herself up to go back out to the supermarket. Which she does not.

Tossing a half-used packet of frozen chicken into the microwave to thaw, she pours herself a glass of pinot in celebration, pants be damned. This discovery could be the kind of earth-shaking, academic triumph that will open doors she'd never dreamed of knocking on. She'd acquire an antique desk, a book-lined office, and a gaggle of graduate students. Best of all, she'd be an expert in the field she started out to study, not the one where the winds of available research subjects had pushed her. The copies she'd made after work tonight ought to help her start building her case.

She chops vegetables and piles them onto a plate. The microwave pings as she stirs instant bonito broth, miso, and sesame paste together in her tiny electric hot pot, then adds splashes of sake and sweet rice wine. Toting it to the table, she plugs it in, twisting the knob to "high." By the time she has assembled her bowl, chopsticks, and reading material, the pot is bubbling merrily.

Topping up her wine, she settles onto her cushion, scrapes the chicken and vegetables into the fragrant broth, turns down the heat. Pulling the first article on Saburo from the stack, she begins to read.

This one is from the *Journal of Japanese Art Studies*. She sips her wine and highlights paragraphs detailing the leading expert's text analysis of Saburo's first volume of poetry, *The Road to Destiny*. It's the paper that first suggested the poet had encountered the potter in the early 1700s, on his first poetry pilgrimage. Citing word pairings, the author posited that Saburo had spent time somewhere deep in the countryside with either a potter or priest, in a year with a legendary typhoon. The poet had set out on his poetic journeys during rainy season only once, on his first trip. Taken with the facts that somewhere along the line Saburo had acquired a tea bowl made by Yoshi Takamatsu, and that a writing box believed to have belonged to him had recently been discovered in the town nearest Takamatsu's kiln, it strongly indicated that he'd met the Pottery Priest, may even have known him well.

She ladles a spoonful of cooked hot pot into her bowl. While it cools, she tackles the next document, her undergraduate advisor's dissertation. It was the talk of the Japanese literature world when it was published, because her professor was the first to suggest a connection between *The Eight Attachments* and the tea bowl now known as Yabō.

At the time, her future advisor was rooming with a doctoral candidate in art history, who'd been examining the calligraphy on the box containing Saburo's "lucky" tea bowl and said she was sure it had been altered. Until then, that tea bowl had been known as Unmei—Auspicious Fate—but her professor's roommate had performed tests on the box and discovered that the original characters had been rubbed out and new ones written over them. Using modern technology to detect traces of the scrubbed-away ink, they'd been able to reconstruct the tea bowl's original name, Yabō. "Ambition," not "Auspicious Fate." Which, her advisor had pointed out, is the sixth of Saburo's *Eight Attachments*. She'd gone on to suggest that the potter's influence on Saburo's work extended far beyond the volume published shortly after he returned, that in fact—

Shitshitshit! Smoke is pouring from the *nabe* pot. Robin scrambles to pull the plug, grabbing a dish towel to snatch the boiled-dry pan and fling it into the sink. She twists the tap and steam billows up as the cold water hits the desiccated nuggets of vegetables and chicken now welded to the bottom. At least this time she got to it before the smoke alarm went off.

24.

Feudal Japan

MARCH, 1704

Shigaraki

At the fork where the path to Yakibō's farmhouse meets the road, Saburo turns to bow his farewells, one last time. Goatee freshly trimmed and topknot fashionably oiled for the first time in months, he puts a cheerful face on his departure, but his smile fades as he strides away, knowing he's about to betray the man who just sent him off with a full stomach and his blessing.

He rounds the bend, and the trees finally hide Yakibō and Hattsan from view. From the bridge ahead, he'll double back through the forest, following the stream to the hut. By the time he gets there, Hattsan should be on the other side of the hill, chopping the wood they gathered yesterday, and Yakibō will be puttering around inside his kiln, arranging his latest batch of pottery for the spring firing.

The stream roars with snowmelt as the poet approaches the battered wooden bridge. He glances around to make sure he's alone, then cuts into the forest, slipping and sliding up the hill, scrambling through the knee-high bamboo that carpets the ground. When the trees are thick enough to hide him from the road, he stops to catch his breath and adjust his sandal, then pushes on, keeping the torrent on his left. He's just beginning to think he missed the hut when he spies its mossy roof through the trees ahead. He stops, listening for the sound of Hattsan's axe in the distance. There it is. *Thwock, thwock.*

Melting icicles over the crooked door drip dark lines onto his back as he ducks inside. He stops to let his eyes adjust, and the six tea bowl boxes lined up on the shelf emerge from the darkness. Crossing, he snatches up the one labeled Ude-jiman, hoping he was wrong about its being empty. But Yakibō has already broken his attachment to Pride— it's too light to have anything inside. His disappointment increases as he lifts Mikudasu, Kanzen-shugi, and Gankō. All empty.

The old fanatic must be getting pretty close to enlightenment, he thinks sourly, since he's already managed to rid himself of Pride, Arrogance, Perfectionism, and Rigid Thinking, as well as First Love.

Yabō is the only one left. He unties his bundle, setting the box atop his belongings. But when he stretches his carrying cloth up around the addition, the corners don't quite meet.

He groans. When he landed on Yakibō's doorstep, his traveling cloth had held only a change of clothes, his writing supplies, and a magnificent lacquer box filled with strips of fine paper for jotting haiku as poetic inspiration arose. But during his time in Shigaraki, belongings that might actually keep him alive on his journey had joined them, and his clothes had multiplied. The kimono he'd arrived in (chosen because it fit his romantic image of an itinerant poet, even though it was made of laughably impractical silk) had been traded for thick, homespun leggings, hemp robes, a warmer cloak, and a shaggy waterproof cape. He's wearing the wide conical hat that will shield him from rain and sun, but two pairs of straw sandals (for when his current ones wear out), plus a set of wooden *geta* clogs to keep his feet out of the mud, have to be carried too. He hadn't realized how bulky everything would be, and last night he'd been too drunk on sake and a sense of his own destiny to realize that adding the tea bowl to his already strained carrying cloth would be a problem.

But it is. If he wants to take Yabō, he'll have to leave something behind. He considers the options. Not the footwear. It's miserable to limp along in worn-out shoes. And not the flint, knife, or pot, because he'd learned the hard way how unpleasant it is to spend a cold, hungry night far from an inn. That left things that weren't lifesaving necessities. He'll need the brushes, ink sticks, and inkstone for writing poetry, but what about the writing box that holds his strips of blank paper? He gazes at its glossy golden lid, lavishly patterned with a design of clouds and dragons. His father had commissioned it from the finest lacquer artist in Kyoto as a going-away present, but it's bulky. If he takes it out, the tea bowl will fit.

But he can't leave it behind. It's too valuable. Saburo shudders, remembering how unpleasant it is to be the target of his father's ire. He can't return without the writing box. But he could come back later for it, couldn't he? He could sneak back along the stream, the way he came today, after he has a stack of fine poems to put inside it. Yes, that's what he'll do. He'll hide the writing box now, and come back for it on his way home.

A nightingale trills outside the hut, and in the silence that follows, he becomes aware that the regular chopping sound of Hattsan's axe had stopped some time ago. If Hattsan has already finished splitting the pile of wood they'd collected yesterday, he'll soon be hauling it in to dry. *Hauling it to this hut.*

Stuffing the slips of blank poetry paper between his folded clothes, he casts about, looking for somewhere to hide the lacquer box. Dig a hole in the earthen floor? No time. Stash it outside? It'll be damaged by weather. The best he can do is wrap it in his hand towel and thrust it behind the stacked logs, poking it down as far as he can with a stick of kindling. Unless Yakibō and Hattsan burn through the woodpile faster than usual, it ought to stay hidden until he sneaks back in a few months to retrieve it.

He hastily knots his traveling cloth with the tea bowl inside, slings it over his shoulder, and hurries back to the road the way he came.

25.

Toting the copies she fell asleep over last night, Robin shoulders through the glass door at Coffee Tanuki and is cheered to see that at least one of the eight million Shinto gods is smiling upon tonight's footnote mining. Not only is a quartet of chattering moms just leaving a corner table on the main floor, her favorite guy is working the counter. He always remembers she likes her medium latte in a to-go cup, and he never fake-compliments her on her Japanese. Plus, he swirls the foam atop her coffee into the café's adorable raccoon dog mascot, even when he's busy. In America, that would nearly be enough to vault him into her outer circle of friends, but here in Japan, she doesn't even know his name. She's been coming here for almost two years, and they've progressed to companionable chatting about the coffee and the weather while he counts out her change and stamps her point card, but she knows from mortifying past experience that's as close as they're likely to get.

She steps up, smiles, and orders. By the time her latte arrives, she has already pulled out the article on Saburo's writing box and uncapped her highlighter. She glances up to thank the coffee artist for today's *tanuki* face, then begins reading.

This piece appeared three years ago in *Archaeology Quarterly*, written by an art historian who discovered a lacquerware box on display in the back room of a small museum near Yakibō's old kiln, and claimed it had once belonged to Saburo.

Robin soon discovers why the paper hadn't been published in a more scholarly journal: it wouldn't pass peer review. Though the author had traced the box back to the artisan who had made it for Saburo's father, that only suggested that the poet had crossed paths with Yakibō, not that the potter had inspired Saburo's work.

But that's not the only intriguing discovery the author had made. The museum's archives also yielded six haiku written on scraps of paper made in Kurodani. Saburo's known works had all been brushed on paper from Kurodani, and although the sloppy handwriting bears scant resemblance to the fair copies of the poet's work, the sheets were discovered among some old ledgers owned by the same family that donated the writing box.

The author's text analysis made a strong case that they were drafts of a poem in Saburo's first famous work, *The Road to Destiny*. The scrawled lines play with various combinations of the words snow, sweat, hard labor, salt, and sake, and whoever wrote them was obviously striving for the same meaning as the final version:

> Hard labor in winter
> Makes sweat taste saltier
> And sake sweeter.

The author also pointed out that Saburo's privileged upbringing was unlikely to have provided opportunities to do the kind of physical labor that inspired such insights, so the poem had probably been based on experiences he'd had on his journey.

Several poems written during his first pilgrimage mention the tea bowl now known as Yabō, so it must have been acquired soon after he set out. Add that to the fact that the winter months referenced in the poem coincided with when he passed through Shiga prefecture, it was likely that Yakibō the Pottery Priest was the hermit/priest/artist he had studied with along the way. The author suggested that the tea bowl Yabō may have been offered as payment for the kind of physical work that elevated an end-of-day drink to a reward, or that Saburo had received the tea bowl as a token of the mutual regard that grows through shared labor. Either explanation would shed light on one of the minor mysteries surrounding Saburo and his "lucky" tea bowl, namely, why a poet toting all of his belongings on his back for three hundred kilometers would have packed something as useless as a tea ceremony utensil.

It's convincing, but Robin wishes the author had more concrete evidence of Saburo and Yakibō's meeting. She flips to the footnotes. The Shigaraki Museum & Visitor Center is listed as the owner of both the writing box and the poetry drafts. Would it be worth visiting, to see if she can dig up more?

She searches the footnotes for the donor's name. Hayashi Ceramics. Waking up her laptop, she keys in a search. The lone result is a website for some sort of merchants' collective called Shigaraki Pottery Town. The subpage she lands on is headlined Hayashi Ceramics, and a single paragraph explains that it has been in business since the eighteenth century, taking its name from the family of the current owner, whose ancestor apprenticed under the famous potter/eccentric, Yoshi Takamatsu.

Yakibō's old kiln is still in business? Coffee forgotten, Robin scans the primitive webpage, searching for contact information. The nearly unreadable black characters on a brick-red background grow blurry when she enlarges the window, and the postage-stamp-sized photos look like they were shot with a version 1.0 phone camera. No GPS map, no email link, just an address and landline number at the very bottom.

It's so badly designed, someone who hadn't spent much time in Japan might dismiss it as a dead end, but Robin is as thrilled as a prospector who'd just uncovered a seam of gold. The page is so unreadable and unfriendly to search engines that the Hayashi kiln just might be as undiscovered by other scholars as it is by the internet.

26.

It's only June, but Kyoto is already stifling. Even within the stout walls of the castle, it's unpleasantly warm, and Saburo's irritation with his wife isn't helping. The poet smooths his distinguished, graying goatee and straightens his stiff, new, court kimono, even though it doesn't need straightening. Footsteps whisper past in the corridor outside the room where he waits to meet the warlord of Yodo Castle.

As if it weren't unnerving enough to be summoned by the new *daimyō* without explanation, why couldn't his wife learn to hold her tongue? She's given him three sons and a daughter, and is still as beautiful as on the day he'd met her, but her understanding of what it means to be a supportive helpmeet leaves much to be desired. How hard would it have been to say something encouraging, instead of bemoaning the fact that he'd agreed to meet Lord Inaba on *butsumetsu,* a bad luck day? As if he had a choice.

The more he tries not to worry about it, the more he worries about it. And then he worries about worrying, because dwelling on thoughts of bad luck might attract it.

He should try to distract himself by writing a poem. Yes, that's what he'll do. He casts about the nondescript room for inspiration. The plum blossoms painted on the folding screen? No. They're not the least bit remarkable, despite being picked out in gold. The single bird trilling in the garden outside? That's beneath his notice too. He's already written a famous poem about *uguisu*. But what about that small spider, sitting in its web up in the corner? That has possibilities. Had it been allowed to live on purpose, or was it merely missed by the servants?

Voices approach in the corridor outside, and he spins toward the door, but they soon fade. He plucks at the chin tie of his hat. Is it too loose? It *is* too loose. What if it slips when he bows before Lord Inaba? What a disaster if it fell off, right in front of the man whose favor could vault him into the loftiest heights of Kyoto society! He summons the servant standing at attention outside the door.

The factotum fumbles around under Saburo's chin, and the poet begins to regret fussing with his valet's work. Now it's too tight. He opens his mouth to demand that the hapless retainer fetch someone who knows what he's doing, when a guard in Lord Inaba's livery flings open the door, announcing that he's here to escort the esteemed poet into His Excellency's presence.

Saburo clears his throat, adjusts the angle of the fan stuck into his *obi*, and follows his escort. The twisting corridors seem to go on forever, and he soon loses all sense of direction. The castle halls all look the same—dark, polished wooden floors, white plaster walls punctuated by sliding paper *shōji* screens concealing unseen rooms. He catches the titter of women's laughter from behind one, and false notes in a beginner's tune on the *koto* coming from another. They move at a snail's pace, since his samurai escort is reduced to scuffing along in the trailing silk trousers that fashionably prevent fighting men from making any aggressive moves indoors.

Just when the poet is beginning to think that the maze will never end, they reach the anteroom of the grand chamber in which the region's new ruler receives his subjects. A thin bamboo blind swagged with impressive purple and red ceremonial tassels conceals a wide opening in the far wall, separating the exalted man in the next room from those seeking his favor.

"Saburo Shibata, Poet of Kyoto," announces the chamberlain. The guards stand aside, allowing him to enter the anteroom alone.

From behind the blind a voice growls, "Pull the damn shade up, Maeda. How am I supposed to talk to this poet fellow if I can't see his face?"

Lord Inaba plans to speak with him directly? Saburo pales and falls to his knees, pressing his forehead to the floor in the bow reserved for the highest authority.

"Come, come," commands the imposing figure now being revealed as the chamberlain raises the curtain. "Get up. I didn't call you here to wear a hole in the *tatami* with your nose."

"Yes, Your Excellency," murmurs Saburo, shuffling forward. He dares not rise any further. It doesn't pay to take a lord too much at his word. He cautiously raises his eyes, only to find Lord Inaba awaiting him in a room so magnificent it takes his breath away. The walls are a deep blood red, entirely plastered in costly *bingara* clay. A carved ceiling of old growth *hinoki* cedar arches overhead, bathing the room in a scent so rare it seldom perfumes any place less exalted than an imperial residence.

The scarred man sitting rather stiffly amid this splendor in his purple silk court robes is relatively new to ruling—it's only been three months since the shōgun commanded the Inaba clan to replace the Todo family and their allies as lords of Yodo Castle—but he's acquiring a reputation as a swift dispenser of justice to anyone who doesn't give him the respect he's due.

"Maeda-san, fetch the poet a cushion. Put it there." Lord Inaba's moustache bristles as he points to a spot directly in front of him. "And bring us some tea. This audience-giving is thirsty work."

When the tea has been poured and Saburo is warily kneeling where he was told, the lord dismisses his retainers, telling them to station themselves in the corridor outside, in case they're needed. Not that a poet poses much of a threat, he jokes.

Saburo forces a polite laugh and waits for the lord to take a sip of tea before venturing to wet his own tongue. Which is, truth be told, parched from nervousness. The *daimyō* finally takes a gulp, peers into its depths with distaste, then refills his cup from the teapot at his elbow.

"I'll never get used to this stuff," he complains. "The tea at my last posting wasn't nearly so bitter." He raises an eyebrow bisected by a thin scar. "I bet you could write a poem about that, couldn't you?"

"Of course, my lord," Saburo quickly agrees. "And a fine metaphor it would be. Are you sure you wouldn't like to use it yourself?"

A bark of laughter. "I'm a fighter, not a poet." Then he heaves an annoyed sigh. "But now it seems I have to be both. These days, it's not enough to keep order, I have to play at politics too."

Saburo compliments him on that astute observation, as though it were his own. In fact, it was the legendary general Hideyoshi Toyotomi who first employed poetry, flower arranging, and tea ceremony as instruments of statecraft. This new lord might be a bit rough around the edges, but he's been well educated for his destiny.

"Now that my clan has taken possession of the castle, I've employed your brother to give me a crash course in tea ceremony," he continues. "But apparently, that's not enough. I need all kinds of other nonsense now, they tell me."

Like . . . poetic scrolls? Saburo's pulse quickens. Had his brother put in a good word for him? He hadn't dared imagine that he'd been summoned to the castle in order to become court poet to the rising star of Kansai, but . . .

"This tea bowl you've written so much about," says the *daimyō*. "What's it called? Fortune? Fate? Something like that?"

"You mean Unmei, Your Excellency?"

"Yes. That's it. Funny name for a tea bowl, isn't it? When your brother first mentioned it, I thought it was a sword." He guffaws at his own ignorance. "Which is why I like it."

He waves the teapot at Saburo (who thinks it safest not to accept being served by such a lofty personage), then fills his own cup again.

"What I'd like to know is, where did you get it? I know I'm

supposed to be able to figure that out by reading those scribblings of yours, but it would be quicker to hear it from you. In plain words, the kind a simple warrior can understand."

He downs half his tea, then sits back, waiting.

Saburo bows.

"I was just a young man at the time, Your Excellency," he begins. "I'd been studying with a disciple of the esteemed poet Bashō, when something he said inspired me to give up my fine clothes, take up my traveling staff, and follow in the footsteps of his master." He leaves out the fact that the life-changing words had been so critical of Saburo's poetic efforts that he'd fled the master's salon, vowing never to come back. Over the years, the story has been retold so many times that he no longer notices how the fabric of the legend hangs on the facts the way a court gown hangs on a wooden stand.

Warming to his subject, he tells of being caught in a typhoon (which had—in the saga's current version—assumed hundred-year ferocity), becoming lost in the woods (so far from civilization that he'd later been inspired to write a poem on that very subject), and being rescued (near death, not drunk) by the reclusive master potter Yakibō. It was at midnight on New Year's Eve that, after drinking tea (not sake) together and pondering the Four Noble Truths (not secretly scoffing at them), the artist known as the High Priest of Pottery had gifted him the tea bowl named Unmei (which is what he had renamed Yabō after a rainstorm and careless packing had smeared the characters the potter had instructed him to write on the lid. He'd taken the mishap as a sign from the gods that they approved of him giving it a new name, one more in keeping with its new owner's aspirations.)

"After I received Unmei," he tells Lord Inaba, "the saintly hermit sent me forth with his blessing, and from that day forward, my luck changed. I carried it over hill and vale, across rivers and mountains, and it inspired me to write *The Road to Destiny* poetry collection that was received with," Saburo bows his head modestly, "my first small measure of acclaim."

The rest—the critical praise, the way would-be poets now regularly appear on his doorstep, begging him to take their money and teach them to be great poets too—he modestly omits, simply concluding, "The rest is history."

He bows deeply, to signal the end of his narrative.

"A fine story," says Lord Inaba, his voice warm with approval. "And that's exactly what I need right now. I've called you here today—"

The poet holds his bow, heart pounding.

"—to tell me where this mysterious High Priest of Pottery lives, so I can send someone to fetch me one of those lucky tea bowls."

Saburo nearly pitches face-first onto the *tatami*. All the *daimyō* wants from him is a miserable tea bowl? Disappointment overwhelms him, then curdles into something worse. Fear. If Lord Inaba manages to hunt down the Pottery Priest, he'll learn the true story. That Saburo hadn't been given his famous tea bowl, he stole it.

"Poet?" the warlord barks. "Is something wrong?"

Saburo coughs, takes a gasping breath.

"Sorry, my lord, I get these spells sometimes . . ."

What's he going to do? He dares not refuse. But how can he say yes, without turning everything he's built into a smoking ruin?

"I would be honored to serve your lordship in any way I'm able, but it's been many years since I saw Yakibō," he waffles. Could he get away with claiming ignorance? "If you remember from *The Road to Destiny*, I chanced across his kiln by getting lost, so I'm not at all sure I can remember how to get there."

Lord Inaba frowns. "You should be able to retrace your steps, though. Isn't that whole book about your journey? It has to be somewhere between here and that town you stopped in. The one with the persimmon tree."

Too close. The first person the *daimyō's* lieutenant stops on the streets of Shigaraki will point them straight to Yakibō's kiln.

"Well remembered, my lord." Think, *think*. "But his kiln could be anywhere within two days' walk from there, and I'd be embarrassed to send Your Excellency's retainers to comb the forest for a single twig, if you know what I mean."

The warlord is frowning even more deeply. He's not buying it.

Saburo is out of excuses. There's only one way to make sure Lord Inaba's minions don't learn his secret.

"Won't you allow me to go on this quest instead? The man who made Unmei is an avowed hermit, and he'll certainly hide himself from such awe-inspiring persons as your retainers. But he knows me, Your Excellency. I'm sure I can persuade him to give you the luckiest tea bowl he has."

"Fine. Just don't order something specially made," the *daimyō* growls. "Artisans fuss over things when they know it's for the Castle, and before you know it, the thing that should have been finished in a month takes a year. Any old lucky tea bowl from this holy hermit will work just fine, but I need it as soon as possible. Too many of my new subjects are still loyal to the Todo clan, and I want to have a firm grip on their allegiance by the time the harvest is due, so they don't siphon off supplies to those who would prefer to bring back their old masters." He tosses back the rest of his tea. "So. What do you need? Horses, servants? How soon can you leave?"

"I'll set out right away, Your Excellency," Saburo gabbles, weak with relief. "I need nothing but my staff, my traveling cloak, and the opportunity to serve you."

27.

Feudal Japan

J U L Y , 1 7 2 4

Shigaraki

Lord Inaba's money pouch weighs heavily under Saburo's traveling kimono, and his feet burn from the unaccustomed walking, but that's not what's slowing his steps as the hills begin to take on a familiar shape. The closer he draws to Yakibō's kiln, the more his misgivings grow.

When he first set out, his relief at dodging certain disaster had lent him a certain optimism. He'd even entertained the notion of buying a bottle of Yakibō's favorite sake, knocking on his door, and suggesting they let bygones be bygones. They could spend a pleasant evening revisiting their old arguments as artists and equals. They could even invite Hattsan.

But by the time half-remembered landmarks begin to appear, the layers of fiction his story has acquired over the years have sloughed away, and he has to face the bald truth that although he departed with Yakibō's blessing, he's more likely to be greeted with a curse.

And that's not even his biggest problem. Now that every step is bringing the past back with uncomfortable clarity, he's reminded that the contents of the bulging purse entrusted to him will never be accepted in exchange for one of Yakibō's precious "attachments." Nothing he can offer the Pottery Priest will tempt him to part with a single tea bowl. Not silver. Not rank. Not fame. Nothing.

Saburo plods on, so caught up in brooding on the impossibility of his task that he doesn't realize how close he's getting, until the acrid smell of wood smoke penetrates his gloom. His chin jerks up. Is he already—? No, this path leads to Old Taro's. If only he could turn here instead, hand over some of the *daimyō's* silver and ask Old Taro to make a tea bowl for him. If the rival potter had even a fraction of Yakibō's talent, that's exactly what he'd—

His sandals slap to a halt, and his bark of laughter launches a cloud of twittering birds from a nearby bush. Why hadn't he thought of it before? Yakibō's beloved "attachments" aren't for sale, but his other pieces are. Special orders, some of them. Why not a tea bowl? If he could be talked into making a new one—a normal one, without all that Buddhist baggage—how would that be different from ordering a miso pot or a sake flask? He'd need a go-between of course, and he'd have to conceal who it's intended for, but . . . yes, that's what he'll do. The intermediary will cost him a string of Lord Inaba's coins, but the Pottery Priest cares little for money, and there ought to be plenty left over to keep himself in comfort and sake at a local inn until the new tea bowl is made and fired.

He tramps on, planting his walking stick with renewed vigor. The sun comes out and glints off the river, and even his blisters hurt less, now that he has a plan.

His surge of good cheer lifts him through the outskirts of Shigaraki, depositing him on the main street. Not much has changed. The tea merchant still displays his wares in Yakibō's pots out front, but a new noodle stand has set up shop across from the temple.

He'd better keep his head down, just in case. It wouldn't do to be recognized by anyone who remembers him from the days he used to be known about town as Tōhai-kun, the Frozen Poet. The streets seem busier than twenty years ago, a little more crowded with—

He glances up as the townsfolk around him shift aside to make way for a file of armed men, escorting a government official. Saburo cranes his neck, curious. Tall hat, brocade robes. The regional magistrate. This one looks younger than the bearded old uncle who held the office twenty years ago, though, and he's . . . no, he can't be. Surely this new magistrate isn't the underling Saburo shared an occasional flask of sake with, back when he was just a clerk, and Saburo was just a potter's apprentice?

A potter's apprentice who disappeared with his master's prized tea bowl.

He draws a sharp breath. Anyone who has heard the Pottery Priest tell the tale will not call what he did "rescuing." He darts into the nearest shop. Even after twenty years, the magistrate could order him flogged for thievery. Or worse. His hand flies instinctively to his nose, as if he heard the swordsman sharpening his blade.

Bending over a bin of *daikon* radishes, he pretends to inspect them until he's sure the magistrate's retinue has disappeared. Pulling his hat lower, he pokes his head out to check both ways, then slinks out to the street and scurries back the way he came. He dares not look up until he's safely inside a hostelry in the neighboring village, where nobody will look at the name on his traveling papers and connect it to the poet better known in Shigaraki as a thief.

Safe in the privacy of the inn, he relaxes a little. But he knows that the time it will take for a tea bowl to be made and fired will already stretch Lord Inaba's patience to the limit, so he can't hide in his room for long.

That evening, he dresses in a brown kimono that shows the kind of false humility a prosperous artisan or a merchant with social aspirations might affect. It adheres to the strict laws that govern how much wealth each class is allowed to display, but is lined in the kind of gaudy and forbidden silk that can be "accidentally" revealed with a kick of the foot while walking.

Joining the townsfolk in the village's sake shop, he hunches over his cup at a corner table. Which of his fellow drinkers would make the best go-between?

By the time he reaches the bottom of his second flask, he's decided on a middle-aged man whose companion excused himself early to go home to his new wife. The balding drinker who's now finishing his sake alone is apparently the town's tea merchant.

Saburo picks up his empty flask and stands, but as he makes his way through the crowded hall for a refill, he jostles the table of the lone tea-seller hard enough to topple his sake bottle. Apologizing profusely, he insists on replacing it with a new (and better) one. When they're both seated at the table with full cups, and pleasantries have been exchanged, he confides that although he's traveling for business, he'd hoped to acquire a gift for his father-in-law while in the region.

"Regrettably, I haven't yet found something that might appeal to him," Saburo says, refilling his companion's cup. "He saw a tea bowl in Kyoto that he admired very much, and I discovered that it was made by an artist from Shigaraki who goes by the name of Yakibō. Do you know him, by any chance?"

"As a matter of fact, I do," says the merchant. "But I'm afraid he's past taking on any commissions. My son-in-law is the apothecary in Shigaraki, and he told me that the old man's apprentice stopped buying his master's usual remedy a couple of weeks ago. He must no longer be hoping for a cure, poor man."

No longer hoping for a . . . Yakibō is *dying*?

"Are you all right?" The tea seller is peering at him strangely.

"Yes, I'm just, uh, I'm sorry to hear the news he's not well, that's all." Yakibō can't be dying. He can't be. "I wish I'd come sooner."

"Eh, you'd have to have come a lot sooner," says the tea-seller, topping up Saburo's cup. "He's been sick for almost a year, and his apprentice has been running things for longer than that. Must be five years ago now—or is it six? No, it's five—Hattsan took over after that hard winter when our pond was frozen well into the spring. The tea crop was so late that my storeroom was nearly empty by the time the new batch of leaves finished fermenting." The merchant drains his cup and smacks his lips. "But if it's a tea bowl you're wanting, I doubt Hattsan can help you. He makes perfectly serviceable water jars and grinding bowls, but he's no artist. For tea ceremony ware, I really think you'd be better off with . . ."

The tea seller prattles on, but the blood is roaring in Saburo's ears and he doesn't hear a word.

How could Yakibō be dying? For every step of his journey, he'd wondered how the potter might have changed over the years. Had he become wiser, crazier, angry at life, at peace with life, free from his attachments, burdened by new attachments? The one possibility that had never crossed Saburo's mind is that the pottery master who seemed more like a force of nature than a mortal man might be *dying*.

The tea merchant is looking at him with interest, but Saburo has no idea what question he's just been asked. He has to get out of here. Abandoning the half-full flask of sake and his startled companion, he blurts that he's not feeling well and stumbles back to his room.

Collapsing on his futon, he stares up at the woven bamboo ceiling. If he'd been far away in Kyoto, where weeks can go by without thinking of his old mentor, the news that Yakibō wasn't long for this world wouldn't have troubled him so much. But here, within walking distance of the dying man, he can think of nothing else.

He tries to tell himself he's only upset because he needs the potter to make a tea bowl for the *daimyō*, but it seems like only yesterday that they'd shared the camaraderie of keeping the kiln fires burning for three days and three nights. Cold wind buffeting their backs, they had passed the sake bottle back and forth, filling each other's cups, while the Pottery Priest waxed eloquent on what it meant to be a poet or an artist or merely a man, navigating this earth for his allotted span. The truth is, Yakibō had taught him everything worth knowing.

Saburo pulls the covers over his head, but it doesn't shut out the fact that the potter is about to die with bad blood still between them, and he's close enough to do something about it.

He turns to the wall. Squeezes his eyes shut. Sleep is what he needs. A few hours of blessed oblivion. He'll decide what to do in the morning.

But despite the three flasks of sake, he tosses and turns, itchy with unconfessed sin. His guilt grows, as unrelenting as a headache, too painful to ignore. By the hour of the Rat, his freshly awakened conscience is insisting he take a hard look at what he did twenty years ago and call it by its true name. By the hour of the Ox, he can no longer escape the dread certainty that if he doesn't set things right before Yakibō dies, he'll carry that burden for the rest of his days. And by the hour of the Tiger, he's begging the gods to make a deal. If they'll keep Yakibō alive until morning, he'll go straight to the farmhouse at first light. Prostrate himself before his old master. Admit what he did. Beg for forgiveness.

Finally, he falls into an exhausted sleep.

The demons that tormented Saburo in the night have shrunk to a more manageable size by morning, and a slightly more optimistic inner voice suggests that they might even have been a little exaggerated. The curse of a creative mind, as it were, throwing shadow puppets against the wall. Nevertheless, the prospect of spending any more nights in their company makes Saburo shudder, so he sticks to his plan.

But instead of dashing out the door at dawn as if all the *oni* in hell were after him, he takes the time to dress himself in his finest kimono and oil his topknot before setting out. It's a fine day, with a clear, blue sky arching overhead. Warm, but not too hot yet. He detours to the local temple to make an offering, then, buoyed by the discovery that the astrological forecast for today is *tomobiki*—good luck all day, except at noon—he begins to plan how best to obtain the forgiveness he craves. Swinging his walking stick, he's soon deliberating between a glittering array of words in which to cloak his apology, discarding and replacing them until he has assembled an oration that would be worthy of the *daimyō* himself. By the time he crosses the bridge near Yakibō's kiln, he's even congratulating himself on the elegant way he likens his sorrow at having wronged the potter to the bitter tears of the goddess Amaterasu.

Turning up the path to the farmhouse, he takes a moment to appreciate the shrilling of the summer cicadas. Why are they so much

louder and more poignant in the woods than in town? And the trees—
they seem bigger than the last time he walked this way. They're certainly encroaching on the path, although that might be because last
time they were winter-bare, and now they're wrapped in lush green
robes. The bamboo, too, has spurted up between winter's dried stalks,
in fountains of freshly striped green and gold.

It's hotter here, away from the river, where the sultry air isn't
stirred by even a hint of a breeze. He mops at his forehead with his
hand towel, swats at a mosquito. The sooner he delivers his apology,
the sooner he'll be able to escape to somewhere cooler. Perhaps he'll
enjoy a bowl of refreshing *sōmen* noodles and a flask of cold sake, once
the gods are satisfied and his demons banished. Tucking his fan more
securely into his *obi*, he climbs the hill, puffing a little, but it's not long
before Yakibō's farmhouse swings into view. As he draws near, he sees
that the blackened cedar siding has weathered to a silvery gray, and the
front door has been replaced, although it's rotting in the same corner
as before. The crack across the entry stone has widened in two decades
of freezing and thawing, its seam of moss no longer winter brown, but
brilliant green and pushing up a miniature glade of pale blue flowers,
nodding on delicate stalks.

He stops a few steps short, preparing himself. Yakibō will be old.
Ailing. Perhaps in pain. But no matter how sick he's become, the man
who devoted his life to freeing himself from his sins will certainly
welcome the chance to put things right between them before he faces
another turn on the Wheel of Rebirth.

Holding that thought, Saburo steps up to the front door. Knocks.
Waits. Waits some more. Has the old man become hard of hearing?
He knocks again, louder, just as the door slides open, revealing a sour-
faced figure, balding and stooped.

Neither recognizes the other.

Saburo is first to venture, "Hattsan?"

Gets a puzzled look in return.

But . . . he can't have changed as much as the potter's apprentice!
Threads of silver brighten his own hair and goatee now, but Hattsan

no longer has to shave his tonsured head, and his thin topknot is nearly white. Saburo is wearing a pleasant expression he likes to think of as "benevolent wisdom" on his prosperously rounded face, but Hattsan seems to have suffered some grave misfortune that stripped the flesh from his bones and dragged the corners of his mouth down into twin parentheses of disapproval.

"It's me," the poet enlightens him. "Saburo."

"You!" Surprise smooths the apprentice's face for an instant before the dour creases return, deeper than before.

"Hattsan?" calls a querulous voice from within. "Who's there? Is it the priest?"

"No," his apprentice replies. He stands aside. "It's the Frozen Poet."

"Saburo?" A pile of quilts next to the hearth stirs and a disheveled graying head pokes out. "Saburo, is that you?"

"Yes, master." He steps over the threshold. "It's me."

The vast room seems to have shrunk. Or maybe it's just that the corners aren't lost in gloom, battened down tight against winter's chill. Today, every shutter has been thrown wide to welcome any passing breeze that might freshen the stale air.

Saburo delivers the proper honorific greeting and draws nearer to the figure lying beside the hearth. He can't ignore the slightly nauseating odor of chronic illness, but he does his best to disguise his distaste. Sweat beads his forehead. Even though it's stifling inside the house, the hearth fire is leaping and crackling as if snow lay knee-deep all around.

"I'd know that voice anywhere," Yakibō says, struggling to sit. "But I never thought I'd hear it again in this life."

Hattsan crouches to assist his master, and Saburo is shocked by how shrunken the once-robust potter has become. Shoulders bowed, his spine now curves protectively around some inner hurt. Even wrapped in two quilts, he seems no bigger than Saburo's youngest son. His neck is as skinny and corded as a rooster's, the skin across his cheekbones stretched tight, strangely pale for a man once at home in the elements.

The potter aims his filmy eyes toward his visitor.

"Come. Sit." He pats the *tatami* with one knob-jointed claw. "Hattsan, is there any tea?"

Saburo seats himself cautiously, wondering what to make of this reception. He's not detecting even a hint of a grudge that's been nursed for twenty years. It's almost as if Yakibō has forgotten about the stolen tea bowl. Could his illness be eating away at his memory? Poor old codger. The poet's resolve wavers. Might his apology do more harm than good? Perhaps it would be better not to say anything, not to awaken memories best left—

"Tell me," Yakibō says, interrupting his dithering. "Did you ever become the poet you wanted to be?"

Saburo's head snaps up, slightly stung that his reputation hasn't preceded him.

"I did, yes. In fact, my first success—my first *humble* success—was a collection I began writing while I was here. I even have my own disciples now," he can't help adding.

"Good. That's good." The blind potter accepts a cup of tea from his apprentice. Takes a slurp. "And why did you come back?"

Bam. He'd forgotten how direct people are in the backcountry. They haven't even begun to check off the pleasantries that would be expected in Kyoto, but this is the opening he'd planned to arrive at by a tactful and circuitous route, so he'd better take it.

Setting down his cup of tea, he straightens his spine, composes his hands on his knees. Bows deeply, eyes respectfully lowered, even though Yakibō can't see him.

"I came here today to beg your forgiveness, master."

Puzzled pause.

"My forgiveness?"

Oh no. This *is* a mistake. Yakibō's mind is too far gone. He backpedals.

"Yes, I wanted to say I'm sorry for the regrettable . . . thing . . . I did."

No reply.

He cautiously clarifies, "The, uh, regrettable thing I did . . . twenty years ago."

"Oh, *that*," the potter says, setting his cup on the floor. "You mean stealing Yabō?"

Saburo is as shocked as if ice water had just been flung in his face. He casts about for the words he'd so carefully chosen, but they've deserted him. His flowery phrases are of no use, now that Yakibō has called him the thief that he is.

All he can do is gracelessly cry, "Yes, master! I truly regret taking your tea bowl! Please forgive me!" Knocking his forehead against the floor, he bleats the words of utmost apology, *"Moshiwake gozaimasen, moshiwake gozaimasen!"*

A log subsides in the hearth, sending a plume of sparks toward the roof. Sweat drips from the tip of his nose onto the frayed straw mats as Saburo holds his face to the floor, praying that his crude utterance will still be worthy of absolution.

What comes instead is a loud rapping at the door.

A visitor? Now? What terrible timing. Should he hold his bow? Or sit up to see who's here? Hattsan decides for him, already moving toward the door. Still half-crouching, Saburo twists around to see who it is. The silhouette of a mountainous man in white robes blocks the light streaming onto the stone entryway. It's Reverend Uchida, the priest who had pointed out the hidden depths of his first great poem. Then the man steps inside, and Saburo sees his mistake. Unless the old priest is aging backward, this must be his son.

"I'm sorry, am I interrupting something?" young Uchida asks, bewildered at the tableau.

Yes, yes you are.

But Yakibō welcomes him with, "No, of course not, not at all. Come in, come in. In fact, your timing is perfect." A bout of coughing interrupts him, but he holds up a hand, bidding the priest be patient. When he catches his breath, he continues, "I asked you to come out here today to help me take care of that attachment we discussed, but now that Saburo here has returned," he waves a hand toward the crouching poet, "I believe we can attend to both of them at once."

The young priest turns to Saburo, surprised.

"You're the Frozen Poet? The one who—"

He snaps his mouth shut, spots of color appearing on both cheeks.

"Yes," Yakibō answers for him. "The one who stole Yabō. And he's come all the way to Shigaraki today to make amends."

"After all these years," the priest marvels. "He really brought it back?"

"We were just getting to that part," Yakibō says.

They turn to the poet, expectantly.

Why are they . . . *oh no.* Yakibō thinks he's here to give the tea bowl back? But that's . . . impossible. Surely he doesn't— But he does. Saburo feels a hot flush of shame. Even after twenty years, the Pottery Priest can still make him feel like he's the only blind man in the room. How could he have forgotten that he's dealing with a man who believes words are meaningless without action? That attachments to this world can only be broken by hurling them against a rock?

But what can he say? Perhaps the potter will accept a partial truth.

"I'm afraid I didn't bring it with me."

Yakibō's brows draw together. "I don't understand. If you came here to apologize, why did you come without Yabō? Where is it?"

Now he's really in a corner. If he admits he never intended to return it, his presence here, his apology, the way he abased himself (not just before Yakibō, but in front of Hattsan and that gaping boy of a priest as well) will all be for nothing. He'll have to slink off with his tail between his legs, gods unappeased, demons still on his back. He'll be worse off than if he'd never come. Sweat slides in a long itch down his chest. Saburo opens his mouth, but he can't say it. He can't admit the tea bowl is still in Kyoto.

"I left it in my room at the inn," he lies, abandoning all hope of absolution. Now he just wants to get away without a painful scene that will replay in his head for the rest of his life.

"I see," Yakibō says. Then he brightens. "But the day is young.

While you're fetching the tea bowl, perhaps Uchida-*bōsan* can bring us the temple drum. There should still be plenty of time before nightfall to do things right."

No, no, no, he needs more than an hour or two. He needs to be far away, before they realize he's not coming back.

"I . . . I'm afraid I have other business to conduct this afternoon," he stammers. "Perhaps tomorrow? Or," really stretching it, "the next day?"

"I can come back tomorrow," the priest offers.

"All right," the potter agrees, subsiding into his nest of quilts. "Tomorrow it is."

Saburo manages to take his leave with a modicum of dignity, but as soon as the door slides shut behind him, his knees buckle. Defeat and shame beat a twin tattoo in his head as he lurches back toward the road. He isn't forgiven. He has made promises he can't keep. He'll have to leave right away. By tomorrow he'll have to be so far away that even if they set the magistrate's men on his trail, they won't catch him before he's out of their jurisdiction.

And then the biggest failure of all draws a howl from deep within. He has no tea bowl for the *daimyo*, and no way of getting one. The potter is beyond making one, and the only Yakibō tea bowl left in the entire world is sitting in his own treasure house, back in Kyoto.

Or . . . is it? A crow calls, the cicadas screech. What had Yakibō said to the priest? *I asked you to come out here today to help me take care of that attachment we discussed.*

There *is* another tea bowl.

The poet's robes flap about his ankles as he flees, driving himself down the path as if swarmed by bees, trying to outrun the unthinkable.

But even now, a small part of him knows he will return tonight, with his traveling pack on his back. That he will find that tea bowl and take it, before the potter has a chance to destroy it.

A sliver of a moon has escaped the branches of the trees overhead by the time Saburo decides it's safe to emerge from the grove where he's been lurking since sundown. Nobody with legitimate business will be traveling at this hour, so there's less risk he'll be recognized, but he still hurries along with his head down, keeping a wary eye out for high-waymen.

He hears the creek near Yakibō's farmhouse before he sees it. Swollen with the summer monsoon, it dashes against the bridge's stonework before roaring beneath.

He crosses, plunging up the hill at a spot wide of the stream's former banks, which are well underwater now. Pushing through the waist-high bracken by the feeble light of the crescent moon, he swears as he slips on a patch of mud. By the time he limps into the shelter of the trees, his robes are soaked to the knee and he's breathing hard, but there's no time to stop and rest. He has to finish his business at the hut and be well away before dawn.

Keeping the sound of the tumbling torrent to his left, he pushes on, angling into the trees, but brambles that hadn't been nearly so vig-orous in wintertime waylay him, and shrubs that hadn't been nearly so twiggy snag at his cloak. Rocks and logs lurk unseen beneath the knee-high bamboo until his shins bark against them, almost as if they were lying in wait. If only he had a knife to hack through this miserable—

And then a ghostly gray trunk looms up ahead, and he spies the tattered straw garland ringing the hollow tree. He must have aimed too far to the right and missed the hut, but at least now he knows where he is.

The sacred *shimenawa* rope has been frayed by many winters, its tassels straggling and uneven. But what jolts him like a centipede bite is how wrong he'd been the last time he was here. Leaves now sprout from every ghostly branch, all the way to its crown. The old tree isn't dead. It hasn't lost its power at all.

He turns to make his way back toward the hut, but a prickling sense of unease stops him. If the gods still live there, ancient and watchful, they must be powerful gods indeed, to keep a hollow tree alive. They could thwart his mission if he continues without paying his respects.

He returns to the tree, fumbling in his money pouch for the

smallest coin he has, then parts the bracken to place it between the tangled roots. And there, nestled at the foot, lies a small mound of weathered one-*mon* pieces. He mutters a short prayer, then counts them. Six. Does that mean the potter has made six trips to the flat rock, sacrificed six tea bowls?

But there had only been five boxes left in the shed after he took Yabō.

How many new "attachments" had Yakibō discovered?

Saburo slashes back toward the shed and soon spots the roof, peeking out above a leafy stand of wild azaleas. The thatch of chartreuse moss has grown thicker with the years, and the thumb hole in the door is choked with green velvet. He works a finger through and yanks it open. Long-dead pine needles rain down as he ducks inside.

He lights the stub of candle he'd pinched from a lantern at the inn. The lengthening flame illuminates a sight more beautiful than paradise itself. Eight boxes sit on the shelf. *Eight.*

One stride takes him across the packed earth floor. He knows the tea bowl named Ude-jiman is long gone, and the boxes labeled Mikudasu, Kanzen-shugi, Gankō and Hatsu-koi are empty too.

The fifth reads . . . Yabō.

What? He snatches it up. There's no mistake. The handwriting is different, of course, but . . . Had Yakibō made a new tea bowl to replace the one he'd stolen?

Of course he had! And the box in his hand is too light to be anything but empty. Which means the potter had not only made another tea bowl to represent "ambition," he's already broken his attachment to it.

The poet frowns. If the potter already broke his attachment to Yabō, why is he demanding that Saburo's tea bowl be returned? The old fanatic doesn't need it anymore, but he still wants to destroy it?

Saburo's face grows hot, recalling the moment they all turned their eyes on him. Hattsan, cold and righteous. The priest, boyish and naive. The potter, blind, but his righteous vision burning brighter than ever. The way they'd ganged up on him. Made him feel small. So convinced they're right.

But what makes Yakibō think he's better than that peacock who clutched the Sesshū scrolls to his chest as his body went up in smoke? He's not! He's just as selfish.

And suddenly, Saburo's not sorry anymore. He was right to have rescued Yabō. And he's right not to bring it back. He replaces the sixth box and is reaching for the seventh when he catches sight of its name and snatches his hand back as if burned.

Fukushū. Revenge. Not just anger, *revenge.*

His soul shrivels. Now he understands why the potter wants Yabō back. If there's an unbroken tea bowl inside this box, it means that for all these years, his old master has been harboring a cold fury toward him, and he hasn't yet given up his desire to make Saburo suffer for stealing Yabō.

He picks it up.

It's heavy.

A sour taste fills his mouth. If this is the only tea bowl left, he'll have to make a choice. He can leave it here and disappoint Lord Inaba, or take it, and deprive Yakibō of the means to break his attachment to punishing his one-time apprentice.

He pushes Revenge back onto the shelf. Praying that the eighth box will hold something he can take to the *daimyō* instead, he reads the name brushed on its lid. Hikitoru. He rubs his chin. Strange choice. The characters can be read any number of ways. "Taking back what's yours"? "Retiring to a private place"? Or could it be implying *iki o hikitoru:* "to draw one's last breath"?

That must be it. If Yakibō is making his peace with dying, giving up an attachment to drawing one's last breath would be fitting.

Hope beating in his chest, Saburo picks it up and . . . it's not empty! The tea bowl is wedged so tightly inside that he has to work to get it out, but as the wrapping falls away, he draws an astonished breath. Even in the guttering light of the candle, it's a thing of beauty surpassing his wildest expectations. Lord Inaba will be pleased. Beyond pleased. He'll be so grateful, he might even—

The poet stiffens, hearing a rustling in the bushes outside. What if it's Hattsan, coming for firewood? He listens some more. Silence. Probably just an animal, but he'd best be on his way.

Snatching up the discarded tea bowl wrapper, a slip of paper flutters from its folds. He stoops to retrieve it, holds it in the candlelight. The potter's seal is impressed beneath the priest's fussy script, with a vermilion stamp bearing Reverend Uchida's name right next to it. *If I breathe my last before letting go of Hikitoru, break this attachment for me.*

Break it? To hell with that idea! He flings the note to the dirt floor with the contempt it deserves, then rewraps the bowl and stows it among his belongings. Turns to go. Hesitates. Could the lacquer writing box he'd abandoned here so many years ago still be hidden behind the woodpile? Back then, he'd feared the potter's wrath too much to come back and retrieve it, but it wouldn't hurt to check. He grabs a stick and pokes around behind the logs. It encounters something, but he can't be sure it's the writing box, and he can't reach it with his arm. He'd have to unstack all the logs in front of it to find out, and he doesn't have time. He'll have to leave it.

Hoisting his burden onto his shoulders, he blows out the candle and tosses the still-smoking lump into the wet bushes as he slips and slides down the hill to the road.

28.

Nori hastily scrubs her rice bowl and props it on the drainer, then has second thoughts and dries it. She puts it away, along with the other wet dishes she'd upended on the dish towel. Not that the expert from the auction house will be setting foot in the kitchen, but it's good to know that if she does catch a glimpse, it won't give the impression of a single woman living alone, eating off sad, solitary dishes. She wipes down the counter, eyeing the condiments arrayed along the backsplash, tidies them into a more pleasing arrangement.

She's decided to receive her guests upstairs in the apartment, rather than down in the shop. The second floor's front room is far from impressive, but at least it doesn't reveal that the family business is mass-produced restaurant dishes, not rare art pieces. It wouldn't do to make Eriko Hashimoto wonder how the proprietor of a modest restaurant supply shop came to own a potentially priceless tea bowl. It's a question she's been worrying over herself, but the stubborn-as-a-stone grandmother who knows the answer is refusing to share it.

Nori opens the cupboard to take down their best teapot—a lovely old piece of blue and white Kutani-ware, brushed with a spray of bush clover and berries—and is instantly dismayed. Early April is the wrong season to serve tea from an autumn-themed pot. Is there time to run down to the shop and dig out the wisteria-motif one that her father had bought, but never sold? April is a little early for wisteria, but it would be a whole lot better than—

Her phone alarm chimes, reminding her that the art expert will arrive in twenty minutes. The blue and white teapot will have to do. She rinses and dries it, setting it on a black lacquer tray blessedly free from seasonal references. Two unchipped Nabeshima teacups join it, thankfully decorated with a nice, safe, Four Seasons design. Nori adds another cup, even though it has a hairline crack. She can use that one herself. Finally, she opens the canister of expensive—if slightly stale—tea reserved for guests. Spooning some into the teapot, she adds a dash more, for luck. She'll need it, because once again it's *butsumetsu*—bad luck all day. Naturally, she'd forgotten to check the astrological calendar before agreeing to the meeting.

Nori carries the tea tray to the main room. Stopping in the doorway, she frowns. There's nothing quite like seeing a familiar place through the eyes of approaching guests to highlight its faults. The stained ceiling, the cracks left unpatched after the last earthquake, the low, black lacquer table, dulled by years of service in the shop's office before being retired for home use.

But there's nothing she can do about any of that now. And once Eriko Hashimoto sees what's inside Hikitoru's wooden box, she won't be paying attention to the décor. Returning to the kitchen, Nori fetches the electric hot water pot, setting it on the floor and plugging it into the single boxy outlet. Her phone pings with another reminder. Ten minutes.

She squares Hikitoru's box on the table, then shifts it closer to the place where she plans to sit. She'll put art expert Hashimoto in the most honorable spot—framed by the *tokonoma* alcove—with Robin Swann beside her.

The doorbell buzzes. They're early. Nori whips off her apron and flings it onto its hook in the kitchen, then trots to the entryway.

Waiting outside on the landing is a slight woman in a luxuriously plain black coat. Chin-length hair frames a face that's middle-aged, but expertly made up. Behind her stand Robin Swann and a third, unexpected, visitor. A square, granite-faced man.

Crap, she only has two decent pairs of guest slippers.

"Hashimoto-san?" she says, with her best customer-welcoming smile.

"Eriko Hashimoto," the woman confirms, bowing. "You've met my assistant, Robin Swann. And this is Mr. Anzai."

Nori invites them in. Digging through the slipper bin to find the least-shabby pair for the mystery man, she tries to guess how Anzai fits into the picture. Hashimoto didn't refer to him with the honorifics she'd use to introduce a superior, but he doesn't strike her as an underling. A colleague? A Yakibō expert, perhaps?

Ushering them into the main room, she rethinks the seating. Pointing the art expert and the man of unknown rank to the more honorable side, she gives Swann the seat next to hers. The foreigner manages to tuck her awkwardly long legs beneath her to sit *seiza* with the rest of them, but even sitting, she's making the biggest room in the house feel small.

Eriko Hashimoto, on the other hand, radiates cat-like elegance. Her severe navy suit has never hung on any shop rack, and the pearls gracing her neck are of a size and quality that Nori has never seen outside a jeweler's window. Half-glasses hang from a tortoiseshell chain, and the crease between her eyebrows is carved deep from passing judgment on artifacts and people alike.

But what about Anzai? He looks older than Hashimoto-san, but that might be because she dyes her hair and he doesn't. His dark suit isn't cheap, but it's not fashionable either, so no help there. His face would be entirely forgettable, if it weren't for his sharp eyes. That, plus his military brush cut, makes Nori think security, not art. Chief of security, maybe? Is Hashimoto-san planning to make her an offer and take Hikitoru with them when they go?

Nori pours.

"What a lovely teapot," murmurs the art expert. "I've always been partial to bush clover motifs."

Crap, she noticed. Setting the cup on a saucer, Nori hands it to Hashimoto with a pained smile, then does the same for the others, giving Robin Swann the one with the crack.

They ease into the business at hand with small talk—the unseasonably cold weather, the current museum exhibit featuring pieces that passed through the auction house on their way to the loaners' collections—then finally circle around to the reason for their visit.

"Okuda-san," Hashimoto says, "on behalf of Fujimori Fine Art, we're honored that you brought your treasured tea bowl to us for evaluation."

Evaluation? Ha. As if she hadn't already acknowledged its value by cutting her trip short.

"On the contrary, the pleasure is all mine," Nori replies. "My grandmother and I are honored that you're sparing us your valuable time. Would you like to see Hikitoru now?"

"If it's not too much trouble," comes the dry reply.

Nori removes it from its box, setting it on the table to unwrap it. Hashimoto-san's eyes widen in appreciation as it's placed in her hands.

Then she surprises Nori by handing it to Anzai.

"Well?" she asks. "Is this it?"

Nori blinks. Was she wrong about his being a security guy?

Anzai sets it on the table and opens his briefcase, withdrawing a tape measure and a photocopied form, which he offers to Hashimoto.

"Twenty-five centimeters," he calls out, measuring the circumference the long way. "Twenty. Fifteen." Width and depth.

Hashimoto checks the measurements against the paper.

"It's the right size."

They both turn to Nori.

"Where did you get this tea bowl?" asks Hashimoto.

"It belongs to my grandmother."

"Where did she get it?"

"I don't know. It's been in our family a long time, I think."

"Since 1945?" asks Anzai.

"1945? Why 1945?"

"Because that's when it was stolen."

"*What*?"

"Shortly after the March 10th firebombing destroyed Senkō-ji temple," Hashimoto says, "the tea bowl named Hikitoru disappeared from their treasure house and was never seen again." She pauses. "Until two days ago."

"No. That's impossible. How could it be stolen if it's been in our . . ."

"That," says Anzai, "is what we'd very much like to know."

He pulls a badge from his pocket and the blood drains from Nori's face. He doesn't work for the auction house. He's an inspector with the Tokyo Metropolitan Police.

Pulling out a notebook, he flips to a half-filled page.

"I understand that the owner of record is Chiyo Okuda, is that right?"

"Yes," Nori squeaks.

"And she's your grandmother? She lives here with you?"

"Yes."

"I'll need to ask her a few questions."

"I'm sorry, but that won't be possible."

"Why not?"

"I'm afraid she's not here. At the moment."

"Perhaps you can call her, then. She can't avoid talking to us, and she'd probably be more comfortable answering questions here than at the police station."

"With all due respect," Nori says, struggling to maintain a calm veneer, "she can't. She's . . . indisposed."

"Is she 'indisposed' or 'not here'?" Anzai snaps. "I find it hard to believe she's both."

"She *is* both," Nori retorts, irritated that the inspector is trying to catch her in a lie she hadn't told. "She's in the hospital, if you must know. And she can't be disturbed."

Stop reacting, scolds the 'Baa-chan in her head. *Take the offensive.*

Nori turns to the ceramics expert. "Not to be rude or anything, Hashimoto-san, but if Hikitoru has been missing since 1945, why isn't that public knowledge? There's nothing online about it being stolen."

"It was on the list of objects dug from the temple's wreckage following the attack," the art expert replies. "But a month later, when the head priest returned to the treasure house to look for an incense burner, it was gone."

"How do you know?"

Hashimoto pushes the copy she'd received from Anzai across the table. The old-fashioned characters across the top spell out "Tokyo Metropolitan Police," and the blanks are filled with spidery, hand-brushed *kanji*. It's a police report.

Nori snatches it up and reads. The facts penned in its official boxes paint a dismal picture of the chaos that reigned in Tokyo near the end of the war. The address from which the tea bowl had been stolen is listed only as the block where the temple stood, because it, and the surrounding neighborhood, had been reduced to charred rubble. The period in which it had disappeared was a lengthy twenty-one days. It had vanished sometime between March twelfth, when it was dug from the rubble, and April fifth, when the head priest discovered it gone.

"You'll notice that Hikitoru wasn't the only thing missing." Anzai draws Nori's attention to the "Description" section.

War fan; 35.5 cm X 55.5 cm; iron and paper folding fan, black with gold Oda clan crest; wooden storage box is water stained, dated Tenshō 1 (1573)

Noh dance fan; 33 cm X 55 cm; *make-shura-ōgi* style, setting sun and wave pattern on gold; wooden storage box is signed by maker "Jumatsu-ya"

Tea bowl; 23 cm X 23 cm X 18 cm; black Raku-ware, square

sides, split foot, white plum blossom motif on one side; wooden box dated Tenmei 14 (1794)

Incense burner with cover; 7 cm X 7 cm X 8.3 cm; round Hirado style with three small feet and handle in the shape of a horse, white porcelain with blue decoration of maple leaves

Tea bowl, named Hikitoru; 25 cm X 20 cm X 15 cm, Shigaraki-ware, rounded sides, red-ochre clay with gray-green glaze. Box is stamped "Yoshi Takamatsu"

Sake flask, named Hatsu-kamo; 10 cm X 10 cm X 25 cm, Bizen-ware, "wild duck" slumped gourd shape, brown and black clay with golden spatter design. Box is stamped Terami Enkichi, dated Hoei 3 (1706)

Nori rereads the last entry and swallows, her throat suddenly dry. She's never set eyes on the first four items, but that Bizen-ware sake flask—or its identical twin—had been sold to cover the cost of repairing earthquake damage to the Okuda & Sons building in May of 2011.

Anzai takes back the form.

"I regret to inform you that the rightful owner of the tea bowl Hikitoru appears to be Senkō-ji temple, and it's my duty to see that it's returned to them."

"No. You can't. This is all a big mistake. My grandmother would never—" What *would* 'Baa-chan do now? "How do you know this tea bowl is the same Hikitoru? Maybe there's more than one. Or maybe this is a copy. Or the stolen one is a copy. You can't take this one until you prove it."

Suddenly uncomfortable, the art expert glances at the inspector before saying, "Naturally, the tea bowl will have to be authenticated before it's returned. But," she's quick to add, "that shouldn't take long. Swann-san is an expert in Edo Period ceramics, and her preliminary assessment strongly suggests this is indeed the missing tea bowl, Hikitoru."

"Fine," Anzai says, snapping his briefcase shut. "I'll give you a week. But until ownership is confirmed, the tea bowl will be stored in the police evidence locker. You may conduct your examination there."

"No," Nori cries. "You can't."

Hashimoto unexpectedly agrees.

"With respect, Anzai-san, storing it in your evidence room is out of the question. I don't think you realize the value—and fragility—of this object. It would be more prudent to store it in the safe at our office."

Anzai is shaking his head.

"If you're concerned about security, don't be," she argues. "At any given time, we have art treasures worth over a hundred million yen in our care, and we'd be out of business if we didn't protect them from both thieves and damage. Does your storage facility have padded floors, in case it's dropped? Is it environmentally controlled, to minimize atmospheric degradation?"

Anzai considers her questions, has no answers.

"If we did agree," he says, "would it be guarded around the clock?"

"Yes, and not by human beings alone. After the Acheson heist five years ago," Hashimoto says, referring to an inside job that netted the thieves over a hundred million in antique jewelry, "we decided to shift our trust to technology instead of personnel. Guards can be bribed; CCTV cameras, electronic tags, and a state-of-the-art safe can't. Our new system is probably more secure than what you've got at police headquarters."

When the inspector doesn't contradict her, she adds, "Our security chief can outfit both the bowl and the box with tracking devices that will set off our security gates if they're taken off the premises, and I'd be happy to invite you back to the office with me to supervise."

Anzai relents. "All right. But I'll have to discuss this with my superior before any decisions can be made. Excuse me while I make that call."

29.

Feudal Japan

A P R I L , 1 7 4 3

Kyoto

"I'm working," Saburo growls at the graying disciple who inexplicably remains with him, after so many years. Lord Inaba's court poet scowls at the characters he has just brushed across the page. Still not right. The sheet crumples in his fist, ink still wet.

"Tell him to go away."

"I did," his number one follower says, in a tone that tells Saburo he's not going to give in so easily this time. "But his servant is waiting for a reply, and he sent *this*."

Coins clink softly inside the doeskin bag he lowers onto the poet's writing desk.

"And this."

He hands the poet a letter, sealed with the family crest of Lord Inaba's chamberlain.

"I really think you ought to reconsider," insists the disciple, a little less deferentially. "These pleasant rooms are ours at his behest, after all."

Saburo picks off the seal and scans the contents, casts it aside.

"Does the son have any talent?"

"I think he might," says the disciple diplomatically. "Given time. And a little teaching."

Which his loyal follower would provide, since Saburo takes little notice of the would-be students who continue to pound at his door despite his refusal to take them on. In fact, the more he refuses, the louder they pound.

All he cares about is finishing his masterwork, and it's not going well. Which makes no sense—in the years since he became court poet, a day hasn't passed when he hasn't pondered the Eight Attachments.

In his first years as court poet, he'd enthusiastically turned his hand to the work demanded of him—"coaching" the *daimyō* in the niceties of composition, while actually ghostwriting poems he could pass off as his own when court society required. But when he sat down to his own work, he'd been utterly unable to compose the poignant—yet uplifting—verses that had originally garnered him so much acclaim.

Try as he might to marshal words into sentiments that were insightful and inspiring, they always veered off in dark directions. If he wet his brush to convey an undiscovered facet of self-confidence, or the joy that comes from hard work yielding mastery, he would rise from his desk hours later to find the paper filled with bitter musings on pride, rigid thinking, ambition.

It took him years to realize the true nature of the deal he had made with his demons, on that long-ago day when he'd tied Hikitoru into his traveling bundle, leaving behind the potter's deathbed wish. Yakibō's spirit now hovers at his elbow day and night, twisting his words. He fears that it will haunt him, not only until he dies, but into the next life and the next, that it will dog him throughout eternity until he finds some way to appease it.

The poet frowns at the pale leather bag still sitting on his desk. His disciple has disappeared, which means he has probably interpreted Saburo's silence as a tacit "yes." Another unknown face will join the small circle that surrounds him on the rare occasions when he agrees to hear them recite their meaningless efforts. He's far kinder to them than his own master had been, mostly because he spares them only

a sliver of his attention. The rest of his mind is occupied with whatever Attachment is sitting on his desk, as he examines each link of the
chain, trying to understand it well enough to break it.

30.

Present-Day Japan

FRIDAY, APRIL 4

Tokyo

Robin perches on the edge of a visitors' chair in the Senkō-ji temple administration offices, waiting for the clerk to fetch the archivist. She shifts uncomfortably. Japanese chairs are too low for her, and she feels slightly ridiculous in them, like a fifth grader assigned to a desk for six-year-olds.

After the awkward meeting at Nori Okuda's shop, Inspector Anzai had accompanied Hashimoto-san back to the Fujimori Fine Art offices to supervise the security tagging and sign the paperwork for storing Hikitoru in their safe, but Robin had been dispatched to Senkō-ji, to confirm that their records did, in fact, list Hikitoru among the temple's possessions prior to its theft in 1945.

It's a task she's more than happy to perform, because she can use her auction house credentials to start nailing down the tea bowl's ownership in an unbroken chain, tracing it back to the hands of the potter himself. Hikitoru's provenance will have to be airtight before she can use it to bolster her claim that Yakibō's tea bowls are tied to Saburo's *Eight Attachments*. Senkō-ji's records are the logical place to start.

But her knee is jiggling as she waits, because even though the tea bowl is now safe from disappearing into the clutches of a rival auction house, the window for proving her theory has narrowed dramatically. Inspector Anzai has allowed them a week to do the testing, with the understanding that Hikitoru will be handed back to Senkō-ji on the following Monday and its recovery announced to the media. The moment the existence of a previously unknown Yakibō tea bowl becomes public, a flock of ravenous scholars will converge on it like seagulls on a sandwich. Unless she can get an unbeatable head start and—

"Excuse me, are you the honorable Swann-san?"

A young shaven-headed priest is bowing to her and smiling with crooked teeth, holding her business card.

"Yes," she says, rising and bowing, trying not to tower over him too much. "The most-humble Robin Swann, of Fujimori Fine Art."

"Your servant, Haneda," he replies. "I understand you'd like to search for some information in our archives?"

"If it wouldn't be too much trouble."

"No trouble, no trouble at all," he says, sounding quite cheered to have a visitor interested in his dusty sphere of influence.

She follows him as he trots down a corridor, right, left, right again, to a small office deep in the building. A large metal desk that's home to a sleek laptop anchors the room, and the walls are lined floor to ceiling with bookshelves. But much to Robin's dismay, they're nearly bare. Only two shelves are filled with toppling ledgers.

The earliest year brushed on the spines is 1948. She stifles a groan. Why had she assumed the records survived the firebombing, when the temple hadn't?

The priest points her to his visitor chair, seating himself behind the desk and folding his hands across his belly.

"So, what brings a Japanese art authenticator here today?"

"Something I doubt you can help me with, since I see you lost all your records in the war."

"What do you mean?" He seems genuinely puzzled.

"I'm interested in an object that I believe the temple acquired in the Edo Period, but it looks like your records don't go back before 1948."

"1948? Oh," he says, following her gaze to the bookshelf. He laughs. "Those are just the ones I haven't gotten around to scanning yet. Our records go back to 1607, the year the temple was founded. When I took over from the old archivist four years ago, I pointed out that the basement where they'd been stored has done a great job of saving them from fire, but not from water. They were slowly being consumed by mold, and the oldest scrolls were already nearly illegible. I was given permission to scan them and construct a database while we renovate the storage area." He smiles at Robin's obvious relief. "So, what are we looking for?"

She opens her handbag and hands him the copy of the 1945 police report.

"I was hoping you could tell me something about the fifth item on this list."

His eyes dart over the document.

"What is this?"

"A police report, filed by the head priest of this temple in 1945."

He skips down to the descriptions.

"These things were all stolen from us?"

"That's what I'm here to confirm."

He studies the list.

"Which item are you're interested in, again?"

"The tea bowl named Hikitoru."

"Is there some reason you're asking about it now?" His interest sharpens. "Has it been recovered?"

Shit. "I'm not at liberty to discuss that, because it's . . . it's a police matter."

She should have asked about everything on the list. Now he knows this is about Hikitoru. What if he tells someone and word gets out?

In her most authoritative Art Expert voice, she says, "On behalf of Fujimori Fine Art and the Tokyo Metropolitan Police, I'm afraid I must ask you to keep this confidential for the time being. At least until a positive identification has been made."

He considers her request.

"Will our records help you do that?"

"I hope so."

"Well, then." He taps in a password. "What would you like to know?"

"I'd like to know when Senkō-ji acquired Hikitoru. And how. If possible, from whom."

"Of course."

He purses his lips thoughtfully, fingers flying over the keyboard.

"My guess would be that an object like that was a gift. Senkō-ji used to be home to the Kinkokoro Jizo, a wooden figure that was famous for healing." He scans the screen, types some more. "Sadly, it was destroyed in the firebombing during the war, but for four hundred years it was much visited, especially when there were outbreaks of infectious disease. Valuable objects like tea bowls were frequently given as offerings."

"If it was a gift, would your records show who the donor was?"

"Sometimes they do, sometimes they don't."

He scrolls, stops. His face lights up.

"Here it is. 'Hikitoru. Tea bowl.' Given to the temple in the year Tenmei 8."

He opens a utility to convert the ancient Japanese calendar system—which restarts at Year One every time a new reign begins—to modern reckoning.

"1788," he announces.

"Is there a record of the donor?" Robin asks, hardly daring to hope.

He clicks back to the database.

"Yes. A Lord Inaba."

Inaba? It's a name she knows well, but she associates it with the poet, not the potter. Saburo had served as court poet to a Lord Inaba from 1724 until his death in 1753. If Hikitoru was given to Senkō-ji in 1788 . . . no, it couldn't be the same one. Maybe this Lord Inaba was his son. Or his grandson. If it was even the same family—Tokyo is a long way from Kyoto.

"How famous was this Kinkokoro Jizo?" she asks. "Would

a *daimyō* from Kyoto come all the way to Tokyo to ask for its help?"

"I doubt it," says the archivist. "Kyoto's got plenty of healing Jizos of its own. But of course, the shōgun insisted that his warlords spend every other year living in the capital, so they wouldn't have the time or the money to stir up rebellion in the provinces. At any one time, half the *daimyōs* from as far away as Kyūshū were—"

"Excuse me, but why wasn't I informed that we had a visitor here without an appointment?"

The archivist jumps, his eyes saucering. Robin twists in her chair to find a man wearing the gold-embroidered vestments of a head priest glowering at them from the doorway. He's older and rounder than the archivist, but there's definitely a family resemblance.

"I . . . forgive me," stammers the junior priest, on his feet, bowing. "You were in the middle of the Yanos' funeral service, and I thought—" He gestures toward Robin. "This is Swann-san, from the Fujimori Fine Art auction house."

The man in the doorway gives her a curt bow before laying into Brother Haneda.

"Who gave you permission to bring this foreign female into our innermost archives, asking questions I haven't approved?"

Robin winces. It obviously hasn't occurred to him that she might speak Japanese.

"Somebody found a tea bowl that was stolen from us during the war," babbles the archivist. "And Swann-san was asking—"

"Tea bowl? What tea bowl?" the head priest demands.

Before Brother Haneda can dig himself any deeper, Robin steps forward, formally extending her business card with two hands and a stiff bow.

"It may be a piece named Hikitoru, Your Reverence."

Shock slaps across the head priest's face, hearing her address him in perfect Japanese. He gives her a tight-lipped smile that doesn't reach his eyes.

"Your Japanese is so good."

Robin has lived in Japan long enough to know what that means: *It can speak.*

Without anything in the way of an apology, the head priest swings his attention back to the archivist.

"This stolen tea bowl. Does it belong to Senkō-ji?"

"Yes, it was given to us in 1788," Haneda replies eagerly. "A gift from a Lord Inaba. And the fact that it's named means it must be a significant cultural property, don't you think? If it's been recovered, perhaps we could put it on display with the—"

"Is our property in this person's possession?" interrupts the head priest.

"I . . . don't know."

He turns to Robin for help.

"Someone brought it to the auction house where I work, for authentication," she says stiffly.

"Who?"

"I'm not at liberty to say."

"Was it the thief?"

"I can't say."

"When you discovered it was stolen, did you turn this person over to the police?"

Robin doesn't answer.

The head priest regards her with ill-disguised irritation.

"I can see that it would be more fruitful to speak with your superior." Turning to the archivist, he says, "Find out his name. I'll be contacting him without delay to discuss the return of our property."

31.

Feudal Japan

DECEMBER, 1753

Kyoto

借り逃げを
やっと止められる
ひきとるの

Kari nige wo
Yatto yamerareru
Hikitoru no.

Finally, I can stop
Running from my debt
The one named Hikitoru.

Saburo reads over the lines of his death poem. Sighs. It will have to do. He stamps it with his seal and sets it aside for his number one disciple to find when he's gone. Before laying down his brush for the last time, he pulls another piece of paper to him, and with a trembling hand, sets down his final wishes. There must be no mistake. He'll only be able to move on to the next life unencumbered if he pays his debt in this one.

Saburo has sinned more than he ought, had more success than he deserved, and his reputation is greater than he ever dreamed possible. But now it's time to follow the old Pottery Priest into the next life, hoping that if their paths cross again, he'll be forgiven for the wrongs he's done him in this one.

As the ink dries, his mind wanders back to the long-ago winter that changed his life. The fierceness of the kiln fire, sparks blasting through the tiny stoking windows as he and Hattsan fed the dragon within. A rabbit bounding ahead of him down a mountain path, as snow drifted down in feathery clumps. A sudden guffaw erupting from the man who'd never been able to see, but who saw farther than most.

He folds the note and wraps it around the scroll onto which he has copied the eight verses it has taken him nearly forty years to write. Not bothering to rinse his brush, he leaves it on the writing table and calls his servant to help him rise from his desk and ease him onto his bed.

He asks the man to put some more wood on the fire, thanks him, and closes his eyes. His work is nearly done. It won't be long now. Both he and the scroll resting between his dry old hands will soon be smoke, rising toward heaven.

He is ready.

32.

Present-Day Japan

FRIDAY, APRIL 4

Tokyo

Still fuming over her treatment at the temple, Robin stops herself before slamming the door to her apartment, easing it shut with a polite click instead. She doesn't want to give her neighbors any reason to label her a Bad Foreigner. It only takes one instance of making too much noise or failing to put out the recycling properly to undo years of tiptoeing around and washing every bottle and can before sorting them into the proper bags.

Instead, she'll channel her anger into squeezing every last drop of information from Hikitoru before handing it over to Senkō-ji's narrow-minded head priest. Eight years of living with the polite, subtle discrimination directed toward outsiders has taught her to recognize a bulletproof glass ceiling when she sees it. Once that old fossil gets his hands on Hikitoru, a foreign woman won't get near it, no matter how many degrees she has.

So. Ten days to nail down the provenance and connect Hikitoru to Saburo.

The authentication tests will only take two—a fact she declined to mention to both her boss and the police. She's ninety-nine percent sure that the numbers will prove it's the right age, with the right chemical signature, to have been made by Yoshi Takamatsu. The real challenge won't be connecting the tea bowl to the potter, but using the bowl to connect the potter to the poet.

She brews a pot of industrial-strength coffee and carries it to her low table, then plops onto her cushion. Highlighter in hand, she resumes harvesting citations from where she'd left off last night.

This piece had been published in a popular international poetry quarterly, not a scholarly journal, but the author is a respected professor at an elite university. A quick skim promised it will provide a quotable overview of the current thinking on Saburo's death poem, which also revolves around the word *hikitoru*, like the poet's eighth *Attachment*.

The famous poet's date of death is a matter of record, but there's little information about what actually killed him at the ripe old age of sixty-nine. One commonly held theory is that his disappointingly prosaic final poem and the crazy deathbed request he left behind point to dementia, but epidemiological studies also make a case that he could have succumbed to one of the periodic fever outbreaks, virulent enough to cause delirium.

Fortunately for poetry lovers, the note instructing Saburo's literary heirs to burn his last great work was tossed into the fire instead, and *The Eight Attachments* has become one of the world's most-studied pieces of Japanese literature. The eight elegant poems on the subjects of "pride," "arrogance," "perfectionism," "rigid thinking," "first love," "ambition," "revenge," and "taking back what's yours" have generated thousands of pages of analysis in the two and a half centuries since he'd written them. Even Saburo's bafflingly mundane death poem had been dusted off and imbued with deeper meaning.

At first reading, his final verse seems to suggest that the poet died in poverty, that he had frittered his fortune away on wine, women, or gambling, and was regretting his frivolity on his deathbed, but that interpretation was quickly dismissed by Saburo devotees as far too obvious, and not nearly dignified enough. For the next several hundred years, the finest literary minds set about divining deeper insights.

One school reads the character "debt" as "loan," and asserts that the aged poet was ready to stop running on borrowed time and be reborn.

Buddhist scholars, of course, subscribe to a more spiritual theory—that the poet was exhorting his followers to stop trying to escape their attachments and face them instead.

Others interpret the final line as "taking back what's mine," arguing that the poet intended to cap decades of not publishing a single verse with a final crowning achievement. That he knew the eight poems he'd left behind would be his legacy-assuring masterpiece, and the falsely humble gesture of asking they be destroyed was a brilliant ploy to make them the most talked-about piece of literature since *The Tale of Genji* was passed around, one tantalizing chapter at a time, behind closed doors.

But Robin doesn't subscribe to any of these theories. Not anymore. The existence of a second Yakibō tea bowl with the same name as one of the eight attachments suggests another meaning altogether. The word *hikitoru* doesn't mean taking back, seeking enlightenment, or hoping for posthumous glory. *Hikitoru* is the name of the tea bowl sitting in Fujimori Fine Art's safe.

The poet owed someone a great debt, and that tea bowl is the key.

33.

Present-Day Japan

FRIDAY, APRIL 4

Tokyo

Nori charges through the hospital's automatic doors and stalks down the hallway. Standing before the elevator, she punches the button repeatedly until it arrives. How could those double-dealing, so-called experts from the auction house do this to her? How could 'Baa-chan do this to her? Where did she get that miserable tea bowl, anyway? Did she know it was stolen?

The head nurse looks up from her charting. Hustling out from behind the desk, she meets Nori halfway down the hall, diverting her into an unoccupied room.

Fear eclipses Nori's fury.

"What happened? Is it my grandmother? Is she . . . did she . . . ?"

"No," says the nurse. "Sorry, I didn't mean to scare you. There's been no change in her condition. But . . ."

"But what?"

The nurse lowers her voice, even though there's no one else in the room.

"She's ah, had a visitor. Two visitors, actually."

She pulls a pair of cards from her pocket, both embossed with the five-pointed star of the Tokyo Metropolitan Police. One of them belongs to an assistant inspector whose name Nori doesn't recognize, but the other is Anzai's.

"Do you have any idea why the police were inquiring about your grandmother's health?"

"Did you tell them she's unconscious?"

"Yes, but they wanted to see her anyway," the nurse replies, uncomfortable. "I told them she was unresponsive, that she needed peace and quiet. But they insisted."

"Insisted on what?"

"Asking her questions."

"What kind of questions?"

"About a tea bowl."

"A tea bowl?"

"Yes," the nurse says, shaking her head. "Some stolen tea bowl. I can't believe they barged in here, demanding to question one of my gravely ill patients about a crime that happened over seventy years ago."

"Did my grandmother answer?"

"Of course not. But I was worried that if she could hear them, she'd be distressed, so I asked them to leave." She lifts her chin defiantly. "I told them I'd call them if she woke up, then shooed them out the door."

Nori thanks the nurse profusely, bowing herself out. Back in the hall, she aims for her grandmother's room. Now it's her turn to ask the distressing questions.

She slips through the door slotted with Chiyo Okuda's name and slides it closed behind her. Contemplates the grandmother lying in the bed across the room.

The grandmother who's more conscious than she lets on. The grandmother who always knows more than she tells.

34.

MARCH, 1945

Tokyo

I t's been the coldest March in living memory, and still too soon to know if the cherry trees left standing will ever bloom again.

Chiyo Okuda picks her way through a landscape that has become as alien as the moon. The world she knew has been reduced to mounds of blackened spars and crushed tile; even the parts that didn't burn are twisted and charred. Will she even recognize the remains of Okuda & Sons when she finds it?

The shells of a few brick buildings and the gravestones around the temple are all that still stand amid the ashes of the kitchenware district. New landmarks, in a city of the dead. One week ago, fire rained down from enemy bombers flying so low that she'd seen the flames reflected in their vast, shiny underbellies as they delivered the war to her backyard.

She can make out the rough outline of streets beneath the still-smoking debris, but it's hard to get her bearings, because she has to look and *not* look at the same time. Rescue brigades have begun to remove the coal-black figures that used to be human, but so far, they've only gotten around to collecting those caught fleeing when the bombs fell. It's still far too possible to stumble across remains of your neighbors or their pets if you venture too far into the ruins.

Which is why Chiyo is nervously picking her way down the middle of what used to be a street, keeping her chin high, focusing on the angular remains of buildings, nothing smaller. She's beginning to despair of ever finding her way when her eyes fall on a familiar shape. The monument is blackened and leaning crookedly, but still standing, at what used to be a shrine sacred to *rakugo* storytellers. It marks the place where fifty-three traditional tales deemed too irreverent to perform during wartime had been buried. Standing with her back to the stone, she scans the surrounding area. The bigger ruins off to the left must be what's left of Senkō-ji, the Buddhist temple.

No wonder she hadn't recognized it. The imposing wooden sanctuary is gone, reduced to a mountain of charred timber. Only the plaster-walled treasure house still stands. Figures are moving in and out of the roofless shell, so she heads that way. The priests look like refugees too, in their grimy, burn-spotted clothing, handkerchiefs tied around their noses and mouths to filter the stench beginning to rise from the surrounding rubble.

She pulls up her own kerchief and offers to help dig out the valuables buried when the temple's roof collapsed. They're being moved to the treasure house as they surface, making them marginally safer from looters, if not the weather.

She isn't just being neighborly. Priests are the first to hear who needs a funeral and she might learn who else from the neighborhood has survived. Every soul from Kappabashi will have to pass through Senkō-ji on its way to the afterlife, and she's told that requests for services are already flooding in. In the days to come, the priests will be chanting sutras day and night.

At noon, she excuses herself and thanks the young priest who refills her water jar from the temple's rain barrel. Making sure the lid is tight, she stows it in her carrying cloth, along with the borrowed spade and the plain rice ball she brought for lunch. Water is a welcome bonus for her few hours' work at the temple—it's become more precious than gold in the wake of the attack. Percussion bombs were dropped just before the wave of incendiaries, shattering the water pipes and blocking streets with toppled buildings, so the fire brigades were unable to fight the flames when the bombs fell. In one night, a quarter of Tokyo had been blasted back to the age when water vendors hauled buckets through the streets.

She reties her kerchief and turns her back on the treasure house. Shading her eyes, she gazes toward distant buildings never visible from the temple before. Tiny figures move on the banks of the river that traverses the burnt-out landscape, its water so befouled by the countless bodies still being pulled from its icy grip that it's dangerous to drink from. Of course, the desperate still do. Before she returns to the refugee barracks tonight, she will detour to its banks, asking again for news of her grandfather and brother.

She knows that the bridge their volunteer fire detail was assigned to protect had been consumed in a roar of flames, as bombers targeted points clogged by panicked citizens trying to escape the inferno closing in from all sides. She'd spent the first week after the disaster frantically roaming the riverbank, asking anyone and everyone if they had seen her brother and grandfather. She hadn't given up, even after discovering that nearly all of those who hadn't burned to death had drowned. At first, as she watched bodies being hauled from the water with long poles and stacked like cordwood on its banks, she stubbornly clung to the hope that her family would be among the lucky ones whose members had merely gotten separated in the chaos. But as week one turned into week two, and sad shakes of the head were the only answer she got to her questions, she began to accept they were never coming home. Unlike her mother, she's given up hope of finding them alive. Now all she wants is something—anything—to chant the sutras over, because that would at least spare her mother from being haunted by their untethered spirits.

But today's main mission is to find what's left of their shop. Setting off in the general direction of where it once stood, she spots a few scattered residents in the distance, sifting through the ashes. Thin sounds of weeping suggest that what they're uncovering is worse than they expected, but she's holding onto the hope she'll find something worth salvaging. Unlike chopsticks and lacquerware, pottery doesn't burn. If their building didn't take a direct hit, there might be enough dishes left unbroken amid the ashes to start anew.

She thinks she's prepared herself for the worst, but it's still shocking to discover the heavily charred signboard that has been reduced to the "O" of Okuda & Sons. It sits atop a heap of cracked tiles and burnt wood—all that remains of where her family had lived and worked for generations.

She clenches her jaw. *Don't cry.* She knew the building would be gone. Everything in it would be gone. There would be nothing left of their house, their belongings, or the street where they lived.

But she's wrong. Nearly every shovelful holds a memory, and that's far worse. A short unburnt length of doorframe, pencil lines still marking how much she and her brother had grown each year. A broken triangle of the rice bowl she'd eaten from since she was a baby. Pretend they're not ours, she tells herself fiercely. Pretend they belong to someone else. But by the time she drags a charred futon off to the side and spies a smiling red fish gleaming at her from the rubble beneath, her throat is so tight that all she can do is hastily scuff ash back over it and walk away. Eyes stinging, shovel in hand, she stalks to a spot closer to the street. Dig, toss, dig, toss.

But the more she ignores what's back there, the more she can't ignore it. She throws down the spade and returns to the ashy grave of the cheerful Ebisu god whose porcelain belly she had rubbed on her way to school every morning. All that survives is one arm wrapped around the red fish of good fortune.

Even the god of luck has run out of luck. A sob escapes as she drops to her knees, hunching over what's left of the once-cheerful figure, bitterly homesick for the everyday life she hadn't appreciated until it was gone. She weeps, envying the Chiyo who thought squid for dinner was the worst thing that could happen to her. The Chiyo whose greatest chore was scrubbing the front steps. Now she'd give anything to have those front steps back, to look out the kitchen window on the life that had disappeared and would never be the same again.

The sun continues across the sky, and presently her tears dry and her breathing calms. She's lost more in the past week than in all of her thirteen years, but each shock is armoring her a little more against the next one. Her bouts of grief are becoming shorter, even as her mother's are getting longer.

She dusts the ash from her hands. Rises wearily to her feet. If they're going to have any future at all, someone will have to make it happen. Her brother and grandfather are missing, and her mother is drowning in a sea of grief, so she's the only Okuda left standing. With a final sniff, she wipes her face on her kimono sleeve, wraps what's left of the God of Prosperity in her last unburnt handkerchief, and buries it in the blackened wasteland that used to be their garden.

Then she gets back to work. By late afternoon, her arms ache and there are blisters across both palms. She stops to take stock of her progress. She has cleared enough rubble to reach the layer of broken pottery, but so far, unbroken dishes have been few and far between.

The shadows are lengthening and the temperature dropping. If she wants to make it to the river before the rescue workers go home, she'll have to get there before sunset. Piling her meager finds onto her spare carrying cloth, she knots it around them. She'll clean these up and sell them at the unofficial market near Ueno Station. That might keep them in rice long enough for her to dig up the rest.

She knocks the ash from the spade and shoulders it, then wearily sets out toward the river to ask after her grandfather and brother. Tomorrow she'll return, and dig some more.

35.

S tanding at her grandmother's bedside, Nori aims her words at the too-serene face.

"The police were here, 'Baa-chan. Of course, you already know that."

The monitors beep. Her grandmother doesn't stir.

"Did you know Hikitoru was stolen, back in 1945? I saw a copy of the police report. After Senkō-ji burned in the firebombing, it was stolen from their treasure house."

No response.

"How did it end up hidden under our *tokonoma*, 'Baa-chan?"

Nori studies her face, but isn't rewarded by so much as a twitch. Frustrated, she turns to the window and parts the curtains. It makes no sense. Where had someone in her family gotten a fancy tea bowl? Their shop doesn't sell tea bowls. They've never sold tea bowls. None of their customers are the kind of people who fuss around with tea ceremonies. What would possess someone in the Okuda family to buy something like that, when they didn't have two yen to rub together?

Unless . . . they hadn't bought it.

That lone remaining bundle under the *tokonoma*. The stack of workman's clothing that's not the least bit valuable. Dark clothing, made for a man. There's more than one reason for hiding something.

Who had the clothes belonged to? 'Baa-chan's grandfather had died in the same firebombing that destroyed Senkō-ji, and her father never came home from the war. That left—

She whirls to face her grandmother.

"You had an older brother, didn't you, 'Baa-chan?"

She leans over the bed, watching her grandmother's face.

"You never told me much about him, just that he was too old to be sent to the countryside with the schoolchildren, but too young to be drafted, so I know he didn't die in the war. He was still alive in 1945, wasn't he?"

No response. But Nori doesn't need one. If 'Baa-chan's older brother had become a shameful blot on the family register, that explains why she always changes the subject when Nori asks about him.

Times were hard—she'd heard plenty about *that*—and the Okudas had lost everything but the clothes on their backs in the firebombing. Her grandmother had only been thirteen when the war ended, but to hear 'Baa-chan tell it, she'd saved the family all by herself. She'd been the one who scrabbled and scraped and worked like a demon to pull together the means to start over.

But if that were true, she must have been an unbelievably industrious teenager or incredibly lucky, because a year after the bombing raid that flattened everything in northeast Tokyo, the Okuda store had been up and running again. It was one of the first shops on the block to reopen.

How was that possible? Where did they get the money? What had her elder brother been doing while 'Baa-chan was out dumpster diving for the limp vegetables she'd famously turned into pickles to keep them alive?

Nori can't believe that the other Okudas had been lazing around on their futons, letting the youngest kid to do all the work. She'd bet her last yen that 'Baa-chan's older brother had been busy providing for the family too, in ways her grandmother wasn't at all eager for her to know about.

36.

Wartime Japan

MARCH, 1945

Tokyo

It's been raining off and on for two days since Chiyo discovered that her brother had survived—in a manner of speaking—and her grandfather hadn't.

Now she and her mother stand in line, alongside the tent erected as a makeshift temple near the pile of charred beams that used to be Senkō-ji. They've been waiting since early morning, taking turns standing in the circle of shade cast by the waxed paper parasol they share, now so accustomed to the mingled scents of burnt wood and incense that they don't notice them anymore. As the daylight fades, Chiyo unwinds her shawl, draping it over the one her mother already clutches around her shoulders.

She stretches her aching back. How much longer? The droning sutras being chanted for the dead rise and fall, simultaneous funeral services sending discordant notes through the thin canvas walls. The next mourners in line shuffle inside as those from a just-finished rite stagger out. Some clutch makeshift urns filled with ashes, some carry even smaller mementos of the deceased. But most are empty-handed, their loved ones entombed in mass graves, along with tens of thousands of other victims whose earthly remains were too mingled by the bombing to separate.

Chiyo holds a tobacco tin. She loops its carrying cloth over her wrist and turns to her mother to adjust her *obi* cord, which has slipped as the hours lengthened. Her mother wears the borrowed black kimono being passed around among the mourners in the refugee barracks. Little decent clothing had escaped the bombing. Most women had fled in cheap cotton *monpe*, the farmers' pants that are warmer and more practical than kimonos for a hardscrabble, wartime existence. The rest wore everyday cotton kimonos altered in the same way as Chiyo's— split and resewn into a sort of jumpsuit. Hers had sported a purple and white arrow pattern until she'd taken it to be dyed yesterday. Now it's a deep, solid indigo, more fitting for a funeral.

"O-kaa-san, move up," she whispers to her mother, gently prodding her as the line advances a notch. Her mother's body complies, but her mind is elsewhere. She has barely spoken a word since Chiyo came home with the news that she'd seen Grandfather Okuda's smashed and melted hardhat being pulled from the wreckage of the Kototoi Bridge. A compassionate relief worker had given her the tobacco tin filled with ashes that she now holds, but Chiyo had seen the aftermath of the bridge bombing and doesn't really believe that what's in the tin had once been part of her grandfather.

That's not what she told her mother, though. She needs O-kaa-san to believe that the ashes the priests will soon chant sutras over are his. Her grandfather's ghost must be sent on its way, so it will stop tormenting them.

Even as a child, Chiyo had scoffed at ghosts, but in the aftermath of the bombing, she's heard so many tales of survivors being visited by loved ones wrenched from this life before their time, she's developed a grudging respect for the power the dead can wield over the living. Grandparents have been seen moving among the wreckage of the houses where they'd died, searching for doors that no longer exist. Babies cry in the night. And her grandfather has been haunting her mother. Every night since the attack, O-kaa-san has jolted awake, her face a mask of horror, wailing that her father's specter is standing at the end of her futon in his volunteer fireman's coat, asking when they're going home.

But everyone knows that the dead linger only because survivors refuse to let go. The haunting will stop once her mother gives Grandfather Okuda's spirit permission to journey on to the next life.

They inch up two more notches. Only one group ahead of them now. Maybe they'll make it to the temporary hospital where her brother is being cared for before sundown.

"If you'll come this way, please . . ."

The priest at the door invites them into the tent, escorting Chiyo and her mother to another priest kneeling behind a makeshift table built of blasted bricks and a board. The seated priest's glasses are mended with tape, and she remembers him from her stint digging out the temple's treasures. He doesn't seem to recognize her, though, so she says nothing as he offers his condolences, then gestures for them to sit. He asks their names, and the name of the deceased.

"With regard to the *kaimyō*," he says, tactfully addressing the question about her grandfather's after-death name to Chiyo when he sees her mother is too shell-shocked to answer. "Will your honorable grandfather be satisfied with a four-character name for use in the eternal everlasting, or do you wish to honor him with more?"

Chiyo doesn't know what to say. Everyone receives a new name when they die, but she has no idea how they get it. She pictures the columns of *kanji* characters inscribed on the black and gold funerary tablets they'd snatched from their home altar the night of the bombing. She's pretty sure the names on them are longer than four characters.

"We'd like to honor my grandfather as much as possible, of course," she says.

The priest bestows an approving smile.

"Very well. The eight-character after-death name will be two hundred yen, in addition to the funeral."

"Two hundred yen?" she gasps.

That's outrageous! Two hundred yen would feed them for months.

Noting her distress, the priest quickly adds, "Of course, a six-character name is still quite honorable. A hundred and fifty yen. Plus the cost of the funeral."

"How . . . how much is the funeral?"

"Three hundred yen." Then he adds, somewhat reluctantly, "That of course includes a four-character posthumous name for inscription on the *ihai* tablets."

Three hundred yen. That's a big chunk of the money they have left. She turns helplessly to her mother, whose unseeing gaze is fixed on her hands, folded passively in her lap. Did she even hear what the priest said?

They can't afford to part with three hundred yen, but what choice do they have? She turns back to the priest, desperate.

"I . . . we lost everything in the bombing. Our family owns Okuda & Sons. You know, the pottery shop? Right around the corner? We . . . we can't afford three hundred yen. We barely escaped with our lives. Is there any way . . ." she swallows, "any way that you could do it for less?"

Shuffling back from the table on her knees, she bows so deeply that her forehead bumps the tent floor.

The priest radiates profound discomfort.

"Just a moment, please."

He disappears, returning a few minutes later with a middle-aged man dressed in lavish green brocade robes. The intricately patterned silk, shot through with gold, strikes Chiyo as incongruously opulent in the grimy tent.

"Okuda-san," says the head priest in a smooth voice, his deferential bow including both Chiyo and her mother. "We're very sorry for your loss. These are terrible times. For all of us."

He pauses, drawing attention to the suffering all around.

"It's a terrible thing that you have lost your beloved grandfather and father," he nods to Chiyo and her mother, "but most regrettably, we are all in the same boat, and priests must eat too. Three hundred yen is already a special compassionate rate, because we want to be sure that everyone can afford to shepherd their loved ones safely to the other side. But I fear we can't reduce it any further, if we wish to rebuild the temple and serve the community. Because you're our dear neighbors, however, you can pay us half now, and bring the rest when you're able."

He bows, preventing further negotiation.

Chiyo's face burns. He didn't offer them even the slightest break. She lowered herself for nothing. She manages to produce appropriate words of gratitude, but her thoughts are murderous. He should be ashamed! Profiting from the misery of the very people he's supposed to be helping. The temple's treasure house is stuffed with valuables— she'd seen with her own eyes how much had survived the bombing. Why doesn't he sell some of those, instead of squeezing people who have nothing left?

But it would be a bad idea to alienate the priest she's counting on to send her grandfather's spirit on its way, so she holds her tongue. With a face like stone, she opens her purse and counts out a hundred and fifty precious yen.

She'll have to join those who scavenge through the refuse of the marketplace for discarded food, but she can't afford to let her grandfather's ghost haunt them any longer. Her mother has to be jolted out of her twilight existence and dragged back to the land of the living. Her brother is worse than dead, and Chiyo can't rebuild their lives alone.

37.

Present-Day Japan

SATURDAY, APRIL 5

Tokyo

Nori stands before the Okuda family grave, feeling slightly guilty. She ought to have brought flowers and lit some incense, even though she's merely stopping by to check the year 'Baa-chan's brother died.

The tomb in which generations of Okuda ashes are laid to rest stands among other graves that date to the early 1800s, its once-shiny granite obelisk weathered to a dull gray. The small altar at the foot hasn't been swept since last summer, and still holds curls of ash from the incense they'd lit during their annual O-bon visit. The Okuda burial place resembles every plot in the sprawling ghost metropolis that surrounds Senkō-ji temple, except that a newer slab had been erected to one side, when it became fashionable to commemorate individuals whose ashes are interred there. Above the most freshly carved name (her father's) are five more. Her grandfather (who had taken the name Okuda when he married 'Baa-chan), her grandmother (whose name, Chiyo Okuda, is already carved into the stone, but filled in with red paint that will be removed when she dies), 'Baa-chan's grandfather Okuda and his wife, and the name Nori came to see, her grandmother's elder brother.

He'd died in 1946, sixteen years after his birth. Which meant he'd survived the 1945 firebombing that had sent so many to the surrounding graves, but something else had felled him within a year.

Accident? Sickness? Hunger? Or had 'Baa-chan's brother made the mistake of stealing something worth killing for?

38.

Wartime Japan

APRIL, 1945

Tokyo

The astrological forecast for the last day of March is *butsumet-su*—a bad day to embark on new ventures—which is why Chiyo is crouching amid the ruins of Okuda & Sons, waiting for midnight. At twelve o'clock, the astrological calendar will tick over to *taian*, and she's counting on twenty-four hours of uninterrupted good luck to deliver a turning point in her family's fortunes.

She'd learned that lesson the hard way. On her first attempt to sell her scavenged pottery, she'd walked all the way to Ueno Station and sat by the roadside from dawn to dusk, but by the end of the day, her load wasn't lighter by a single teacup. Everybody and his brother were trying to turn their battered belongings into something that would fill their aching bellies. The motley collection of Okuda & Sons dishes she'd spread on her carrying cloth hadn't attracted a single glance from shoppers hurrying by. She'd trudged back to the refugee camp, where the woman living next door had laughed and said, what did you expect? Today is *butsumetsu*. If you learn nothing else from this crazy war, it should teach you to respect how much depends on luck.

After that, she knew not to attempt anything important before consulting the stars. She became better at turning a profit too. Dealers who displayed a wide selection of wares attracted more customers and better prices, so she became a steady supplier to one of the more successful stalls. Soon she was selling enough to stop dipping into their savings and start adding to it.

Until her brother was released from the hospital.

Out of danger, they'd been told, even though his burns were so severe he might never walk or talk again. His bellows of pain and despair echoed through the barracks day and night. Between the additional mouth to feed and his never-ending need for ointments and bandages, it quickly become clear that even if she sold every piece of unbroken pottery buried in the shop ruins, they'd never have enough money to rebuild.

Which is why she's squatting by the skeletonized bushes behind the wreckage of Okuda & Sons tonight. She chose the lucky day nearest the full moon so she can make it across the broken landscape without mishap. But the bright moonlight will also make it easier for the priest guarding the temple's treasure house to spot her, so she's dressed head to toe in deepest indigo, her grandfather's work clothes freshly dyed to blend with the shadows. She scoops up a handful of ash and washes her hands with it to blacken her pale skin, then rubs soot all around her eyes, until only the whites gleam in the darkness. Then she unrolls the long indigo strip she'd sewed together from scavenged rags. She winds it around her head and face, leaving a narrow slit so she can see. Knotting it under her chin, she tucks in the ends and shakes her head to make sure it's secure, then stuffs her carrying cloth inside her jacket.

Clack-clack. The neighborhood watchman's sticks send the reassuring message that all is well, even though nothing is. There's little left to steal in the burnt-out kitchenware district, but patrols had resumed within days of the bombing to provide routine and a sense of purpose to those suddenly finding themselves with none.

Chiyo hides behind the mound of debris until he passes, then listens until diminishing claps tell her he's far enough away that she can pick her way toward Senkō-ji, unseen.

Two blocks of houses and shops used to stand between, but they've been reduced to a low obstacle course. Crouching, she darts in short bursts toward the burned-out temple until the broken wall that encircles the cemetery looms before her. Squeezing through a gap in the masonry, she slinks down an avenue of blasted gravestones toward the place where the temple's valuables are kept.

The reinforced storehouse had faithfully protected the temple's wealth against fire for hundreds of years, but it was no match for bombs dropped from the sky. The walls and iron door were stout enough to remain standing, but the roof is gone. She has investigated it thoroughly in the past few days, and decided to clamber up and over via the rain barrel from which the priest had refilled her water jar. Once she's inside, she'll have her pick of the treasures she helped stack there.

The only real barrier is the guard. She peers out from behind a tomb, searching the darkness. There he is, a slumped figure, sitting beside the padlocked door. For ten long minutes she watches, but he doesn't move. Then his head droops and he emits a snore.

Thanking her lucky stars, she creeps around to the opposite side, gathers her strength. Up and over, with only one scrabbling scrape. She has to inch precariously along the top of the wall for a meter or so, until she's above the stepped cabinet she remembers from digging duty. Lowering herself onto its top, she spiders her way down, leaping softly to the packed earth floor. Listens. The wind bangs a loose shutter against the wall. The snoring stops. Her nerves stretch as taut as a kite string in a stiff breeze. If the guard begins wrestling with the rusty padlock on the door, she'll have to abandon her mission and flee.

She surveys the shelves, but there's no time to pick and choose. Trusting the gods to lead her to pieces of value, she piles six small boxes of different shapes onto her carrying cloth. Knots it around them.

She stands, shouldering her plunder. As soon as she's on the other side of the wall, she'll be a thief, a looter. If she gets caught, the wartime police will show no mercy.

Mouth set in a thin line, she begins to climb.

39.

SATURDAY, APRIL 5

Shigaraki

Tramping up the muddy track, Robin is glad she dug out her rubber boots before boarding the bullet train early this morning. Tokyo was cold and overcast, but rain had apparently come down with rural determination in the mountains near Shigaraki last night. Countless rivulets are now joining the twin streams carving the tire tracks leading to Hayashi Ceramics even deeper.

Robin had spent the past hour examining the writing box and poetry fragments at the town's small museum. When she asked if there were any other places nearby with Saburo or Yakibō artifacts worth seeing, the curator had smiled and told her that the Hayashi family actually had a little museum of their own now. Their eleven-year-old son had come to her office a few months ago, asking to take the poetry drafts back. He wanted to earn money for a Hanshin Tigers baseball jersey by setting up an exhibit. The curator had convinced him to leave the fragile paper scraps in the museum's archival storage, but she gave him color copies and offered to pay him ¥250 for every museum patron who asked to see the real ones. Robin had laughed and promised to give him the agreed-upon fee when she stopped by the kiln later.

The grass growing between the tire tracks is tall enough to wet the tops of her boots, and she's cheered that this road doesn't look much traveled by Saburo scholars. Up ahead, she glimpses an old-fashioned farmhouse between the trees. Like most in the area, its cedar siding is charred black against insects and oiled against the weather, with a band of white plasterwork winking at her from beneath gray-tiled eaves. Before the entrance lies a single, massive, stone step, split by a seam of vibrantly green moss. A wooden plaque next to the door announces "Hayashi Ceramics," and tacked below are two rain-rippled notes in plastic sleeves.

In an unnecessarily fancy font, the top one reads:

HAYASHI POTTERY, POETRY, & BASEBALL CARD MUSEUM
Please ring bell for tour

The other is handwritten. "For kiln business, please go around to office in back."

Robin rings the bell. As a tractor rumbles past on a nearby road, the heavy wooden door slides open a crack and a foxy puppy head pokes out at knee height, barking a welcome. Just as quickly, a hand grabs its collar and hauls it away, a woman's voice calling, "Just a minute."

An interior door slams, and a moment later, the owner of the voice appears, opening the door wide enough to give Robin a view of her harried face. It's haphazardly smeared with something greasy and white. The streaks match those covering the toddler she balances on one hip, who had apparently applied it with a liberal hand to her own face, clothes, and hair before sharing with her mother.

"Sorry, the last time the puppy got out—Oh!" Her face radiates dismay as she realizes her visitor is a stranger. And a foreigner. "I'm so sorry. You're not . . . I mean, I was expecting—"

"My name is Robin Swann," Robin says in her friendliest Japanese. "I was hoping to walk through your museum, but it looks like I caught you at a bad time. Should I come back later? I guess I should have called first."

"No, no, please come in," says the woman, obviously relieved that she won't have to dust off her middle-school English. She opens the door wider to invite Robin into the stone-paved entry. "I'm so sorry, I—" She winces as her daughter grabs her hair in one chubby cream-covered fist. "Never fall asleep when you think your toddler is napping."

Robin laughs in sympathy as the girl squirms, wanting to be let down.

"I'm sorry my English isn't as good as your Japanese," Mrs. Hayashi apologizes, shifting her daughter to the other hip. "Did you say you're interested in the museum? My son's out back helping my husband with next week's firing, but I can get him to show you around, if you like." Her brow furrows. "I'm afraid the signs are all in Japanese, though— will that be a problem?"

"No, that's fine." Robin had learned to read Japanese before she could speak it.

"Just a minute, Babylump," Mrs. Hayashi chides the toddler, now kicking her hip. "If you don't mind waiting here a moment, Miss Swann, I'll go find my son, Mamoru."

Robin has just finished idly translating a framed Ikkyu poem hanging crookedly above the shoe cupboard when the woman reappears with a boy in a Hanshin Tigers t-shirt. His hair sticks up in tufts, as if he'd been a moving target while it was being cut. Catching sight of their visitor, he darts his mother an uncertain glance.

"*Hajimemashite.*" Robin bestows the most respectful of greetings on him with a small bow. "My name is Robin Swann. I hear you're the local expert on pottery, poetry, and baseball cards."

"This is Mamoru," his mother says, propelling the boy forward and clearing her throat in a hinty sort of way.

Reminded, the boy bows.

"*Hajimemashite.*"

Pleasantries observed, his mother says, "Can you please take Miss Swann out to your museum now, and answer any questions she has?"

"*Hai.*"

He slides his feet into a pair of mud-flecked boots. Not bothering to zip them up before hunching into his parka, he clomps outside. Then he turns and fixes her with a solemn gaze, extending one skinny arm. "Right this way, please."

He leads her around the house and up a well-worn path into the woods. Shy at first, he warms up as she peppers him with questions. Yes, he'd been to a Tigers' game. Last year, for his birthday, when he turned eleven. The new puppy's name is Hanako. She's only six months old but he doesn't think she's as smart as their old dog. They can't let her out without a leash, or she might run onto the railroad tracks. His sister's name is Sakura, but everyone still calls her Babylump.

"Is that the museum, up ahead?" Robin asks, spotting a building through the trees.

"No, that's the New Kiln, where my dad works."

The long, low structure rambles down the side of the hill they're climbing, its thick walls punctuated by tiny blackened windows, through which the flames are fed day and night during a firing. All along the side, split logs are stacked waist-high under waterproof tarpaulins. The tang of wood smoke lingers in the air.

"Why is it called the New Kiln?" she asks. "It doesn't look that new to me."

"It's not, really. It was built by my great-great-great-great-great-great-great-grandfather Hattsan, the one who took over from Yakibō himself. We just call it that, because it's newer than the Old Kiln."

"This isn't the one Yakibō used? What happened to that one?"

"It's still here," says Mamoru, looking slightly uncomfortable. "It's just that, well, it's haunted."

"Haunted?"

"Yeah. That's why my dad let me make the museum in its storehouse. But don't worry," he adds quickly, "the ghost doesn't come out during the day."

"Have you ever seen it?"

"Well, no," he admits.

"So how do you know it's haunted?"

"Because that's the reason the New Kiln was built. My granddad told me that after Yakibō died, every pot they tried to fire in the old kiln exploded. For no reason. They asked the Shinto priest to come out and bless it, but it didn't help. Then they asked the Buddhist priest to come, and he couldn't help either. The *o-bōsan's* ancestor said that Yakibō's spirit was refusing to move on to the next life."

"Why?"

"Dunno. I guess you could ask him."

"Ask who?"

"The priest. He lives at the temple outside town. It was his ancestor who couldn't get rid of the ghost. O-bōsan knows a lot about the olden days."

"What's his name?"

The boy stops, forehead wrinkled in thought.

"Dunno. We always just call him O-bōsan. But you'll know him when you see him." He starts walking again. "He used to be a sumo wrestler before he was a priest."

Huh. Robin had never met anyone with a calling to be both. As they reach the top of the New Kiln, she spies another building through the trees.

"Is that it?"

"Yeah." The boy flicks it a nervous glance. "Um, could you wait here just a minute while I, uh, get things ready?"

He runs off before she can answer. She watches him stretch up toward the door lintel of the long shed behind the kiln, then jump a couple of times until his hand brushes something off the top ledge. It falls to the ground and he digs it from the bushes, then wipes it on his pants and jiggles it in the lock. When the boy doesn't reappear within a few minutes, she wonders if he's forgotten about her, so she walks to the open door and knocks on the frame.

He looks up guiltily, a grubby feather duster in his hand.

"Sorry, I'm supposed to clean the museum every week, but . . ."

"That's okay," she says. "I can see things just fine with a little dust on them. Why don't I tell you if I need to look at something special, and you can clean it off for me?"

A table with baskets of curling postcards and a cash box faces the entrance, flanked by board and brick shelves set up as a "gift shop." She politely glances at the modern Shigaraki-ware teacups and sake sets lined up like soldiers, then raises her eyes to what's beyond.

The room's shelves are laden with cracked and broken Shigaraki-ware of all shapes and sizes. Her breath catches. Is it possible that . . . ?

"Ahem," the boy hints. A sign taped to the front of the table reads, "Admission ¥500."

"Oh, sorry." She digs in her purse and hands over a big golden coin. It clinks into the box.

"Also," she digs deeper, "I stopped by the museum in Shigaraki to see the poems you donated, and the curator asked me to give you this." She hands him another ¥250.

The boy thanks her with a small, pleased smile and sorts the coins, diligently locking them in the box. Then he drags the table aside, unblocking the entrance.

"This way, please."

But the pottery on the shelves is a disappointment, once she gets close enough to read the inkjet-printed tags taped in front of each grouping. It had all been made by Mamoru's ancestors. Three broken water jars and a cracked grinding bowl are all that's left of Yakibō's original apprentice's work, but the collections increase in quality and quantity as she makes her way around the room, finishing with an array of impish raccoon-like *tanuki* figures, representing Mamoru's father's take on the legendary trickster.

After politely admiring the display, Robin says, "Thank you for showing me these fine pieces made by your ancestors, Mamoru-kun. But I'm curious—do you have anything made by old Yakibō himself?"

"Of course!" Mamoru replies, then admits, "At least, they might be. They're in the next room."

They? He has more than one? Could the rest of the tea bowls that inspired Saburo be here, in this amateur museum in the middle of nowhere? Undiscovered, unstudied . . . ?

She dashes to the door, then stops, confused. All that's displayed on the tables that line the walls in the next room are baseball cards. Lots and lots of baseball cards.

Except for one nearly bare card table, set by itself in a corner. Atop it sit some color copies in plastic sleeves and five small shards of pottery. She crosses to get a closer look.

The smallest fragment is no bigger than the coin she paid for admission, the largest nearly the size of her palm. Three of the pieces are crossed with swashes of gray-green melted ash on both sides, one is bare clay that shades from red to ochre and is studded with "dragonfly eyes." The last is iced with deep glassy green.

Even someone with no experience identifying Edo Period pottery could see that these are different from the pottery in the first room. Thinner, finer, the glaze applied with an abstract, almost modern, sensibility. But Robin is an expert, and she'd spent hours examining Hikitoru just yesterday. She'd bet her dusty bottle of Dom that these had been made by the same hand.

"Where did you get these?" she asks the boy.

"Found 'em."

"Where?"

"Out back. In the woods."

"Are there more?"

"Dunno. Might be."

"Can you show me?" She senses his hesitation. "I know they belong to you and your family. I promise not to take any or tell anyone where they are. I just want to see."

"Okay. This way."

Mamoru pulls up his hood as he heads out the door, with Robin close behind. Swishing through the wet bushes overhanging the path, the boy follows a faint trail that's little more than a *tanuki* track. He stops only once, before the shell of an ancient gingko tree girdled with a fresh straw rope and paper charms. Robin joins him to pay her respects, then Mamoru leads her a few steps further and stops.

"Here," he says. "This is where I found them."

Fat raindrops plop onto her head from the overhead branches

as she regards the small clearing. There's no excavation, no cave of wonders, just a carpet of moss, surrounded by cedars, with a table-sized hunk of the local granite peeking out from the bracken on the far side.

"Where, exactly?" she asks.

"Here." He waves his hand vaguely at the clearing.

"They were just lying on the ground?"

"Yeah. I mean, when I saw a corner sticking up I had to dig a little, but yeah."

Where there were five, there would be more. She advances slowly toward the big rock, eyes avidly scanning the velvety green, but spots nothing. Which, she tells herself, is a good thing. Until a proper excavation can be organized, it would be best if those precious fragments stayed buried, undiscovered, beneath centuries of pine needles and moss.

"Would you like to find out for sure if Yakibō made the pottery shards in your museum?" she asks the boy.

"Yeah! But . . ." he squints at her. "How are we going to do that? The lady at the museum told me you need special machines and stuff to test them."

"Well, guess what?" Robin says. "It so happens that I work in a place with those machines, and I know how to use them. If you let me borrow those pieces, I can return them to you with an answer by the end of the week."

Robin solemnly stamps her name seal on the "loan agreement" that Mamoru's mother helped her son compose on the family computer. Ceremonial signing completed, she wraps the Yakibō shards in a Hello Kitty handkerchief loaned by Mrs. Hayashi, and tucks the precious package into her purse, promising to send them back as soon as she's completed the tests.

Walking back to town, she barely notices her surroundings. How many broken tea bowls lie beneath that clearing in the woods behind the Hayashi kiln? And how did they get there? If the fragments in her purse really were made by Yakibō, the site behind the kiln would become a significant archaeological site. The clearing would be laid out with a string grid, serious-faced graduate students crouching with paintbrushes, logging each piece into a site map before transferring them to experts who would put the puzzles back together. Papers would be written, grants would flow in from—

BEEEEP! A turning bus startles her, and she jumps back onto the curb just in time. How could she already be back in town?

And what's that delicious smell? Suddenly ravenous, she backtracks to a noodle shop. Taking a seat at the counter, she inhales a bowl in less time than it took them to make it. Washing it down with near-scalding tea, she calls up the train schedule. Time to hightail it back to Tokyo and get to work.

Well, shit. She's just missed the poky local train, and there won't be another for an hour. How's she going to kill an hour in a small town in the middle of nowhere? The only thing they seem to sell in the nearby shops is those lucky *tanuki* figures, and her apartment is cluttered enough.

Maybe she should try to find the priest the boy mentioned. Ask him about Yakibō's ghost. Colorful tales sometimes hold a grain of historical truth, and maybe he'll tell her something that helps tie the potter to the poet.

Waiting for her change, she asks the gap-toothed proprietor how to find the local temple. The wizened auntie drags her to the door, wordlessly pointing. Across the bridge spanning the river is an imposing gate, marked with carved and gilded characters that read "Heizan-ji."

Built of cedar beams that interlock like a massive wooden puzzle, the portal is as tall as a two-story building. Generations of pilgrims have stickered the gate with samurai-era graffiti—small rectangular patches of *washi* paper, printed with quaintly old-fashioned names. Passing beneath, she cranes her neck toward the ceiling and wonders how three enterprising sojourners had managed to tag the underside of the roof.

The temple beyond isn't especially large, but looks prosperous and well kept. Its gold-leafed roof carvings gleam in the midday sun, the path is swept, the gravel freshly raked. Weeping cherry trees flank the entrance to the main sanctuary, with its red-lacquered beams and spreading, upturned eaves. Nearby, a stout tower with a tile roof supports an enormous bronze bell, with a suspended log striker. Racks ten-deep in prayer plaques surround a venerable ginkgo tree, greening with the spring, and family graves stretch out behind the main building, sheltered by old-growth cedars. The complex is bounded by an administration building—its wood pale and new, but built in the traditional style—and a gated garden with housing for resident priests. Midday on a Saturday, multiple plumes of smoke rise from the temple's great bronze incense urn, and there's a line at the offering box.

Robin joins it. When the requisite coin has been tossed, prayer offered, etiquette observed, she angles back toward the stand that sells everything from protective amulets to wooden prayer plaques.

"Excuse me," she says to the priest manning the counter. "The son of the potter at Hayashi Ceramics mentioned that one of the priests here might be able to tell me about the ghost that haunts their old kiln. I believe he used to be a sumo—"

"Are you looking for me?"

Robin turns. Beaming down at her is the only Japanese man she's ever had to look up to. The priest wears simple linen robes, but they must have been custom made, because even though he's no longer as mountainous as a ranking sumo wrestler, he's still boulderishly huge. Beneath his priestly shaven head, a smile broadens his high cheekbones and crinkles his eyes into half-moons. She finds herself smiling back.

He introduces himself as Uchida. She explains why she's here, and he invites her to accompany him to his office. They stroll toward the administration building, exchanging pleasantries—the fine weather, the beauty of rural Shiga—as he swings a knobby wooden cane, favoring a stiff left leg.

When he mentions the unusually large amount of snow still on the ground in the mountains, Robin replies that even Tokyo had suffered a multi-day, traffic-snarling snowstorm in January.

He gives her a wry smile.

"That's something I don't miss about city life. The snow covers up the dirt and ugliness for a while, but it shows through again all too soon."

"How long did you live in Tokyo?"

"Only long enough to get this." He flourishes his cane. "Thankfully, I blew out my knee within a year."

"'Thankfully'?"

"Keeps anyone from expecting me to kneel during long services," he confides. "I get to use a chair."

"You weren't sorry to turn your back on a sumo career?"

"Quite the opposite," he says with a short laugh, "since it wasn't me who wanted one. If I hadn't been twice the size of every kid in my class since kindergarten, I wouldn't have taken up wrestling at all. I'd have preferred sitting with my nose in a book, to tell you the truth."

She gives a snort of sympathy. "I know what you mean."

"Let me guess . . . basketball?"

"Yeah."

They share a moment of companionable bitterness, then he ushers her into an office noticeably warmer than the rest of the temple. A small space heater purrs in the corner, and religious texts line the walls. His desk is pleasantly messy.

Once she's seated in a far more comfortable chair than she'd enjoyed at Senkō-ji, with a fragrant cup of roasted green tea steaming before her, Uchida asks her to say more about the reason for her visit. He listens, gazing into his teacup, while she explains her scholarly interest in the poet Saburo—specifically, in his poem cycle, *The Eight Attachments*. How she'd gone to Hayashi Ceramics in search of evidence connecting the poet to Yakibō, because a piece made by the potter had recently been brought to her for authentication. She's sure that the existence of the tea bowl he'd named Hikitoru indicated a—

Uchida's head snaps up.

"Hikitoru? It's been found?"

"I still have to perform some tests," she replies, "but yes, I'm pretty sure that the tea bowl I saw last Friday was the one Yakibō called Hiki-toru."

"When will you know for sure?"

"By next Monday. I might finish sooner, but just between you and me, I'm trying to delay handing over the results for as long as possible. As soon as I give the report to my boss, the tea bowl will be returned to the temple it was stolen from. And the head priest there . . . well, let's just say that a foreign woman is the last person he'd allow to study it."

"I'm sorry," Uchida says, perplexed, "but which temple are you talking about?"

"Senkō-ji. In Tokyo. Hikitoru was reported stolen from their treasure house in 1945. According to the police inspector in charge of the case, that makes them the owner of record."

"But . . . they're not."

"What do you mean?"

"Because long before it was stolen from Senkō-ji, it was stolen from us."

"From *you?*"

"In a manner of speaking. Yakibō entrusted my nine-times-great-grandfather with his dying wish. But my ancestor couldn't fulfill his vow, because he needed that tea bowl to make the offering, and it was stolen before he had the chance."

"The same ancestor who tried to exorcize the ghost in the Hayashis' Old Kiln?"

"Yes." Uchida searches her face for a long moment. Then he grabs his cane and levers himself to his feet.

"Come. There's something I want to show you."

He stumps out of the building and she follows him through the gate to the priests' private garden. Picking her way along well-worn stones sunk into a carpet of pillowy moss, the clamor of the outside world recedes. In this gently sculpted landscape, the quiet music of a waterfall trickling over smooth stones is interrupted only by the cheeps of tiny green birds, flitting through a plum tree's leafy branches. Cedars that were giants long before she was born shade a red maple whose lacy parasol of leaves cascades to the ground around a gnarled trunk. The priest steps up onto the stone threshold of a small house at the very end. Even if she hadn't seen the characters spelling "Uchida" next to the entrance, the way he opens the door and walks inside without hesitating tells her this is where he lives.

He doesn't have to duck as he enters, and neither does she. As he fetches her a pair of slippers that's not three sizes too small, he explains that when he took over the temple from his father, he used his patrimony to rebuild the head priest's house to his scale.

"It's a luxury," he admits, a bit sheepishly. "But when you spend most of your waking hours feeling like an ox in a teahouse, it's good to come home to a place where you don't have to worry about bumping your head every time you turn around."

"I know what you mean." Does she ever.

The house is new, but constructed in the time-honored way. Planed wooden beams frame plaster walls the greenish-gold of fresh hay, and the *tatami* mats beneath her feet are smooth and springy. The main room is bare except for a low table in the center, surrounded by three plump cushions with backrests, and a short wooden chair. Uchida disappears into the kitchen. A hot water pot gurgles, and when he returns with the tea tray, he pours a cup for her, inviting her to sit for a few moments while he retrieves what he wants to show her.

The sliding doors to the cupboards lining the walls are brushed with a flock of sparrows, but Robin barely glances at them, because even the most enchanting of paintings is no match for the lush landscape framed by the window that stretches across the lower half of the far wall. Viewed from her seat at the low table, the composition of waterfall, maple, and tumbling stones rivals anything she's seen hanging in a museum.

Uchida returns, carrying a bulky indigo-dyed carrying cloth, its faded wave design stretched over a collection of angular objects. Lowering himself stiffly to the chair across from her, he sets the bundle on the floor next to him and unknots the corners. He lifts out a *kiri*-wood box that's been polished by time, and sets it on the table. The characters brushed across the top read *"Hatsu-koi"*—First Love—and the stamp in the bottom left corner is Yoshi Takamatsu's.

Robin snatches it up, in disbelief. First Love is the fifth of Saburo's *Eight Attachments*. She pries off the lid. Empty.

"What happened to the tea bowl inside?"

Uchida's only answer is to line up six other boxes next to it.

Ude-jiman. Mikudasu. Kanzen-shugi. Gankō. Yabo. Fukushū.

"What . . . ? How . . . ?" She picks them up, one after the other, but they're all empty.

"I can see that you know what these are." Uchida takes a sip of tea.

"The Eight Attachments," she whispers. "Where are the tea bowls they belong to?"

"Long gone. Except—you now tell me—Hikitoru." He inclines his head. "Which, I hope you'll agree, ought to be returned to me, not to that temple in Tokyo."

"This is . . ." Unbelievable. She can't take it in. "Where did you get these?"

Uchida refills her teacup, then his own. His backrest creaks as he leans back.

"Shortly before he died, Yakibō asked to see my nine-times-great grandfather. He made him promise to use the tea bowl he'd named Hikitoru to perform a ceremony on his behalf after he died, because he'd become too sick to do it himself. After the funeral, my ancestor accompanied Yakibō's apprentice back to the kiln so he could fulfill his vow, but Hikitoru was gone. These empty boxes are all they found.

"They couldn't figure out who could have taken it, because nearly everyone in town had been at the funeral. I'm sure they looked for it, but finding it didn't become a priority until Hattsan's next firing. When he went to unload the kiln for the first time after Yakibō died, every piece was broken. When it happened again, two months later, the apprentice became so convinced that the ghost of Yakibō was haunting the kiln, he abandoned it and began constructing a new one. That's when my ancestor realized the seriousness of the vow he'd made—Yakibō's spirit would refuse to move on to the next life until he fulfilled his promise.

"But by then, Hikitoru had been gone for months. The thief's trail was cold. It wasn't until later that summer that he had a small stroke of luck." He tops up her teacup. "Orders for tea bowls began to pour in to local potters after the *daimyō* of Yodo Castle in Kyoto conducted a grand public tea ceremony with a Shigaraki-style bowl, and they became wildly fashionable. Every member of Lord Inaba's circle wanted one, and retainers arrived in droves to commission them. My nine-times-great-grandfather overhead a samurai who'd been lucky enough to be present at the tea ceremony describe the unusually shaped tea bowl that had been used, and knew it must be Hikitoru.

"He packed his bag and went to Kyoto, determined to tell Lord Inaba that Hikitoru was stolen, to insist that it be returned. Of course, he learned pretty quickly that a poor parish priest didn't have a prayer of getting closer to the Lord of Yodo Castle than the outermost gate. He did manage to discover the name of the thief, though. Twenty years before, an itinerant ne'er-do-well had repaid Yakibō's hospitality by stealing a tea bowl from him, and that very same wastrel had risen to become the *daimyō's* court poet."

"Court poet? But . . . Lord Inaba's court poet was Saburo!" Her eyes grow wide. "Are you suggesting that the tea bowl he brought back from his pilgrimage wasn't a gift? That Saburo *stole* Yabō from Yakibō?"

Could that be true? Her gaze falls on the box with the characters for *yabō* brushed across the top. She picks it up.

"But if he stole the tea bowl named Yabō, what's this?"

The tiny, precise handwriting on this box doesn't look anything like the elegant calligraphy on the one marked Unmei. She searches her phone for a photo, compares it to the box on the table. Passes the phone to Uchida.

"The tea bowl in that picture is one of Yakibō's few known works," she explains. "It was called Yabō, before the name on its box was changed to Unmei. If the one that belonged to your box was the real Yabō, is that one a copy? Or is it the other way around?"

The priest studies it, unsure.

"My ancestor's account only mentions Hikitoru, but the potter's apprentice told him that Yakibō made a number of tea bowls before he chose one to represent his 'attachment.' Perhaps he gave one of the rejects to the poet . . . ?"

But Robin doesn't reply. If the boxes on the table really had contained Yoshi Takamatsu tea bowls representing the *Eight Attachments*—tea bowls that must have existed long before Saburo penned his masterwork, since their maker died before those eight classic poems were written—Yakibō *did* influence Saburo. This is the proof she needs. But she'll only be able to turn this discovery into a glorious academic career if . . .

"Will you let me study these boxes?" she pleads. "Prove what you've just told me is true? The implications for Saburo scholarship are . . . are . . ." She throws her arms wide, at a loss for words.

The priest regards her thoughtfully.

"Yes," he says, setting down his teacup. "But I want something in return."

"Anything in my power."

"My ancestor returned from Kyoto empty-handed. But he passed down Yakibō's deathbed obligation to his son, who passed it down to his son, and so on, until finally, it's been passed to me. If you return Hikitoru so I can perform that ceremony and put his spirit to rest, these boxes are yours. With my blessing."

"Yes," she agrees, stunned by his generosity. "Thank you. Yes!"

But Hikitoru is in Tokyo. And her boss has agreed to hand it over to the head priest of Senkō-ji a week from Monday.

"I'll need proof," she says. "To show my boss and satisfy the police. We'll need to prove that you're the rightful owner. Do you have any documents that authenticate the oral history? Did Yakibō record his wishes, so he could be sure they'd be carried out after he was gone?"

"Not in any detail. But my ancestor did. When he realized he was dying and wouldn't be able to fulfill his vow, he wrote down exactly what the potter had asked him to do. That's how I know what happened."

"Is it signed?"

"It is. But it's stamped with my ancestor's seal, not the potter's."

"Is it dated?"

"Yes, the year he died. Genbun 2."

Robin consults her phone and converts it to a modern date. 1737. *The Eight Attachments* wasn't discovered, clutched in Saburo's cold, dead hands, until 1753. The tea bowls predate the poems by more than a decade. Proof doesn't get more ironclad than that.

"Do you have that document here?" she asks. "Can I see it?"

"I do," he says, "but I'm afraid you can't."

"Oh." She's taken aback. "Why not?"

"It was meant to be read only by those charged with fulfilling the vow."

"But . . ."

"I'm sorry."

"All right." She tries another approach. "But if I'm not allowed to see it, could you read it over again? Look for a loophole in the wording, something that would allow us to . . . ?"

Uchida is shaking his head.

"My nine-times-great grandfather did try to, ah, 'interpret' Yakibō's instructions when they discovered Hikitoru was gone. After the first kiln disaster, he tried performing the ceremony using a different piece of Yakibō's pottery, but the next time Hayashi-san stoked the kiln, everything exploded again. The potter's spirit refused to be satisfied with anything but Hikitoru." Uchida spreads his hands helplessly. "I'm afraid I have to fulfill his instructions to the letter."

Robin sighs. She believes Uchida's tale, but her boss will want more than an oral history. If the priest allowed her to borrow the account his ancestor had written, the paper could be tested and dated. That would keep Hashimoto-san from handing Hikitoru over to Senkō-ji until more evidence is gathered. Without it . . . well, all she can do is try.

She clicks on her phone camera.

"Let me take pictures of the boxes to show my boss. I'll do everything I can to persuade her that Hikitoru should be returned to you."

40.

Present-Day Japan

MONDAY, APRIL 7

Tokyo

F or the first time in forever, Robin wakes up before her alarm. She faces the mirror, cheeks flushed with the fever of discovery, eyes shining with an anticipation she hasn't felt in years. Between the boxes calling to her from Shigaraki, and Mamoru Hayashi's pottery shards burning a hole in her handbag, she's never felt more alive. She dresses with care, considering it a good omen that even her hair is cooperating today. She'll need all the luck she can get, to convince her boss that Hikitoru ought to be returned to Uchida-*bōsan*, rather than that small-minded priest at Senkō-ji.

When the elevator opens on the twenty-second floor, she waves a cheerful "Good morning!" to the receptionist and breezes through the security gate. Stopping before Eriko Hashimoto's door, she straightens her jacket, and raps twice.

"Come."

"Good morning," Robin says, entering the light-filled office.

Hashimoto-san is at her desk, frowning over some paperwork. She looks up, and removes her reading glasses.

"Oh, it's you. Can you go straight to the lab this morning? I'm getting some pressure to deliver results on that Yakibō tea bowl. That lot of Bizen-ware can slip a day or two, if you don't finish testing it by the end of the week."

"Understood. But before I get started, may I show you something?"

Perching on the visitor chair, she recounts her weekend visit to Shigaraki, reciting Uchida-*bōsan*'s tale of thwarted obligation. Finally, she passes her phone across the desk, displaying the seven boxes bearing the names of Saburo's *Attachments*.

"You see?" She can't keep the excitement from her voice. "If the tests on Hikitoru prove it was made by Yakibō—and I'm certain they will—it won't just be another example of his work. It'll be the eighth in a set of tea bowls that correspond to Saburo's *Eight Attachments*. The implications for Japanese literature will be absolutely groundbreaking. The study of one of Japan's most important works of poetry will be . . ." she waves her hands, searching for the right words, ". . . changed forever!"

But the crease between her boss's eyebrows only deepens.

"I'm sure the head priest of Senkō-ji will be very gratified to hear that," she says. She passes the phone back, mouth pressed into a grim line.

"No, don't you see? He isn't the rightful owner," Robin insists. "Hikitoru was stolen from Shigaraki long before it was given to Senkō-ji, which means that Uchida-*bōsan* is the rightful heir."

"Where's the proof?"

"This is the proof!" She holds up the photo. "How could he have these other boxes if his story isn't true? I know we need to run tests to authenticate them and match them to the one in our safe, but once that's done, there shouldn't be any question."

Hashimoto is shaking her head.

"I'm not sure Mr. Fujimori can be convinced of that, but you're welcome to try."

"Mr. Fujimori?"

Why would the big boss be involved in this? His specialty is selling art, not authenticating ceramics.

"The head priest of Senkō-ji was on the phone to us before you'd even left the temple on Friday," Hashimoto tells her, face pinched with distaste. "He's demanding that the tea bowl be returned without delay. I tried to tell him that we can't deliver it to Senkō-ji until it's authenticated, but he insisted on speaking to . . . someone else."

A *man*. He'd insisted on speaking to a *man*. Hashimoto-san's tight smile says she's no more pleased than Robin to be dismissed for that reason.

"We should at least hold onto it until Uchida-*bōsan*'s claim can be investigated," Robin argues. "It's only fair. It would be wrong to give it to Senkō-ji without—"

"I don't disagree," Hashimoto says, cutting short her pleas. "But it's out of my hands. You'll have to persuade Fujimori-san. I wish you luck, but be prepared for him to be . . . unreceptive. His interest is in making the most profitable decision for the company, and I'd be very surprised if he doesn't already have an agreement with Senkō-ji to represent them if they sell Hikitoru."

41.

Present-Day Japan

TUESDAY, APRIL 8

Tokyo

N ori sips her bitter Metropolitan Police tea as she waits for Inspector Anzai. The interview room looks exactly like the ones in TV detective dramas, with one mirrored wall, a small table bolted to the floor, and two hard chairs facing each other.

You're here as a witness, she reminds herself, not a suspect. At least, she doesn't think she's a suspect. How could she be? She hadn't even been alive when Hikitoru was stolen in 1945.

So, why does she feel guilty, even though she has nothing to confess?

Every infraction she's ever committed returns to haunt her. The five thousand yen note she'd found on the street, but didn't turn in to the police box. The lipstick she'd stolen on a dare in middle school. The—

"Thank you for coming in to assist us with our investigation," says Inspector Anzai, striding through the door. He slaps a folder on the table, and Nori jumps as if zapped by a live wire. Even upside down, she can read her name on the thick file. How could the police have so much information on her in such a short time? She wipes her palms on her skirt, shifts in the uncomfortable seat.

"As I mentioned on the phone," the inspector begins, "you've been called in to make an official statement explaining how you came to be in possession of the stolen tea bowl, Hikitoru."

She swallows. What's in that folder?

"Do I need a pen?"

"That won't be necessary. My colleague will take notes." Anzai shifts his gaze briefly to someone behind her.

She twists to see. The small desk in the corner is now occupied by an assistant inspector with a laptop. Feeling outnumbered, she turns back to Anzai.

"Let's start with the day you first saw it."

She shades the truth, recounting how her grandmother had showed her the family heirloom hidden in a . . . a secret place in the house.

Anzai pounces on her hesitation and drills in.

She doles out the truth as parsimoniously as possible. There's a storage space beneath their *tokonoma* alcove. No, she'd never guessed it was there, even though she'd lived there all her life. Yes, as far as she knew, her grandmother was the only person who knew of its existence. The only person *alive* who knew, she amends.

But the inspector is soon peppering her with questions she doesn't want to answer. Palms sweating, face like a poker player, she begins to lie. To the best of her knowledge, the hiding place has never been opened in her lifetime (except to retrieve the stolen sake flask her grandmother sold after the earthquake). The space was empty, except for the tea bowl (and a stack of men's clothing, fit for a thief). Nori hadn't shown Hikitoru to anyone but Robin Swann at Fujimori Fine Art (and her grandmother's pawnbroker, Miura).

"Did you know the tea bowl was stolen?"

"No!" How many times does she have to say it? "Do you think I'd have taken it to the biggest auction house in Tokyo if I'd known it was stolen? How stupid do you think I am?"

"Good question," Anzai replies with a faint smirk. "What about your grandmother? Did she know?"

"No." If she did, she'd have warned me.

Then it hits her. 'Baa-chan *did* try to warn her. Hadn't she frowned right after Nori mentioned her plan to show Hikitoru to the experts at the auction house? Hadn't 'Baa-chan gripped her hand and refused to let go? 'Baa-chan had been trying to—

"I'm sorry, is there something you'd like to add?"

Anzai is looking at her strangely.

"No," she says quickly. Can't let him guess that her grandmother is more conscious than she lets on.

"Are you sure?"

"Sure about what?"

"That your grandmother didn't know," Anzai repeats. "If that tea bowl really is a family heirloom, why didn't she tell you about it until now?"

"It's just how my grandmother is. She never tells anybody anything, unless they need to know."

"But why now?"

"She . . . a few years ago, she started having 'spells,'" Nori admits. "She tried to hide it, but they've been getting worse. Maybe she was worried that if anything happened to her, I'd need to sell the tea bowl to make ends meet."

"But if she was looking out for your welfare," Anzai counters, "why did she tell you to sell something that would land you in jail?"

"Land me in—*What*?"

"The brass will want an arrest to go with the announcement that we've solved a major cold case. If we're unable to find out who stole Hikitoru in the first place, we'll have to settle for you."

42.

Chiyo zigzags through the crowded streets, making her way toward the maze of alleyways surrounding Ueno Station. As shortages grow, so does the station's unofficial marketplace, as buyers and sellers of legal and not-so-legal goods gather to do business.

The silk cloth that had ferried the Okuda ancestors' death tablets to safety on the night of the bombing is now knotted around boxes containing two fans, an incense burner, two tea bowls and a gourd-shaped sake flask. She hurries along as quickly as the crowd will allow. It's nearly noon, and today her luck is scheduled to change from bad to good as soon as the clock strikes twelve. She'll need all the time and luck she can muster to find a buyer before sundown.

She'd spent the morning improving her chances. Her grandfather always told her the more desperate you are to sell, the more it pays to look like you don't need the money. So she'd scrubbed her face, pulled her hair up in a twist to look older, and pinched her cheeks to give the impression she had plenty to eat. She'd borrowed a mostly undamaged kimono from a refugee woman who had stubbornly refused to dye it for mourning, and draped her mother's shawl over her red coat's burned patches.

Mincing toward the outskirts of the market with kimono-hobbled steps, she marvels at how unchanged everyday life is, in the unbombed parts of Tokyo. Linen curtains hang before the entrances of uncharred wooden buildings, housewives shop, children squabble, dogs chase cats. Fragrant grilled chicken smoke follows her, and the call of the roasted sweet potato man rings out as he pushes his cart through the streets. Ordinary life now strikes her as unbearably exotic, almost as if she'd journeyed to a foreign country.

She clutches the stolen boxes tighter as the crowd jostles her along, then slows as the lane is narrowed by hollow-eyed bombing victims who have spread their blankets on the ground along either side. She averts her eyes from the battered household goods they're desperately trying to turn into enough cash to feed themselves. Orphaned rice bowls, matches being sold by the piece, blackened kerosene heaters for which fuel has become vanishingly scarce.

As the crowd spills into a wider avenue, refugee blankets give way to tables and stalls lining the street, and she slows to scan the merchandise. The goods here look less pitiful, but the crowd of shoppers still flows briskly along. Most are saving their meager yen for those who deal in rice, boiled sweet potatoes, miso, anything that will supplement the government rations that aren't nearly enough to live on. Her own stomach growls as the fragrance of ramen broth wafts from a noodle stand, but she ignores the temptation. Lunch is a luxury she can't afford.

Chiyo lets the crowd steer her, searching right and left for stalls selling more expensive goods. But as offerings of secondhand household junk and used clothing give way to unappealing displays of grubby carrots and homemade pickles, her hopes falter. Had it been a mistake, bringing valuables to this place? Her biggest problem might not be unloading the goods before the theft becomes known, it might be finding a buyer at all.

She reaches an intersection, not sure which way to turn. Even standing on her tiptoes, it's impossible to see if any of the stands ahead deal in goods more costly than the mismatched dishes she brings here after digging duty. Dizzied by the sheer number of people milling in every direction, she makes her way to the side of the street to gather her wits. Hungry, thirsty, her head is beginning to pound. But time is racing by, and there won't be another good luck day until next week. Upending an empty wooden crate, she climbs onto it to get her bearings. Every able-bodied man between seventeen and forty is either farming or fighting, so the market crowd is made up mostly of old men, women, and children whose schooling has become spotty or nonexistent since the war news turned bad.

Oof.

"Watch where you're going, young man!" a matron barks at a gangly youth in a schoolboy cap who has just careened into her at the stand next to Chiyo.

The boy sweeps off his cap, but as he bows and apologizes, Chiyo spots his other hand emerging from the deep sleeve of the woman's silken wrap, holding a rice ball that he deftly drops into his book bag. None the wiser, the matron accepts his apology, then turns back to the counter to receive her package of used clothing. The boy glances up, catches Chiyo watching. She gives him the tight smile of a fellow thief, and he flashes her a crooked grin in return. Then his eyes widen in alarm and he melts back into the crowd.

Chiyo swings around to see what spooked him. A pair of sharp-eyed patrolmen is moving through the throng, scanning faces as they saunter along, their long bamboo nightsticks swinging by their sides. The younger of the two is looking in her direction. He turns to say something to his partner, and Chiyo hastily steps down, heart in her throat.

Now they're changing course, angling toward her through the crowd. She squeezes between the used clothing stall and the pickle vendor, tugging her burden through the tight space to the no-man's land behind the stalls. Scurrying along as quickly as her kimono will allow, she hears a commotion behind her and is nearly bowled over when the pickpocket bursts through the line of stalls and races toward her. The younger patrolman isn't far behind. Chiyo flattens herself against the wall as they barrel past. The policeman's partner pops into the alley just as the swifter one catches up with the running boy, grabbing his jacket, throwing him to the ground. The boy's hat goes flying and he rolls onto his back, holding up both hands in surrender. The police loom over him.

She can't hear what he's saying, but they allow him to stand without using their nightsticks. The boy dusts himself off, digs into his bag, and hands over the stolen rice ball. Instead of arresting him, the first policeman breaks it in half to share with his partner and, with a wave, they continue on their way. The boy watches them go, then retrieves his cap and swats the dust from it. He looks up to find her standing there. She shuts her mouth.

"You okay?" he asks, stopping a few paces from her. "You look lost."

"I'm fine."

"Haven't seen you here before."

"I . . . uh, it's my first time."

"No kidding," he says with a laugh. Eyes her bundle. "You buying or selling?"

She clutches it tighter. "None of your business."

"Don't worry. Whatever you've got in that fancy silk carrying cloth is way above my pay grade."

He takes a step closer, but she doesn't hear his next question, because over his shoulder, she sees a man emerge from between two stalls farther along, clapping a gray fedora onto his head.

Is that . . . ? No, can't be. She hasn't seen the youngest Itoh son since the night of the bombing. But when he pokes a cigarette between his lips and cups his hands around it to light it, she's sure.

"Itoh-kun!" she cries.

He's too far away to hear. Hitching a bulging bundle more securely onto the shoulder of his Western-style suit, he sets off so purposefully that he's almost to the next corner by the time she figures out what's wrong.

Tetsu Itoh is walking without a limp. How is that possible? He'd been sent home after the battle of Guadalcanal with a bum leg, and has been staggering around the neighborhood with a crutch ever since. Too crippled to return to the fighting, too crippled to volunteer for fire duty. Had he been *faking*?

She's so shocked, she nearly misses that his carrying cloth is tied around wooden boxes just like hers. He must be here to sell too. And anyone who can afford to waste a match on a cigarette must be doing well. She hurries to catch up with him.

Before the war, the Itohs had been no more successful than the Okudas, but judging by how the youngest son is dressed now, that's changed. And he's navigating the market without hesitation. He's been here before, knows where he's going. She drops back, keeping the gray fedora in sight. Maybe he'll lead her to the kind of buyer she's looking for.

Sure enough, they're soon in a part of the market she's never seen before. Crowds are thinner, and the stalls display goods that are whole and unbroken, some actually new. Cigarette lighters, winter coats trimmed in fur, real leather gloves. She can almost pretend it's not wartime.

Itoh stops, taking a few last puffs on his cigarette before pinching it out and stowing the nub in his pocket. At least some economies die hard.

She bends to inspect a pair of gloves as his gaze sweeps her way. Can't let him know she's following him. His family doesn't deal in boxed wooden art objects any more than hers does, which means neither of them has come here to sell goods that are rightfully theirs.

When she looks up again, he's gone. Has she lost him? No, there he is, coming out of that stall at the end, with a man in an even snappier hat and sharper suit.

She follows them into the backstreets of the surrounding neighborhood, to a quiet lane of wooden-fronted shops and expensive-looking teahouses, with stands of bamboo and unlit lanterns outside. They disappear into one of them.

She stops outside, hears the lock click behind them. There's no curtain hanging in front, no light showing through the shutters that blind the windows facing the street. Judging by the lack of signage, this dealer does business by invitation only. Should she knock while Itoh-kun is still there, or wait until he leaves?

If she forces him to make an introduction, that would pave her way. But what if he refuses? Denies knowing her? If she were him, she'd want as few rivals as possible. She retreats to the shadowy entrance of a shuttered tobacco shop across the street and makes herself still and small, waiting for him to leave.

A woman in full white-face makeup and a kimono worth more than everything in the Okuda store emerges from a teahouse down the block, and lights a cigarette. Cherry blossom ornaments twinkle in her elaborate hairdo, as she tips her head back and blows smoke up into the clear blue sky. Before she finishes her second cigarette, Itoh reappears, tucking his folded carrying cloth into his jacket. As soon as he's around the corner, Chiyo stands, smooths her hair, and steps up to the dealer's door to knock.

He opens it, minus his hat. Up close, he's more handsome than anyone she's ever met, and she blushes at herself for noticing. A thin pencil moustache draws attention to his chiseled lips, and his lazy eyes give her the once-over, settling for a beat on her silk carrying cloth, before returning his gaze to her face.

"What can I do for you, young lady?"

Flustered, Chiyo has trouble answering.

"I'm . . . I'm a friend of Tetsu Itoh."

No flicker of recognition.

She kicks herself. Itoh-kun had been smart enough not to use his real name. She tries again.

"The thing is, he uh, said he was coming here today to sell some things, and if I met him here before noon, he'd introduce me. But it took longer to get here than I thought. Is he already here?"

"I think you just missed him."

"Oh no! Am I too late?"

"That's all right." He eyes her bundle again, then stands aside, inviting her in. "We'll just have to introduce ourselves."

Inside, he bows, telling her his name is Yoshizaburō Arashi. She follows his cue, introducing herself as the actress who was cast opposite the film idol in *The 47 Ronin*.

"Did you have something you'd like me to take a look at, Miss?"

"Yes, if it's not too much trouble."

She follows him through a shuttered showroom that's luxuriously appointed in the exotic art deco style fashionable before the war. It's the most opulent place she's ever been, and she has to remind herself not to gawk. Once they get to the back room, though, she relaxes. It had obviously been a workshop, although the tools that once hung on the wall pegs are missing, and the workbench is now cluttered with wooden boxes like the ones she brought.

The dealer makes a fresh pot of tea and sets a cup before her on a lacquered saucer. Clearing a space at one end of the long counter, he switches on a lamp and seats himself on a wooden stool. Chiyo unpacks her burden, hands him the first box.

She sips her tea as he examines the pieces one by one, encouraged by his approving murmurs and the speed with which he assesses them. He must really know his stuff, she thinks, watching him expertly turn one of the tea bowls in his slender fingers and snap open the black and gold war fan.

Finally, with a practiced hand, he reknots the cord around the last box and stacks it with the others.

"This is a fine selection, Miss." He steeples his hands before him. "And in very good condition. I'll give you four hundred yen for the lot."

Four hundred yen? That's all?

"But . . . but . . . that sake flask is over two hundred years old!" she objects. "And this tea bowl has a name. See? Hikitoru. It alone should be worth more than four hundred yen!"

"Perhaps in happier times, it would be," he says. "But there's a war on, and I'm afraid four hundred yen is the best I can do."

Her eyes sting with tears. How could she have risked so much for only four hundred yen? The goods in the boxes are worth a lot more than that, she knows they are. But if she doesn't take this offer, she'll be back on the street, and what are her chances of finding another buyer before the theft becomes public knowledge, and she can't sell them at all? She bites her lip. She can't refuse. But she can't bring herself to say yes, either. What would her grandfather say? Don't let your desperation show. Don't be too eager.

"Can I . . . think about it?" she asks.

"Think about it?" The dealer's face hardens.

She begins to stack the boxes on her cloth.

"Hey, what are you doing?" His voice grows less friendly. "What's there to think about?"

She reknots the carrying cloth, her fumbling fingers betraying her growing conviction that this was a mistake.

"Four hundred yen is a lot of money," he says, moving closer. "You're lucky I'm being so generous, considering."

She freezes.

"What do you mean?"

His mouth widens into a menacing grin. "Where did you say you got these, exactly?"

She feels her face grow hot.

"I thought so. You're not really in a position to refuse, are you?"

She rises, clutching her bundle.

"Thank you for your offer, but I'm afraid I have to go now."

His hand latches onto her carrying cloth.

"Don't be so hasty."

She tries to pull it away, but his grip tightens.

"You can leave these things with me. For safekeeping."

"No," she cries, struggling to free the boxes. "Let me go."

Then a rock smashes through the window, skittering across the wooden floor in a shower of broken glass. The dealer lets go and lunges toward the window with a curse.

That's all the opening she needs. She scrambles for the door.

The dealer turns to stop her just as another missile demolishes what's left of the glass and hits him on the back of the head. He falls.

She scurries through the showroom, out the front door, then hikes up the front of her kimono and runs. She doesn't stop until a stitch in her side forces her to slow to a walk. Breathing hard, she slumps against a postbox and hangs her head.

When she recovers enough to look around, she doesn't see a single familiar landmark. She's drained from her ordeal, but the lengthening shadows and deepening chill remind her it will soon be dark. She'll have an even harder time finding her way back to the refugee barracks if she doesn't push on.

A shopkeeper points her at the glinting water of Shinobazu Pond at the end of the next cross street. If she follows the shoreline, it will lead her back to the refugee camp.

43.

TUESDAY, APRIL 8

Tokyo

Robin charges out of the Fujimori Fine Art building and strides toward police headquarters, seething from her encounter with the head of the auction house. She'd perched on a chair outside Mr. Fujimori's inner sanctum for forty-five minutes, waiting for him to squeeze her in between appointments, but she'd barely warmed the visitor seat in his office before she was out the door again.

Interesting tale, he'd said. Did she have proof? His frown said it all, as he silently regarded the photo of the empty boxes and passed it back. If she managed to find something more convincing before they delivered the tea bowl to the head priest of Senkō-ji next Monday, by all means bring it in. Until then...

She stalks across the vast concrete plaza toward the skyscraper housing Tokyo Metropolitan Police headquarters. How is she going to stop this train wreck?

The stoic-faced policeman standing guard with his wooden staff bars her path, asking what business she has there.

"I'm here to sign a statement. A *witness* statement," she snaps, in case he suffers from the national misconception that foreigners are responsible for most of the crimes keeping him in business.

He lets her pass. She sails through the big automatic doors, gives her name to the receptionist, then sits on the edge of the last empty chair, waiting to be summoned by Inspector Anzai. Her knee jiggles. She stills it. Nips at a hangnail, then drops her hand to her lap, closing her fist around her smarting thumb.

Why do encounters with Japanese bureaucracy always do this to her? Seems like every officer crossing the lobby is eyeballing her. Because she's a foreigner? Because she's female? Or do they sense she has a profoundly illegal bag of marijuana gummy bears shoved into the toe of her snow boot at home? Her underarms prickle. She's never been able to figure out a safe way to get rid of the unwanted gift from the spectacularly irresponsible college friend who visited four years ago. Bury it in her kitchen garbage on Burnable Trash day? A neighborhood dog might sniff it out. Flush it down the toilet? What if a plumber came to snake the clogged drain and—

Wait, is that Nori Okuda?

It is. The spiky-ponytailed shopkeeper is crossing the vast lobby, aiming for the automatic door, eyes vacant, face shell-shocked. What had Anzai said to make her look like that?

"Miss Swann? This way please?"

She jerks to attention, follows the constable to a waiting elevator.

But nobody seems to want her in their office for very long today. Ten minutes later, a succinct account of her first meeting with Nori Okuda has been stamped with her name seal, a vague answer about when to expect test results on Hikitoru given to Inspector Anzai's assistant, and she's back out on the plaza. Her own attempts to find out whether the police had discovered anything that might help her establish Hikitoru's provenance died a quick death against the brick wall of "sorry, police business."

She blinks in the glare. If only people who weren't gangsters could wear sunglasses in Japan without seeming rude. Squinting as she makes a beeline for the shade of the plaza's token trees, it isn't until she steps into their shifting shade that she recognizes the solitary woman slumped on a bench beneath them.

"Okuda-san?" She stops a few feet away.

Nori glances up, eyes red, face puffy. Quickly turns away.

"Are you okay?" In all her time in Japan, the closest she's come to seeing a Japanese woman lose her composure in public was the stunned face and rapidly blinking eyes of a fellow grad student who spotted her fiancé emerging from a love hotel, and not alone.

Robin perches on the other end of the bench and says, "I saw you coming out of the elevator. What happened?"

Nori flinches away, repeating, "It's fine. I'm fine. Really."

But any idiot could see she's not. If Robin had been Japanese, it would have been inexcusably rude to ignore the body language screaming "go away," but she hasn't forgotten how to be a blunt foreigner, and the poor woman seems so alone.

"Let me buy you a cup of tea, at least."

"No. Thanks. Really." Nori jumps up, grabs her purse. "Sorry. Excuse me." She sketches a head bob that barely counts as a bow and hurries away, stiff-legged, across the plaza.

Confounded, Robin watches her go. What had upset her so deeply that she'd barely made it out of police headquarters before breaking down? Anzai must have threatened her, but with what? Nori hadn't done anything wrong, not really. Her tea bowl was stolen, but she hadn't even been alive in 1945, so she couldn't be the thief.

She might know who was, though. Robin starts back toward the office. They really only had Nori's word for it that the tea bowl had been in her family since 1945. What if it hadn't been? What if it had changed hands multiple times since it disappeared from Senkō-ji's treasure house? Just last week she'd read an article about how stolen art—especially art too famous to sell—is being used by criminals as collateral in black market deals. What if—

No, that's ridiculous. A Kappabashi shopkeeper, neck-deep in arms running or drug trafficking? She's got to stop watching so many gangster movies.

But it's a legitimate worry. If there had been multiple "owners" since 1945, who else might try to get their hands on Hikitoru after it's handed over to one of the claimants? She needs to find out if there are other players. And who they are.

Inspector Anzai might know, but they'll be building snowmen in hell before he shares.

He's not the only one with that information, though. If she can get past the anger and hurt, Nori Okuda might help her. Maybe they can help each other.

44.

Wartime Japan

A P R I L , 1 9 4 5

Tokyo

Chiyo drags her feet to a bench on the deserted lotus-viewing boardwalk that borders the Shinobazu Pond, shoulders aching beneath the burden that feels twice as heavy as when she set out that morning. She drops onto an empty seat, her cheeks wet with despair. All around her, the dry stalks whisper, *thief, thief,* in the shivery breeze. What's she going to do now? She has no money, no buyer, and if anyone guesses her carrying cloth is filled with stolen goods, she'll—

"You should be more careful who you do business with, you know."

Chiyo nearly jumps out of her skin. It's . . . the pickpocket from the marketplace?

Snatching up her bundle, she squeaks, "What are you doing here?"

"Followed you."

He plops down on the far end of the bench and occupies himself digging around in his jacket pocket, looking away politely while she tidies her face with a corner of her kimono sleeve. Drawing out a half-smoked cigarette and a magnifying glass, he leans into the last patch of afternoon sun and focuses the rays on the end of his fag until it begins to smolder. He sticks it between his lips and takes a drag.

"Did I kill him or just knock him out?" he asks, blowing smoke from the corner of his mouth.

"That was *you?*"

"Best strikeout I ever pitched."

The memory burns. How long had he been standing outside that back window, witnessing her humiliation? A resentful bow hides her mortification.

"Thank you," she says stiffly. "For your, uh . . . help."

"You're welcome." He parks the cigarette in a corner of his mouth and tucks away his magnifying glass.

"You shouldn't be smoking, at your age, you know," she scolds, trying to wipe the smug look off his face.

"If I'm old enough to train for homeland defense, I'm old enough to smoke," he retorts. Then admits, "At least, I will be next month."

He's barely older than she is. She forgives him his bravado.

He stands.

"Come on," he says. Walks away.

She stares after him, then grabs her burden and catches up, planting herself in his path.

"Where are you going?"

"To someone who'll give you a fair price for your stuff."

"Who?"

"You'll see."

"*Who?*" she insists.

"My mom."

"Your *mom?*"

"Yeah." He takes a drag on the cigarette and blows the smoke out with a world-weary twist of his lips. "My dad and my brothers are off fighting on some godforsaken island in the South Pacific, and someone's gotta run the family business."

She falls in beside him.

"What kind of family business?"

"Pawnshop."

"She runs it alone?"

"I help."

He pinches out the spark at the end of the fag and carefully stows the remnant in an envelope he draws from his jacket pocket.

"My name's Miura, by the way. What's yours?"

"Okuda. Chiyo Okuda," she tells him, forgetting to lie.

"Nice to meet you, Chiyo-chan."

He leads her through the backstreets of Ueno, promising "it's just two more blocks" when her feet start to drag. It's really more like four, but as they make their way down a quiet lane toward a building displaying a door curtain dyed with the characters for "pawnshop," it's the boy's steps that slow, then stop. He studies a large black car parked out front.

"I think we'd better wait until that customer leaves," he says.

She gapes at the shining beast.

"Your customers ride around in *cars*?"

These days, it's pedestrians and bicycles that clog the streets of Tokyo. Every drop of oil is being funneled into the war effort, and gasoline is so severely rationed that even the rich can no longer afford to drive. A car could only mean—

A man emerges from the doorway, flipping the curtain aside, his military bearing marking him as the one kind of person who can swan around in an automobile without being unpatriotic. He turns to receive a silk-wrapped box from the woman who follows him out. His driver is standing at attention next to the open car door by the time he straightens from his bow, but the woman maintains her deep, ninety-degree obeisance until they have pulled away and rounded the corner.

The boy resumes walking, motioning for Chiyo to follow.

"'Kaa-san!" he calls.

His mother turns. She'd probably never been beautiful—her nose has a pronounced bump, and her features are too sharp to be fashionably feminine—but she's so elegantly dressed in a willow-patterned silk kimono that it doesn't matter. Her still-black hair (where does she manage to get dye of that quality during wartime?) is pinned up in a traditional *nihongami* hairstyle, a reminder of a more gracious era.

When Chiyo gets close enough to be introduced, the sharp eyes behind Mrs. Miura's gold-rimmed spectacles miss nothing, but her voice isn't unkind as she holds the curtain and invites them inside.

While the boy explains why he brought her back with him, Chiyo tries not to be distracted by the costly merchandise gleaming everywhere. The shop feels like a pirate's cave.

Mrs. Miura leads them down the hall to the office.

Chiyo sets her carrying cloth on the well-used black lacquer table. Cups of tea are poured, snacks offered. Feet tucked neatly beneath her as she kneels across from Mrs. Miura, she nibbles on a rice cracker, nerves on edge as the pawnbroker's wife removes her glasses and sets them aside. The boy kneels at his mother's side, sharing the circle of light from a powerful lamp.

Together, they work their way through the boxes. Once he asks, "Kutani or Hirado?" and when his mother refuses to answer, he grimaces and gets up to consult the reference books bowing the shelves along one wall. Occasionally, she passes him an object and he inspects it with the magnifying glass before muttering a cryptic comment like, "Jumatsu-ya."

Then she hands him one of the tea bowls. When he says "Yes?" after hefting it, she tells him to flip it over and check the foot. When he looks up, puzzled, and says, "Fake?" Chiyo stiffens with alarm, but his mother just smiles and says, "No. Look at the date on the box. It's too old. Signing one's work is a modern conceit."

After rewrapping each piece, Mrs. Miura pencils notations and figures into a notebook. Chiyo's surreptitious attempts to read them upside down meet with failure, so she studies the small office instead.

The Miuras appear to have been in business for nearly as many generations as her own family. About the same number of bookkeeping ledgers are lined up atop the filing cabinet as sat on the shelf at Okuda & Sons before the bombs fell, and although the Miuras' wall calendar is a slightly different design than the one that hung on the wall on Kappabashi Street, it also features a weeping cherry tree for the month of March. The oddest similarity is that the Miuras' resident Shinto gods occupy a shelf high up in the far corner, just like the deities in the Okudas' office. They live in an identical wooden shrine building, with the same offering bowls set before it. She's oddly comforted by this piece of home, almost as if the Okuda family gods had temporarily relocated and were still watching out for her.

In the silence, her stomach growls and she shrinks as the boy's mother looks up. But Mrs. Miura merely offers more tea, urges her to take another rice cracker. In fact, she says, taking in Chiyo's hollow cheeks and pale skin, help yourself to as many as you like. Mrs. Miura returns to her task, and Chiyo finishes her second rice cracker rather more quickly than the first, her hand stealing across the table for another.

Mrs. Miura opens the last box. It holds one of the fans. She passes it to her son, who gingerly unfolds it, revealing a gold quince blossom crest on a black ground.

"Oda clan?" he guesses.

"Yes."

He snatches up the box, looking for the date. "Do you think there's a chance . . . ?"

His mother smiles.

"Doesn't matter, as long as the buyer thinks so."

Chiyo badly wants to ask what she means, but Mrs. Miura is already repacking the fan and hooking her glasses over her ears. Picking up her pencil, she ticks down the figures she's written, adding them in her head. She makes a notation and circles it, then puts down her pencil.

Chiyo leans forward, praying she'll be offered enough this time to make it worth the risk.

"Well, Miss Okuda, with the exception of the war fan—which has understandably seen some hard use—these pieces are all in good condition. These three," Mrs. Miura says, moving the boxes containing the dance fan, the incense burner, and the plum blossom tea bowl to one side of the table, "aren't one-of-a-kind, but they're nice pieces, so they'll be fairly easy to sell." She picks up the war fan's box. "This one is in the worst condition, but could end up fetching the most."

"It could?"

"If it's offered to the right buyer," she says. "But that will require some groundwork."

"Groundwork?"

The boy explains, "War fans were used by samurai, for signaling during battle. This one belonged to someone in the Oda clan—you can tell by the quince blossom crest. But it's the date that's makes it interesting. The Battle of Nagashino happened in Tenshō 3. Which means this fan could have been used by Oda Nobunaga himself."

Oda Nobunaga? The legendary warrior who had unified all Japan?

"How can we find out for sure?" Chiyo asks eagerly.

"We can't," Mrs. Miura replies. "There's no way to know if he used it or not. But," she adds, a gleam kindling in her eye, "if the right whispers reach the right ears, some collectors might be willing to pay a premium, just for the possibility."

Chiyo is impressed. Maybe the gods *are* looking out for her. She nudges the boxes containing the tea bowl named Hikitoru and the gourd-shaped sake flask into the spotlight.

"What about these?"

"Those are . . . more challenging," Mrs. Miura admits. "They're named, which means they're one of a kind. That makes them more valuable, but it also means they have . . . cultural baggage."

"What do you mean?"

"You might not be able to sell them for years."

"Years?" She doesn't have years. She needs the money now. "I see. But . . . the others? Can they be sold right away?"

"That depends on how soon you mean by 'right away.' They're collectors' items, so if you want to get full price, finding the right collector is important. That can take time."

"How much time?"

Mrs. Miura considers the boxes on the table.

"I could probably get a satisfactory sum for the first three within a month. The Oda fan . . ." She regards it, considering. "Getting the best price for that depends, frankly, on how the war goes. There are quite a few collectors of what we call 'traditional Japanese cultural items' in the current government, but their purse strings tend to be looser when the news from the front is good."

Which it hadn't been lately.

"How much difference will it make if we're not so picky about the buyer?"

"I'm afraid it could be thousands of yen."

Thousands? Not hundreds, *thousands!*

Mrs. Miura is totting up a new total. She sets aside her pencil.

"By my estimate, the incense burner, the dance fan, the plum tea bowl, and the war fan could fetch something in this range, if we find the right buyers."

She pushes her notebook across the table, turning it so Chiyo can read the sum.

"Seven to ten thousand yen?" Chiyo squeaks. That would feed her family for years, might even rebuild the store!

"Of course," Mrs. Miura reminds her, taking her notebook back and scribbling two more figures beneath, "minus our commission, that means you would net something more like this."

She pushes it across the table. Three-point-five to five.

Oh. Right. Pawnbrokers don't work for free. Then Chiyo does the math, and rounds on the boy, incensed.

"*Fifty percent?* I thought you said you were taking me to someone who would give me a fair price! Taking half is . . . it's not fair!"

"Actually . . ." The boy glances at his mother. "It is."

Mrs. Miura explains, "That's the going rate for objects with . . . special circumstances."

"'Special circumstances'?"

"The instant you untied that carrying cloth, I could smell Senkō-ji temple burning to the ground." She flicks through the stack of papers on the corner of the table and pulls one out, hands it to Chiyo. It's a police circular, dated April 5th, headlined, "BE ON THE LOOKOUT FOR STOLEN GOODS."

The blood drains from Chiyo's face. Every item on the table is described in detail.

"In the future," Mrs. Miura advises her in a dry voice, "maybe you shouldn't try to unload everything all at once."

45.

TUESDAY, APRIL 8

Tokyo

The train eases to a stop at the station nearest Miura's pawnshop. Nori stops in the ladies' room to swipe the weepy smudges from beneath her eyes, then beeps herself out through the ticket gate, pulling her muffler up. Head down against the wind, she hurries past the Korean restaurant, determined to get some answers from the only man who might be able to help her.

Daiki cracks open the door. "Oh. It's you." Awkward silence. "So . . . did you find another buyer?"

"No. Can I come in?"

"I guess."

He unchains the door and lets her in.

As it closes behind her, she says, "I need to talk to your grandfather."

"Why?"

"The police have Hikitoru."

"What? Why?"

She describes her meeting with the experts from the auction house, tells him how they'd ambushed her with the police report and confiscated the tea bowl.

"They say it's stolen," she tells him. "That it was stolen from Senkō-ji temple in 1945."

"What?"

"Your grandfather didn't tell you?"

"No."

"But he knew, didn't he?" she insists. "I think that's why he wants to charge fifty percent commission. If Hikitoru can only be sold to someone who doesn't care if it's stolen, that's a lot less outrageous. But how did he know?" She leans in. "I need to talk to him, Daiki. I need to find out how he knew it was stolen."

The boy looks doubtful.

"He's not feeling very well today, but I'll go up and ask."

By the time he reappears, Nori has nervously picked up and set down half the dusty merchandise in the shop.

"Come back to the office," he says. "My *o-jii-san* is waiting."

Miura is seated at the table in his stiff, out-of-date suit, fresh comb marks in his thin hair. He bows and invites her to sit, as the boy closes the office door.

"Daiki tells me the police have Hikitoru."

"Yes. I showed it to some auction house experts, because I thought fifty percent commission was unreasonable. But now I understand. They told me it was stolen from Senkō-ji temple, in 1945."

Miura won't meet her eyes.

"You knew, didn't you?"

He contemplates his gnarled hands, clasped before him.

"And I think you know who stole it."

No answer.

"Please help me!" she implores. "If the police don't find out who took it, they're going to arrest me instead."

His head snaps up.

"I think I know who it was, and I think you do too," she blurts. The words tumble out. "There was a stack of men's clothing hidden in the same place as Hikitoru. Dark clothes, like a burglar might wear. My grandmother had a brother she doesn't talk about, an older brother who died right after the war. I think he stole that tea bowl, along with the other stuff in the police report. Please," she begs, "the truth is, my grandmother is really sick. She's in the hospital. She can't give them a statement. You're the only one who was around in 1945, the only one who might be able to tell the police what they need to know. Will you help me? Please? Go to the police and tell them the thief was my grandmother's brother?"

Miura coughs. Dabs at his mouth with a handkerchief. Sighs.

"I can't," he finally says. "Because it wasn't."

He raises a hand, anticipating her protest.

"It's not that I have a problem with lying to the police when necessary," he explains, "but the facts are too easy to check. Your grandmother's brother was so badly burned in the firebombing, he never recovered. The hospital sent him home after the next attack—they needed his bed for those who were even worse off—but someone had to feed him, wash him, and change his dressings day and night until he died."

"That's . . . terrible." She pauses, digesting the news. "But if it wasn't him, who was it?"

It couldn't have been 'Baa-chan's grandfather, who died in the same firebombing that destroyed Senkō-ji. And it couldn't have been 'Baa-chan's mother, whose failure to help with even the most basic survival tasks still inspires diatribes half a century later. But that left—

No.

"'Baa-chan?" she whispers. "It was '*Baa-chan*?"

Miura's silence says it all.

Her *grandmother* stole the tea bowl? The same grandmother who punished her for shoplifting a single lipstick by making her scrub toilets until she'd earned enough money to pay for it? The grandmother who marched her to the drugstore to make a full confession and a formal apology? That grandmother was a *thief*?

"Stop," Miura says, reading her face, shaking his head. "You don't know what it was like, near the end of the war. Every day, death and destruction could rain down on us again at any moment. We were so hungry, we scavenged through the rubbish for anything edible, and we made tea from anything green. Every day, we thought it couldn't possibly get worse, and then it did. The only people who survived were those who were willing to do whatever it took to stay alive, and," he sighs, "the ones who'd been breaking the law before the war had a head start. Those of us who were new at it, well . . . we had to help each other."

Wincing as he rises, he allows Daiki to steady him across the room to a *tokonoma* alcove between two bookcases. He kneels, reaching beneath the lip of the wooden slab to fiddle with a latch. The boy shifts the heavy lid for him. The old man returns to the table with a narrow wooden box. He opens it, offering Nori the contents.

She takes the war fan, unfolds it. Looks up, confused.

"Gold on black, Oda family crest." She recognizes it from the police report.

"Made in the year Tenshō 1," Miura affirms. He turns to his grandson. "Do you know what the Oda clan was doing a few years later, in 1575?"

"Uhh . . ." Daiki consults his phone. "That's the year Oda Nobunaga won the Battle of Nagashino." His eyes widen. "Do you think this fan belonged to *him*?"

"It might have," his grandfather says. "And that's the story we'd have told collectors, if it hadn't been way too hot to sell." He turns to Nori. "But I'm trusting you to keep that to yourself. My mother told your grandmother that we got an excellent price for it, even minus our exorbitant commission."

Nori sits there, stunned. So that's how 'Baa-chan got the money to rebuild the store. Her grandmother had stolen the goods, and the Miuras had sold them for her. Or not, as the case may be. Which made the obligation she owed them even greater.

She bows over the table, murmuring words of utmost gratitude. But her heart is filled with despair, because now she can't press Miura to tell the police what he knows. Not when it would shift the police crosshairs from herself to the old man and her grandmother instead.

46.

WEDNESDAY, APRIL 9

Tokyo

Robin steps into the office elevator thirty minutes early, to avoid being trapped for twenty-two floors with higher-ups who'd been known to seize that opportunity to saddle captive underlings with extra work. Half an hour is a small price to pay for avoiding hours of overtime, and between now and Monday, she needs to spend all her waking hours proving Hikitoru had never rightfully belonged to Senkō-ji. In five short days, it will be handed over to that chauvinistic head priest, and another scholar will scoop the discovery right out from under her.

But giving in to her frustration isn't going to help. While she tries to figure out how to keep Hikitoru from disappearing into the black hole of Senkō-ji, she can test Mamoru's pottery pieces and find out if the Hayashis are sitting on an archeological treasure trove.

She unlocks the door to the lab, takes Hikitoru from the safe, and unwraps the shards Mamoru had found in the woods. Her eyes flick back and forth between the tea bowl and the fragments, comparing the color of the clay, the nuances of the glaze, the thickness of the wall.

Side by side, they appear to have been made by the same artist. She sets to work proving it.

By the end of the day, she's as sure as anyone can be. The chemical signatures of both the tea bowl and the shards match the published test numbers belonging to Yabō, Yoshi Takamatsu's other Shigaraki-ware bowl. And the thermo-luminescent samples she'd prepared yesterday confirm they're all the same age.

She picks up the palm-sized piece. What was it part of, before it was broken? A tea bowl? A water jar? Is the rest of it buried out in the woods behind the Hayashi kiln? She imagines the fanfare that would accompany such a find. The press conference, the dramatic photo of the first reconstructed piece on prestigious journal covers . . . and the balding, gray-haired head of the scholar most likely to be directing that research. Because unless she manages to get her doctorate, it won't be her. She won't even be on the team.

She lets out a moan of frustration, confronted with the same dilemma she's been wrestling with since her bosses refused to accept the seven empty boxes as proof that Hikitoru belongs to Reverend Uchida. She has to return the tea bowl to Uchida in order to see the document proving his ownership, but she has to prove his ownership in order to persuade Fujimori-san to return the tea bowl.

If only the police hadn't taken it away from Nori Okuda. She's sure she could have talked Nori into letting her borrow Hikitoru long enough for Uchida to—

That's it.

Owning the tea bowl isn't the key to getting access to Uchida's document—performing the ceremony is.

Pawing through her purse, she retrieves the priest's number, taps out a message.

Uchida-san,

I just finished testing that tea bowl, and I'm sure it's the Hiki-toru you're looking for. How soon could you be ready to perform the ceremony your ancestor described? If I brought it to you Saturday morning, would you have time to do it on Saturday afternoon?

She reads it over, corrects a typo.
Send.

47.

N ori guiltily snaps to attention as a last-minute shopper steps into the store. It's been a long, dreary day, with few customers to break the tedium, but her grandmother would skin her alive for being buried in her phone instead of ready to greet them, even those who arrive ten minutes before closing.

"*Irasshaimase*," she sighs. Welcome to our shop. But not really.

The latecomer charts a course through the displays like a barge squeezing through a neighborhood canal, a shopping bag from a fancy department store grasped in one fuzzy-gloved hand.

Stopping short of the counter, she ventures, "Okuda-san?" from behind her muffler.

Her accent. Her height. What's Robin Swann doing here?

"I'm sorry to bother you at the end of a long day," the intruder begins, unwinding her scarf as if she plans to stay a while. "I, uh, wanted to see how you're doing."

"How kind of you," Nori replies stiffly. Put that scarf back on.

"So . . . are you all right?" Robin persists.

"I'm fine."

The truth is, Nori is hungry, her feet hurt, and she wants to close up shop, but the 'Baa-chan in her head is reminding her she's still on duty for five more minutes.

"Thank you for taking the trouble to stop by," Nori says, without enthusiasm. Please leave.

"Oh, it's no trouble." Bright smile. "On my way home, actually."

Wrong answer. And the mouth-watering aroma of grilled chicken wafting from that shopping bag is nearly unbearable. Irritated by Robin's inability to take a hint, Nori is forced to be more explicit. She begins to tidy the sales desk.

"I'm afraid you caught me about to close up shop, so . . ."

"Great! I was hoping you'd say that."

Huh?

"I stopped by the Mitsukoshi food hall on my way," Robin explains, setting the shopping bag on the counter, "and picked up a few things for dinner. There's plenty for both of us, if you'd like to share?" She tips the bag, offering a view of the contents.

Nori stares, astonished, confounded. What kind of person would walk up to a near stranger and offer food? In *public*. From a *bag*. Is this barbarian really suggesting they share a meal from take-out cartons? It's time to put a stop to this, leave no room for misinterpretation.

"That would be. . . a little difficult," she says firmly.

"Oh no! Did you already eat? I thought if I came early, before you got off work . . ."

What the—? Everybody knows that "a little difficult" is Japanese code for "impossible." Someone who's as fluent as Robin Swann ought to—

Wait. Those unnaturally blank round eyes. Could she be misunderstanding on purpose? She is. She's playing dumb, refusing to take "no" for an answer. That's why she cornered Nori at work, knowing it would be unthinkable for a shopkeeper to be rude to a customer.

Politeness be damned! "I'm sorry. I can't eat with you."

Surprised look. "Oh."

Good. She's getting the message.

"Are you vegetarian, or something?"

"What? No!"

The big pigeon stands there, confusion written all over her face.

That's it. Nori is done with being shoved around like a little marker on everybody's *go* board. Done with Anzai, done with 'Baa-chan, and most especially done with Robin Swann.

"How can you not understand?" she says, in a voice that would freeze a freshly crushed hand warmer. "Would *you* eat with someone who set you up?"

"Set you up?" Robin looks shocked. "You mean . . . last Friday?"

No need to dignify that with a reply.

"But I had nothing to do with that," Robin protests. "Hashimoto-san didn't tell me that your tea bowl was stolen. Or that Mr. Anzai was with the police. I found out the same time you did."

Nori doesn't care. "You're still on the team trying to put me in jail."

"Jail?" Robin blinks. "What do you mean, 'jail'?"

"If they don't find out who stole Hikitoru, the police say they'll arrest me instead. For 'intent to sell stolen goods.'"

"What? They can't do that!" Robin's brow furrows. "Can they?"

"I don't know. They say they can."

Robin bristles. "But that's wrong. Everything about this is wrong. I've been trying to tell them, but they won't listen. The police . . . my boss . . . *her* boss . . . they all think they can ignore anyone who's below them, that we'll just shut up and go away. But you know what? I'm not going to let them get away with it. Not this time. I'm not going to let them ignore the truth."

The truth? What truth?

"I've been doing some investigating," she says. "The real crime involving Hikitoru has nothing to do with you. It happened long before 1945."

"What?"

"It was stolen from someone else, long before it was stolen from Senkō-ji."

"It was?"

"Yes. But . . . I can't prove it."

"Oh."

"Not yet, anyway. But together, I think we might be able to."

Together? Nori takes a step back, feeling the hope radiating off of Robin like heat from a New Years' bonfire.

"I don't understand," she replies, wary.

"Explaining might take some time." Robin lifts the shopping bag, inclining her head toward the open office door. "Eat while we talk?"

Nori relents. "All right. I have to be at the hospital at seven to visit my grandmother, but I'll listen. Wait in the back room while I close up shop."

By the time she joins Robin in the office, a feast that only a foreigner could have assembled is laid out on the low table. Japanese grilled chicken skewers, Chinese potstickers, spicy eggplant, crab croquettes, seaweed salad, and two kinds of cake—chocolate and green tea—plus a tall can of Premium Malts. The outlandish combination would never appear on a Japanese menu, but after Nori fetches dishes and chopsticks to satisfy her sense of decency, she surrenders to the decadence, helping herself to specialties from six famous makers. She hasn't eaten this well since before her grandmother became ill, and it must have showed, because as she sets aside her third bare skewer, she catches Robin observing her with a small crooked smile.

"Sorry," Nori says, swallowing a mouthful of yakitori. She guiltily nudges the plates of food closer to Robin. "I'm eating more than my share. I didn't realize how hungry I was." Reluctantly, she reaches for her purse. "How much do I . . . ?"

"Nothing. You don't owe me anything. I—" She winces. "I'm sorry I had anything to do with landing you in so much trouble." Then she startles Nori by scrambling to her feet, nearly upsetting the table.

"*Moshiwake gozaimasen! Moshiwake gozaimasen!*" she cries, bowing as stiffly and deeply as a fallen pop idol.

"Hey, no, stop it." This is too embarrassing. "Sit down. Please. Don't say that." The absurd level of formality is way out of line, but

Nori sees the look on Robin's face. She actually means to be sorry, not insulting. "You don't have to apologize, all right? And certainly not like *that*."

"Like what?"

"Like . . . I don't know . . . a politician caught with his pants down." As Robin self-consciously folds herself back onto her cushion, Nori gives in to her curiosity. "Is that the way people apologize in your country?"

"No!" Robin gives a nervous laugh. "But . . . isn't that how you do it here?" Now she sounds worried. "I mean, that's the right phrase, isn't it? The one they use on TV?"

"You learned to apologize by watching TV?"

"Well," Robin cringes. "Sort of. I mean, I took four years of classical Japanese in college—had to, so I could study medieval Japanese literature—but as soon as I got here, I found out it was completely useless for talking to real people. I can read *The Tale of Genji* in the original, but when I tried to order a beer, everyone would burst out laughing. Finally, someone explained I wasn't exactly making mistakes, but only poets from the 1700s talked like that. From then on, I made myself watch TV for two hours every night: news, high school dramas, gangster movies, anything but period pieces. I guess it worked, because now I can usually order a bowl of noodles without being the funniest foreigner in the room." She grimaces. "The only time I accidentally revert to medieval bard mode is when I meet clients for the first time." Shooting Nori an embarrassed look, she says, "That's why you thought I was an idiot the first time we met, isn't it? You didn't want Hikitoru being evaluated by someone who couldn't even speak normal Japanese."

"No, of course not," Nori quickly replies. Then she admits, "Well, maybe a little. But I thought you were doing it on purpose. To put me in my place. Which," she concedes, "I deserved. I thought because you weren't Japanese, you couldn't possibly know anything about, uh . . ."

". . . an obscure Edo Period potter named Yoshi Takamatsu? If it makes you feel any better, there are only about five foreigners who do.

And I was wrong to be offended that you didn't know I was one of them."

Robin tops up Nori's beer, then Nori surprises herself by taking the can from her and returning the favor.

"Thanks." Robin's mouth quirks up at the corner. "Shall we start over?"

She raises her glass, and after a slight hesitation, Nori does too. They sip, then Robin shifts to a more comfortable position and asks, "Are you ready to hear how we might be able to make the police case against you go away?"

Nori sets down her glass and says, "I'm listening."

"Okay." Robin takes a deep breath. "Anzai-san is threatening to prosecute you for 'intent to sell stolen goods,' right?"

"That's what he says."

"But what if he doesn't know who the goods were stolen *from*? Or when?" She explains how she went to Shigaraki and discovered that Hikitoru had originally been stolen from the potter himself, more than sixty years before it was given to Senkō-ji. That Yakibō had made Uchida-*bōsan*'s ancestor promise to make an offering with it on his behalf, but the tea bowl had disappeared before the priest could fulfill that vow. That Uchida-*bōsan* has a document corroborating this story, but it can't be made public until after he performs the ceremony that his ancestor promised the dying potter."

She leans in.

"But what if Hikitoru was returned to Uchida-*bōsan* just long enough for him to do what he has to do? He doesn't need to own the tea bowl, he just needs to use it to perform the ceremony. Once Yakibō's spirit is laid to rest, he can give Hikitoru back and show me his ancestor's document. It'll prove that Senkō-ji never really owned it, their claim on the tea bowl will disappear, and so will the charges against you."

"Do you really think that could work?"

"I'm sure of it. The thing is, I need to borrow Hikitoru and take it to Shigaraki to make that happen."

"Your boss will let you do that?"

"Not in a million years. But the ceremony needs to be performed before Monday, or they'll arrest you and hand Hikitoru over to the head priest at Senkō-ji. Which neither of us wants, right? I think I've figured out a way to get it out of the office . . ." Her eyes slide away. "But I can't do it alone."

Ah. There it is. Now she knows why Robin made a special trip to Kappabashi, bearing a bag of expensive food.

"You want me to help you."

"It would be worth it, wouldn't it?"

"Unless we get caught."

"Which we won't. Look, I've worked at Fujimori Fine Art for over three years, and I know their security systems inside and out. If we 'borrow' it tomorrow, I can take it to Uchida-*bōsan* first thing Saturday morning, and have it back in the safe before anyone arrives for work Monday morning. If you agree to help me, we can work out the details tonight."

Robin is trying to keep the pleading from her voice, but Nori can hear it, and she doesn't understand why the art assistant is willing to commit what is—no matter how she tries to pass it off as "borrowing"—grand theft. Robin Swann has something important riding on this, something she's not telling. Until Nori finds out what it is, she isn't about to get into any more trouble than she's already in.

"No," she says. "Unless you tell me why you're really doing it."

Robin flushes.

She's right. There *is* another reason. She sips her beer and waits.

Haltingly, Robin begins to explain. Her unfinished doctorate, her dream of studying Saburo's poetry instead of working as Hashimoto's pottery-testing minion. Her stalled life in Japan. The loneliness of being a stranger in a strange land, but how little awaits her back in America if she doesn't get her degree.

"And then you walked into my office with Hikitoru," she says. "If I can connect it to Saburo's *Eight Attachments* and those empty boxes of Uchida's, I can write a paper that will change Japanese poetry scholarship forever. And," she adds, a little shame-faced, "after they give me my doctorate, I'll be able to quit my job as a lab slave and get paid to do what I love instead." She drains the last of her beer, then sets down her empty glass with a twisted smile. "So. Now you know everything. Not such a selfless do-gooder after all, am I? Feel free to kick me out now."

"Why?" Nori says.

Robin looks up, surprised.

"My grandmother taught me never to trust people who claim they're doing something for noble reasons." She divides the last of the beer between their glasses. "But self-interest? That I understand." She picks up her glass. "So, what's the plan?"

48.

N ori closes her eyes, takes a moment to gather her thoughts as the elevator rockets to the twenty-second floor. Head down, don't look up at the cameras. She nervously tightens her grip on the ordinary Shigaraki-ware tea bowl she'd found in the back room when she was looking for Hikitoru, and prays that the receptionist won't recognize her in the mom-like black dress and wig that had been left behind in her parents' abandoned room, relics from the funerals and other occasions when her mother had found it expedient to appear in a conservative black bob rather than her usual bleached curls.

The doors open on the Fujimori Fine Art lobby. It's impossible to avoid glancing nervously at the graying uniformed guard who had attempted to inspect her carrying cloth when she was here before, but she makes it across the plush carpet and speaks her lines to the receptionist without any further blunders, remembering to identify herself as Ai Tanaka, the forgettable name that's on her visitor badge.

When Robin appears, she's wearing the white lab coat again.

"Good morning." Her coconspirator bows deeply. "Are you the

esteemed visitor who hailed our humble organization from the lobby, with a request to authenticate an Edo Period tea bowl?"

"Yes," Nori replies.

"On behalf of the executive director, I extend our thanks for this generous opportunity," Robin continues. "We would very much like to examine your tea bowl, but I fear you have caught my humble self in the midst of some important tests in the lab. I deeply apologize for not being able to give you my undivided attention at this moment, but if you will forgive me for monitoring the equipment while we speak, I can examine your admirable tea bowl there."

Nori murmurs her agreement and follows her down the hall.

So far, so good. She watches as Robin swipes her keycard outside a white room with workbenches lining three walls. As they cross the gray industrial carpet, she manages not to look up at the cameras glaring down at her from all four corners, but it feels like being at the beach without any sunscreen. They aim for the white counter across the room, which is cluttered with glass labware, squeeze bottles labeled with chemical names, tiny power tools, and an assortment of electronic probes that Nori can't even begin to guess the purpose of. A collection of Bizen-ware teacups occupies much of the workspace, along with one object she recognizes: Hikitoru's wooden box.

Robin flips the notebook closed and pushes aside a pair of measuring calipers to make room to unwrap the bowl, then takes the box from Nori and pries off the lid. Taking out the ordinary Shigaraki bowl, she removes its gold brocade wrapper and gives it a cursory once-over. Is obviously not impressed.

"I'm sorry to disappoint you, Tanaka-san," she says, for the benefit of the security cameras, in case they capture sound as well as video. "This bowl wasn't made in the Edo Period. I'm afraid it's a modern piece."

"How do you know?" Just like they practiced. Don't overdo it. "How do you know, without testing it?"

"I've authenticated hundreds of pieces of pottery, Miss Tanaka. I know a modern tea bowl when I see one. For one thing..." Robin hefts it. "It's too heavy." Flips it over. "And there's a potter's mark, which means it's not old enough to be from the Edo Period." She rewraps it in the gold brocade. "I'm sorry it's not what you hoped it would be."

Now come the lines Nori would never have the nerve to speak in real life.

"Nothing you've told me is proof. Would it be possible to get a second opinion? From your superior, perhaps?"

Offended, Robin replies, "I can't waste her—I mean, that's completely unnecessary. Look, if you don't believe me, I can prove it."

With the brocade-wrapped decoy in one hand, she crosses to a black-hooded machine in the corner.

"This thermo-luminescence chamber measures the accumulated radiation a ceramic piece has absorbed since it was made," she explains. "The older a piece is, the brighter it glows. A tea bowl made centuries ago should have visible luminescence."

Last night, Robin had explained what thermo-luminescence testing actually is—the analysis is done by scraping a tiny sample from the piece and affixing the dust to slides read by an array of equipment sitting at the other end of the counter, not by looking at it inside the apparatus shrouded by a big, black hood. The hooded device is a tabletop photo booth, used to shoot authentication details under controlled lighting. But if Robin is ever questioned about the security footage, she'll say this was the quickest ruse she could think of to get rid of a walk-in attempting to pass off a cheap modern piece as something more valuable.

She flips a switch on the photo booth and takes the ordinary Shigaraki bowl inside. Unwraps it.

"I should have a reading in . . . ah! I knew it. There isn't the faintest glow coming off this tea bowl." She emerges and invites Nori to take her place. "See?"

Inside the hood, all Nori can see are the decoy and Hikitoru, which Robin had placed inside to photograph before she arrived. She nervously flips it over, checks the foot. No security sensor. Good. Robin must have found the right solvent. She backs out.

"All right. I can see it's not glowing." Time to be irritated, defensive. "Tests can be wrong, you know."

"Not these tests. Our equipment is extremely accurate."

Robin ducks back inside and wraps Hikitoru in the gold brocade from the other bowl. She emerges and packs it into the box belonging to the decoy, then hands it to Nori.

"I regret to say, this is not the sort of piece we can represent."

Wilted with faux disappointment, Nori follows Robin back out to the lobby.

A different guard has come on duty while they were in the lab. A young man, with a military haircut. He steps between Nori and the elevator with a crisp bow.

"I'm sorry, Miss, but all packages leaving our security area must be inspected."

"That's all right, uh," Robin reads his nametag, "Hato-san. I'm Robin Swann, Hashimoto-san's assistant. I'll vouch for Miss Tanaka. I was with her the whole time she was inside the security gate." She pushes the elevator button.

The guard regards her impassively for a moment, then turns to Nori.

"I'm afraid I must insist. Company policy. If you'd be so kind . . . ?" He reaches for the box in her hands.

Oh no. Nori was afraid this would happen. What are they going to do when he—

"Allow me," Robin commands, intercepting the bundle. "I wouldn't want to be held responsible if you drop it," she adds, using her haughtiest Art Expert voice. "The only thing in this box is the tea bowl Miss Tanaka brought with her. But if you *insist*, I'll show you it's a Shigaraki red clay bowl with gray glaze, from the Sakamoto kiln, just like it says on the lid."

Robin shows the guard the kiln stamp on the box, then opens it and peels back one corner of the brocade to give him a glimpse of Hikitoru's red clay and grayish glaze.

"See?" She tucks it in again, begins rewrapping the box. "Unfortunately, this one isn't an example of their Edo-era work. I wish it were."

The elevator pings.

Robin raises an eyebrow. "Are we done here?"

The guard bows and retreats.

"Thank you for coming, Miss Tanaka," Robin says, handing Hikitoru back to Nori. "I'm sorry to disappoint you."

The doors eclipse their mutual farewell bows. Nori exhales, but her pulse is still hammering.

Hold it together. Almost there. Robin will go back to the lab now, pack the decoy tea bowl in Hikitoru's box and lock it in the safe. It matches Hikitoru's description closely enough that if the guard who performs the random weekend security checks opens the box, he'll mark a Shigaraki-ware tea bowl as present and accounted for.

The doors part.

Shoulders back, chin up, Nori returns her visitor badge at the gleaming hardwood desk, and walks Hikitoru out through the doors, to freedom.

49.

Present-Day Japan

SATURDAY, APRIL 12

Shigaraki

F our hours, four trains, and two bottles of green tea later, Robin gathers her empties and steps onto the platform at Shigaraki Station. Clutching the carrying cloth with Hikitoru inside, she squints in the mid-morning sun. Up before dawn, she didn't dare sleep on the train, all too aware she was holding her future in her lap.

She pushes the tea bottles into the recycle bin, stops in the last ladies' room she can be sure of for a while, then makes her way to the curb outside. Stops to fill her lungs with fresh mountain air. It's a beautiful day, and that feels like a good omen. The sky is a clear and promising blue, the air warmer than when she was last here. She studies her phone map, planning to walk the kilometer and a half to Uchida-*bōsan*'s temple, when a boxy, compact car rolls up and stops at the curb.

"Swann-san?"

The king-sized priest is leaning toward her across the passenger seat, calling to her through the open window.

"Good morning! Want a ride?"

She finds herself grinning in reply, and not just at the prospect of catching a lift. There's something about the genial priest that gladdens her heart, and as she pulls open the passenger door, she's struck with a giddy premonition that this will be a day she'll remember for the rest of her life.

"Thank you," she says, folding herself gingerly into the small car. It sags slightly beneath her, but although it looks much too small to accommodate two larger-than-average passengers, it's surprisingly spacious inside.

"It's great not to have to slouch, isn't it?" Uchida says, as she cautiously straightens her spine and discovers her head doesn't bump the roof. He pats the dashboard. "Looks like a sake crate on wheels, but that's a small price to pay for headroom, don't you think?"

They exchange smiles, sharing a moment of outlier solidarity before he drops his gaze to the bundle in her lap.

"Is that it?" he asks.

"Yes. As promised."

"I was surprised to get your message," he admits, putting the car in gear. "How did you convince your boss to return Hikitoru without the proof you said you'd need? You must be the most persuasive woman in all of Japan."

"Trust me," she says, with a short laugh. "You don't want to know."

She'd thought long and hard about how much to tell him. In the end, she'd decided not to burden him with the questionable means she'd used to get the tea bowl here today. She doesn't want to give him any reason not to perform the ceremony that's the key to gaining access to his ancestor's document. What he doesn't know won't hurt him. The moment that tea bowl is back in the office safe on Monday morning, it'll be as if it had never been gone.

He regards her thoughtfully.

"However you did it, thank you. Have you eaten?" he asks, before turning onto the street.

She thinks about the two bottles of green tea she'd drunk on the train, but she has too many butterflies in her stomach to eat now.

"I'm fine. Maybe we'll have time for lunch afterward, before I catch my train back to Tokyo. Are we going straight to the temple?"

"No, we're headed to the kiln. I've arranged with the Hayashi family to conduct the ceremony where my ancestor was supposed to perform it."

Robin settles in for the drive, wondering aloud what the town had looked like the last time Hikitoru had passed this way. Uchida tells her that it now sprawls considerably closer to the kiln than in Yakibō's day, but as they pass through the outskirts, he points out a few landmarks that have been there since the potter's time. The noodle shop where she'd wolfed down her lunch on that first day had begun as an itinerant vendor's cart, back in Edo times. The rice fields by the riverbank had been under cultivation by the same family since before Yakibō was born.

He clicks on the turn signal and Robin spots the track she'd walked, just a week ago. So much has changed in such a short time. The trees are now misted in green, the brown sticks poking from the bamboo have burst into bouquets of purple azaleas, and the twin tire tracks are now lined with a riot of yellow daffodils on either side.

They bump slowly up the rutted lane. At the top, Uchida sets the parking brake and the little car rocks as they climb out. Robin stands holding Hikitoru while the priest rummages in the back seat.

"Would you mind carrying this?" he asks, handing her a shopping bag from the local sweets maker. He emerges with his cane and three bulging carrying cloths, not bothering to lock the car before they make their way to the house.

Mamoru and his mother must have been watching from the front window, because they're already standing in the doorway with welcoming bows. Mamoru has dressed in his Hanshin Tigers jersey for the occasion, and Mrs. Hayashi is looking prettier and less harried without smears of sunscreen all over her face. The puppy can be heard whining behind a distant door, as the little girl toddles into view. Her hair bow is slightly awry, but her company-is-coming pinafore is still unsullied.

Pleasantries are exchanged over tea. Robin has to muster every ounce of patience she possesses, wondering how Uchida can fail to feel as itchy as she does. The priest presents the sweets he brought, with a murmured deprecation of their worth, and shows no haste as they are opened and sampled—the mother showing her appreciation of the local rice cakes with compliments on his choice of maker, the children wolfing down more than they'd have been allowed if there hadn't been guests. The priest even accepts a third tea refill as the children run off to play, asking how Mr. Hayashi's newest *tanuki* figures are faring in the marketplace.

Finally, he hands his teacup back to Mamoru's mother, and while she clears the table, he unties the smallest blue carrying cloth. Inside are a bamboo whisk, an elegant carved case containing an L-shaped scoop, and a plain lacquerware tea caddy, gleaming with the patina of regular use.

Robin smiles. Why hadn't she guessed that the ritual Yakibō had requested would be a tea ceremony? No wonder it couldn't be performed without Hikitoru.

"If you wouldn't mind," Uchida says to Mamoru's mother, "some hot water, please? And a bowl? Doesn't have to be fancy."

The priest carefully wipes each utensil with a soft cloth and lines them up on the table while she fetches an iron teapot, beautifully wrought with a dragonfly design. As she sets it on a trivet at the priest's right hand, a ghost of steam curls up from its spout. She hands the priest a mixing bowl, which he places on the floor by his side.

Without another word, Uchida unwraps Hikitoru and sets it on the table. Mrs. Hayashi lets out a soft sigh, and Robin feels a shiver of anticipation, seeing it for the first time in the role it was designed for.

The priest closes his eyes, takes a deep breath, and exhales. They settle into the silence, allowing it to separate the ceremonial from the everyday. Then he opens his eyes, pours a splash of hot water into Hikitoru to warm it, swirls it, and dumps it into the mixing bowl. Pulling a folded handkerchief from his robe, he dries the tea bowl and measures out a scoop of vibrant green powder. Tips it in, adds a brief pour of hot water.

Robin is enjoying his skill at whipping it to a froth with the delicate bamboo whisk until she remembers what comes next. And panics. What if he offers the tea bowl to her? How is she supposed to hold it? How is she supposed to drink it? She knows there's a right way, but can't remember what it is. The only tea ceremony she's ever been to was a "cultural experience" performed for the foreigners studying the objects from Jakkō-in's treasure house by an elegant woman in a museum-worthy kimono. Robin had tried to experience the serenity that's supposed to flow from practicing the ancient art, but all she really felt was clumsy and ignorant. The organizer had assured them that nobody expected foreign students to know how to do things the right way, but it was painfully clear that there *was* a right way.

Now she's desperately trying to remember the details. This might be one of the defining moments of her life. She doesn't want to blow it.

Uchida sets down the whisk and holds up the bowl. With a gentle smile, he hands it to their hostess.

Whew.

As Mrs. Hayashi takes it between her hands, her face lights up. She examines the tea bowl, then looks over its rim at the priest, eyes shining.

"It's extraordinary."

"It is, isn't it?" He beams.

Bees buzz outside the open window, crows call and answer, the children's voices rise and fall as they play in the room next door. Mamoru's mother turns the tea bowl three times, admiring the swashes of glaze and the artful drips, noting its fine points with the practiced eye of someone who breathes kiln smoke every day.

"It's astonishing that something this beautiful was made by a blind man," she remarks, before setting its delicate rim to her lips. Closing her eyes, she takes a long, appreciative sip. Turns it, takes another from a different spot, does it once more. Then she gazes into Hikitoru's emptied depths with a satisfied smile and passes the bowl back to the priest.

He cleans it, repeats the ritual, offers it to Robin.

This time, she's ready. As she takes Hikitoru between her palms, she understands: nobody can fully appreciate a tea bowl until they use it as intended. With tea inside, it's warm, almost alive. The bright green *matcha* shimmers like a jewel in its red clay and ash-glazed setting.

She turns it full circle, marveling at how every splash and spatter of molten ash tells the story of its birth in the kiln. She lifts it to her lips, and the tea swirls into her mouth with an intensity that makes her feel more alive than she's ever felt. Turn, sip. Turn, sip. The shape of the rim fits her mouth like a lover's kiss. Saburo himself might have drunk tea from this bowl! Yakibō too. Happiness flowers and sparkles within her as the experience connects her with them across the centuries. When she finally lowers Hikitoru to take a last look at the green pool of crackled glaze at the bottom, it shines like a memory of the tea, a dream caught in amber.

She raises her eyes to meet Uchida's, and the corners of his crinkle, enjoying her moment of revelation. She hadn't expected to be moved by the ceremony—had, in fact, been looking forward to its conclusion, so she could study the all-important document—but now she wishes this sublime feeling could stretch on and on.

But it can't. Uchida is waiting. Reluctantly, she hands Hikitoru back.

"Well," he says, breaking the spell. "I believe old Hikitoru was happy to be used again, don't you?"

"Yes. And thank you," Mrs. Hayashi bows low over the table. "Forgive me for saying so, but I'm glad it wasn't found until now, so I could drink from it, just once in my life."

The priest returns her bow, then he rinses the tea bowl and wipes it dry, as if he were washing nothing more precious than the lunch dishes. He cleans the rest of the utensils with the same casual, unhurried movements, then reboxes Hikitoru, stowing everything back in the carrying cloths. Heaving himself upright with his cane, he thanks Mrs. Hayashi for allowing him to fulfill his nine-times-great-grandfather's vow. Looping the two unopened parcels over his other arm, he asks Robin to hand him Hikitoru.

"That's okay," she says. "You've got your hands full. I can carry it."

He smiles.

"No, why don't you wait here and enjoy another cup of tea? I'll be back before you know it."

"Back? From where?"

"There's one more thing I need to do before my obligation is satisfied." He gently takes the tea bowl from her. "It shouldn't take long. The sutra is short."

Mamoru's mother leads the priest out through the kitchen and Robin trails them as far as the back door, gnawing at her lip as the solitary figure stomps off toward the woods. She turns to Mamoru's mother.

"I'm sorry, but I don't think Uchida-*bōsan* understands how nervous this makes me. Hikitoru is on loan from the company I work for, and I'm responsible for it. I know it's important for him to chant his sutras, but I'm not supposed to let it out of my sight. If you'll excuse me . . ."

She slips out the door before Mrs. Hayashi can object, and strides up into the woods after the priest.

He's not hard to follow, having no reason to muffle the crunching and swishing of his passage through the knee-high bamboo encroaching on the path. Robin stays back far enough to make sure that the rustling of her own passage doesn't reach his ears, but when he unexpectedly halts before the hollow gingko where she and Mamoru paid their respects, she turns to stone where she stands, hoping he won't turn around. Uchida merely bows his head, though, giving the old gods their due, then continues on his way. He slows as he enters the clearing where Mamoru found the pottery shards, and sets his burdens on the ground by the flat boulder. He opens the pumpkin-sized one, revealing the carved wooden drum that's struck to punctuate the chanting of the sutras.

Then he unties the smaller bundle, unwinding the hand towel that's wrapped around the contents. A glazed clay bowl disappears into the former sumo wrestler's ham-sized fist. Robin hastily ducks behind a venerable pine as he doubles back, limping to the bank of the nearby stream. Hopping a little and stretching his stiff leg out to the side, he braces himself and dips water from the racing rivulet. Some sloshes out as he maneuvers to stand, but there's still enough to pour over the boulder in the clearing, leaving its pale granite surface wet and gleaming. Then he sets the dipping bowl on the moss and unpacks Hikitoru.

He arranges the tea bowl front and center on the glistening rock, then picks up the drum. Drawing himself up to his full height, he stands for a long moment, still and silent as an ancient cedar. The tree limbs overhead dance with the wind, casting coins of light all around him as he composes himself before beginning the chant.

Tock.

The single drumbeat echoes through the forest and dies away. Then the Sutra of True Faith rings out in Uchida's deep and sonorous voice. Rising and falling, rising and falling, the hypnotic cadence fills the space between the trees. Robin has been resisting the urge to celebrate until everything is said and done, but as the verses build toward the moment when the last barrier to her shining new future falls away, she can no longer suppress a surge of joy.

Tock.

Arm still raised, Uchida stands there like a statue, allowing the final beat to fade into the forest.

A bird twitters in the distance as he lowers the drum and picks up Hikitoru. As he holds it between his hands and raises it like a chalice, Robin feels an almost-physical connection between herself, the priest, the tea bowl, the universe—

Then he hurls it.

Clay explodes against granite, shattering the silence. Time seems to slow as Robin watches shards of the priceless cultural treasure bounce off the rock and arc through the air in all directions, into the bushes, onto the moss.

She doesn't hear herself scream, but Uchida spins around, startled. "Swann-san?"

"No!" she wails, flailing toward him through the bracken. "No!"

Falling to her knees, she snatches up one of the pieces. Sharp corners, raw edges. Bright ochre clay, like the margins of a wound. She can't believe what her eyes are telling her, but she's holding the truth in her hands.

Hikitoru is gone.

Destroyed.

And not just the tea bowl. Her career. Her future. Her life.

"Why?" She raises her stricken face to Uchida. "Why didn't you tell me?"

"I couldn't." He shakes his head sadly. "You'd have stopped me."

"Yes! I would have!" She takes a ragged breath. "*Why?*"

"Because that's what Yakibō made my ancestor promise to do for him," the priest replies, "so his spirit could escape the cycle of rebirth. The desire to get back the tea bowl that had been stolen from him was his last remaining attachment to this world. And breaking Hikitoru—the tea bowl he made to represent that 'attachment'—was his final wish."

"I don't understand. I don't—" Tears brim and overflow, twin tracks burning down her cheeks.

It can't be returned to the safe now. She'll be accused. Arrested. She and Nori Okuda will be locked away until they are old women. She doubles over, weeping.

Uchida moves around her quietly, rummaging in the bushes, picking up the pieces of what used to be Hikitoru.

When the ugly sounds being ripped from her chest finally quiet and she's able to open her swollen eyes a slit, seven fragments are lined up before her on the moss.

"The breaks are clean," says Uchida in the compassionate voice he must use with the bereaved. "Now that Yakibō's spirit has been released, I believe the tea bowl can be mended. I know an artist who still knows how to do it the old way, with gold."

"It doesn't matter," she says, in a dull voice. "By then, I'll be in jail."

"What do you mean, you'll 'be in jail'?" He frowns. "I know you're upset, but it's not a crime to break a tea bowl."

"It is if it's stolen."

"Stolen? What are you talking about? For the first time in hundreds of years, it's *not* stolen. It's back where it belongs, and has fulfilled the purpose it was made for. It was never truly owned by that temple in Tokyo, and that's the truth. I thought you believed me."

"I do." She hangs her head. "But my boss didn't. She wanted more proof. So, I . . . I borrowed it. Without permission. I thought that as long as I put it back in the safe before anyone missed it, you could perform your ceremony. After you did what you needed to do, you could show me your ancestor's document and I'd use it to convince my boss that Hikitoru should be returned to you. Then I could study it and write my paper, and everyone would be happy. But I never thought . . ."

The blood drains from Uchida's face.

"Why didn't you tell me?" His despair now mirrors her own. "If I'd known, I wouldn't have . . ."

He sits down hard on the boulder that had served as both altar and instrument of execution, burying his face in his hands.

Robin slumps on the moss, heartsick and spent. A lone cuckoo calls. The drone of a distant airplane grows louder, recedes. A breeze stirs the ferns. The small sounds of the forest emerge around them, then abruptly fall silent as Uchida grabs his cane and rises to his feet.

"How many people know what Hikitoru looked like?" he asks.

Without waiting for an answer, he scoops up the dipping bowl, limps across the clearing to stand before her.

She climbs to her feet and he passes her the bowl. The familiar shape settles into her palms and for a moment, she thinks this was all a bad dream. He hasn't destroyed Hikitoru after all.

But there are more "dragonfly eyes" in this one's unglazed clay, and although the dipping bowl too settles into her hands as if made for them, it's ever so slightly rounder. It's not Hikitoru.

But it *is* another Yakibō tea bowl. She stares at it in disbelief.

"Where did you get this?"

"From my nine-times-great-grandfather. Remember how I told you that nothing survived the next firing after Yakibō died? My

ancestor suggested to Hattsan that they try to fulfill the vow by substituting a different piece of Yakibō's pottery for the missing Hikitoru,
and that's when he learned about the rejects. The apprentice told him
that Yakibō made many tea bowls before he chose the one to represent
his 'attachment.' After he narrowed the candidates down to three, he
offered the others to the gods and waited a while before breaking them,
in case they wanted him to choose a different one. The apprentice led
my ancestor to the *kami-sama's* hollow tree, and they found two tea
bowls stacked inside. They broke one in the failed exorcism. That," he
nods at the one in her hands, "is the other."

Robin looks down at the tea bowl, shocked. This was a *reject*?

"I know it's not the one that the potter chose to be Hikitoru,"
Uchida says. "But it could have been. I was thinking that maybe . . ."
He purses his lips, struggling to overcome his discomfort with decep-
tion, "you could substitute this one instead. It's not like you'd be trying
to pass off a fake. It really is a Yakibō tea bowl, and I believe it was
made to represent the same 'attachment' as Hikitoru. That's all your
boss cares about, right?" He peers anxiously into her face, searching
for a sign of hope.

Robin shifts into an island of sunlight, holding the exquisite tea
bowl that Uchida had used as a humble water dipper. It does have the
same shape, the same delicate walls. It's made from the same red-ochre
clay, studded with the same tiny chips of white feldspar. If she tests a
new sample, swaps out the photos she took on Friday for shots of this
one, alters the description to fit . . .

Her shoulders sag. Who is she trying to kid? Eriko Hashimoto
is an expert in Japanese ceramics and she knows exactly what the
real Hikitoru looked like. The swashes of glaze, the constellations of
imperfections in the clay. Her boss won't be fooled, not for a second.
It's kind of Uchida to try to help, but unfortunately, the substitution
will never—

Then she looks up and sees the desolation on his face, knows that
he feels responsible for landing her in life-destroying trouble.

But it's not his fault, she thinks bitterly. It's mine. I allowed ambition to goad me into bending the rules. I cut corners that ought not to be cut. He shouldn't have to suffer for my failings.

"You're right," she says, arranging her mouth into something she hopes will pass for a smile. "I'm sure nobody will notice the small differences between them." She bows deeply, holding the bowl. "Thank you for your generosity, Uchida-*bōsan*."

Robin waves a brave and falsely hopeful farewell to the priest before stepping onto the train to begin her long trek back to Tokyo.

Finally, she can give in to sheer, unadulterated misery. Fortunately, the train isn't crowded this afternoon, so her fellow passengers can give a wide berth to the alarming foreigner who's hunched into the seat by the window, dabbing at her blotchy face and running nose with a wad of damp toilet tissue.

But wallowing in despair doesn't help Robin feel better, it only conjures up unpleasant variations on what will happen next if she can't figure out how to get herself and Nori Okuda out of this mess. For the next four hours, towns and rice fields zip past unseen as she racks her brain, cobbling together plans, shooting them down.

She's no closer to a solution by the time she stands, swaying and exhausted, on the local that drops her at Tawaramachi, the station nearest to where Nori lives. She drags herself to Kappabashi Street under a blindingly bright full moon, which makes the steep flight of stairs up to the Okuda flat seem even darker. She's running on fumes, but Nori is expecting her, and she can't put off telling her partner in crime the terrible truth. She rings the doorbell, wishing she could be anywhere but here.

All too swiftly, Nori is standing before her, vibrating with nerves. Her eyes latch onto Robin's nylon grocery bag.

"Did you get it? The document?"

"Yes. I took a photo. It's on my phone."

"Okay, good," Nori breathes a sigh of relief, missing the defeat in Robin's voice. She sets out a pair of guest slippers, then runs ahead to switch on the light in the main room.

"Come in, sit down," she calls over her shoulder, disappearing down the hall toward the kitchen. "I'll make us some tea."

The cord pull is still swinging over the low lacquer table as Robin drops onto the same floor cushion she'd occupied before. Dreading the next half hour more than she's dreaded anything in her life, she unties the cord from around Hikitoru's wooden box and frees the dipping bowl from Hikitoru's old wrapper. No point in delaying the inevitable. She sets it in the middle of the table.

Nori returns with the tea tray and deals out the Four Seasons cups and saucers, then takes her place across the table and pours. Full teacup in hand, her smile falters as she belatedly reads the disaster written on Robin's face.

"Is something wrong? What happened? Is there something wrong with the paper that's supposed to get Inspector Anzai off my back?"

"No, that's not the problem. It says exactly what Uchida-*bōsan* said it did. But . . ." she can't bear to look Nori in the eye, "while he was performing the ceremony, Uchida-*bōsan* broke Hikitoru."

"He . . . *what?*" Nori snatches up the dipping bowl. "Is it cracked? Where?" She examines it inside and out. "I don't see it." Puzzled, she flips it over.

"That's not it. That's not Hikitoru."

"What do you mean, it's not Hikitoru?" She stares at the bowl in her hand. "This is a *fake?*"

"Not . . . exactly. It was made by Yakibō too, but . . ."

Robin sets a Shigaraki sweets box on the table and lifts the lid. "*This* is Hikitoru."

Nori stares at the jumble of broken pottery and snatches up one of the fragments in disbelief. Her eyes shift back and forth between the sharp-edged piece in one hand and the unbroken tea bowl in the other, as Robin explains how the priest had smashed Hikitoru in the woods behind the Hayashi kiln, and tried to make things right by replacing it with Yakibō's reject Hikitoru, the tea bowl he'd used as a water dipper. By the time she finishes, the broken piece is clutched, forgotten, in Nori's curled fingers, her expression congealed into blank shock.

"I'm so sorry," Robin says, losing her battle with despair. "Ever since I left Shigaraki, I've been trying to think of a way out of this mess, but nothing works. Hikitoru might be able to be repaired, but there's no time, and if I try to pass this dipping bowl off as the real thing, my boss will spot it. I even thought of faking a robbery, but the company's security systems are too complicated. Too much could go wrong. If I got caught, we'd be in even worse trouble than we are now. I just . . . I can't—" Her voice breaks. She buries her face in her arms and sobs, "I'm so sorry. I'm so sorry."

Cats squabble in the alley outside, a distant siren wails, but no words of forgiveness come from Nori. And Robin doesn't blame her. Not one bit.

When she finally raises her head, Nori's gaze is fixed on the dipping bowl, but she doesn't look as angry as she deserves to be. Obviously, it hasn't hit her yet.

Not knowing what else to do, Robin begins to gather up the discarded wrapping and cord.

"I don't get it," Nori finally says.

Robin wilts, not sure she has the strength to go through it again. "What don't you get?"

"Why this is the end of the world."

If Robin could sink any lower, she would. In a defeated voice, she explains again. "Hikitoru is broken. We can't put it back in the safe now. Once they discover it missing on Monday morning, all hell is going to break loose."

"Yeah, but . . . do you really think they'll guess this one isn't the real Hikitoru? Because I sure wouldn't. If my grandmother were here, she'd say, 'they'll buy it if you sell it, sweetheart.' I mean, the way I see it, all we have to do is—"

Her words bounce off Robin's ears, the dipping bowl swims in and out of focus. It's not Hikitoru and never will b—

"What time did you get up this morning?"

"What?" Robin blinks.

"Not to be rude or anything," Nori says, eyeing her critically, "but you look like you just fought ten bouts in the sumo ring. And you didn't win. We've got thirty-six hours to come up with a plan, but you're not going to be much help until you get some sleep." In a kinder voice, she adds, "If you're too beat to make it home, I could pull out my parents' old futon . . ."

Robin is suddenly aware of how sore her feet are from walking in the "good" pumps she'd put on a lifetime ago, and how much her back aches from eight hours hunched in a train seat. She's more tired than she's ever been in her life. Maybe things *will* look better in the morning, if she faces them in clean clothes and sneakers. She swipes her ravaged face on her sleeve.

"Thanks for the offer," she replies, trying to muster a smile. "But I should go home. Take a shower. And . . . I've got this goldfish. It's probably pretty hungry by now."

"Okay," Nori says collecting the tea things. "Meet back here in the morning? Early?"

Robin staggers to her feet. "I'll bring coffee."

"Make mine black. And would you mind picking up some rice balls from the little supermarket on the way from the subway station? The tuna ones are the best."

50.

Present-Day Japan

SUNDAY, APRIL 13

Tokyo

N ori yawns, lifting the new tea bowl and the carton of pottery shards from the secret hiding place. She carries them down the hall to the kitchen, where dawn is just beginning to pinken the curtains hanging over the tiny window. Kneeling on a worn cushion, she places the tea bowl atop the once-bold oilcloth on the low table, its plaid now scrubbed down to pale reds, yellows, and greens. Then she lines up the pieces of Hikitoru, contemplating them like a jigsaw puzzle. The doorbell peals.

Robin is on the landing with two coffees and a supermarket bag. Her eyes are still bruised with fatigue, but she's standing straighter. She greets Nori with a weak smile.

"Good thing we decided to meet early. A peewee baseball team came into the market right behind me and hoovered up the rest of the tuna rice balls."

Robin follows her to the kitchen and her smile fades a little, at the sight of the pottery shards. They sit and sort out the coffees—white for Robin, black for Nori.

"*Itadakimasu,*" they both mutter, blessing their rice balls as they unwrap them.

"Thanks," Nori says, "for breakfast. And for getting a photo of that thing the priest's grand-whatever wrote. At least I won't have to worry about Inspector Anzai hauling me off to jail tomorrow."

"Don't thank me until we figure out how to make that permanent," Robin warns, taking an exploratory sip of coffee, then a bigger one when she finds it cool enough to drink. "The thing is . . ." She puts down her cup. "I've been thinking about this all night, and once we get you off the hook for 'intent to sell,' there's no reason you should share the blame. For any of this. Unless you looked up at one of the security cameras while we were in the lab, you can walk away. There's no reason for us both to go to jail."

"There's no reason for *either* of us to go to jail."

Nori balls up her *onigiri* wrapper and takes it to the trash. She returns, looking down at the dipping bowl.

"I still can't believe this isn't Hikitoru. I'd never have known if you hadn't told me. Why would it be so impossible to swap this one for the one that got broken?"

"My boss will know. Instantly. She's one of the top Japanese ceramics experts in the country. If she doesn't spot the differences in the clay and glazing pattern, she'll know by the shape. Even I could tell. The moment she picks it up, she'll know it's not the real one."

"Well, maybe it's not *the* Hikitoru, but it's *a* Hikitoru," Nori argues. "It's at least the bronze medalist, maybe even the silver. Passing it off as the first-choice Hikitoru wouldn't even be a crime."

"Hashimoto-san still won't let us get away with it."

"What's she going to do, tell her boss?"

"For starters. Then the police."

"As my grandmother would say if she were here, 'so what'? Your word against hers."

"Yeah, but who would believe a lowly authentication assistant over the Japanese Ceramics Expert?"

"Believing isn't proof."

"Until they check the pictures. Or someone who saw the real Hikitoru backs her up."

"Like who? Who's seen it, besides your boss?"

Robin sips her coffee, thinking. "I'm sure she showed it to Fuji-mori-san."

"Is his eye as good as hers?"

"No," Robin admits. "He's not actually an art expert at all. I bet all he saw when he looked at Hikitoru was a fat stack of ten-thousand-yen notes. He'd believe Hashimoto-san over me, of course, but you're right—he wouldn't swear to it. Not to the police. But let's not forget that Inspector Anzai got a good look too."

"I bet all he saw was 'Case Closed' stamped across that old police report, though," Nori counters. "He wasn't paying much attention to what Hikitoru actually looked like, just that its size and shape matched the description. This bowl is slightly rounder, but I measured it last night before I went to bed, and it's less than a half centimeter off in each direction. Close enough to pass. What about the head priest of Senkō-ji, though? Do you think they showed it to him?"

"No, by the time Fujimori got involved, Hikitoru was under lock and key in the lab, and there are no names on the sign-out. I'm pretty sure they did their deal over the phone."

"Anybody else?"

"That's it, I think."

"Okay." Time for another rice ball. Unwrapping it, Nori asks, "What about photos? Does your boss have photos of the old Hiki-toru?"

"No. I just took the authentication shots on Friday, and haven't put them in my report yet."

"Didn't you take some the day I first came in?"

"You're right." Robin grimaces. "But I could delete those from the intake file and substitute new ones."

"Good. What about the internet? I searched pretty hard, but . . ."

"I did too, until I realized that if there were any photos of it out there, some Yakibō scholar would have pounced on them long before now."

"What about books?"

"Hard to know." Robin ponders the question. "Photography hadn't been invented when Hikitoru began gathering dust in Senkō-ji's treasure house in 1788," she says, thinking aloud. "And if the temple had photos, wouldn't they have been given to the police when the theft was reported? The only time pictures could have been taken was after it was stolen in 1945. Do you know who had it before your grandmother got ahold of it?"

Nori hasn't told a living soul that she knows the identity of the thief, but she can hardly keep that from Robin now. She opens her mouth to answer, but it's surprisingly hard to admit.

"Nobody took pictures of it after it left the temple," she says. Maybe Robin will just take her word for it.

"How do you know?"

Crap. Nori rises and crosses to the small window.

"I'm sure there aren't any photos," she says, "because it went straight from the temple's treasure house to ours. My grandmother is the one who stole it."

"Your *grandmother* was the thief?"

Nori hangs her head. Being related to a thief is almost as shameful as being one yourself.

"But . . . that's the best news I've ever heard!"

She whips around to find Robin grinning for the first time since she returned.

"I was afraid that there might have been a whole string of shady owners between 1945 and now," she explains, "and we'd be lucky if they were just thieves, not drug runners or arms traffickers. I was worried they might come after Hikitoru, once they hear it's surfaced. I can't tell you how relieved I am that your grandmother had it the whole time."

Sounding more optimistic, Robin says, "Okay. Next steps." She picks up the dipping bowl and eyes it critically. "I need to go into the office this afternoon and delete all the photos I took of the other Hikitoru, and substitute shots of this one instead. And I should probably redo the thermo-luminescence testing too, so the numbers in the authentication report match the dipping bowl exactly."

"Is there time?"

"If I prepare the samples this afternoon and let them cure overnight, I could run the analysis before work tomorrow."

"What about the security sensor? You saved the one you took off Hikitoru, right?"

"I did, but," worry casts a small shadow, "I had a hard time finding the right solvent, so it got a little banged up while I was scraping it off. When the security chief takes it to the lab to remove it before the press conference, he'll know it's been tampered with."

"I don't think we need to be too worried about that," Nori says. "If you manage to convince your boss that Uchida-*bōsan*'s document raises too many questions about Hikitoru's ownership, there won't *be* a press conference."

51.

S omething buzzes as Robin steps through the security gate in the still-dark Fujimori Fine Art lobby. But it's not the alarm, it's her phone. Who would be messaging her at this hour of the morning? She excavates it from her bag. Uchida-*bōsan*? What's he doing up so early?

Swann-san,

I haven't been able to sleep all night, worrying about your meeting with your boss today. I deeply regret not insisting that you take the original documents supporting my temple's claim to the tea bowl, and since there's no time to messenger them now, I've decided to bring them myself. Right now, I'm standing on the platform at Shigaraki Station, waiting for the first train. I should be in Tokyo by 10:30. I hope that's not too late. I'll come straight to the address on your business card, unless it would be more convenient for you to meet me somewhere else. Let me know?

Uchida

Ten-thirty. That'll be cutting it close—the press conference is scheduled for two. But if she can delay talking to Hashimoto-san until he arrives, there should still be time to stop the handover.

Gratitude blooms. She hadn't realized how much she dreaded doing this alone. The priest's solid presence backing up the authenticity of the dipping bowl will be as much of a comfort as the evidence he's bringing.

She sends him a warm reply, thanking him and promising to postpone the meeting until he gets there. Then she unlocks the lab and gets to work.

After feeding the dipping bowl samples she'd left curing overnight into the thermo-luminescence tester, she perches on a lab stool, nipping at a cuticle, waiting for the machine to render the results. They finally pop up on the monitor and she scans them.

Just as she thought. They're so close to Hikitoru's, she could have used the old numbers and saved herself the trouble of running new tests. Still, it's a relief. She'll need all the ammunition she can get when she shows them to Hashimoto-san this morning. It hadn't been hard to pretend a confidence she didn't feel when Nori was coaching her in the art of salesmanship yesterday, but bluffing her way through the substitution while looking Hashimoto-san in the eye will be another matter.

She turns to her laptop and substitutes the new numbers for the old in the authentication report. Then she checks to make sure that the dipping bowl photos she came into the office to shoot yesterday were saved in place of the old ones in both the report and the intake form she'd filled out on the first day Nori brought Hikitoru to the office. All good. She deletes the old ones permanently from the hard drive. The report is now an airtight authentication of the dipping bowl that she'd switched into Hikitoru's box yesterday before locking it back inside the safe. If anyone insists on testing it, there will be nothing to fuel suspicions that this isn't the same tea bowl Nori brought in for authentication two weeks ago.

Now what? The only thing left to do is wait. She makes her way down the hall to her cubicle, flipping on the lights. How can she occupy herself until Uchida-*bōsan* arrives? Draping her jacket on the back of her chair, she switches on her computer and begins researching the proper way to put together a Japanese letter of resignation. If all goes well, she's going to need one when it's time to quit being a lab slave and launch her career as a Saburo scholar. When the prescribed phrasing is finally typed in, the lines formatted, and the envelope addressed, she still has two hours until the priest arrives, so she dives into proofreading a report for the head expert in the Buddhist Sculpture department. She has just hit "Print" when her phone buzzes. Could Uchida be early?

"*Moshi-moshi?*"

"Hashimoto here. I need you in my office right away."

Lack of pleasantries: not a good sign. She glances at the clock, and is surprised to see it's already past ten, but Uchida-*bōsan* won't be here for at least twenty minutes. She has to stall.

"Of course," she replies, crossing the room to straighten the printer paper as the first page of the Buddhist Sculpture report glacially emerges. "I'm in the middle of printing a report for Kato-san right now, but if you give me a few minutes, I'll—"

"No. Now." Click.

Uneasiness ratchets up to dread. She hadn't sent the Hikitoru authentication to her boss yet, but what if she jumped the gun? If she's already accessed the report, seen the pictures . . .

Armoring herself with fresh lipstick, she buttons her suit jacket. Spine straight, shoulders back, she marches down the hall to Hashimoto's office. She smooths her skirt, tugs her jacket into place, and knocks.

"Come in."

Her boss is at her desk, her face set in hard lines of disapproval. No need to ask why—the dipping bowl sits front and center, unwrapped.

"Sit down."

She does.

"Where is it?"

"Where is what?"

"The Yakibō tea bowl. Hikitoru."

She looks from her boss to the piece on her desk.

"I don't understand."

"I think you do. This," she nudges the dipping bowl toward Robin, "is not it."

"It's not?" Wrong, wrong, wrong. *Sell it, sweetheart.* "What do you mean?" she amends, fixing the dipping bowl with a puzzled look. "I just finished testing it early this morning. Have you seen my report?"

Her boss swivels her laptop so Robin can see the screen. The freshly fixed authentication document is zoomed in on the main photo.

"I don't understand." Robin glances back and forth between the picture and the real thing. "They look the same to me."

"Oh, they are. Which is how I know you're involved." Hashimoto picks up the dipping bowl, regarding it with a jaundiced eye. "Unless all the hidden impurities in a piece of centuries-old pottery spontaneously exploded in the safe over the weekend, this piece has far too many 'dragonfly eyes' to be Hikitoru." She turns it to display the offending side. "Where did you get this forgery?"

"It's not a forgery." That, at least, is the truth. "I ran the numbers, just this morning. It's an eighteenth-century tea bowl, made by Yoshi Takamatsu. Look at the test results. Compare them to his known works. The numbers don't lie."

"Since you're the one who put them there," Hashimoto says in a cutting voice, "I'm quite sure they do."

Raising her chin defiantly, Robin says, "You're welcome to send it out to an independent lab for testing, if you don't believe me."

"We don't have time for that."

"You'll just have to take my word for it, then."

"The word of a thief?"

She opens her mouth to protest, but Hashimoto is clicking open another window.

The CCTV footage from Friday plays. Paralyzed, Robin watches herself and Nori silently act out their parts in fuzzy black and white, substituting the decoy Shigaraki tea bowl for Hikitoru. Without the dialogue, it's far too easy to see what they're up to. How could she have thought this amateurish ruse would fool anybody?

"I don't know what you did with Hikitoru after you and your accomplice took it out of the office on Friday," Hashimoto says, "but you can either tell me where to find it, or I'll call Inspector Anzai and have him arrest you right now." She picks up her phone.

"No," Robin yelps. "Wait." Her own phone buzzes. Uchida. He's in the lobby. "I can . . . I can explain."

Hashimoto sits back, arms crossed.

"There's a man in the lobby right now who can back up what I'm about to tell you. A priest. He came this morning, from Shigaraki."

"The priest who claims that Hikitoru belongs to him?" Hashimoto scoffs. "He's hardly a disinterested party. For all I know, you're working together."

"We are, but not in the way you think. He's here to back up what I tried to tell you last week." *Stop reacting*, scolds Nori's grandmother. *Take the offensive*. Robin puts some conviction into her voice and says, "The discussion we really ought to be having, is why Mr. Fujimori is planning to hand over a culturally important property to someone who isn't the rightful owner. Hikitoru really was stolen long before it was given to Senkō-ji. Uchida-*bōsan* brought proof."

Hashimoto's lips thin to a skeptical line, but she lifts the receiver of the phone on her desk and calls reception.

"Is there a priest out there waiting to see me? I understand. Yes, she's with me. Please bring him back."

They sit in fraught silence until the receptionist knocks and announces the shaven-headed, sumo-sized figure filling the doorway in his crisp linen robes. One hand is wrapped around the head of his knobby cane, and the other grasps a tote bag with a long wooden scroll box poking from the top.

"*Hajimemashite*," he rumbles in his sonorous voice, bowing to Hashimoto, who rises to return the greeting. Then he turns to Robin and says, "Swann-san," with a reassuring smile. He takes the proffered seat, declines an offer of tea.

Hashimoto folds her hands before her.

"I apologize for being rudely direct, Uchida-*bōsan*, but we're scheduled to return the tea bowl Hikitoru to the head priest at Senkō-ji in three hours, and I hope you're here to tell me where it is. I also understand you feel that you have a claim to it. Perhaps you can show me the evidence you brought."

"Gladly," he says, drawing the scroll box from his bag. "With my own apologies for getting right to the point, are you familiar with my nine-times great grandfather's relationship with the potter, Yoshi Takamatsu?"

"Swann-san told me that he was the priest who conducted Yakibō's funeral service. That he claimed to have been entrusted with a deathbed wish to perform a ceremony using Hikitoru, but the tea bowl was missing when he tried to retrieve it. Miss Swann's theory," she casts a withering glance at Robin, "is that it was stolen by the poet Saburo."

"Yes," Uchida confirms, ignoring her tone and removing the scroll from its box. "That's exactly what happened, according to this document signed and sealed by my ancestor. When he realized he wouldn't be able to fulfill his vow before he died, he wrote this eyewitness account, including details of the offering he'd been asked to perform. It has been passed down from head priest to head priest through my family, until it—and the obligation it represents—came to rest with me." He rises to offer the scroll respectfully, with both hands, to Hashimoto.

The art expert receives it and inclines her head. "With your permission . . . ?"

He assents.

She raises her reading glasses, unfurls it. Her brows knit as she reads, the lengthening hush punctuated only by the ticking of the clock that Robin is usually too busy to notice. A gust of wind buffets the tall glass windows, and the room dims as a cloud blows in front of the sun.

The art expert gasps, whipping off her reading glasses to stare at the priest.

"He promised to *break* it?"

"Yes."

"That's not . . . that's not what *you* intend to do, is it?"

"No, it's not," he replies, face serene. "It's what I already did."

"*What?*" She blanches, and shoots to her feet. "But that's . . . you can't! Tell me you didn't!"

"I was merely fulfilling my vow," he said calmly, "using the tea bowl that was entrusted to my ancestor by the potter who made it. The only reason it survived this long was because the dying man was too sick to do it himself."

"That's completely beside the point!" the art expert sputters. "That tea bowl, it . . . it wasn't yours to break! This document," she flaps a dismissive hand at the scroll, "says nothing about giving the tea bowl to your ancestor."

"But this does." The priest reaches into his tote bag and pulls out a stiff envelope, passes it across the desk.

As Hashimoto slowly lowers herself back into her chair and extracts the fragile scrap of paper inside, Uchida explains, "That was written by my ancestor, at the blind potter's behest. Yakibō wasn't sure he'd be able to break his last 'attachment' before he died, but he wanted to make certain that his final wishes were respected and that nobody would prevent Hikitoru from being broken after he was gone. I don't know if the thief saw this note and ignored it, or dropped it unaware, but it was left behind when my ancestor discovered the tea bowl missing." He nods at the scrap of paper in Hashimoto's hands. "I'm sure you recognize Yakibō's seal. The one next to it belonged to my nine-times-great-grandfather. This document clearly gives whoever found Hikitoru the permission—and the obligation—to break that tea bowl on behalf of Yakibō's immortal soul."

The art expert's mouth is opening and closing, struggling to find the words to express her outrage and dismay.

He holds up a placating hand. "I understand why you're distressed,

Hashimoto-san. Swann-san's reaction was the same. Which is why I gave her a tea bowl to replace it, one that was fired in the same batch as Hikitoru, according to Yakibō's apprentice at the time. The tea bowl sitting on your desk is one that Yakibō might have chosen to represent his final 'attachment,' had he not settled on the one that I broke." He folds his hands across his mountainous bulk and nods at the dipping bowl. "From your company's point of view, nothing essential has changed. You're still in possession of a genuine Yoshi Takamatsu tea bowl that was made to represent the eighth of the 'attachments' that inspired the poet Saburo."

Hashimoto is still pale, but his words seem to be getting through, because the calculating crease has reappeared between her brows.

Robin stands and bows.

"Hashimoto-san, I sincerely apologize for surprising you with news like this. I know that Uchida-*bōsan*'s documents will have to be tested and investigated before you and Fujimori-san can acknowledge his ownership of Hikitoru, but I hope you'll agree that what we need to do right now is postpone that press conference."

Robin does a final save on the Bizen-ware report and sends it to the printer. Two o'clock has come and gone, and the press conference didn't happen. Fujimori-san is probably fuming in his office, after making a reluctant call to his would-be client at Senkō-ji. Across town, the head priest will be gnashing his teeth. Hashimoto-san probably got stuck with breaking the news to Inspector Anzai, and is undoubtedly packing up Uchida-*bōsan*'s documents and the dipping bowl to ship to the most nitpicky independent lab she can find.

Robin's phone buzzes. She checks the name on the screen and sighs. She's been expecting this call.

"Miss Swann. Could you come to my office, please?" Her boss's chilly tone turns the request into a command.

"Yes, ma'am, I'll be there as soon as I finish printing out the Bizen-ware report."

Hashimoto hesitates, but she must need that authentication badly enough to wait a few minutes, because she concedes, "All right. Bring it when you come."

Robin crosses to the printer, watching it spit out the last Fujimori Fine Art document that will ever bear her name. Leaving the pages to emerge on their own, she returns to her laptop to click open the letter of resignation. After inserting today's date, she queues it up to print after the Bizen-ware report.

While she waits, she looks around the tiny cubicle she's called home for the past three years, feeling a twinge of loss. There won't be much to pack. Just the photo of her team after their first crazy auction and the framed woodblock reproduction of Hasui's "Zōjōji Temple in a Snowstorm" that they'd given her for working around the clock to rush their authentications and save their butts, after the previous authenticator quit.

The printer wheezes to a halt, and she tidies the Bizen-ware report into a plastic sleeve, then looks over her *taishoku todoke* before stamping it with her seal and folding it into the envelope inscribed with the three characters for "formal letter of resignation." Slipping it into her purse, she walks down the hall and stops before Eriko Hashimoto's office. Knocks.

"Come in."

She enters, with a polite, "Please excuse me for intruding."

Her boss is sitting at her desk, hands folded, and she's not alone. Mr. Fujimori stands behind her, short and stout, his face so akin to the God of Thunder painted on the screen in the lobby that she'd have been stifling a "separated at birth" laugh if the situation hadn't been so grim.

Hashimoto's mask of propriety is back in place, but today's stressful events have taken a toll. The lines around her mouth are more pronounced, and the skillfully concealed crow's feet around her eyes have surfaced through her makeup.

Coming to a stop before her desk, Robin catches a faint whiff of . . . tobacco? She didn't know Hashimoto-san smoked.

All in all, though, this tableau is no worse than she expected. And not as bad as she'd feared—at least they didn't invite Inspector Anzai to the party. They must not be planning to have her arrested. Not yet, anyway. She places the authentication report atop her boss's in-tray, then stands there, not sure what to do next.

"Please sit," says Hashimoto.

She does. Obviously, they're not going to let her go until they extract their pound of flesh. She pulls her letter of resignation from her purse, and holds the envelope ready in her lap.

"I believe you know why you're here," says Hashimoto.

"Yes, ma'am."

"Your conduct over the past few days has been unacceptable."

"I understand."

"Your actions have embarrassed this company."

Only "embarrassed"? Frankly, she was expecting "damaged." Cancelling a press conference at the last minute is embarrassing, but losing Senkō-ji's potential commission is worse than that.

Robin bows her head.

"I understand."

"What you've done is not only unorthodox, it's borderline illegal."

Merely "borderline"? They must have decided that it wouldn't be profitable to reveal that the original Hikitoru had been replaced by a different Yakibō tea bowl.

"I understand."

"Considering these grave circumstances, I'm sure you agree that it would be difficult for us to continue to employ you."

Wow, that was fast. She was sure they would—

Fujimori coughs, and Hashimoto quickly adds, "Of course, in the interest of continuing your pursuit of a career in the art world, it goes without saying that you will refrain from embarrassing yourself or this company by engaging in unprofessional behavior, such as divulging confidential information about objects we represent, or our clients."

Ah. They're worried she'll reveal the substitution. That's why they're threatening her with never working in this town again. Well, she can agree to that without a second thought. She doesn't care which tea bowl Yakibō chose to represent the eighth of Saburo's *Attachments*, only that he did.

"I understand." The clock ticks. The moment lengthens. Was that her cue? She shoots to her feet. Bows deeply.

"*Moshiwake gozaimasen*," she cries, extending the letter of resignation with both hands. "Please accept my humble resignation."

Hashimoto rises and takes it with due formality.

"Accepted," she says wearily. "Please give me your keycards. You can collect your personal things on your way out."

Robin zips the coin locker key into her purse and hurries toward the café where Uchida and Nori are meeting her. She has moved past numb, and the feelings now surfacing are as jumbled as the box of belongings she just stowed at Takara-chō Station.

On one hand, she's relieved. Maybe even slightly elated. Uchida-*bōsan*'s scroll and note have been sent out for testing, and once they come back, her former employer will have no choice but to give the dipping bowl back to him, signed, sealed, and authenticated as made by Yoshi Takamatsu in the eighteenth century. And from now on, she'll be able to spend all day, every day, researching and writing the paper connecting Yakibō's tea bowls to Saburo's poems.

On the other hand, she's out of a job. Even she has to admit that calling the paltry sum in her bank account "savings" would earn her a Pinocchio nose.

Five minutes after five. Nori checks again to see if Robin messaged her about being late. She studies her shoes, then peers down the alley, looking anywhere but at the man standing nearby. He was outside the cafe when she arrived, also apparently waiting for someone who's running late. Big enough to have been a sumo wrestler in a former life, he has to be the priest Robin told her about, the one who broke Hikitoru. But that's not a conversation either of them wants to have before Robin introduces them properly, so he's also looking at anything but her. Out of the corner of her eye, she catches him checking his watch, then turning to study the menu tacked up outside the café.

"Okuda-san! Uchida-*bōsan*!"

They both pivot toward the wild-haired foreigner waving and trotting in their direction, then exchange slightly embarrassed half-smiles, now that their suspicions have been confirmed.

Robin slaps to a halt and breathlessly introduces them, then leads them inside, hustling to claim a table that three schoolgirls are just leaving. The priest offers to get the coffees, trundling back to the cashier to order.

Nori is dying to quiz her about what happened today, but as they slide into their seats, Robin asks, "How's your grandmother? Any change?"

"No, she hasn't opened her eyes. Yet." The old faker.

"How are *you* doing?" Robin is searching her face for the source of her frown. "I mean, is business . . . ?"

"Better," Nori reassures her. "I even made a big sale to a walk-in this morning. I don't know how I'm going to deal with the medical bills if my grandmother doesn't come home soon, but I hope—no, I'm *sure*—she's going to wake up any day now."

She'd better. Because it really roasts Nori's sweet potatoes that she'd been forced to fumble around in the dark when her grandmother got sick, instead of being trusted with the emergency plans. 'Baa-chan needs to start treating her more like a partner.

"When she does wake up," Nori grouses, "the first thing I'm going to make her tell me is where she hid the savings. It's ridiculous that I've been relying on selling that stupid tea bowl to make ends meet, and it's high time she started to show a little more trust. I mean—" She breaks off abruptly, hearing a polite cough, feels her face grow hot. How long had the priest been standing there? She hopes he didn't hear her moaning about money.

"Coffee and tea are on their way," he announces in his deep voice, pulling out the spindly chair next to Robin. He eyes it dubiously before gingerly lowering his bulk onto it.

As soon as he's settled, Nori looks from Robin to the priest. "Now that we're all here, don't make me wait any longer. What happened?"

They both start talking at once, then they look at each other, and laugh. One green tea, one black coffee, and a latte arrive. Uchida cedes right-of-way to Robin for the first half of the story, taking over at the point where he entered Hashimoto's office.

"I don't know what happened after I left, though," he concludes, sipping his tea. "I assume the press conference was called off?"

"It was, but first Hashimoto-san had to break the news to Mr. Fujimori, and he was anything but pleased. In fact," Robin says apologetically, "I might be taking you up on that offer to come to Shigaraki and study those boxes a little earlier than you expected. Now that I, uh, don't have a job anymore."

Uchida's cup freezes halfway to his mouth.

"They fired you? After all we . . ."

Robin shrugs. "You've never worked for a Japanese company, have you?"

"But . . . how hard will it be for you to get a new job?"

"Without a reference?" She laughs. "Pigs will fly. But with any luck, my next job won't be at an auction house, so I won't need one. Once the news of Hikitoru's recovery becomes public, I'll have to work day and night to prove that Yakibō's tea bowls inspired Saburo's poems, or someone else will get there first. It's probably a good thing I don't have a day job to get in the way."

Uchida still looks worried.

"Yes, but what will you live on?"

"Don't worry, I've got some savings. And I've been meaning to go on a diet anyway," she jokes. Uchida doesn't laugh. She changes the subject. "Hey, I almost forgot to warn you—Fujimori-san might be calling you."

"Your boss's boss? Why?"

"I got the feeling during my, uh, 'exit interview' that he's hedging his bets. If your ancestor's documents check out and he can't do business with the head priest at Senkō-ji, I'd be surprised if he doesn't turn around and try to sign you up instead."

"To sell Hikitoru?"

"Yeah. Or rather, 'the-tea-bowl-known-as-Hikitoru.' Which is what they'll call the dipping bowl, to keep from being sued, in case rumors about it not being the original get out."

Uchida ponders that.

"If I agree, will they give you your job back? I mean, could I *make* them give you your job back?"

"Probably." She smiles. "But I was serious when I said I don't want it. The best way you can help me now is to be the rightful owner of 'the-tea-bowl-known-as-Hikitoru' and let me study it. And," she adds, lowering her voice, "if you could be regrettably unavailable to show it to other scholars who ask to see it, that wouldn't hurt either."

"Got it." But he's not giving up quite yet. "What if we sold the other one?"

"What other one?"

"The one I broke. Didn't I tell you that I know a guy who still repairs pottery the old way, with gold? What if we got the original Hikitoru fixed, and sold it? I know it won't be as valuable as before it was broken, but I see mended tea bowls in museums all the time, and it ought to fetch something." He turns to Nori. "The two of you could split the proceeds."

He *did* overhear. Embarrassed, Nori tries to protest, but he holds up a platter-sized hand to stop her.

"Look, my life is a simple one," he says. "If I do my job right, the people I serve will support the temple in return. That's enough for me. The kind of money I'd get from selling that tea bowl would be a burden on my immortal soul. And," he bows apologetically, "I owe you—if you'd never taken Hikitoru to Swann-san, I'd never have gotten out from under the obligation that's been hanging over my family all these years." He looks at Robin. "And you paid for my vow with your job. If I can sell Hikitoru and help you both stay afloat while you deal with the fallout, it's the least I can do. So, when Fujimori-san calls, why don't I ask him what kind of terms he's offering?"

"No!" Robin yelps. "When Fujimori-san calls, I want you to tell him exactly where he can stick his 'terms.' I don't want him to make one yen off that tea bowl. He tried to give it away to the wrong priest, remember? And he tried *hard*."

"Okay, fine. Is there another auction house we could try? An arch-competitor, perhaps?"

"Wait," Nori says. "Before you do that—" She lowers her voice. "I know a guy."

52.

Present-Day Japan

TUESDAY, APRIL 15

Tokyo

W hat the . . . ? Nori rounds the corner onto 'Baa-chan's ward, ten minutes after the start of visiting hours. Is someone having a party in one of the hospital rooms? She can hear it all the way down the hall. Worse, it's getting louder, the closer she gets to her grandmother's room.

She reaches the half-open door and discovers why. The other bed is occupied again, this time by a bird of a woman with wispy white hair. She has an oxygen tube clipped to her nose, and an IV line just like 'Baa-chan's, but she's holding court propped against her pillows, very much not in a coma. She's surrounded by a gaggle of women all on the far side of seventy. By the way they're loudly exchanging baffling non-sequiturs, they're all a little hard of hearing.

Her first instinct is to shush them, so they won't disturb the still figure in the window bed, then stops herself. Anything that jolts her grandmother back to reality would be a good thing.

As she steps into the room, the flock interrupts its twittering long enough to inspect her. They apologize for the noise, then the one in a matronly mauve kimono swirls the blue privacy curtain around them.

They lower their voices a little, but by the time she has shed her coat and pulled her chair into its customary spot, they've forgotten her and are back at full volume.

She takes her grandmother's hand.

"Hey, 'Baa-chan. How are you doing today?"

She searches her grandmother's face for an answer. Doesn't get one.

"Well, guess what?" She moves closer, so she won't have to shout to be heard above the chatter. "I'm not going to be arrested. And," she brings her mouth right down by her grandmother's ear, "neither are you."

She pulls back, searches her grandmother's face. Nothing.

"Come on, cut the act." She drops the hand. "I know you're awake. It's time to stop pretending. You're safe. The police won't be coming back to ask you about Hikitoru. Not ever." She raises her voice. "Did you hear me? I said, you can wake up now. The police are NOT coming to get you!"

The chatter across the room abruptly stops. A bespectacled face peeks from behind the curtain.

"Sorry." Nori half-rises from her seat with an apologetic bow. "My grandmother sometimes doesn't have a very good grip on reality. *Sumimasen*," she apologizes again.

The woman looks unconvinced, but she retreats behind the curtain. Nori eases back into her chair as the chatter resumes.

"'Baa-chan!" she hisses. "I'm serious. There's no reason for you to fake it anymore. Listen to me. That tea bowl Hikitoru was stolen by someone else, long before it was stolen by you. That's right, I know all about what you did, and you've got plenty of explaining to do. But it turns out that some famous poet beat you to it, by a few hundred years. And the police aren't going to come after you for stealing something that was already stolen goods."

She leans closer, willing her grandmother to show some sign she's heard. Nothing happens.

Enough. She pushes away from the bed.

"Fine. Don't believe me." She snatches her coat from the back of the chair and pokes one arm into a sleeve. "I guess you need to hear it from Inspector Anzai himself. I'll just stop by the police station on my way home and—" She almost misses it.

One eye cracks open, just a sliver.

"'Baa-chan?"

The eye opens a little more, shifts its focus to her.

"'Baa-chan? You're awake? 'Baa-chan . . . !"

Her grandmother's lips curve into a smug smile. Nori drops back into her chair, so overcome with relief that she doesn't register that the smile is bigger on one side than the other.

Everything is going to be all right. Her grandmother is back among the living. Nori is so relieved, she's . . . she's *furious*.

"I knew it! I knew you were faking. How long have you been conscious, anyway? Why didn't you tell me? Why didn't you trust me? I wouldn't have told anyone. I wouldn't have let you get arrested." The eye slides away as her scolding intensifies, but now her pent-up worry is pouring out in an unstoppable torrent. "It's high time you started trusting me more, you know. What if I hadn't figured out where you hid that tea bowl? They'd have switched off the lights, that's what. And the internet too. Oh no, don't pretend to go back to sleep when I'm talking to you. You can't get away with that, not anymore."

But her grandmother's face has subsided back into beatific serenity. Nori glares at her. Pokes her. Shakes her shoulder. But 'Baa-chan is the most stubborn person she knows. When no more signs of consciousness appear, she gives up. No use calling the nurse now. Her grandmother will decide when to make her recovery public, and not a minute sooner. She turns to check the weather through the window, buttoning her coat.

"'Ou din't need help," comes a voice from the bed.

Nori spins around.

"I knew 'ou could figger i' ou'."

Her grandmother's eyes are closed, but she's smiling even wider than before.

Nori sinks into the chair, overcome with love and exasperation. She takes the thin hand in both of hers again and holds it tight. But just as she bends down to kiss the papery cheek, the good eye snaps open.

"Now tell 'e ev'ything. F'om the 'eginning. An' don't leave a'ything out."

53.

N ori leaps up the stairs from the subway station, and hits the sidewalk running. A last-minute customer had taken a maddeningly long time to decide between the Green Oribe ramen bowls and the brown ones from Mashiko, so she's late. If she sprints, she'll only have to apologize for ten tardy minutes, not fifteen. She pelts around the corner near the Miura pawnshop and spots Robin and Uchida-*bōsan* loitering out front. Waving, she surrenders to the stitch in her side and slows, apologizing to Robin as she arrives.

"Sorry," she pants. "Ten minutes to five. Customer. Couldn't decide." She swallows and sketches a bow toward the priest. "Uchida-*bōsan*. Hi. Sorry."

He says hello and smiles genially in return, unable to return her bow properly because his hands are full. He's toting two outsize bundles, the angular corners of their contents advertising that three empty tea bowl boxes are packed in one, four in the other.

Robin carries two smaller parcels wrapped in indigo cotton, their faded wave patterns knotted around single boxes.

Nori squints at her. Something's different. Is she wearing . . . lipstick?

"Are you sure about this dealer?" Robin is asking, surveying the pawnshop dubiously.

A flimsy plastic bag tumbles past them in the crisp breeze, catching on the accordion bars protecting the too-shiny kimono and the not-shiny-enough swords in the window. Nori can tell the expert's eye is flagging half the goods in it as knock-offs.

"Don't worry," she reassures Robin, ringing the bell. "Miura-san is too smart to put the good stuff out front." While they wait, her gaze settles on the boxes in Robin's hands. "You brought them both?"

"Yep. You said we could trust this guy, right? I thought he might want to see them side by side. 'The-tea-bowl-known-as-Hikitoru' arrived by armored art courier last Tuesday. And the other one came back from the goldsmith yesterday. Wait 'til you see it. It's—"

The door eases open with the now familiar sticky sound, and Daiki's suspicious eye appears in the gap.

"Oh, good." He grins at Nori. "What took you so long?"

The chain rattles and the gap widens. The boy sizes up her looming companions as they step into the cramped shop and clears a wider path through the teetering stacks of clutter, saving the introductions until they can include his grandfather.

"They're here, O-jii-san," he announces, sliding open the office door to frame Miura, standing behind the table.

Even though Robin's words of greeting are absurdly archaic and Uchida's head accidentally sends the overhead light swinging, the pawnbroker gives them a courtly bow and murmurs the proper honorific welcomes due to sellers of highly desirable goods. He doesn't allow his eyes to dwell too long on the bundles they carry until all are settled around the table and have steaming cups of tea before them. There are only four cushions, so Daiki resumes his place of honor, standing behind the old man.

Even then, the niceties must be observed before diving into the business at hand.

"How is your grandmother?" he asks Nori.

"Better," she replies. "Although I feel kind of sorry for the nurses in the rehab wing. The stronger she gets, the more she insists it's time they let her out of 'prison.' They say it'll be another month before she's made enough progress on her left side to go home, but she thinks that's too long. They caught her halfway down the hall yesterday, limping along with her walker, overcoat half on, trying to escape. I suspect that the day she actually makes it as far as the front door, they'll breathe a sigh of relief and just let her go."

They all laugh, and Miura shifts his attention to Robin.

"Pardon my curiosity, but are you, by any chance, the Swann-san who was on the team that authenticated that Yakibō tea bowl they discovered at Jakkō-in? The one called Waterlily?"

"Yes," Robin says, looking surprised that he's familiar with her work.

"I thought so. Perhaps you can enlighten me on something I've been wondering about. Why was that tea bowl named after the species called 'Gekka Bijin' in Japanese?"

"Funny you should ask—one of my colleagues is writing a paper on that. It's kind of a sad story. The tea bowl was a gift from a nun who came from the same town as Yakibō. They were contemporaries, oddly enough, although they couldn't have known each other, since she was the daughter of a high-ranking government official and he was just an artist. She was barely sixteen years old when she died, just a few months after becoming a nun. The tea bowl was among her possessions, and went to the convent after her death. Its storage box was blank except for Yoshi Takamatsu's seal, so they labeled it with the nun's posthumous name, which was Gekka Bijin. It's a variety of water lily that has a beautiful fragrance, but blooms for only one night."

The old man sits back, satisfied. "Thank you. I've always wondered. It's not easy to find information about Yoshi Takamatsu's work."

"That's because there aren't many of us studying him. But," she says, beginning to unwrap the boxes bearing the names of Saburo's *Eight Attachments*, "there will be."

She lines them up before the old man. One by one, he examines them, shaking his head in amazement while she fills him in on their history, concluding with the update that she'd spent the past three weeks in Shigaraki, working with Uchida to document them.

The priest passes her one of the two remaining boxes and clears the others from the table.

The familiar characters spelling *hikitoru* are brushed across the top. A faint aroma of charcoal emanates as Robin wiggles off the lid and lifts out the wrapped dipping bowl. She places it before Miura.

"May I?" he asks.

"Please do."

Switching on his lamp, he angles it closer, then peels back the brocade. A look of wonder suffuses his face as he lifts the dipping bowl, examining each side, peering into its depths.

"How is it that no one knew this existed, until now?" he marvels.

"I asked Uchida-*bōsan* the same thing." Robin turns to the priest with a smile.

"And I told her no one had ever asked." He smiles back.

"It's truly astonishing." Miura gazes at the jewels of green glaze winking in the lamplight. "And you say there were more? What a shame they were destroyed." He raises an inquiring eyebrow at Uchida. "I don't supposed you'd consider . . . ?"

"No," says the priest, glancing at Robin. "I plan to hang onto this one." His eyes crinkle at the corners. "At least until it's been thoroughly studied."

He hands Robin the last box, but she passes it to Nori.

"Will you do the honors?"

Everyone leans a little closer. Nori unwraps the original Hikitoru, telling herself not to expect too much. It will no longer be in pieces, but it will still be broken. No matter how meticulously the *kintsugi* artist has mended it, this won't be the same tea bowl that thrilled her to the core when she first lifted it from the shop shelf.

But as it emerges from the brocade wrapper, a collective sigh goes up. The pieces are now held together by seams of burnished gold. Nori cups it between her hands and is startled to discover it hasn't lost its magic. In fact . . .

"I don't know how it can be more beautiful than before," she says, lifting it into the light. "But somehow, it is." She studies it for a long moment, then passes it to Miura. "Too bad it's not more valuable too."

"I wouldn't be so sure about that," he says, running his thumb over the dull gold mends, admiring the quality of the workmanship. "You have to understand something about collectors. Some things are valuable because they're beautiful. Others, because they're rare. But the ones that are most valuable are beautiful *and* rare . . . and they have a story."

"Oh," she says. "Like the war fan?"

"Yes. Hikitoru was exceptional before it was broken, of course, but this," the golden rivers gleam in the lamplight, "*this* Hikitoru looks like it has a story. Buyers might actually pay more for it *because* it's broken."

"Yes, but . . ." Robin's face fills with regret. "You know we can't tell anyone it's the real Hikitoru, right? I mean, I don't know if my ex-boss kept it to herself about the substitution, or if it was Fujimori-san who decided to sweep it under the rug, but the minute the police showed that dipping bowl to the media and announced they'd solved the cold case, 'the-tea-bowl-known-as-Hikitoru' officially became the *only* tea bowl known as Hikitoru."

"Of course it did," Miura agrees. "But this one has a different story, and I suspect buyers will like it just as much."

"What are you planning to tell them?" Nori asks, curious.

"Well," Miura says, regarding the tea bowl thoughtfully, "A little bird," he flicks her a glance, "told me that this tea bowl was broken by a priest. A priest," he quickly adds, catching the alarm on Uchida's face, "whose name remains shrouded in mystery. I heard it was broken in a secret ritual, in order to fulfill a vow made to its maker on his deathbed. That maker, as everyone knows—or will, once Swann-san's paper is published—was a famous potter who believed that breaking his tea bowls would free him from his sins. And not only did he act on his obsession, he inspired a famous poet to write about it." Miura sits back. "With a story like that, I wouldn't be surprised if its sale price beats Snow Bride."

Nori grins. That's the best news she's heard in weeks. "How soon do you think . . . ?"

"We'll have to wait until Miss Swann finishes her paper. Do you have any idea when might that be, Swann-san?"

"November," Robin says. "My research is ahead of schedule, thanks to Hirosh—I mean Uchida-*bōsan*'s, help, and the first journal I approached jumped at the chance to publish it. If I make the submission deadline, it will be the cover story of the annual *Japan Review*."

"Congratulations," Miura says, with a pleased smile. "That's exactly the kind of splash that bidding wars are made of. And I'm sure we can be ready to sell by then, if we start laying the groundwork now. Can you afford to wait that long?" he asks Nori.

"I think so. I suspect my grandmother has been calling our past due accounts behind my back, ever since her speech improved enough to use the phone. I nearly had a heart attack when I overheard her talking to one of them yesterday—she sounded so pitiful, I thought she'd had another stroke. She made a miraculous recovery the moment she hung up, though. In any case, checks are coming in nearly every day."

"Glad to hear it." He looks around the table. "So, that's settled? If it's November we're shooting for, Daiki and I will get to work right away, polishing up the story."

Nori crosses her arms.

"*If* we agree to let you represent us."

Miura stiffens.

"I beg your pardon?"

"We haven't discussed your commission yet."

"You really are Chiyo Okuda's granddaughter, aren't you?" He shakes his head. "But there aren't any 'special circumstances' now, so this sale will be much more straightforward. Shall we say . . . twenty percent?"

"Fifteen," Nori counters, glaring.

"Seventeen." He glares back.

"Fifteen percent of ten million is a million-five," she points out. "And that's if you do a lousy job and it doesn't sell for any more than Snow Bride."

"All right, all right," Miura concedes. "Fifteen it is." Then he laughs. "Your grandmother would be proud."

EPILOGUE

TWO YEARS LATER
Tokyo National Museum

Fifty-seven minutes until she can clock out, but she's nearly finished. There's just the National Cultural Treasures room left to clean, and then she can sit down on one of the hard benches and call her mother. Her *o-kaa-san's* forgetfulness is beginning to worry her, because sometimes she doesn't remember to eat the lunch left for her in the fridge. It happened again last week, and by the time her weary daughter pushed through the door after trudging home from the station, O-kaa-san had been famished and raging.

Dredging the heavy ring of keys from the pocket of her smock, she picks through them, then slides open the panel hiding the lock on the first exhibit. During opening hours, the lighting in this gallery is kept low, inviting visitors to stand in awe before each of the glowing jewel-box displays and speak in hushed whispers of the spotlit treasures within. On Mondays, though, when the museum is closed to all but curators and the cleaning crew, every corner of this room is garishly lit, so her supervisor can spot any speck of dust left behind or—she'd heard from Kimiko that this had actually happened—fingerprints left by someone who'd been lazy about wearing gloves.

Who would be stupid enough to do that? Not her, that's for sure. She needs this job. Pulling on her white cotton gloves, she draws her feather duster from the cart and goes over the brass incense burner (seventh century, Kyoto), then moves on to the lacquer writing box (eighteenth century, Kyoto) and the dragon-headed pitcher (eighteenth century, Nara).

Slotting the duster back in her cart, she unlocks the next window, but the eighth-century gilt bronze water pot she expected to find there is gone. In its place is a new object. The museum must have acquired another National Treasure for its collection. This one is a tea bowl that's both rough and smooth, seamed with gold.

Could something that's broken still be a National Treasure? She's worked here long enough to know that plenty of broken things are still mysteriously worthy of being displayed with great reverence, but she's never seen one in this room before.

The name of the maker means nothing to her, but centuries ago (according to the tag) it had been owned by a poet. His name she knows. Everyone does. Is that why this tea bowl is so special?

She flicks the feather duster vigorously against a clean cloth to rid it of any fluff it might have picked up from the other displays, then reaches in to dust the new acquisition. But as she's pulling back to relock the window, she spies a dark fleck beneath the clear acrylic stand that supports the tea bowl like a crown jewel.

Dead spider. Just her luck. Why did it choose to die in the one spot her duster is too fat to reach? She's going to have to move the tea bowl to get rid of it. Reaching in with both gloved hands, she gently lifts the bowl from its stand.

As its slightly oval shape settles between her cupped fingers, a sigh escapes her lips. The objects she cleans are always old. Beautiful. Irreplaceable. But none of them have ever made her feel like this. The tea bowl curves into her palms as if it had been made for her alone. For the first time in all the years she's worked in the museum, she wonders whose hands held it last. How many lips had tasted tea from its delicate rim?

A smile steals across her face, and she forgets all about her ailing mother, her tired feet, and her aching back.

ABOUT THE AUTHOR

Dear Friend,

Thank you for choosing *The Last Tea Bowl Thief*—as a reader, I know how precious those stolen moments of relaxation are, and I'm honored you chose to spend them in Japan with me. If you know someone else who might enjoy *The Last Tea Bowl Thief,* I'd be forever grateful if you'd pass it on. I've always thought that a recommendation from a friend is the finest way to discover new books, and sharing a good read is one of life's great pleasures.

With warmest regards,
Jonelle

JONELLE PATRICK is the author of five novels set in Japan, and has been writing about Japanese culture and travel since she first moved to Tokyo in 2003. She writes and produces the monthly news-letter *Japanagram*, and blogs at *Only In Japan* and on her travel site, *The Tokyo Guide I Wish I'd Had*. She teaches at writing workshops, appears as a panelist at *Thrillerfest*, and was the keynote speaker at the Arrow Rock Writing Workshop.

A graduate of Stanford University and the Sendagaya Japanese Language Institute, she's also a member of the Mystery Writers of America, International Thriller Writers, and Sisters in Crime. She divides her time between Tokyo and San Francisco.

AUTHOR'S NOTE:

What's real and what's not, in The Last Tea Bowl Thief

One of the most delightful things about reading good international mysteries and historical novels is that the fiction is built on fact, and you can learn all kinds of interesting stuff while enjoying a good tale.

All the places in *The Last Tea Bowl Thief* are real towns and neighborhoods, and I'd like to think the pottery stores of Kappabashi Street and the landscape surrounding the village of Shigaraki would feel quite familiar to you if you were to visit, especially in the spring.

Jakkō-in (the convent where Yoshi's Kiri is sent) is also a real place with a healing Jizo figure that became even more legendary after being tragically destroyed in a great fire. Amid the ashes, mourning nuns discovered a metal box filled with over 3,000 smaller Jizo statues that had been secretly concealed within the great wooden figure, and the replica they commissioned to replace it became a powerful and much-visited symbol of rebirth.

The main Buddhist temples in *The Last Tea Bowl Thief* (Senkō-ji, Sengen-in, and Heizan-ji) are all based on real temples that exist in the places they're situated, but I've changed their names and appearances to keep from tarnishing their noble histories with less-than-admirable priests and unlucky incidents. The *rakugo* storyteller's temple is also real, and there really is a monument marking where fifty-three *rakugo* stories deemed too irreverent to perform during wartime were buried.

I made many visits to the Nihon Minka-en traditional farmhouse park outside Tokyo and Komorebi Village at Showa Kinen Park in Tachikawa, to get a feel for what it would be like to live in Yakibō's old farmhouse. I'm deeply grateful to the long-suffering docents who demonstrated fascinating details about Edo Period daily life, like the way the "dirt" floor of the kitchen area had been infused with lime, so spilled water would wick away, leaving the floor dry and hard again within seconds.

Yodo Castle has been reduced to its stone foundations, but you'll recognize its interior if you wander the halls of Ni-jō Castle in Kyoto or Hikone Castle in Shiga prefecture. Lord Inaba's audience chamber is a real suite of rooms in Nomura House, a high-ranking samurai's residence in Kanagawa that's been beautifully preserved right down to the red bingara clay walls and secret cubbyholes in the corridors surrounding it, where guards would be stationed in case they had to leap out to defend their lord.

Chiyo Okuda's wartime existence came to life thanks to the excellent curation of wartime living spaces and models of the black markets at the Edo-Tokyo Museum. I discovered very quickly how little information and how few photos have been published (especially in English) about the firebombing of Tokyo, but the curators and staff at the 東京都復興記念館 (Tokyo Reconstruction Memorial Museum), and the 戦災資料センター (Center for the Tokyo Air Raids and War Damage) gave me access to obscure historical photos and unpublished maps of the bombing—horrifyingly complete, with wind directions—to show the spread of the inferno.

The philosophy taught to Yakibō by his mentor Takanori jumps the historical gun a little, as the ideas so eloquently expounded by Soetsu Yanagi wouldn't become widespread until the Mingei movement popularized them two centuries later. The curators and staff at the 日本民芸館 (Japan Folk Crafts Museum), 甲賀市信楽伝統産業会館 (Shigaraki Traditional Industries Museum), and the 滋賀県立陶芸の森 (Shigaraki Ceramics Cultural Park) assembled beautifully curated exhibitions of rare Tamba-ware and Shigaraki-ware pieces that I was lucky enough to see, and the catalogs for those exhibitions were a goldmine of information about the what, how, and when of Japanese wood-fired ceramics. The staff at the Sōtō-en ceramics company, in the town of Shigaraki, whose magnificent wood-burning *noborigama* kiln has been in constant use since Yakibō's time, were also very generous with their expertise.

Finally, *The Last Tea Bowl Thief* relied on many sources (in both Japanese and English) for a solid foundation of facts to build the fiction on, and if you'd like to learn more, here are some excellent places to delve deeper:

Everyday Life in Traditional Japan by Charles J. Dunn
江戸衣裳地図鑑 (*Encyclopedia of Edo Era Clothing*) by Hitomi Kikuchi
Art by Buddhist Nuns: Treasures from the Imperial Convents of Japan by Patricia Fister
Daily Life in Wartime Japan by Samuel Hideo Yamashita
The Great Tokyo Air Raids published by the Tokyo Memorial Association
Japanese Wood-fired Ceramics by Masakazu Kusakabe & Marc Lancet
日本のやき物信楽伊賀 (*Japanese Ceramics: Shigaraki & Iga*) by Rinko Otsuki
The Japanese Pottery Handbook by Penny Simpson, Lucy Kitto & Kanji Sodeoka
The Unknown Craftsman by Soetsu Yanagi (adapted by Bernard Leach)

Two notable things that are fictional in *The Last Tea Bowl Thief*: There is no Sorasenke School of tea ceremony (because I didn't want to cast unflattering aspersions on the actual schools), and the story of the Edo

Period aristocrat who was cremated with his Sesshū scrolls is based on a modern-day Japanese tycoon's threat to take two of his Impressionist paintings (a VanGogh and a Renoir) into the flames with him. The paintings disappeared after his death, but it was later discovered that they had been sold.

I've tried to make the world of *The Last Tea Bowl Thief* as believable and factual as possible, but if I made any mistakes in that regard, the errors are no fault of my sources and are strictly my own.

ACKNOWLEDGMENTS

To Mika Kawana, who navigated me around the extremely off-the-beaten-track backwoods of Shigaraki and Jakkō-in, and helped name those elusive tea bowls, my gratitude and friendship forever.

Heartfelt thanks always to April Eberhardt, of April Eberhardt Literary—I'm so lucky to have the world's most lovely, most capable, and most tireless agent.

Heaps more thanks to my excellent editor Dan Mayer, for his expert insight and advice, and for being so delightful to work with. Also bowing in deep gratitude to production manager Marianna Vertullo, copyeditor Patrick Smith, and cover designer extraordinaire Jennifer Do for transfiguring my heap of words into a thing of literary beauty, with all the apostrophes pointing in the right direction. And to Ashley Calvano at Seventh Street Books, along with Dana Kaye, Samantha Lien, and Hailey Dezort of Kaye Publicity, thank you for helping put *The Last Tea Bowl Thief* into the hands of so many fine readers. You're the best.

If you made it all the way through this book without being

annoyed by words used too often, Japanese customs that make no sense, and infuriating errata, you'll join me in thanking my long-suffering manuscript readers, who pointed all that stuff out to me, so you don't have to. Thank you from the bottom of my heart to Lisa Hirsch, JT Kalinka, Mary Mackey, Susan McCarthy, Chris Nolan, Marcia Pillon, Mac Salman, Paula Span, and Craig Tanisawa. The book was made infinitely better by your thoughtful questioning and benevolent criticism. I'm also grateful to the members of my real-life book club and other assorted friends who helped me figure out how to balance the narrative between the past and the present. Judy Avery, Connie Ballmer, Clarissa Daniel, Suzi Finney, Sue Henry, Annette Pollack, Steve Pollack, Emily Sellers, Anne Staland, Stuart Statland, and Sandra Sutton. I'm talking to *you*!

And finally, to my family, always and forever, my love and gratitude is utterly boundless.

CHARACTERS

EDO PERIOD (1700s)

TAKAMATSU family
Ceramic artists, specializing in tea ceremony ware

Yoshi Takamatsu – eldest son (later known as **Yakibō**)
Nobu – Yoshi's younger brother (later known as Honzaemon IV)

SHIBATA family
Hereditary Masters of the Sorasenke school of tea ceremony

Saburo Shibata – third son, poet

OTHERS

Kiri – Yoshi's beloved, daughter of a government official
Sachi – Kiri's maid
Rinkan – abbot (*rōshi*) of Sengen-in monastery

Takanori – Yakibō's mentor, Shigaraki-ware pottery master, friend of Rinkan-*rōshi*

Hattsan – Yakibō's apprentice

Lord Inaba – head of the Kyoto region's ruling family, commander of Yodo Castle

Uchida – head priest of Heizan-ji Temple in Shigaraki, friend of Yakibō

PRESENT DAY

OKUDA family
Owners of the Okuda restaurant supply pottery store

Nori Okuda – granddaughter

Chiyo Okuda – grandmother, current proprietor (also called O-baa-san or the more familiar **'Baa-chan** by her granddaughter)

ITOH family
Owners of the rival restaurant supply store next door

Tetsu Itoh – current proprietor, same generation as Chiyo Okuda ('Baa-chan)

MIURA family
Pawnbrokers

Miura (Senior) – grandfather, current proprietor

Mariko – Miura's daughter

Daiki – Miura's thirteen-year-old grandson

HAYASHI family
Ceramics makers, owners of Hayashi Ceramics in Shigaraki

Mamoru – eleven-year-old son, descendent of Yakibō's apprentice, Hattsan

FUJIMORI FINE ART
Auction house

Eriko Hashimoto – art expert, specializing in Japanese ceramics
Robin Swann – assistant to Eriko Hashimoto
Fujimori – auction house owner

OTHERS

Anzai – Tokyo Metropolitan Police Inspector
Haneda – archivist at Senkō-ji Temple, son of the head priest
Uchida – current head priest *(o-bōsan)* of Heizan-ji Temple in Shigaraki, descendent of the Uchida-*bōsan* who was Yakibō's friend

GLOSSARY OF JAPANESE
WORDS AND PHRASES

JAPANESE PHRASES:

"Haji-memashi-te"—Formal greeting when people meet for the first time

"Irasshai-ma-se!"—"Welcome to my shop/restaurant." Greeting when someone arrives at a shop (used only in commercial situations)

"Ita-daki-masu"—"I humbly receive this food." Typically said before eating, like grace

"Kanpai!"—"Cheers!" Typical drinking toast

"Moshi-moshi"—What people say when they answer their phones

"O-kaeri"—Acknowledgment that someone has just come home. Meaning: "Welcome home"

"O-tsuka-re sama-deshita."—"Thank you for working hard today." Typical end-of-work departing words, said to coworkers. Colleagues often shorten it to the more casual, *"O-tsu-kare-sama."* Literal meaning: "You really became tired by working so honorably."

JAPANESE WORDS:

butsumetsu—The least lucky day in the Japanese astrology calendar. It's bad luck to do anything on this day (except have a funeral)

daimyō—A regional warlord serving under the shōgun in the samurai era

hanko—The small personal seal used instead of a signature in Japan

kami-sama—Shinto gods, worshipped at Japanese shrines

kanji—The multi-stroked characters used to represent Japanese words

kintsugi—The art of repairing broken pottery by sticking the pieces back together with gold

mon—The smallest unit of money in the Edo Period

nihongami—A traditional Japanese woman's hairstyle featuring rolled and pinned sections, often decorated with combs and seasonal ornaments (now worn mostly by *geisha*)

o-baa-san—Grandmother

obi—The wide sash worn with a kimono

o-jii-san—Grandfather

o-kaa-san—Mother

onigiri—A sticky rice ball, usually wrapped in seaweed with a savory filling

ō-sōji—The deep housecleaning that takes place once a year before New Years

seiza—Sitting on folded legs with back straight and feet tucked under your body

senshō—A day in the Japanese astrology calendar that predicts good luck all morning, but bad luck after noon

shimenawa—A rice straw rope that marks an area or natural feature as sacred to the Shinto gods

shōgun—Military dictator who governed Japan during the samurai era. The emperor was still the official ruler, but he had no political power

shōji—Old-fashioned Japanese sliding windows/doors, framed with wood and covered with paper instead of glass *taian*—The luckiest day in the Japanese astrology calendar. Taian brings good luck all day to any endeavor (except having a funeral, which should be avoided)

tokonoma—A built-in floor-to-ceiling alcove in traditional Japanese rooms, used to display seasonal art and flowers

torii—The pi-shaped gates at Shinto shrines

tatami—The woven straw mats that cover the floors in traditional Japanese houses

uguisu—Japanese nightingale, a bird known for its elaborate song

yen—Japanese unit of money. Roughly: 1 yen = 1 cent (USD)

zazen—Meditation practice of Soto (Zen) Buddhists

HONORIFICS USED WITH NAMES:

-san—Added to someone's name like Mr., Mrs., Ms. or Miss.

-chan—Added to the name of a childhood friend or a young woman (instead of *-san*), to show a close relationship.

-kun—Added to the name of a young man or young professional colleague (instead of *-san*), to show a close relationship.

-rōshi—Added to the name of an abbot at a monastery

-bōsan—Added to the name of a Buddhist priest, equivalent to Reverend

o- —Added in front of someone's title to show respect (for example, *o-bōsan*)

DOES YOUR BOOK GROUP READ LITERARY FICTION, HISTORICAL FICTION OR MYSTERIES?

Choose *The Last Tea Bowl Thief* for your next get-together!

DISCUSSION STARTERS

Do you believe in luck?
"Good luck" and "bad luck" are often used to describe situations or events that we're powerless to control, and the characters in The Last Tea Bowl Thief *are typically Japanese in their respect for (and fear of) what fate dishes out.*

- Think of a point in your own life that changed your entire future. Did good or bad luck play a part? Where would you be now if things had been different?

- Can you think of ways the characters in *The Last Tea Bowl Thief* tried to influence their luck? Do *you* think we can influence luck? What are some things you do to get more good luck/avoid bad luck?

- Look up today's date on a Japanese lucky day calendar website (seiyaku.com is a good one). What kind of day was today? Did today's forecast accurately predict what kind of day you had?

Is stealing ever right?

There are three generations of thieves in this story. If we give each of them the benefit of the doubt and believe they acted from the best of intentions, one steals to save a thing of beauty from destruction, one steals to survive, and one steals to right an old wrong and advance scholarship.

- Were Saburo, Chiyo, and Robin right or wrong to steal the tea bowl?

- What could they have done instead? Could they still have achieved their goals? How might their lives have been different?

More food for thought & discussion starters are at lastteabowlthief.com

Make your book group memorable with
***The Last Tea Bowl Thief* extras**

- Narrated video slideshow of the real Japanese places and scenes in *The Last Tea Bowl Thief*

- Original cocktail/mocktail recipes inspired by *The Last Tea Bowl Thief*

- Easy homemade tea ceremony sweets recipe

- How to make real tea ceremony tea (*matcha*) and where to buy it

For all these goodies, and more, visit
***The Last Tea Bowl Thief* website:**
lastteabowlthief.com